praise for when oceans rise

"A **spellbindingly fresh reimagining** of The Little Mermaid that will **bewitch readers** until they reach the final page. Malaya is **a compelling protagonist entrapped** in a conflict that will resonate with the realities of many young women. You can't help but to root for her as she traverses through alternate timelines rife with creatures from Filipino folklore and her own personal demons. **Alvarez is a brilliant new voice** to watch in the world of fantasy fiction." — **Priyanka Taslim, author of *The Love Match***

"Malaya, you are the captain of your life. You decide which oceans to sail. You don't wait for the ocean to take you." (This has to be my favourite line in the book.) In a nutshell, this is **an emotional ride that navigates the waves** of an abusive relationship. The emotions in this cautionary tale are **raw and relatable**, and will sweep you off your feet. **Beautifully woven** with the magic of rich Filipino culture, Alvarez's remarkable debut will stay with you beyond the last page." — **Joyce Chua, author of *Land of Sand and Song***

"Simply stunning! Robin Alvarez weaves together the **perfect blend of modern retelling and mythical fantasy** in *When Oceans Rise*. Prepare yourself to be swept away in this gorgeous and courageous story of loving yourself after heartbreak." — **Dana Swift, Author of *Cast In Firelight***

"*When Oceans Rise* is an exciting story with **a lot of heart and emotion**. Malaya's emotional journey rang true." — **Wendy Parris, author of Field of Screams**

"Set against **a rich and beautiful setting**, *When Oceans Rise* is **a stunning book** both inside and out." — **Rebecca Ryan, author of *My (Extra)Ordinary Life***

"A gorgeous debut about **gods, monsters, and the courage it takes** to love (and free) yourself. When Oceans Rise deserves a place on every shelf." — **Gigi Griffis, author of *The Wicked Unseen***

when oceans rise

ROBIN ALVAREZ

CJM
CREATIVE JAMES MEDIA

This is a work of fiction. All of the characters, organizations and events portrayed in this novel are either products of the author's imagination or are used fictitiously.

Published in the United States by Creative James Media.

 Printed in the United States of America. For information, address Creative James Media, 9150 Fort Smallwood Road, Pasadena, MD 21122.

www.creativejamesmedia.com

978-1-956183-16-0 (trade paperback)

First U.S. Edition 2023

content warning

Before you read this book, you must know that the main character, Malaya, undergoes mental and physical abuse from someone she loves. If you have never experienced this, you may think Malaya's choices and behaviors are nonsensical. At times, they might even infuriate you. It can be difficult to understand the manipulation one is under when being gaslit, especially when one has not gone through this themselves. That manipulation will often seem so subtle to outsiders yet so significant to those experiencing the abuse. Likewise, if you've experienced abuse, the situations presented in this novel can be quite triggering. If you are not ready for this journey, I understand. However, if you are ready, just know that while this will be difficult, Malaya will come out on the other side, just as her name suggests: free.

For more specific information about the abuse depicted in this novel, go to robinalvarez.com.

To my husband and family, who indulge my eccentricities and support me endlessly.

For those who are voiceless, who feel like they are too much, who find themselves incredibly lost: be weird and feel deeply, for we have found each other.

I don't believe in the occult.

It's not that the supernatural isn't readily available, what with my Irish grandmother claiming ties to a famed line of Celtic witches and my Filipino heritage rich in mythological superstitions and homeopathic healing rituals. The information has been offered, but I've held it at arm's length like one holds a pot of three-day-old rice as far from their burning nostrils as possible. Perhaps growing up in a mixed-race household, with twice the culture to consume, is just a little much. It's hard to be both without feeling guilty that I'm letting one side down. One could argue that it's much easier not to embrace either side fully.

Or maybe I don't believe in the occult because there is no magic in my life.

Practical Magic plays for the second time tonight, fifth time this week, as I light sage to cleanse the space—otherwise known as the sacred living room. Though burning sage cleanses people and places of negative energy, I'm using it to smudge the smell of cigarette smoke wafting through the open back door. Mom and Tita Blessica are "de-stressing" over a cutting comment a friend of theirs made about my little brother Eric supposedly punching a hole in the wall when *their* son had sheetrock dust on his shoe. Dad pointed it out, causing laughter among the other dads, but Auntie Jeslyn hadn't thought it was funny because she pretended to cancel this Saturday's Filipino party so that we wouldn't come.

I was thrilled about the whole thing because it meant Mom saying yes to this impromptu sleepover with Hannah, Penny my best friend, Stephanie, who concocted the idea. Stephanie had never seen *Practical Magic* until a week ago when I put it on while we were working on a group project. After that, she became obsessed with a witchy-themed sleepover, especially after my Tita Blessica promised to do some palm readings.

"Grant will be mine," Hannah says, grinding red rose petals into a fine powder with a wooden mortar and pestle set Mom bought at the Asian Market years ago. She does a little mad scientist laugh, her arm making comically exaggerated circles until the bowl tips over.

"Oh no! I foresee a messy future for you two." I press my finger against the reddish powder and drag it between her eyebrows and down her nose like Gillian does to Sally in the movie. My sister, Gabrielle, laughs from the other end of the couch, and I flick the remaining powder in her direction.

"Don't get that love crap on me!" Gabrielle flinches.

"Right. Because you would *hate it* if Josiah was suddenly obsessed with you!"

Gabrielle tosses a throw pillow at my head, causing me to bump into Stephanie, who's been deep diving into her phone for several minutes now.

"What are you up to?" I pull one of my curls over my upper lip like a mustache so when she finally looks up, it's with wide-eyed amusement.

"Just making plans to pick up some seaweed later so we can make face masks to attract *the one*." The *click click clicking* of her phone goes unbroken.

"I don't know if I want to be with anyone who's attracted

to stinky sea slime. And why does that plan involve so much texting?" I reach for her screen, but she pulls away, her eyes sparkling.

"You'll just have to wait and see!"

"Well, while you three are obsessed with love," Penny says, pulling out a black ribbon and *The Craft,* which is the only witch movie to give me consistent nightmares, "I will be placing a binding spell to protect myself from those who wish to do me harm."

"Who is trying to hurt you?" Gabrielle's brow furrows.

"My chemistry teacher Mr. Winer." Penny's lips purse. "I swear to God, if he gives me one more F, my mom will kick my—"

"HEY, Mom," I raise my voice warningly as the backdoor closes. I'm not sure if Mom would scold my friend for cussing, but she sure as hell wouldn't let me hang out with her anymore if she thought Penny was "corrupting" her precious daughters.

Mom and Tita Blessica must not have heard because they come over to the coffee table to look at the mess of herbs, dried flowers, and essential oils splayed over it. Hannah found the best love potions Pinterest had to offer, but honestly, she might be making her own concoction based on whatever she could find in her mom's garden and my pantry.

Tita Blessica's nose crinkles. "If you want it to work, you'll need an *Albularyo* to seal the relationship."

"Where do I get one of those?" Hannah sits up eagerly.

"It's not a thing, it's a person, and she's right here." Tita Blessica gestures to Mom.

"*Ano ba*?" Mom's forehead knits. "I'm not an *Albularyo*."

"Floribeth, you have healing hands," Tita Blessica turns Mom's palm over.

It's not untrue. Mom has reduced swelling and muscle aches by placing her fiery palms on people, though I'd never heard of the term *Albularyo* before. "It's likely you come from a long line of *Albularyos.*" Tita Blessica takes my palms and presses them together, binding her own hands around mine, though she speaks to Hannah instead. "Put your potion in your palms and press them together like this. Floribeth will bind the love when she places her hands around yours."

While offering her hands to Mom, Hannah utters words of amazement at how Tita Blessica even knew it was a love spell. Meanwhile, Tita sits cross-legged on the floor, pulling me down with her. Without warning, she traces lines across my palms. A hush falls over everyone as they squeeze in closer. It creates a beautiful blend of floral scents.

"Your true love ... *Ang* true love *mo* is coming," Tita Blessica whispers as if the words *true love* took her breath away. It stole mine. In my periphery, Mom shifts closer. Tendrils of smoke from the burning sage weave between Tita and me. "He won't see you coming. You are about to step into a new phase of your life."

"Blessica," Mom says, but her voice doesn't seem to reach Tita Blessica, whose eyes are so distant it's like she's seeing into another world.

"He will make you believe in magic because you will create magic together."

Goosebumps run up my arms. How could she know I don't think there's magic in my life?

"Blessica," Mom's voice is harder—a warning.

"Who is it?" Stephanie sits up on her knees, inspecting my palm.

Tita Blessica's head shakes minutely like she can't find a word in a word search though she knows it's right before her eyes. "I can't see. It's like he's close, but it feels like he's a world away. Give me something," she seems to be talking to the universe rather than any of us, and no one dares to move. "But how will you know it's him? How will you know? Shirtless. He will be shirtless the first time you meet him."

"That's enough, Blessica." Mom pulls my hand away from Auntie, bringing her back from whatever realm she'd become lost. "It's all a bunch of nonsense." Mom's grip on my arm is firm, but her voice shakes. Why, if it's all fake? She's always been uptight about boys, but is there something more here?

"I'm sorry, that's all I got for now—"

"And it better stay that way," Mom interjects before Tita Blessica can even suggest trying again later. They move to the kitchen, and their argument is loud and in Tagalog, so I can't understand them.

"Come on," Stephanie says, picking up her car keys.

"Come where? It's so late." Despite my protest, I shove my feet into my pink Vans.

"I told you; we need seaweed! No better time to head to the beach than in the middle of a heated argument."

My shoulders slump. There's no way Mom would be okay with me going out this late. There's also no way she'd say yes with all my friends watching. Still, I slink into the kitchen.

"Mom," I mutter a few times before touching her arm. She blinks like I appeared out of nowhere. "Can I go out with my friends to pick up something for face masks?" It's not entirely a lie, but it's not like I'm just headed down to Target, either.

Mom looks over her shoulder at my friends. "Just go, *Anak*." Then she dives back into the fight with Tita. What luck is this? I don't stay long enough to question it as we race for the front door. Gabrielle almost closes the door when Mom shouts that she can't come with us.

Sorry, I mouth when Gabrielle's shoulders slump. The light from the hall widens as she shuffles back inside before casting me into the dark.

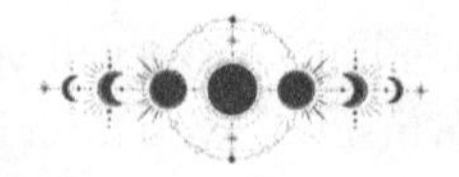

Twinkling embers from the bonfire lift into the sky, dissolving like fireworks before hitting the soft beach sand. A large group of varsity swimmers surround the fire, chatting, drinking, and laughing. The energy is intoxicating.

"We're not just getting seaweed, are we?" I nudge Stephanie with my shoulder as Hannah spots Grant and beelines for him, dragging Penny along. Grant lifts a finger, swiping at the red dust staining Hannah's nose, and she giggles. "Is this what you were doing on the phone earlier?"

"The varsity guys can move fast with the right incentive." She wiggles her eyebrows.

"What incentive?" A gust of sand sweeps and swirls along the beach's surface like fairy dust.

"You'll see." Stephanie's the only one in our friend group who made varsity as a sophomore because she's been a club swimmer since before she could walk. Because of that, she's the only one who crosses over into this exclusive group of upperclassmen. I think we're going to grab a drink by the fire, but she pulls me past the flames and to the shoreline, where a group of people stand in a circle. With only the starlight illuminating the space, it's hard to see who is who.

Soft fabric is pulled over my eyes, casting me in complete darkness, and a blindfold is tied tightly at the back of my head. Instinctively, I reach up to uncover my eyes, but a hand stops me.

"That's no fun," a deep voice whispers near my ear, pulling my hand away from the blindfold. I don't recognize anyone's voice outside of my friend group, but the closeness of his breath against my neck makes me shiver.

"Okay, the name of the game is spin the person!" Stephanie shouts. "That's right; we're playing human spin the bottle. Malaya will be spun a ridiculous amount of times as we circle her, and the first person she finds gets a kiss."

"What?" The word escapes my mouth before I can stop myself.

"Don't worry," Stephanie whispers. "You'll do great. And who knows, maybe you'll even find your shirtless love."

Heat warms my face and neck despite the way the wind whips around us. I don't even dare to protest because I don't want to risk anyone overhearing my embarrassing fortune. Stephanie spins me, and the people circling us cheer. It's infectious, being cheered on for doing nothing more than participating, and my limbs become light. I dip to the side when she lets go, almost tipping over.

There are giggles as I get close to people, but I'm trying to pick out Stephanie's laugh. We've kissed before, so maybe I can get through this with a quick peck and pass the baton to someone else. I swipe the air, and Stephanie's distinctive snort-laugh sounds to my left.

I turn, but my reaching hands don't land on Stephanie's forearms. Hot skin burns beneath my palms, cutting my laughter short.

Shirtless.

A collective "Oooooh" breaks out around me, and my hands slide involuntarily up someone's bare chest as whoever I've landed on steps into me.

Before I've even had time to process, soft lips press against mine.

I'm flooded with warmth as *the guy's* hands pass over my ribcage and press against my back, pulling me against to his blazing skin.

"He won't see you coming," Tita's voice echoes in my mind. Maybe what she meant was *I* wouldn't see *him* coming. And what is happening between this shirtless stranger and me feels magical. But my pesky brain sounds the alarm.

You are kissing a stranger—someone crazy enough to be shirtless on this strangely warm January night in Texas. Clearly, neither of you is in your right mind.

I pull back, pushing up the blindfold.

Silvery-green eyes reflect the distant bonfire, making this beautiful guy look supernatural. Before he can speak, the tide rushes in—crashing against our ankles. Shrieks erupt among the group, and everyone races off, complaining about the cold.

The bursting energy in my chest, like laughter trying to escape, is something I can't explain—a promise of something more. I glance at the endless, black sea, and a dark, indiscernible shadow glides below the surface.

I blink, shaking the strange sensation of being watched away, and find *the guy,* Ian Decker, waiting for me.

Tita Blessica predicting my true love, predicting Ian, puts fear in Mom. After the girls and I get home, Mom pulls me aside to talk about the family curse.

Here's the truth about Mom: she lies.

But that's okay because they're never harmful. They're lies like never pop a pimple because you'll get an infection and die, or never wave to other drivers because they'll think you're angry, shoot you, and you'll die. Before tonight, I would have said that Mom's biggest lie was about *Aswangs*, Filipino mythological creatures meant to keep me in line. When I was little, she used to say things like, "If you don't tell me the truth, the *Aswang* will get you." But now, I roll my eyes whenever she mentions the winged shapeshifter.

Mom presses my shoulders, so I sit. Infused in her pressure is the weight of her intention when she says, "My mother, your *Lola*, was thirteen the first time she fell in love, and she had to die to escape it."

Whatever this lie leads to, it's shaping up to be her most outlandish.

"Die? Come on, Mom. I just spoke to Grandma last week on FaceTime. Remember, she held the phone this close to her face?" I press my phone against my nose, going cross-eyed.

Mom doesn't laugh, her mind far away.

"She fell in love with the sweetest boy in the village, but there was a girl who was jealous of their love—she came from a family of *Mangkukulams,* but their family did not use their magic for good. She put a curse on your *Lola,* who immediately fell ill. A traveling *Albularyo* healed *Mamay* before she could die, but there was still fear that the jealous girl's family would put another curse on my mom. *Mamay* did the only thing she could. She chopped off all her hair, which was so long it swept the ground, and faked her death."

I pick at a thread coming loose on the couch. "Okay, but faking a death is not dying."

"Until you've had to give up a life you've always known, you may never understand the death she suffered." Mom breathes heavily through her nostrils before continuing. "Still, the curse was not gone. Because she fell in love with the sweetest boy, we, her daughters, are doomed to fall in love with the most deceptively sweet boys. Our first loves are tainted as these boys would be appealing on the outside like a fresh dragon fruit but cut into them, and they're rotten to their core. Being with them kills the person you are so that even when you escape, you will never be the same."

I'm silent for so long Mom finally looks up at me. I keep waiting for the part where she laughs and tells me she's kidding, but it doesn't come. Mom is absolutely serious about this lie because she's not ready for me to have a boyfriend. The persistent shaking of her leg indicates she's waiting for a response.

"If the curse makes these guys bad, then why don't you try to save the guys or break the curse, so no one gets hurt?"

"The curse doesn't make the guys bad. It only attracts the worst guys. Makes you attracted to them; puts you under their spell. The guys were always going to be bad."

"Okay." I snort, getting up.

"You don't believe me?" Mom stands as well.

"No. But even if I did, what's the solution? Never fall in love?"

Mom is silent, probably trying to reason out this grand lie in her head. I exhale, conceding that perhaps she's not lying at all. Perhaps she believes the lie her mother told her. Mom goes on about what she and my aunties went through with this curse, how she knows it's real, but I'm too exhausted from the excitement of the beach bonfire to parse through this fabrication with her.

I may not believe her, but I know she wants me to, so I don't bother telling her about meeting Ian. In fact, even as she speaks, the excited whispers of my friends explaining how Ian had rallied the team for the bonfire just so he could see me completely tune her out. At the same time, I'm sent to another world as I relive Hannah describing how Ian purposely stood in front of me just so he could kiss me.

No one has ever pursued me like that. I'd never been made to feel that special for doing absolutely nothing. I'm too high to hear Mom, and the further I get from that conversation, the more it sounds like just another mom lie.

This is especially true a month after the bonfire, just after my sixteenth birthday, when Ian invites me to his house to catch fireflies in a Ziplock bag. He knows I hate flying bugs, so he comes up behind me and tickles my ear, causing me to shriek. He's always finding little reasons to touch me.

"How'd you do on that math test?" I love how he remembers the things I care about. I'd been stressing over that test for a week.

I roll my eyes, groaning into my hands. "I got a low B."

"That's cool." Then reading into my raised eyebrows, he says, "Or it's horrible."

"My mom expects As. A low B is basically a C which is basically an F."

"If I got a low B, my dad would probably throw me a

party," he laughs, but it doesn't reach his eyes which are focused on a leaf he's shredding.

We lie in the grass, examining the lightning bugs in our makeshift lantern when he touches the crease on my forehead. "What are you thinking about?"

I lean into his hand, which caresses my face. "Do you believe in curses?"

A sound like a plate shattering against a wall crashes from within Ian's house.

"Ian, get in here," a voice booms from within the dark walls.

"I'll be right back." His expression darkens, which confuses me because it's so far from the confidence I've come to expect. I sit up on my knees, alert.

The lights never come on in the house, and Ian's voice never climbs higher than his father's shouts, but the anger pouring from the house makes me cover my ears.

Another crashing noise has me jumping to my feet, my palms sweating. I don't know if I should run in there to check on Ian or call the police, but suddenly the screen door swings open, and Ian races outside. He reaches for my hand and drags me to his car while his dad, not even forming fully coherent sentences, throws anything he can reach at us—mail, a tv remote, a half-full water bottle.

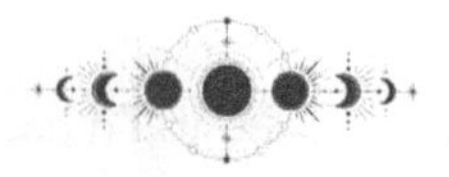

At first, Ian seems to be driving around aimlessly, but eventually, we arrive at Laguna Pool which glows cyan as dusk settles over this small part of our world. He gets out, beelining for the entrance, then notices I don't get out of the car.

Leaning against the open window on the passenger side, he asks, "You coming?"

"I can't climb that fence. If cops catch us sneaking in, Mom and Dad will kill me."

"Relax. I worked here last summer, so I have a spare set of keys."

"Legally?" My voice trembles at his receding back, which shakes with laughter as he leaves me behind.

Ian sits at the pool's edge, and I join him, removing my shoes and slipping my feet into the water. Under the lamp light from the pavilion, I gaze intently at Ian's reflection. Only water swishing in and out of the filters and bugs hitting the orange-yellow light fixture next to the office door breaks the silence between us.

"Earlier, you asked me if I believed in curses." His green eyes seem bluer tonight. "The truth is, I think my dad's a curse. I don't know what I did—" He squeezes one of his biceps, his eyes closing as he grimaces.

"Are you okay?" I hadn't realized he might have actually gotten hurt.

"It's not a big deal," Ian says, pulling his shirt down to reveal the reddened skin around his shoulder. It will bruise.

I reach to touch it but hesitate when my heart accelerates. He grabs my hand, placing it over the spot where he's hurt, just inside his shirt. Electricity pulses through me, making my insides tingle.

"Your hands are so hot." He laughs once. "It's nice."

"Thanks," I breathe, trying to clear my mind but having trouble when I touch him like this. "My aunties call them healing hands."

"A healer, huh?"

"No, not really. It's just something they say—that you can tell when someone's a healer by the heat of their hands. I recently learned that those types of healers are called ... something that starts with an A, but I can't remember. It's stupid."

"It's not." He touches the fraying ends of my shorts, his finger grazing my leg. "I wish I was connected to my family."

My heart aches for him, and I wish I could give him that connection he desperately wants. There's a heavy weight between us, but it's broken when I startle at the thunderous thud of a wooden shutter snapping shut. It evokes the traumatizing memories of things crashing within Ian's house. He flinches.

"I can't go home tonight."

I gaze at his profile; the way the light from the pavilion outlines him, the defeated hunch of his shoulders, makes him seem so fragile. He has no one.

And as much trouble as I would get in if we were caught, I risk it for him when I offer, "You could stay at my house." His eyes widen as they meet mine, sparkling as if I'm his savior, even though I'm not offering anything more than my floor.

He cups my face, pulling me to him as he hesitantly brushes my lips with his. We've shared kisses since that night at the bonfire, but this one is different—more intense in its softness.

"I'd love to stay with you tonight," he whispers, and the way his voice shakes makes me teary-eyed.

He leans in to kiss me again, but I pull away, excusing myself for the restroom to collect myself. I splash water over my face, then clutch both sides of the sink as I steady my breathing. How could someone do that to their kid?

When I go back out there, Ian is nowhere in sight.

Behind me, the office door is open. I peek inside, but it's not what I expect. Because the swim season is over, all water bottles, whistles, and wet towels have been cleared from the place for the rest of the year, leaving the space feeling haunted. Darkness from the back room threatens to spill over the threshold and grab hold of me.

"Ian?" I call out, trying to suppress the trembling. Flip

flops shuffle in the back room, and he emerges reeking of weed. It doesn't shock me since a lot of the guys on the team smoke, but I am surprised he had a stash of weed here.

"You ready to go?" I jerk my thumb back at his car.

"Yeah, I can drop you off at your home if you're ready." Ian shoves his pipe into the fanny pack containing his CPR breathing mask.

My mouth opens and shuts. "Are ... are you staying with me?"

"Not tonight. Tomorrow."

I laugh, but when he doesn't join me, I realize he might not be joking.

"Are you kidding? You said you couldn't go home and wanted to stay with me tonight."

"I did say I couldn't go home. But I meant for a few days. And I really would love to stay with you. But that doesn't automatically mean tonight." I look from him to the place by the pool where we were sitting together. Am I remembering things wrong? What suddenly changed?

Ian avoids my gaze, messing with a red marker from a plastic cup of pens. I try to recall our earlier conversation. *Am I crazy?*

"So, you don't have anywhere to go tonight, but you'd love to stay at my house tomorrow?"

"Well, I could cancel plans with Garrett if you really *need* to hang out tonight." I shake my head one quick time. Okay, so did he make plans with Garrett while I was in the bathroom? And if so, then why didn't he say that?

My shoulders drop. I don't want to be a burden, but I'm bummed that I thought we had plans tonight, and now we don't. "No, don't worry about it. As long as you're safe."

Ian smiles. "Hey, don't be like that. We'll hang out tomorrow night, just like we planned. In the meantime, let me show you something." He tosses the red marker and catches it behind his back before disappearing into the back room. My heart hammers as I follow him into the darkness. I jump when I turn the corner and find Ian crouched low in the shadows. But he only laughs before uncapping the marker and writing our names plus forever near the baseboard behind a filing cabinet because, "That way, no one will see it and paint over it."

Warmth floods me as he documents our night together, and I'm touched that he wouldn't want anyone to erase it. When he drags me to the supply closet and closes the door, he treats me like I'm the sun keeping his world alive. Snatching the marker from his hand, I pull his shirt collar away just enough to draw a heart on his chest as he picks me up and wraps my legs around him.

chapter two

Months later, Ian sneaks into my room in the dead of night. He holds me within the protection of his lean, swimmer arms, creating warmth and love that sets my soul ablaze. His fingers trail up and down my arm as light as feathers.

"Why don't you come to my house?" he whispers in the blackest of hours as I nuzzle my cold nose into his warm neck. My stomach twists.

"I have to ask my mom," I reply in a low voice, so it doesn't wake my sister in the next room. But I already know Mom won't let me go to his house anymore. She's always been strict about boys, but when it comes to Ian, there is no leeway. She calls him "the curse" to Tita Blessica when she thinks I'm not listening.

"No, Malaya," he sighs. "I mean, sneak out."

I freeze, and he peers at me questioningly. The depths of his sea-green eyes ignite a familiar ache in my chest, a primal need to be with him all the time because, in his absence, I'm incomplete. Even the thought of him having to leave at some point tonight causes a hollowness in my gut though he's right here. But while I want to say yes, to make him happy more than anything, the idea of sneaking out makes my hands clammy. I try to relax my shoulders, but the tension in my neck won't release.

"Like at night?" My voice sounds impossibly small, like a child's.

"I did it for you." While his tone is soft, his words say more—implying I should do more.

"Yeah, no ... I could try," I stumble.

He releases his hold of me, placing his arms behind his head, and there's a perceptible shift as chilly air fills the space between us. I cling to him, light from my TV flickering across his darkened face.

"Okay." I stare into his distant expression, trying to infuse my commitment to him in that word. Surveying me, he gives a crisp nod before scooping an arm around me—just one. Though I have his approval, the absence of his other arm is a confirmation that until I meet him halfway, I'll never have all of him.

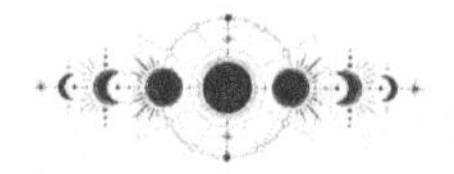

It's the end of summer, and Mom is packing my suitcase in the living room. Taking any advantage she can to separate Ian and me, Mom is sending me off to Virginia, against my will, to visit my dad's side of the family. She's not subtle in her dislike of Ian, and I point that out, hoping I can guilt my way out of this trip.

"Tell me this isn't about the curse again. Your mom left town to break her curse, you left the Philippines to break yours. You think sending me out of the state will break mine? There is no curse."

"Malaya Isla Davies." Mom employs the full use of my name, completely bypassing the softer first/middle name warning.

"I'll get my toiletries bag," I concede, pulling my phone out of my back pocket to text Ian.

He calls me immediately. "You're going out of town?" Am I imagining it, or does he sound a little happy? "You're canceling plans on me for the week?"

"Only because Mom's making me." I flop onto my bed, staring up at my immobile ceiling fan. "She's been so irritable lately. Like Grumpy Cat, only not funny."

"I hate that she's always picking on you." Ian pauses to take a hit from his bong. Then murmurs something to his friend Caleb before adding, "I wish I could take you away from there, but I'm eighteen, and your dad would call the cops. One day though ..."

"One day." I sit up, feeling trapped by my four walls.

"Is there anything I can do to make you feel better? Oh, I know. What if we video chat during your trip, and you can introduce me to your family?"

I sit up, suddenly lighter from the gesture. "You would do that? That's so big."

"Of course, I would do that. I'd do anything for you."

I sigh, an easiness filling me up. "How do you always know how to make me feel better?"

"Because I'm there for you when no one else is."

I feel that more and more with each passing day—lucky to have someone who takes my side no matter what. And just like that, I'm loading my suitcase into Dad's truck and making sure to pack his favorite road trip snack, beef jerky, while looking forward to Ian meeting my family.

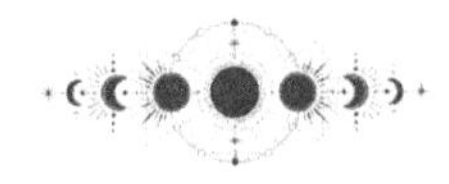

Ian and I text often, and I FaceTime him every night. At first, I'm sick with missing him and can't sleep. Then it becomes more than that.

Four days ago, Ian didn't respond to my texts until well after lunch. No, "good morning, beautiful" message. Two days ago, he didn't call me at all. I spent all night checking my phone for responses to my messages, inspecting my connection, and restarting the device in case of data issues, but I didn't hear from him until mid-morning the following day.

"Hey." His voice is stiff and lifeless, sending warning signals pulsing through my veins. I walk through the open field of my grandpa's untamed property, trying to get as far from prying ears as possible. Yellow wildflowers claw into my leggings like beasts trying to drag me to the pits of hell.

"Why didn't you call?" There's an edge to my voice.

"I was helping my dad with something, and by the time I got done, I was too tired to do anything else. I just passed out for the rest of the night."

"Oh." My voice fails, though my thoughts are firing off questions. What work could his dad need help with when he's got a bad back and no job? Why didn't Ian call during lunch or dinner? And did he expect me to believe they just skipped eating all day? But he does sound tired, so I drop it, adopting a more positive attitude. "Well, my trip is almost over. I can't wait to see you."

"Me too." He's rolling a joint now, his eyes cast downward. I'd waited and waited for this call, but Ian's voice, his face, aren't the assurance I need that we're okay. That he's missed me the way I've missed him. Before I can reach for anything to say that will lighten the mood, Ian says, "I guess I'll let you go."

My throat tightens.

"Okay ..." When we hang up, I'm not just states—but a world away from him. The rest of our conversations are brief, distant. They make food inedible, and interactions with family distracted. We just need to be with one another. Everything will fall into place when we are in each other's arms.

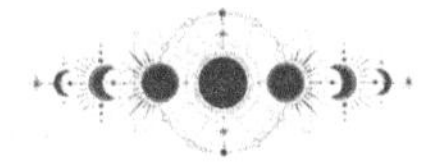

Back from Virginia, I'm desperate for my world to right itself, so I sneak out for the first time in my life.

Humid summer air sweeps my curls behind me as I walk swiftly toward the gulch at the end of my street. I've never snuck out before, but I'm afraid to take my car, worried the noise will wake my parents though their room is at the back of the house. Cicadas hum in the dead of night with such force they conceal my feet patting against the ground.

I approach the end of the sidewalk, where the cement fractures like lightning. Ian's neighborhood isn't far by car, but walking? The unknown makes this an endless task.

But he's done this much for me, right?

Glancing back at my parent's house, fireflies glint invitingly, lighting the way as if to say it's not too late to go back. It wars with the guilt poisoning my veins as I hide beneath the sweeping, ebony shadows of a Weeping Willow. Mom would kill me if she found out I'd snuck out, but instead of all the ways I'd be in trouble, my thoughts go to another conversation she and I had at a much different time in my life.

"Malaya, your virginity is something you can never get back. Once you give it away, it's gone." There was a finality in Mom's words as she turned onto the street that led us to our isolated neighborhood. The main road to civilization disappeared in my side-view window. "You only get one chance to decide if the person you give it to is worth it. That is why you wait until marriage."

While I hadn't waited 'til marriage, I did wait until I was

absolutely in love. What won't I do to ensure Ian and I end up together? Maybe not everyone ends up with their high school sweetheart, but there's no saying I won't. We could be like the couples in the romance books I read—facing adversities but always finding our way to one another. Whatever life throws at us won't matter if we keep walking toward each other.

Staring at my mother's house, I know I'll lose Ian if I don't do this. If I've learned anything from the stories I'd read, it's that a person needs to feel like you're willing to fight for them.

Turning away from home, I embrace the dark ditch below, hopping the mossy rocks that bridge my block to the next. There aren't many streetlights, so with mostly starlight to guide me, I flinch at every noise—the rare car scooting along the far main road, the brush shifting in the wind, a bat flitting so close to my hair that strands get caught in my mouth. There's one piece of advice I'm sure Mom didn't lie about: never stay out after sunset because anything can happen, and you'll die.

My heart hammers in my throat as onyx shadows take on eerie forms. I stare into them to discern that they are not monsters ... yet the shadows crawl.

It's the clouds moving across the moon, I tell myself, but my mind goes to darker places.

The *Aswang*, a Filipino shapeshifting creature known for the *tik tik* noise they make before they attack, stalks me. That sound plays mind games because it doesn't function as a typical monster's roar does. When they are loudest, *TIK TIK,* that means they are farthest away. You still have time to run, and you want to race *toward* the guttural roar. It forces you to fight your every instinct. It's the almost undetectable *tik tik. tik tik. tik tik.* that should scare you because the creature is right over your shoulder, and all is lost.

I tread the edge of the inky-black road overgrown with

weeds that scrape my skin, not a single weapon or defensive skill in my arsenal. I wish I'd listened to Mom about being out at night.

Two car doors slam, *TIK TIK*, and I run.

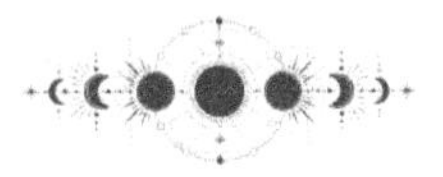

Instead of racing all the way to Ian's house, he asked me to meet him in the band hall parking lot, equidistant from each other.

He seems otherworldly, standing beneath the fire-orange glow of the lamplight rather than waiting for me by his window at home. I run the rest of the way to him. But his arms don't open like I imagined they would every day of our separation, though I fling myself against him. The stiffness in his body, the awkwardness of his hands gently pushing me away, spark that intuition I'd ignored all week. My guts twist as a cold wave of dread flushes my body. Something isn't right and seeing each other is not the cure I hoped it would be.

"What's wrong?" My stupid voice shakes as my smile falters.

I track his stiff walk as he moves out of the fiery light and into the darkness. His green eyes turn silver in the dim stardust; their expressiveness mirroring my confusion.

His torturous confession starts as a dream.

"In this dream, there were two girls ... they wanted me ... in this dream, you didn't exist ..." My heart cracks, rather than beats, within my chest even though, according to him, this is a dream. Yet, my gut is screaming that it's not. My gut shouts that he cheated. Am I breathing? My chest is so tight, I can't tell. Finally, he says, "I just think, if this dream is what I really want, it wouldn't be fair for us to be together."

In an instant, color drains from my world entirely. But my brain refuses to believe this is it. My head shakes as he speaks about our time together as something he'll never forget, though no words fall from my lips. His shirt ripples in the breeze like the ocean's gentle waves when the surf is weak. It's the same color as his iridescent, moonlit hair, making him ghostly.

"Say something," he urges, stepping toward me.

I recoil. "This is what you want? You want to break up because you had *a dream*?"

His eyes shift to the ground. Dropping my head back, I scan the vast night sky for any answer other than the one coming.

"Was it a dream?"

He's silent for too long, and when my gaze returns to him, I know the truth. He wouldn't end us simply because he had a dream. No. This was more. The rose gold feeling of love drains from me, and I'm miles from someone I love.

Rage fills me but not toward Ian. This is Mom's fault. This wouldn't have happened if she hadn't made me go out of town—all because she thought it would break that stupid curse. No, this goes back further. All my life, she'd promised that when I turned sixteen, I could date. But that birthday and its promises came and went. And here I am, having to sneak out just to see Ian. Now I'm suffering for it because he's found something in someone else that he couldn't find in me.

Betrayal shatters me, weakening my limbs, making me dizzy.

I don't know when I started walking away. I don't notice anything around me until Ian pulls me back to him—embracing me as my arms hang by my sides. He's whispering things against my hair, but the words don't make sense.

All I know is that I come away with this idea that this love and this life being over is unacceptable. That he's not ready to give up on us, so neither should I. Is this part of the curse too? Are these my ideas or his? I'm not sure.

Tik Tik.

All I know is I'm not ready to admit I'd trusted my virtue to someone so willing to throw it away.

chapter three

With autumn, I replace my nightly walks to Ian's for early morning hikes—driven by a dark force to cling to him despite what happened. It's as if the shadows of the *Aswang* are whispering me onward, encouraging me not to let go, asking me to forgive but never letting me forget. If I'm cursed, nothing Mom's suggested in all her months of warning me about the curse has worked to release me from this personal hell. I've taken salt baths, cut energy cords, lit candles, and prayed—all to no avail. I can't leave him no matter what I do.

It's like I haven't slept in months, I'm fighting with Mom more, my grades are slipping, and so are my friendships. But since cheating, Ian has become incredibly attentive. He bought me daffodils, which are *his* favorite flowers but are starting to become mine. He texts me every day, calls every night, and when I come over, he strokes my hair as I lie wide awake. I can't sleep because when I close my eyes, my dreams are haunted by the images of him embracing other girls. In some ways, his cheating made him a better boyfriend, and I'm attempting to forgive him because at least he's trying.

As I park my old Mustang in front of the decrepit school gym that houses the pool I should be practicing at, my lights narrowly illuminate the sidewalk to the steel gym doors. Once I cut the engine, my path is cast in darkness. This place marks a quarter distance of my walk to Ian's, saving me some, but never enough, time. I park here and walk the rest of the trip. This way, when my dad drives to work in the mornings, he'll think I'm at swim practice.

The gym doors are a shortcut to the field behind my school, and I pass through them without a glance back. I'll hit after-school swim practice ... maybe. I don't have the energy to do much these days besides sit in my room, gripping my phone in wait. Dew glistens atop the tall grass, disappearing into my jeans as I cut through the immense, star-covered space. Wind bounces off the school buildings, putting me on edge as it echoes in low beastly moans. Maybe if I sink low enough, I can disappear beneath the iridescent spider webs draping across the weeds, and the things that haunt me will leave me alone.

My imagination conjures *Aswangs* built from the absence of light. Their branch-like limbs and beastly gaits threaten to envelop me. Mom has always said *Aswangs* are attracted to lies and use their long proboscis to suck out bits of their victims hearts that had turned dark from dishonesty. That way, they can feed off one child for years before finally killing them. Even in this cool season, this part of the walk makes my palms sweat for the lack of light.

Maybe Ian hasn't cheated again—but distrust is my personal monster growling low in my ears, conjuring images of Ian's arms around other girls. Despite all he's done to make me more comfortable, like tacking up a picture of me next to his bed and inviting me to hang out anytime he's going to his buddies' houses to smoke, I'm haunted.

I've started hiding in the library, sometimes in the occult section, trying to figure out how to break curses, while other times near the self-help books, trying to figure out how to let go and forgive. The curse-breaking stuff just makes me smell like herbs. But I think the self-help stuff is starting to work. Ian's been going to parties every Saturday, something I can't do with him because Mom always drags us to Filipino parties on Saturdays. Last weekend, I got through most of the Filipino party without texting Ian by simply becoming engrossed in karaoke. It felt like the old days, and Mom even sang that mermaid song with me.

I might finally be over the hardest part of Ian's betrayal, and I'm stronger for it. In my gut, I know if I ever got proof of him cheating again, I'd leave him.

But I soon discover that healing is not an easy downhill walk. Trauma involves ups and downs, and today is definitely an uphill battle. Stephanie approaches my locker for the fifth time. Her boyfriend, Caleb, is good friends with Ian, and he's having a party tonight. But Ian forgot to invite me to it. My paranoia keeps whispering *how convenient.*

"I'm sure he'll text you about it soon," Stephanie says. "He probably just forgot to invite you."

It's meant to be comforting, but I find myself burying my face in my locker so she can't see my trembling chin or reddening ears. She pats me on the shoulder, and I manage a thin-lip smile, but my gut says he forgot on purpose.

By the time the party rolls around later that night, Ian and I have texted three times without him mentioning his plans. Ten minutes before the party I call him.

"What are you doing tonight? You want to hang out?"

"Awe baby, I can't. I'm going to Caleb's with the guys."

"Oh?" My heart accelerates. Maybe this is it.

"Yeah, it's just a chill hang."

My shoulders slump as he rushes to get off the phone. I text him a few more times, but they all go unanswered. I feel crazy. I am crazy, and my once beautiful love story has become something I'm ashamed to tell my friends about.

I lie to Mom about the party, telling her that Stephanie and I are going to do face masks and watch romantic comedies tonight. She only consents because Stephanie shows up at the front door right then, proving that we will be together.

We pull up in front of Caleb's to a line of cars parked up and down his street. *Just-a-chill-hang, my ass.*

Inside, there's a general clutter of noise and chatter as people laugh in their groups. Smoke lingers in the air, and beer permeates the atmosphere. Calvin, one of Ian's dealers, nods as I enter. Then he turns back to his friend, pulls out his phone, and texts while he carries on his conversation. I give him a polite smile, trying to ignore the voice in my head telling me he's warning Ian that I'm here.

As I head for the den in the back of the house, Kurt, a sandy-haired beach bum with sunspots, nudges his girlfriend and looks nervously at the back door. Not even bothering with pleasantries as I pass Ian's loyal friends, I turn toward the door. It sits crooked on its frame, so I have to throw my shoulder into it to get it to open. The door makes a loud noise that's muffled by the raucous party. But that noise isn't loud enough for Ian, who is so engrossed in conversation with a thin blonde that he doesn't bother to see who's come outside.

Ian leans against the railing of the rickety porch so close to the attractive girl with the unfortunate root job that you'd think it was snowing out here on this fall night. But this is South Texas, and the word cold is practically mythological. A fantastical story told by northerners to put fear in unwanted tourists.

Though Ian still hasn't looked at me, the girl does. Her friendly smile shows she has no idea who I am. My scowl turns the mood sour quickly.

Ian, noticing his friend's expression, finally checks over his shoulder.

"Malaya?" His surprise is fleeting, immediately replaced

with a bold smile. He takes a step away from the blonde, and it's so smooth you would think he was just shifting his weight to the other leg. "What are you doing here?"

"I was able to get away." I look from her to him. Has anything happened between them? Her expression betrays nothing.

She passes the joint pinched between her fingers to Ian, and her touch lingers. Fiery rage rushes through my body, so I'd swear my hair is on fire.

"I'm going to find ... everyone else," she says, eyes sparkling.

I step aside, so she can get by, angry at myself for being mad at her when she probably has no clue he has a girlfriend. Angry at myself for not being confident enough to confront her. Because maybe if I did, she would tell me what she thought would happen between them. Solidarity between sisters and all that. But I don't even have the guts to look at her face as she passes. Afraid of seeing pity or guilt or even amusement in her eyes. Afraid my anger at him will send a message that I want to fight her. Afraid she could kick my ass with her model height and muscular arms.

After the door closes, there is a deep and fiercely uncomfortable silence. Ian takes a hit from his joint. "You shouldn't be here." His voice takes on that airless quality of someone speaking without breathing. Despite that, there's a tone that suggests he doesn't want me here. My scowl deepens, and he rushes to say, "Did you walk here? You know I don't like when you do that. Anything could happen to you."

He leans forward and reaches for my hand, pulling me into his chest and making me feel foolish for doubting him. I push him away, crossing my arms.

"I didn't walk here. Stephanie drove me. Because *she* actually invited me."

He nods once, like he's connecting my tone on the phone earlier and how I'd found out about the party.

"Is that why you're being irrational?" He strokes my cheek, and angry tears spring to my eyes. "I told you about the party. Remember, you were doing homework when I called to invite you? You didn't really respond to me, so I said if it's okay, I'll just go alone. Then you said okay."

My skin prickles as I immediately want to call him out on the lie ... and yet, there's just enough doubt to cause me to pause. Can the curse affect my memories too? I inhale deeply through my nose, rolling my shoulders back. "I don't remember when I was ever distracted by homework and not giving you my full attention ..."

Ian reaches for me again, his face in a puckered apology as he clutches me to him.

"You've been so tired lately; you just haven't been able to give me the attention you used to. And it's okay. I understand. With all the fighting you've been doing with your mom and your classes getting harder, you don't have time for me."

"But I do—"

He looks down. "No, you don't. But I'll take whatever I can get because you're important to me."

"I am?" My words are a whisper, caught on a breeze.

"Of course, dummy. I can't be without you. I didn't even want to come to this party if you weren't going to be here. To be honest, it hurt when you said I could come alone."

My brow furrows, but at the same time, Ian's arm clenches me more tightly to him as if the thought of me leaving causes him pain. It's almost too tight, but it feels so good to be held that I don't say anything. He *has* been calling me more lately, and I *have* been overwhelmed with homework. I guess it's entirely possible that what he's saying happened and that he's not just saying that so he can party like he's single. The problem is that I can't trust myself to believe him since he cheated, even after all his efforts to fix us.

So, I stand in his arms with my face turned away, mainly because I want to keep frowning and don't want him to see. After all, it's not like I caught him kissing another girl. It's not like I found him in bed with someone else.

We're silent for too long. This position isn't comfortable anymore, but we both hold onto it. The night air is so strangely still that we're standing in his smoky weed cloud. I get the feeling he's hoping the second-hand smoke will force me to calm down. It only puts me further on edge because I'll have to wash my clothes at Stephanie's before going home, or else Mom will smell it.

I exhale as quietly as possible, trying to let go of my anger. Ian takes that as a signal to let go of me, misreading my cues. Then he pulls out his phone and checks the time. I steal a glance at the screen and notice that there is not one notification of my messages. He'd gotten every single one and ignored me on purpose because he was too busy talking to Miss Bleach Blonde.

I step out of his reach, which causes him to drag his eyes away from the screen.

"Why were you out here alone with that girl?" I cross my arms.

"Malaya," he sighs exasperatedly, rolling his eyes. "Not this again."

"Yes, this again." I'm forceful, angry that he's always in these situations. Frustrated that he's the type of boyfriend who just happens to be sitting next to the prettiest girl or even the only girl when there are so many guys he could hang out with instead. Furious that he isn't more proactive about avoiding situations like this when other boyfriends don't seem to have this problem. Enraged that situations like this 'just happen,' as he puts it.

"For the thousandth time, it happened once," he says, clearly talking about the cheating incident. "Once! And I told you about her immediately. If I cheated on you again, don't you think I would tell you?"

Images of him with imaginary girls flash through my mind. But they run wild as an imagination will do when you are not there to experience something and have to rely on the vague details of someone else's account of events. They haunt me the way the *Aswang* does—the way this curse of a relationship does.

I want to scream "I want out" but my lips fuse together from the curse. I barely breathe from this paralyzing pain.

Ian takes my hand, his expression softening. "It's been a long time. Even Stephanie thinks so." Stephanie? When did she talk to him about this? My face burns because I didn't think she knew let alone would side with him. Maybe I should get over it. "You have to start trusting me. You're the only one in my bed." His words ask for forgiveness, but his tone says something more. It suggests that if I don't start trusting him, there will be no us. That's not just my paranoia talking. He's said as much before.

My expression remains rigid, though my insides burn with panic. I don't want to know what life would be like without him. He's my true love. He's the guy who picked wildflowers for me and tucked them in my hair. The guy who built a bonfire for me just so he had a chance to meet me. He's the guy who I thought would be my last everything. I can see all his potential; the man he would be once he was through with this partying lifestyle. We are young, after all. There is so much time for change when we get older.

But I also don't want to feel this way anymore.

Mom tells me I'm in charge of my happiness. That breaking the curse comes down to me. Yet, I can't see joy down either path when I think about staying or leaving. My shoulders slump with the weight of these two paths. I wish there were some magical third option, but as far as I can tell, there is no magic in this world. Only darkness.

"It's not like it's even my fault that we were alone out here," Ian scrambles. "A bunch of us were hanging out, but they went inside right before you got here. I don't even know that girl. You just came at exactly the wrong time."

Ian's not used to me holding my ground, and he fidgets with his lighter, snapping the wheel over and over. But I appear more confident than I am because something catches my eye on the end of the property. It's a flicker of movement in the trees, like a small, old woman standing at the edge of the lawn. Has the *Aswang* shapeshifted into a new form? No back fence separates the yard from the heavy brush, and the creeping vines mix with the overgrown forest, creating eerie shapes in the darkness. Like the shape of the woman standing still among the suddenly breezy branches. Is it the *Aswang* again? Or is it something more terrifying than that demon shapeshifter?

"Malaya," Ian calls for my attention.

"What?" I'm a little too harsh.

"Let's get a drink. That'll make you feel better."

"Fine." I pull my arms close as I look back at the empty spot in the woods.

For some reason, I can't get my eyes to find the same pattern in the brush that framed the woman's outline, and it sends chills running down my spine. *TIK TIK.*

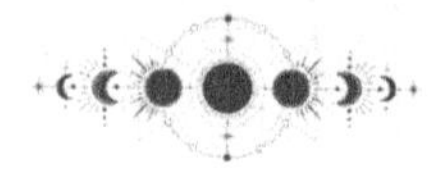

Later, a smaller group of us meet at Ian's for a kickback. Ian pulls me into his room, picks me up, and tosses me onto his bed. My head hits something hard just next to the pillow.

"Ow." I rub the back of my ear, picking up a camera that is almost shoved into the pillowcase. I toss the camera on an old recliner in the corner, so it has a safe place to land.

Though I think nothing of it, Ian's voice is hard as he says, "I've had that for a long time."

My brow furrows, and then I connect his comment to the camera.

"Okay ..." My head shakes as if to clear the confusion caused by the defensive edge of his tone. The whites of Ian's eyes grow as if he's made a mistake, and then, in a beat, he lightens up. Crawling into bed next to me, he kisses me like he's trying to erase any memories of the camera. Typically, that might work, but not tonight.

When he's satisfied, he gets up. "I'm gonna grab weed from Calvin." He smiles like it's my treat.

"I don't care," I mumble, keying in my passcode as I feign interest in my phone. I don't participate in his extracurriculars. All I care about are the things hidden on that camera.

The instant Ian is out of the room, I grab the camera.

For a second, for just a moment, I stare at the black screen. My pulse pounds so that the finger hovering over the power button shakes. This feels like one of those moments I'll never be able to take back.

Then I'm holding the evidence I've been searching for: pictures of Ian at the beach with different girls, in bed with a brunette whose halter top is untied, Ian and some blonde biting his ear. The tattoos on his body mark the passage of time. Not for the first time, my body curls in on itself as I stare at the blinding screen gripped in my fist. Cold sweat from the flood of betrayal causes uncontrollable shivers that give way to interspersed periods of numb calmness as I stare at the oldest picture in the collection.

Ian is wrapped around a pretty, freckled girl, and there's a red marker drawing of a heart on his pec. My chest is heaving, and the tears roll hot down my cheeks. That first night he was supposed to stay with me, the night I was there for him, fell for him because I thought he needed me, he went to someone else.

I'd known he'd cheated once before, but this feels worse somehow. Perhaps because if I'd known what he was really like that early in our relationship, nine months ago, I might have been able to get out before I'd gotten in so deep.

I hadn't been stupid for distrusting him; I'd been stupid for distrusting myself. I have proof that I wouldn't be giving up on something special if I left him.

I'm ending this now. Tonight.

And yet, at his voice filling the hall on his approach, darkness digs its claws into my chest once again. The familiar chill of the curse whispers warnings of love lost forever and conjures images of a friendless, empty existence. When he opens the door, it's like I've lost time. Like I've blacked out somewhere between my conviction to leave him, and the physical action of shutting the camera off and returning to bed. It doesn't make an ounce of sense, but that's what happens.

I understand now. No amount of proof would ever be enough to get me to leave Ian. I'm stuck in a nightmare, and the person I want to save me is also the person causing the pain. My head is so haunted by those gut-wrenching pictures I don't hear Ian after he comes in and starts talking to me.

All I hear is Mom telling me that the curse brings these deceptively sweet guys to kill the person we are. I want to tell her she's right. I'm not the person I was. But I can't face her I told you so. I can't go to her; I can't even go to Stephanie. The only person I'm connected to anymore is Ian.

Tik tik.

Every Saturday night, we attend a Filipino party at Auntie Jeslyn's house. As I push the door open, the Filipino-American environment attacks my senses. My ears fill with the jarring croons of my aunties singing over each other into karaoke mics. The microphones' reverb settings are too high like they'd all piled into the shower or fallen into a deep cave. My nose picks up their margarita breaths mixed with the ever-permanent smell of steamed rice and soy sauce dishes.

While the aunties sit on couches passing songbooks, they gossip about the latest thing they found out about So-and-So or the newest drama at church. They shout for me to join them, but I wave away the binder of song choices.

"No, thank you, Auntie." I smile politely.

Of course, I'm not related to any of them. But "Auntie" is what you call other Filipino women who are your mom's age, even from the moment you meet them, because 'that is the way.' It's the same with Filipino women who are my grandma's age. They are all my Grandma. My sister's friends call me *Ate*, big sister because I am the oldest.

As if on cue, the dads erupt into loud cheering from the patio as they watch the latest game on a small TV hooked up via an extension cord out on the back patio.

"Todd," Uncle Jason calls to my dad from the sliding door. Dad pulls a beer out of a cooler in the dining room before heading to the back porch.

"Malaya, go eat." Mom had sprinted to the karaoke, so she's shouting between the lyrics of a song she cut in on. Her voice echoes through the speakers. She taps the songbook against one leg in rhythm with the music, her other leg tucked under her.

As I enter the kitchen, I pass a table of aunties speaking mixed Tagalog and English: Taglish. Even if I don't speak Tagalog, I understand enough to know that my Tita Blessica is both drunk and on another long-winded rant.

"They say we have no culture." Tita Blessica throws her hands up exasperatedly.

"Who says?" Auntie Jeslyn enters the kitchen behind me so quietly on foot and yet so loudly by mouth that it causes me to jump.

"Everybody. Everybody who is not Filipino."

"Everybody?" Auntie Jeslyn raises a sharply drawn eyebrow.

"Well," Tita Blessica, in her drunken state, considers, "okay, not everybody. But people! They complain we steal from other cultures. who is not Filipino. They complain we steal from other cultures. They say our food is not authentic, but they order from our restaurants. They clap when we perform *Tinikling* at the festivals. But God forbid we try out their dances! They act like we are too stupid to understand because we have an accent, but I speak three languages: Tagalog, Ilocano, and English. Might as well never come here."

"*Hay naku*," several of my aunties murmur in unison.

I've seen people treat my mother less than because of her accent, but I've never heard about the other things Tita Blessica is complaining about. Then again, I'm never seen as a Filipina because of my mixed-race features.

I finish loading my plate with *pancit* and *lumpia* and head back to the living room, where the mood is less tense, though just as loud. Ian has people over at his house, so he hasn't texted me in hours. A pain, which started in my throat at the beginning of the night, has spread throughout my chest. I scroll through social media but don't feel relieved when there's nothing from Ian's get-together.

Tita Blessica comes around the corner with a deck of playing cards held high.

"*Hoy*," she shouts above the laughter and talking.

The room gets about as silent as it can get, considering more than seventy-five percent of its occupants are drunk. Most of us turn to look at Tita Blessica as she slurs, "Time for readings." There's a cheer before Tita Blessica disappears down the opaque hallway that leads to Auntie Jeslyn's master bedroom: the future-telling quarters.

As the night goes on, I continue to see zero Ian-related posts on any social media sites, which is impossible because I'm "friends" with a lot of Ian's friends who document every minute of their life. Why do I have to see every breakfast they have and joint they roll, but this party is somehow not eventful enough to document? In my gut, I sense Ian told them to block me.

How's the party going?

I wait several minutes with no response. My breathing becomes more intense. It gets harder to look up from my phone. When I can't take it any longer, I head for the front door. But then I stop. It would be crazy to walk to his house, right? Maybe I can ask to borrow Gabrielle's phone and see if anyone posted anything by looking through her accounts. I doubt they'd think to block her.

No.

I run my fingers through my curls, letting them fall when I catch the inevitable knots. If I ask to use her phone, she and her best friend, Bentley, would have too many questions. The last time I snuck out during a Filipino party, Bentley almost accidentally outed me by shouting, “Ugh, you’re so lucky you get to go to high school parties!” Of course, I wasn’t lucky. We’re all in high school, so none of us will be allowed to go to a non-Filipino party until we’re in college. I’d just left. Luckily, none of the moms heard.

I exhale, then it hits me. I can borrow Eric’s phone. He doesn’t care enough to ask why.

However, he will probably give me hell about borrowing his stuff because I got him in trouble earlier. This morning Mom attacked me with a Zoom call hosted by an *Albularyo* and populated with a prayer circle made up of Aunties all from her hometown province in the Philippines. It was an explosion of condolences, pity, and chiding for allowing myself to be cursed. I’d refused to participate and shut the laptop. Mom started in on me and what began as an argument about the curse, turned into other faults like my tone and how I fold laundry. We’d just finished snapping at each other about the kitchen not being cleaned her way when Eric had gotten in the crosshairs. “She wouldn’t be so angry at me if you weren’t pissing her off all the time,” Eric had grumbled, pushing his way past me.

Even now, I’m too prideful to apologize. We don’t do that in this family. But he might take my request for help as an admission that he’s right as long as I don’t snap at him when he inevitably makes a comment about how *now* I need something from him, and I definitely need this.

Turning casually, I walk down the dusty hallway. It’s remained unlit for as long as I can remember because nobody feels like changing the lightbulb, no matter how much Auntie Jeslyn complains about it. A random sock litters the corner, and the baseboard gathers dust bunnies that swish back and forth when I pass, reminding me this isn't the typical, pristine Filipino household.

Passing the master bedroom, Tita Blessica stands at the foot of the bed, only partially obscured by an iridescent bead curtain that is the door to that room. Last summer, the boys were roughhousing and tackled each other right through the original door. Rather than buy a new one, Auntie Jeslyn replaced it with this crap which is all the rage at the Asian Market right now.

Tita Blessica's head snaps up, her eyes locking on mine though I hadn't made a sound. The stare sends chills up my neck, though, in normal lighting, I'm not the least bit creeped out by her.

"Don't just stand there. Come here."

I lift my hand to move the curtain aside before I've even thought about what I'm doing. That's how commanding she is. Then I hesitate.

Nobody truly happy goes to a fortune teller, real or not. No, you only go because you want to hear that something in your life will change. So, naturally, I have two concerns. Am I willing to admit that I want a change when I usually don't even let myself think that? And am I just desperate for someone to know what's going on? To force me to change because I'm not strong enough to do it on my own?

The middle-aged woman peers at me in the dim, yellow light of the table lamp, which gives her cat-like orbs for eyes. I get the distinct feeling that she already knows everything I'm going through. There's something about this midnight hour, in this musky setting, with her long hair removed from its normally immaculate bun and the ebony shadows obscuring parts of her aging face that make her a stranger to me.

At this moment, she scares me.

I almost drop my hand that holds the curtain open

between us, but ... this is Tita Blessica. I hug her every Sunday at church when we're giving peace. She's the one who makes my favorite coconut dessert, *palitaw*, just for me because no one else loves it. Her boy is my brother, Eric's, best friend. She was the first Filipino we met when we moved to Corpus Christi and the reason we are part of this community. It's got to be my fear of the dark messing with my head.

"I'm not going to wait much longer." She waves her cards around like an impatient poker dealer asking if I'm in or out. I step inside, more because of her mom-tone than anything else.

Tita Blessica smiles and pats the floral bedspread. I sit on the edge of the quilted surface as she scooches to the center of the bed and begins to shuffle her deck of cards. It's not a set of tarot cards, though from what I gather from previous chatter, she reads fortunes with them in such detail and accuracy that she makes tarot cards look obsolete. Nope, these are just regular playing cards she could have picked up from a junk drawer. She passes me the red-backed deck, and as commonplace as they may be, their weight is like a bag of stoning rocks.

"Shuffle them twice and cut the deck." She closes her eyes to pray. I do as she says, though I'm still unsure why I agreed. Then I remember what sent me walking through this hallway to begin with—Ian. It had only been a few minutes that I'd forgotten my anxiety and dread. I wish it had lasted longer. With as blank a face as possible, I set the cards down.

"Child, what do you want to know?" Her sepia eyes are wide and glued to my face. I'm convinced she's trying to get the answers from my soul; I shift my weight away from her.

"Ugh, nothing specific. Just whatever." I tuck a tress of my long hair behind my ear.

"Just whatever," Tita Blessica scoffs, her accent heavier when she uses sarcasm. I look up in time to catch her eye-roll. "Child, you're miserable."

I jerk back, her words like a slap. I do a very good job of hiding my emotions. At least, I thought so. Besides, I'm not miserable, exactly. Just temporarily in a state of ... everything-could-be-better-ness. "I wouldn't say mis—"

"Don't bother lying to me." Tita Blessica cuts me off, her eyes narrowing. I shiver. "The cards can tell me everything you refuse to admit." Cold waves of dread wash over me as her hand, aged like a fine leather purse, flips a water-worn playing card toward herself before laying it down on the quilt.

A jack.

She does this again, placing a queen of hearts next to the jack, with the edges slightly overlapping, then hums in an I-knew-it way. I imagine myself as the queen and Ian as the jack, though shouldn't he be a king? My throat dries as Tita Blessica places the queen of spades on the opposite side of the jack, the queen of diamonds above, and the queen of clubs below. If this were a poker hand, I'd be winning.

But this isn't poker, and I'm no queen.

The woman across from me pauses her reading, examining my expression, not with pity or sympathy but with the eyes of someone who's been there and *thinks* she knows better. The jade bracelets around her wrist clank as she fills her pre-designed layout with playing cards. All the while, I try to remind myself that I don't have to put any stock in her words.

It does little to comfort me.

Finally, Tita Blessica holds a card up and says, "This is you."

Before looking, I imagine a two of clubs or a four of spades. Something lowly and unremarkable. I certainly wouldn't be a queen like the ones centered around the jack. But in Tita Blessica's hand is an ace of diamonds. I'd forgotten all about the aces. Somehow, this makes me feel better. She lays this card in the true center of the layout.

"Here is your past, present, and future." Each word is

designated its own area with its own set of cards, which her hand hovers above as she moves between the sections.

Tita Blessica begins with my past, and to my relief, she speaks in very general terms with phrases like "good childhood" and "moved around a lot." She already knows these things about me. Listening to this white-washed version of my life is a nice reminder that fortune-telling isn't real. It's just supposed to be for fun. I relax into a slouched position.

However, that relief is short-lived as her hand moves to the cards representing my present.

"He's unfaithful." Her words steal oxygen from the air. "He's a cheater and a liar." Silence spills between us like black ink on a rug, unwanted and permanent. Permanent because even though I don't confirm what she's saying, my utter speechlessness has done that for me. Finally, I shake my head, wanting to deny it but knowing she knows everything. "Oh, he thinks he loves you. In his selfish way, he does. But not enough to keep his eyes from wandering or his hands to himself."

Her words conjure nightmarish images, as realistic as if I'd witnessed Ian cheating. Those damn pictures reanimate themselves. My eyes begin to sting, and I stare intently at a spot on the ground next to a pair of dirty dad sneakers.

Don't cry. Don't cry. Don't cry.

Her cold hand grazes mine. "He won't change. People don't change."

I pull my hand away, standing up quickly. "I have no clue what you're talking about." I turn my head away to swipe tears. I have no interest in hearing the rest of the reading.

"Are you sure? Because ..." Her hands fan the cards as if their word is gold.

I rush to the door, thanking her because it's polite. The beads of the curtain clank like a waterfall of plastic as I shift them aside so that I almost don't hear her say, "It will get worse." I pause, wanting to laugh and cry. How could it possibly get worse? "I know how you could change everything. There's a king in your future. Well, not this future, but in a possible future. And he's the guy you're meant to be with. Would you like to hear how you can be with him?"

She sounds insane talking about other possible futures. There's only one future. Perhaps she's misspoken. Mom once explained that she thinks in Filipino first, so when she speaks in English, sometimes things get lost in translation. I assume that's what's happening.

"The last time I listened to one of your readings about finding my true love, I ended up with Ian."

"Ian is not the one true love from that reading. You only get one *the one,* and he is not *the one.*"

"But you said he would be shirtless and wouldn't see me coming. I met Ian that night." Though now that I'm thinking about it, I was the one that didn't see him coming.

"A lot of people are shirtless. Are you going to fall in love with all the beach bums at the H.E.B.?"

I shake my head. Is it possible I was never supposed to be with Ian?

"You want to know, don't you? You want to know how you can be with him."

"How? You going to tell me to break up with Ian?" I want to laugh facetiously, but knives of pain slice through my throat, cutting off the sound.

Tita Blessica rolls her eyes dramatically. "If you could do that, you would have done it by now. No. You are too ... tangled. What you need is a reset: to be separated as if you two were never together. You can start over."

I turn incredulous eyes on her. "Are you insane?" I ask before slapping my hand over my mouth. You don't talk to aunties like that. It's just not something you do.

Luckily for me, she laughs. "Maybe."

She gestures to the bed next to her, but I hug the doorframe like I'm keeping it from falling apart. Or maybe *it's* keeping *me* from falling apart. Tita Blessica sighs like she's ready to give up on me. If she gives up, I will have no one in my corner. I haven't told anyone what I'm going through, and even though Stephanie knows, she never brings it up. No one else has figured it out. Who knows if they ever will? "Okay. Let's pretend for a moment that what you're saying about my boyfriend is true. Your solution to reset everything is impossible."

"Is it? How do you know?"

"Because if resets were possible, everybody would be doing it."

"Well, it is possible, but it's not easy. That's why not everybody is doing it."

"Why isn't it easy?" I ask, shocked at myself for entertaining this insane idea.

"Because nothing you truly want in this world will ever come easy. Otherwise, those things wouldn't be worth it." When she says stuff like that, it's almost enough to make me forget all the other crazy crap she says.

Almost.

"What about love? Isn't love supposed to be easy when you're with the right person?"

"Not even love," she shouts before lowering her voice. "Damn books and movies, filling your head with nonsense. Love is work on both ends, and when both ends work, it's worth it." She slams her hands down on the cards, on my present. "He will not work for it. Not now, not ever." Then she grabs the king from my future. "But this boy ... this boy will work. And he will love you. And life will *feel* easier with him, even on your darkest day, because you're both willing to try. But you will never have him if you don't make a change."

"If I was meant to be with that guy, then where is he? Why

hasn't he walked into my life and saved me from all this misery? Why haven't I met him already?"

"Perhaps you have, but your current relationship blinds you. Or maybe you haven't met him yet, but when you do, you won't recognize him because you're still with this stupid boy."

I bite my tongue because if it were as easy as letting Ian go and taking a chance on an unknown future, I would have done it by now. But she's right; I'm tangled. Cursed.

"Malaya, you are the captain of your life. You decide which oceans to sail. You don't wait for the ocean to take you. You will not see your king when you're so busy keeping your eyes on this jack of idiots. And your king can't see the real you when this obsession consumes you." I cringe. Is that what Ian is? "This boyfriend dulls your light." Tita Blessica tosses the jack on the ground, too disgusted to even look at him.

"This is stupid." I pick up the crinkled card. "You can't reset life."

"*I* can't. But I know who can."

I can't contain my lip-pressing grimace. I'm barely willing to admit my problems to her. What makes her think I'd trust a stranger? Seeing she's lost me, Tita Blessica gathers her cards.

"Look, I can't make you do anything you don't want to do. This has to be your choice. But if you change your mind and decide to start over, go to the ocean during the next full moon at the witching hour. Let the water wash over your entire body. Do not come up for air. That will be your best chance to start the process."

She waves her hand as if that is all the explanation she needs to give.

"And then?" I let the words linger.

"And then the sea witch will take over from there."

chapter five

With winter comes a numbness that gifts me with its presence right through the holidays, into the new year, and well past my quietly celebrated seventeenth birthday.

Though my morning walks are easier to conceal from Mom than when I was sneaking out at night during the summer, my stomach knots every time she turns her narrowed eyes on me. She's got this weird ability to channel a witch-like instinct as if she's summoning the ancient Filipino *Albularyo* magic of her ancestors.

"How's swim practice?" Mom asks when I get home from school, her jaw flexing.

"Fine." I keep things minimal, digging my nails into my palms concealed within my hoodie pocket to hide how they shake.

Her head tilts as if she's judging my every move. I turn to leave, and she draws me back. "I need you to start taking your brother and sister to school in the mornings."

Energy crackles around me as my senses heighten. "I have practice."

"Can't you go to evening practice?"

"Not with this new coach. He expects mandatory

morning practice." I lie outright to Mom so often I rarely experience that sour twist in my stomach anymore.

Her lips purse. "You can pick them up after practice."

"I won't have time to make it to their schools and still get to first period."

Mom slams her palm against the island, and the burst of anger causes me to jump. "Why did we even get you a car? You think you don't have to help around here? Don't you care about anyone other than yourself? Huh?" Her teeth clench so tightly, and her eyes alight with such fury that my insides tremble. Yet, that doesn't stop me from clenching and unclenching the strap of my backpack hanging off my shoulder. "If you want to keep driving that car, you will drive your sister and brother to school."

Nostrils flaring, I growl, "That doesn't make sense. I don't get out of practice until—"

"—You know what?" Mom cuts me off. "Forget it. Just get out of my sight."

I rush to my room, slamming the door.

I know all the ways I'm wrong, but I don't care. I hate her for yelling. I hate her for picking a fight when we both know this isn't about driving my sister and brother to school. Mom just wants to make sure I have no way of seeing Ian. I heard her telling Tita Blessica that it's her way of combating the curse without saying anything because if she does it always ends in a fight. Somehow, she's figured out what I've been doing every morning, but she doesn't want to say it.

Mom's slippers slap against the tile floor as she storms the hall. She doesn't knock because that isn't a right she believes in. It certainly wasn't a right afforded to her as a child. Snatching my keys off the antique sewing machine desk near the entrance, she shouts, "You don't want to drive your sister and brother? Fine. You don't drive at all."

And there it is, the thing she's after: grounding me from

my car so she can stop me from seeing my boyfriend. She stabs a finger at me and adds, "You want to go to swim practice? I will drive you myself. You don't want to practice after school? You wait for your dad to get you after work."

In a steely voice, I ask, "How do you suddenly have time to drive me around *and* get Gabrielle and Eric to school when two seconds ago you needed me to drive everyone?"

Mom and I glare at each other. Will she admit she knows I've been skipping practice to see my boyfriend and only ordered me to drive my siblings because she wanted to stop me? Did she honestly think I would admit to sneaking out to see Ian?

"You know, for once, I thought you could help me. I do everything for this family. But no. I have to make time because my selfish daughter doesn't want to do this one thing for me."

I scoff because it's the only thing I can do to keep the tears at bay.

"Right, because I do *nothing* for you. I never get you whatever you need at the grocery store when you've forgotten something or clean the house alone because everyone else is busy or stay in when other people my age are out having fun just because you don't like to be alone." I let the moment land, watching Mom's face. What would guilt look like on her? I don't think I'll ever know because her nostrils flare. "Why can't you say why you're angry? *Who* you're angry about?"

Mom's head jerks back, and her mouth opens and closes. After an eternity, she bristles. "I wasn't raised to do that. My mom wasn't like that."

"And how did that work out for you?" Though I honestly want to know, I can't rid myself of my attitude to infuse that maybe she never returned to the Philippines for a reason. Instead, Mom hears insolence for her culture and her child-rearing abilities.

She raises her hand like she wants to slap my smart mouth right off my face, and I flinch. When her palm doesn't come crashing against my skin, I look up. Mom's lip curls instead as a slew of Filipino cuss words spill from her mouth.

"One day, you will have a daughter just like you, and then you will know what it's like to be me." Like an *Albularyo*, it isn't a promise. It's a curse.

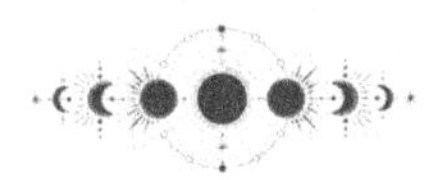

Laughter fills the house as Mom, Gabrielle, and Eric spend the rest of the evening watching Filipino horror movies. I listen from my room, knowing I should probably join them if I want to get on Mom's good side. But I'm still too angry, and I probably wouldn't respond appropriately enough for Mom when Dad inevitably comes out of his room to scare everyone.

So, I just stay away.

Long after the laughter has died and everyone's gone to sleep, I grab the spare car keys hidden in my antique sewing desk and bolt. Any fear I had about taking my car goes out the window tonight. Hopefully, Mom doesn't wake up until after I'd already be gone for swim practice because I have no intention of returning until after school tomorrow.

I didn't warn Ian I was coming, and his face tightens when he lets me in. I'm annoyed too because he has no idea what I've been through today. And yeah, that's my fault for not telling him. But I also blame him for not asking. He barely texted me today, which is becoming a habit again.

I crawl into bed, wanting to sleep, but Ian stands there. The tension in his posture tells me he wants to say something, but what? He's texting, so I close my eyes. Hopefully, he takes that as a signal to let it rest until the morning.

"Malaya, you can't just come over here without telling me."

I keep my eyes closed a moment longer. Today is a never-ending nightmare. Scratch that, this year is a never-ending nightmare. Finally, I sit up, throwing off the covers. "Why not? I have before, and you never complained then."

"Because I could have had plans."

"At three in the morning? Were you just about to go out?" I only notice now that he's not shirtless as he usually is when he's sleeping. Maybe he *was* about to go out or have someone over ...

"That doesn't matter," Ian raises his voice.

"You literally just said it matters. You said you could have had plans." I keep my voice low, so his dad doesn't wake up shouting at us, but there's plenty of irritation in my words.

"What I mean is that it doesn't matter if you know whether I have plans or not. You still should tell me before you come over here."

I laugh humorlessly. "That would help you, wouldn't it?"

"What's that supposed to mean?"

I stand up quickly, wanting to be on the same level as him if we're doing this. "It means that if I warn you ahead of time, you can make sure that no one is here that shouldn't be here. That's why you suddenly want me to do it, right? Because the truth is, what does it matter if I show up here randomly? If you're gone, then I would turn around and go home. And if you're here, then there's no reason I couldn't come in." I've never spoken so brazenly to him before, and it shows. The room seems to darken, and Ian punches his dresser, exploding with fury. I start, then clench my fists.

"It always comes down to that, doesn't it?" He shouts, disregarding his usual attempt at charm to persuade me that I'm wrong. I wait for his dad to scream from his room, but he must be out tonight because the house is dead quiet. *TIK Tik.*

"You still don't trust me, even though I told you I haven't cheated on you again. I'm getting sick of it."

"And I'm sick of your lies and your guilt." My hands tremble with rage and fear because I've said too much. And I can't go back now.

"WHAT LIES?" He screams so hard his entire face is red and shaking. I flinch, and I wish I hadn't.

"I know about the girls." My voice is low, my nostrils flaring. "I looked through that camera with all the pictures of you and your conquests."

Ian's eyes widen, and his nostrils flare. Yet, he remains silent, clenching and unclenching his fists as if he's trying to work out his next move—his next lie.

"I don't know what you're talking about."

"Sure, you do." I recount details from each picture.

"Those girls were from before you."

I scoff, incredulous that he would keep lying. And I take that moment to look at him. I mean, really examine him. There isn't a hitch in his voice. Though he's still angry with me, he isn't fidgeting with nervousness about the lie. Not shifting from one foot to the other. He's even able to maintain eye contact. By all accounts, I'd say he even believes himself.

"Your tattoos are timestamps," I reply.

"What does that even mean?"

"It means I know you're lying because of the tattoos I saw in the pictures. You didn't have any tattoos when we first met. But in each picture, they were there. I could even put the pictures in time order of when you cheated based off your first tattoo on your leg all the way to the most recent one on your bicep. But the one that makes me the sickest is the one from that day we caught fireflies together. The one where I drew a heart on your chest, and instead of spending the night with me—you went to some other girl. You must think I'm pretty stupid, leaving your photo trophies out in the open like that."

"If you saw the pictures, why didn't you say anything? Where are they now?"

I scoff. "Why? Do you want them? Because I'm sure they're somewhere in this giant mess of a room. I haven't kept tabs on the camera. You think I wanted to keep looking at those pictures? They make me sick. You're sick." I press a hand to my stomach, revolted by everything about him.

Ian scowls, dropping the liar's façade he's adopted. The slew of cuss words is the least of my concern as Ian backs me to the closest wall. He calls me every bad thing he can think of and tells me this is all my fault.

"Get out of my face," he yells, though he is the one an inch from mine.

"You're the one in my space," I scream back, trying to get him away from me.

Then the world spins as he flings me onto the bed. I'm gasping for air as Ian pins me down, shapeshifting into a dark silhouette of raging limbs.

Time becomes this mythological thing: freezing at once while simultaneously speeding up. What happens next is the beating of my life, accompanied by cliches like, "Look at what you're making me do to you," as he clutches my throat.

When he's done, he justifies his behavior by telling me that what he did was not that bad because he never closed his fist. I barely register it because I run as soon as he rolls off me.

Slamming my car door, I hit the gas, and my tires spin in the mud before gripping the road. Tears blur my vision, so I can't see the street. I end up on Laguna Shores, a route that doesn't lead home. It is continually wet as the ocean on one side sweeps its low surface. My tires lose traction, and I swerve into the water. As saltwater washes my windshield like the tumultuous rain of a hurricane, I beat my steering wheel, knowing even *this* isn't enough for me to end us.

A new gateway to hell has opened. Ian would do this again, and there is no one who can save me from this curse. But if I allow him to rage against my body, would it be the end of me?

tik tik. tik tik. tik tik.

I have nightmares of monstrous waves.

Watery beasts roaring miles above, crashing down on my body like a meteor pounds craters into the earth, pushing me closer to the freezing ocean floor as if to bury me. Having drowned when I was five and again this summer when a lifeguard training exercise went wrong, I'm aware that water could kill me. Yet, the Corpus Christi side of the Gulf ripples just beyond the rain that pelts my windshield as Gabrielle and I head for a surf session at the jetties.

"I can't believe you're skipping school to teach me how to surf, Malaya." Gabrielle scooches closer to the window to view the sparkling waves. "I can't believe *I'm* skipping school!"

My gaze alights at the excitement in Gabrielle's voice. I'm not one to encourage Gabrielle to ditch because Mom would kill me, but today I cannot summon the guilt. Today, I am full of yeses. Yes, to greasy Taco Stand. Yes, to overpriced shell necklaces at the surf shop. Yes, to a movie after. Today, I want to be anyone but the me I've been lately because the me I've been for over a year now is someone hiding her cheating boyfriend's abuse. She's someone in so deep she can't let him go, someone no one knows anymore. And I'm tired of being her.

That's why I'm finally taking Gabrielle surfing, even

though she's not a strong swimmer. Because hanging out with her is something different, and surfing is the only thing I can count on to free my mind, to free me.

"Just don't tell Mom, or your favorite clothes get thrown out like hot garbage." I poke her face teasingly, but she swats my chipped, manicured finger away.

"Jokes on you. All my favorite clothes are yours." Gabrielle laughs, pulling the neckline of my favorite lace top out of her sweatshirt collar. I try to smack her, but she ducks. Laughter erupts, but I don't feel it in my chest. I'm hollow inside—carved out by the *Aswang* ... metaphorically, of course. I have Mom and Ian to thank for that in more ways than one.

I tug at the hoodie concealing the bruises on my chest and neck. Gabrielle turns the heater on, probably thinking I'm cold, then starts belting out a girl power song that reminds me of summer, and freedom, and possibility. It feels wrong on an overcast day like today, even if I want it to be right.

I make it to the jetties despite nearly bottoming out the car in the soft sand twice. I'm wearing my wetsuit from the waist down, so all I need to do is pull the zip strap up and over my head to conceal the wounds Ian inflicted on me last night. Then I remove my surfboard from the car's roof. Kneeling on the ground, Gabrielle tosses me a flimsy, water-damaged box containing my favorite coconut-scented surf wax. While my arm moves in vigorous circles along the bumpy surface of my board, I scan the sea. There are few bodies in the water; the swells so large surfers go in and out of view as the waves rise and fall.

Gabrielle edges to my side; her eyes are wild with excitement. "You ready?"

TIK TIK.

I love her for saying yes to today, no questions asked.

"Ready for the years of comic relief I'm going to get from watching you!" I mimic the last time I brought her out here.

She'd somehow fallen on her butt on the surfboard, riding the wave in from a seated position because she couldn't figure out how to stand without falling into the ocean. Only Gabrielle.

"Never. Become. A. Teacher." Gabrielle's lips purse, though any attitude she means to project is broken by the smile she suppresses.

Gabrielle sets her surfboard in the sand as I run through reminders of how to pull the board back to break, where to put pressure to carve in case she needs to make a sharp turn to avoid hitting someone, and how to fall safely if she's thrown off.

"Okay, but do I have to stand up?" Gabrielle tucks her board under her arm, her knuckles white with tension. She's always been afraid to try things like this, which is why I was surprised when she started asking me to teach her a couple months ago. I assumed this was Mom's attempt to get me to spend more time with Gabrielle and less with Ian. I shake my head.

It doesn't matter now.

When I first learned to surf, I was obsessed with standing. I felt like I wasn't surfing if I couldn't stand, but Gabrielle is different from me. More thoughtful. More careful. "No. Don't stand if you're not ready. Honestly, it's better if you get a solid feel for catching waves while bodyboarding. You'll be more successful in the long run."

On the other side of the rocks, the water rushes to my toes. I leave my board on the beach while I help Gabrielle practice in waist-deep water. This way, I can push her board if she's struggling to paddle hard enough.

She digs her elbows into the board's edges, rolls off the sides, nose-dives a few times, and pulls back often, missing the waves out of fear. The way she clutches her elbows to herself, she's getting disappointed, and it's messing with her head. But then she catches a wave, and another, and another. Fumbling off the board that she rode all the way into calf-deep water, she jumps up and down, shouting gleefully. I race toward her, water spraying my face as I lift my knees high. A small wave, more forceful than the others, hits the back of my knees, and I collide into Gabrielle. We fall against the spongy sand, laughing as another wave rushes in and knocks me over again. It's supposed to storm later this week, but that impending hurricane is already feeding the ocean.

"Can we try again?" Gabrielle asks. I recognize the addiction in her voice and yearn for the freedom riding grants —the way I'm like a bird gliding above crystalline water. Nothing can touch me out there. Nothing and nobody.

"Of course! But I'm joining you this time." I strap my leash to my ankle.

"What about over there?" Gabrielle asks, pointing to the other side of the jetties.

A guy in his early twenties grunts as he lifts his knees high to step up and over the jetty rocks. His board has taken on damage, and his nostrils flare. He shakes his head at what I imagine is some internal dialogue, and I want to ask him what happened, but his eyes flash. They remind me of Ian's, of the way he's shapeshifted throughout our relationship.

TIK Tik.

"Malaya?" Gabrielle shakes my shoulder, her forehead creased in concern. Had she been talking to me? She must have been.

I smile. "Sorry, I zoned out."

"Yeah, you've been doing that a lot lately."

"That is the only way to survive your constant chattering." I force my voice to be light, ignoring the things that haunt me. "I mean, it's non-stop."

Gabrielle kicks sand at me, and her smile doesn't reach her eyes. "Seriously, though. I wish we could be like this all the time."

"Skipping school? Lying to Mom? I'm in."

"No, not that. I mean ... close." She pauses, biting her lip like she's said something wrong.

"We're close." My tone rises like it does when I'm lying.

"Are we? Because this is the first time we've hung out in forever. You're always with Ian or hiding in your room. Something is wrong, but every time I try to ask you say—"

"I'm fine." My words are short as I try to stand straighter.

"Exactly." Gabrielle's shoulders slump. "You always say you're fine."

Tell her. I command myself. Tell her what your boyfriend is really like. Unload this burden causing your soul to weigh a thousand pounds. "Did Mom put you up to this?" My fingers tense as I grip my board to my side.

"What? No. I swear. It's just you're always fighting with her, fighting with Ian, fighting with Mom about Ian—" Her voice drops off. "It wouldn't kill you to try to get along with her."

It wouldn't kill her to get off my back for once, but I don't say things like that to Gabrielle because then she'd just be stuck in the middle of our fights, and that's not fair to her. That's part of why I don't hang out with her anymore. So instead, I smile, keeping the storm raging inside me from raining down on her.

"Nothing is wrong. People fight. It's nothing out of the ordinary." My bruises pulse beneath my wetsuit. "Now, let's get back out to the surf before the ocean dries up."

Gabrielle humors me with a small laugh at my pathetic attempt at a joke before I rush off.

Atop the second jetty, indigo clouds swirl above the thrashing waves. Water hits the rocks with such force it rains down on fishermen at the end of the seawall. My stomach churns, but my feet plunge forward. I need this escape.

The water warms my wind-chilled body as I drop my

board onto the ocean's surface and guide it with the pressure of my hand to the first sand bar. A wave, easily a foot above my head, forms before me. It's too immense in relation to the depth of the water. Gripping both sides of my fiery-orange board, I launch through the thick, slate-blue liquid. Like a character entering a new world through glass, I slip into the base of the wave, duck diving with the press of my knee against the board.

It's cold but not shocking. My wetsuit warms the water between the ocean and my skin. I'm about to surface when another wave pummels me. It's so powerful my board's fins scrape the ground. Muscles jerk along my spine because waves don't normally break that close together. The next several minutes are a battle of paddling against the most powerful part of the waves: the white water. These swells break before I can dive under them, pushing me back to where I started and rejecting me in a way that sparks belly-knotting flashes of Ian's hammering hands.

I guide Gabrielle to water shallow enough to stand in, making it easier for her to jump on her board rather than paddle. I don't need to do much to catch these monstrously thick swells because just as I turn my board toward the beach, I'm pulled backward and upward by the mighty water. I paddle once before the wave launches me forward. Snapping into a standing position, a thrill shoots through me. My mind clears instantly. The intensity of conquering this wave, this joy, this confidence ... it's the only good thing I've felt all year.

As I pass Gabrielle, who's walking her board back toward the surf, I lean down for a high-five. Water, like diamonds, shatters on contact, and she whoops. Then I lose my balance and, like a bucking bull, my board slams onto the water repeatedly until I'm thrown off. Instinctively, I cover my head, and it's a good thing I do because I hit the ocean floor.

Tik Tik.

The dark water reminds me of the darkness in Ian's room last night. The darkness in Ian. My lungs collapse just as they had last night, and every nerve in my body ignites. I kick off the muddy sand and surface a second later.

"You alright?" Gabrielle calls over my shoulder.

I spit salty water into the air, and the mist reflects a rainbow before the wind sweeps it away. "Fine," I call before heading back out there.

"Let's catch one together," Gabrielle says when I make it back out to her.

"Okay," I say, but I jerk back when I turn my board for that ride. We're way too close to the rocks. Odd, because it hadn't been an issue a second ago. I meet Gabrielle's uncertain eyes, but the tug of a wave sucks me backward. With shaky hands, I pull up on the front of my board, preventing the surge from taking me. Though they're not close enough to touch, I could hit the rocks if I make one wrong move.

My throat tightens. No one else is surfing here, and there must be a reason we're alone.

"We need to go in!" I shout above the roaring currents.

Gabrielle nods, and a wave passes over her right as it breaks. Her hair wraps around her face, and she coughs up seawater. In the brief breaks between the waves, I paddle away from the rocks, pulling cupped hands through the water with all my strength. After years on the swim team, all the a.m. and p.m. practices, this is the hardest workout of my life.

But something is wrong.

I'm not moving forward at all; neither of us is. The direction of the water has shifted since we've been out here, and we're caught in a war between sea and land. For the first time in my life, I'm stuck in a rip current.

I fight to swim to shore when my knowledge of riptides tells me to let it take me out to sea and swim perpendicular to the shore until I'm out of the riptide. Only then can I swim back to the beach. But blackening waves pile one on top of the other, and there is only the blur of a horizon saturated by rain. Lightning flickers in the distance and thunder cracks like a vicious warning not to let go of the inches I've gained, or the ocean floor will be my grave.

Gabrielle is behind me now, but not because I've moved forward. Her muscles must be fatiguing. Mine are heavy weights, pulling my shoulders down. The waves push me toward the jetties, which glint razor-sharp. The cutting sensation of what could happen mirrors the fear sparked by Dad's stomping feet before he storms from his room, screaming inches from my face, as he defends Mom in one of the many fights he knows nothing about. *Tik tik. Tik tik.*

I need to get Gabrielle out of here fast.

Hopping off my board, I grab Gabrielle and push her toward the rocks. My feet barely sweep the ground now, but I hold her surfboard as steady as I can.

"You've got to jump," I shout, as water pounds the jetties, sweeping them clean with such force I imagine Gabrielle being beaten against the sharp edges then vacuumed away. I push her board onto the rocks, and she crawls off quickly. Then I pull myself onto the jetties just as a wave breaks over me. I fall forward, smashing my chin and scraping my bare feet against barnacles, trying to find purchase. I steady on one knee, and Gabrielle tries to grab me, but I knock her hand away.

"Get on the platform," I growl.

Another wave hits me, and half my body submerges into the sea's frothy mouth. Gabrielle makes her way to higher ground, and the ocean is reduced to drips spilling from her limbs.

"Just a little more," Gabrielle urges, throwing her board onto the platform, so it's no longer a weight. "You've got this."

But I don't as I slip back into the wild water when the next big set of waves sucks the rocks dry. I cough up seawater, desperately pulling myself back onto my board for fear of going under.

Waves continue to thrust me back and forth. Is this it? Is this the end?

Who would miss me anyway? My cheating, abusive boyfriend? My parents? I'm sure they'd be sad, but what a relief it would be not to have screaming matches with me every day. Besides, they have my fun brother, Eric, and easy-going Gabrielle. She looks like me, but she's a better version of me. Malaya 2.0. Maybe my parents would even forgive me for everything because at least I saved her.

A wave flips my legs over my head, tossing me off my board. I can't even throw my arms up in cover as I'm submerged in water so dark I could be asleep. Like a rag doll in a washing machine, I topple and whirl with no control over my body. My limbs are as ineffective as my voice was at the timid age of five.

A tear-blurred image of a younger Gabrielle smiling at my baby brother plays behind closed eyes. "Why can't you be like your sister?" Mom's voice cuts me, conflicting with the warmth of her arm wrapped around my slight frame.

I clench my jaw at the memory, haunted by a different darkness than the ocean. Why couldn't I be like Gabrielle? Even at a young age, Mom could see it. I wasn't easygoing. I'm just not built that way.

Another bout of waves crashes down, flipping me over again. But this time, the waves catch my surfboard, dragging me forward. I grab the leash and follow it, hand over hand, as I pull myself to the surface. There's time for one breath before water whales on me, and I go under.

I came to the beach to feel good. I surf because it's a natural high. But the ocean is not giving me what it promised. It's fighting me the way everything in my life fights me, and as usual, I'm not getting anywhere.

As my body twists, my leash tangles around my leg. Pain shoots up my limb, and a groan escapes me as a flurry of bubbles. I fumble to unstrap the rope tethering me to my board, but I can't get the cord unknotted even as the Velcro comes undone.

It will be over soon. It will be over soon. It will be over soon.

Am I talking about these uncontrollable waves or my life? The pressure in my chest and throat crushes my insides as water chokes me. My mind flashes to Ian; his hands close around my throat as darkness closes in from the edges of my vision. I squeeze my eyes shut and cover my head the way I used to when I thought *Aswang*s were lurking.

I wish I could magically change the past. Then I never would've ended up here.

Something warm touches my ankle. I try to jerk away, but it hurts so badly I barely move. Tightly knit bubbles block my view, so I can't see what grazed me, and the white-water rippling above clouds my vision further. Unmistakably, a hand grabs my leg, and I'm freed from the leash. Then two hands find my back, stable in the chaos.

Someone must have dove in to get me. A fisherman? Gabrielle?

With all my remaining strength, I claw my way to the surface. Then my arms become trapped. Something wraps around my body. I writhe. An electric blue light pulses, illuminating the water. It's enough to see veiny serpent-like limbs wrapped around me. *Tik tik.* I scream, and darkness falls around me once again. But no matter how hard I fight, this creature is much stronger than me. With incredible speed, I'm dragged through barrels of rolling underwater waves.

Then I succumb to a world without oxygen.

tik tik.

tik tik.

tik tik.

A shock of chilly air hits my face. Disoriented, I'm hoisted out of the ocean and into the salty air by my midsection—freeing my legs from the heavy water weighing down my lower half—and dropped onto the rough, wet surface. The impact forces fluid to eject from my nose and mouth. I cough to the point of gagging until my airway is clear. Then I rest my face on the damp, smooth rock, shivering despite my wetsuit.

I vaguely recall getting caught in a riptide and serpentine limbs of an unseen beast ensnaring my body. There's a cave-like echoing as tin clacking against a hard surface bounces around me. The ocean howls like I'm inside a seashell. Through narrowed eyes, firelight flickers against a glittering rock wall. A petite figure, possibly a woman, works over the rising embers of the flames. Her head snaps toward my direction as if responding to her name called.

The woman says something in what I think is Tagalog, but I can't interpret it because her voice is low and hissing. Removing her mask of seaweed and barnacles, she Asian-squats before me—feet flat on the ground, perfectly balanced as her face drops to my level. At least, I imagine her feet are flat on the floor; I can't see them beneath her long, tattered skirt. She's holding something that looks like a sage stick but smells like putrid fish. Her blackened mouth and wildly tangled bird's nest hair causes my neck muscles to stiffen.

"Where am I?" A sharp pain shoots through my ankle, and the nightmare of serpents wrapped around my body returns like muscle memory. "Am I dead?"

A smile grows from the woman's obsidian lips, revealing rotten, charcoal-colored teeth and a missing canine. She shakes her head. At least she understands English. My shoulders slump, yet my uncertainty about my safety causes my throat to dry.

"Did you save me?" My voice cracks. Years of being taught not to sound impolite, as politeness is so highly valued in Mom's culture, forces me to add the honorific particle, "po," at the end. *Did you save me, po?* The homeless-looking woman seems appeased.

"Not yet. But I can, Malaya." The woman's scratchy voice stretches out her words, chilling my insides. How does she know my name? She stands, but it's as if her spine is shaped like a question mark the way she hunches. She's got seaweed green homemade tattoos covering her feet and hands. I hate to find out what she used. She glides, rather than walks, to attend to a beaten-up old pot over the pathetic-looking fire.

"What do you mean you *can* save me?" Instinct makes me want to run, but I can't figure out how or even where I'd go. I'm in a vast cavern centered around a hole filled with ocean water. I've never seen anything like it in Corpus Christi. To my knowledge, there aren't any caves at the beach I was surfing at. I can't see another way out, and I don't want to try diving into the shadowy water without knowing where I'm going. Peering into its contents is to look into an abyss.

"What do you think I mean? You're the one who came to me." The woman's accent is thick, yet it's also as if she comes from another century, like the difference between a British accent in a period piece versus a modern one—only Filipino.

"I didn't come to you. I was surfing when I got pulled under."

"Tut, tut, tut." She shakes her head like a mother to a misbehaving toddler. "That's not entirely true, now, is it?" Her mom-stare strikes at my insides, while the softness of her tone says she knows everything the way my mother always knows everything.

Ian. The name seems to reverberate off the walls, though I only think it.

"I don't know what you're talking about." My voice carries in the hollow cave, though it's almost soundless. Her black eyes glint yellow in the firelight.

"Surfing in a riptide like that? You must have had a death wish. That death wish is why you're here." A smile twists back and forth between amusement and utter hatred on the woman's face. Every instinct in my body tells me not to lie to her again.

"I didn't know there were riptides—"

That's when I see it. There's a crevice in the cave wall to the far right, which looks like a possible exit. I force myself up on my injured ankle, and limp/run toward the wall. The woman shouts at me to stop, but I turn the corner and slam face-first into a wall of water. I gasp, sucking in a mouthful of seawater, and step back again. The salt gets in my eyes, forcing them shut as I cough up water.

"Foolish child," the woman hisses, grabbing the back of my neck and swiping the water out of my eyes the way my grandma used to when she bathed me as a small child. The woman lets go, leaving the fishy odor that clings to her hands on my face.

I gag. "H-how? How is this possible?" I shudder at the underwater world that is somehow being held at bay by nothing at all.

"Magic."

My heart hammers. Not an ounce of daylight touches the wall of water, yet the ocean floor is somehow illuminated by the rocks and creatures around it. Seaweed grows so high off the sea ground that it looks like they're blood-colored trees in a forest. I can't be that far down. Can I?

"What will happen if ...."

"If you walk out there?" The woman finishes my thought. "Unless you've suddenly sprouted gills, you'll surely drown."

My gaze darts to the woman's neck as her skin lifts in three even slits to reveal gills. An underwater cave? A mutant woman? A wall made of water held back by magic? My knees weaken, and I stumble to the rocky surface below me. It hurts, so this can't be a dream.

"Oh, god. I'm dead," I mutter aloud before stopping myself.

"Relax. You're not dead."

"Who are you?"

"I'm Maguyaen, but you may call me Auntie Maggie." I nod because knowing her name is nice but not what I meant. She gathers as much from my expression. "You might know me better as Maguyaen, goddess of the wind of the sea." I stare blankly because I know some Filipino mythology, but I've never heard of her. "Or maybe you don't." She rolls her eyes.

"If you're a goddess, then ...." I want to ask, what are you doing in this dump but stop. I try to come up with something else to say, but my brain can't think of anything that won't insult her.

"Then?" She waits, her tone and expression daring me to finish that thought so she can throw a slipper at me as some Filipino women do when disciplining a child.

Finally, I say, "Then ... why would a goddess want to help me?"

"Why indeed ..." she mutters, dissatisfaction in her tone. "I'm here in this ... *dump* ...." She eyes me pointedly, plucking the word from my thoughts and causing my skin to burn with embarrassment, "as punishment. The reason being none of your concern. I play nothing more than a sea witch until this punishment is over."

"A sea witch," I whisper.

The woman cringes, and it's clear that she hates that moniker.

My mind immediately flashes to the last Filipino party Mom made me go to. Tita Blessica was reading my cards, and she'd just got done telling me that I'd never be free of Ian; that the only real solution was a reset.

Tita Blessica's advice to go to the sea witch echoes within me—a misguided north star. Perhaps that's what really drove me to take Gabrielle surfing rather than hiding out at Coffee Waves or throwing medium sums of money at Target.

"Do you know my Tita Blessica?"

"I know a lot of people." She somehow answers my question without answering it.

"She's the one who told me about this place. Though ..." I pause as I try to remember what she said. "She said I was to come during the witching hour, so I'm not sure how I ended up here." When Auntie Maggie doesn't explain the anomaly, I ask, "Can you help me get home?"

"Do you really want to go back home?" She must know about my situation, though I can't tell if she knows everything or can only read my current thoughts.

Do I want to go home, back to the boy who keeps breaking my heart? Even if we break up, I'll bump into him everywhere. No matter what, I will be the loser who couldn't keep his attention, while he won't miss me at all. Do I want to return to friends who've given up on me because I devoted so much time to him that I didn't have anything left to give them? Do I want to return to my family, who I constantly disappoint?

And what's my alternative? Staying here in this humid cavern with its permanent rotten-fish stink? I mean ... it's lovely ... uh ... I grimace, unable to complete that thought politely.

When I don't say anything, Auntie Maggie nods like it confirms what she suspects. "To answer your question. I can help you go back. But consider that people don't stumble upon my cave by accident. Only people who desperately need something can pass through my gates. You came for a reason."

She pours foul-smelling liquid, which had been brewing in her pot, into a stone bowl and passes it below my nose three times before placing it in my hands. As the fumes rise, my eyes water. No, not just water; tears rain down. Images of Ian's flashing fists, of his cheating, of the pain he's caused, and of every wrong decision I've made since being with him flash behind my eyes as if yanked from my mind. I'm brought to my knees, the bowl clanking loudly against the cave floor.

"I'm sorry, Auntie Maggie."

Every drop of the rancid liquid spills, yet the sea witch smiles. "It's just as I suspect. Heartbreak."

My breathing is heavy as I curl over in a sob. Whatever was in that bowl unnecessarily freshened the wounds that are still raw. In one excruciating moment, I experience all the pain I've felt for over a year. All the pain I'd grown accustomed to feeling suddenly renews in my chest, and I can't bear it.

"Make it stop," I moan, weak and worthless.

Auntie Maggie comes down to my level, her skirt squishing. Where there should be legs, water snakes snap at me through the high slit of her ragged skirt. Gasping, I back into a wall.

"You ... you grabbed me underwater. You said only people who desperately need something can pass through your gates, but I passed through because you brought me here."

"Child." Auntie Maggie's voice rises in irritation. "I could only find you because you have a death wish, and that potion," she points to the empty bowl on the floor, "reveals truth. Your truth is ugly. If you were happy, you would have smelled delicious soup. I smell *sinigang*." Her gaze drifts like she's thinking about the deliciously sour meat and vegetable broth. Then that dreamy look vanishes. "But you? It was like poison in your hands because there is poison in your heart."

"I've been poisoned?"

"No, not real poison, girl. The boy, Ian, is poison, and he's not contained. He leaks into all aspects of your life. I'm sure you notice that everything seems to be going wrong."

"Well, yeah, but ...." I can't manage to say what I'm thinking, which is that if I had just been good enough, I wouldn't have lost him, my friends, or my family.

"But nothing ..." Auntie Maggie reaches to stroke my head. Before she touches me, her face contorts as if touching a human repulses her. She attempts a smile, but it looks unnatural. That ingrained politeness, above all else, keeps me still. "You got bad grades?"

I nod because despite the tears slowing, I'm hyperventilating so hard I can't speak.

"Because you're always so tired from staying awake waiting for his calls or calling him to make sure he's not cheating." She knows. That potion didn't just bring up all my pain, it must have shown her every painful memory I've had for over a year as it passed through my mind.

"And your friends don't ask you to hang out because you kept turning them down just so you were ready to hang out with Ian. You were too available to him." She holds both hands up like she's refusing a beverage. "That part is a little on you, honey, but a good boyfriend wouldn't make you feel the need to do that."

Guilt grips my chest, lacing itself with my heartache.

"And your relationship with your parents?"

I suck in a deep breath, hugging my knees so tight my forearms hurt. The new normal in my family is Mom and I arguing. I don't remember the last time I had a real conversation with my father. And too often, I'd inflict my sour mood on my sister and brother.

And yet, even knowing I let all this happen, I can't imagine life without Ian. It's like he always says, he's the only one who's there for me. If I weren't here now, I would be with him, trying to figure out how to make all this okay—trying to get him to promise that hitting me was a one-time thing that would never happen again and knowing deep inside that it wouldn't be.

"I can make all of the bad go away."

I can't dare to hope that her statement is possible as my breath gets caught like a stutter in my throat. "What do you mean? Like, kill him? Because I don't want him dead."

The sea witch lifts one of her serpent limbs, and it curls around her forearm. "I wouldn't waste my magic on an insignificant mortal death. I wouldn't get anything out of it."

Her words strike a nerve. Something about her makes my guts feel wrong. *Tik Tik*.

"I can reset your life. Your emotions. Your *kaluluwa*."

Kaluluwa? Resetting my soul? "Are you talking about going back in time?"

"No, that's too dangerous." It surprises me that her words have a ring of possibility to them. "I'm talking about removing a choice. The choice to be with him. Which will create a ripple effect in your life, undoing all the hurt. I'll let you remember the pain and bad memories, but they won't affect you the way they do now. It will be as if time passed, and your wounds healed."

My next breath is full and filling, like the possibility of removing that pain is oxygen, and I've been deprived. I exhale long and smooth. "How does it work?"

"It doesn't matter how it works." Auntie Maggie waves her hand. "All you need to know is that all this pain, the torment you are putting yourself through, all the decisions you are not strong enough to make, will go away. You won't have to redo those memories, and you won't have missed out on any time. You will simply reenter your life, free from this pain."

Free. That word, so abstract, sounds tangible. I imagine being free from this pain, a chance to pretend like none of it ever happened. Then I remember that none of it will have ever happened. I will never have had my first love. My first real date. My first time. My face falls as I imagine a life without Ian. I would have broken up with him if it were that easy to be without him.

I clutch at my chest as if I can protect myself from the pain with the strength of my grip.

"Oh, my dear," Auntie Maggie coos, stroking the air before my face but not touching me. "It will all be okay. After all, if you accept my offer, you won't have to feel this way much longer."

Though I can't bear losing my first love, I also can't handle another second of things staying the same. All that time I spent convincing myself that all I needed was proof of his cheating and I would leave him could easily translate into months of me convincing myself that he'll never lay a hand on me again until time, and Ian's fists, prove me wrong. I don't want to keep living that way, but I will without help. And if Mom's efforts to break the curse—forcing me out of the state, having me cut energy cords, praying, making me take salt baths, and all the times she attempted counter curses behind my back—wasn't enough, maybe altering the past will be.

Peering into the sea witch's face, her black eyes glint as if she knows she's hooked me.

"What ... what will I have to do?" I ask timidly.

"Do? Nothing!" She stands with a triumphant little hop. "But give ... what will you have to give? That's a whole other thing."

One of the serpents snaps at me as Auntie Maggie glides away, and my skin prickles.

"What do you want?" I cross my arms tightly over my chest in case she wants my soul.

"Oh, nothing too big." She glances around the room as if the thing she needs is of similar value to the rotting objects she treasures. "Just your voice."

"My voice?" I touch my throat. "So, I won't speak again?"

"It's such a small price to pay, don't you think? To reset your past. To be rid of this excruciating pain?" She looks over her shoulder at me.

"What will you do with my voice? What will I do without it?" I think of the little mermaid we'd read about in English class, gesturing wildly at the prince to communicate, and my chest caves. Years of public school have taught me that the overly expressive are subject to ridicule.

"What I do doesn't matter. As for you, well, you'll be fine. You live in a world full of communication! You'll text, and message, and social-platform-whatever to your heart's content. You'll hardly miss the thing."

It did seem like such a small price to pay. I would get a chance to start over, and it's not like I couldn't communicate. There are so many ways to talk to people without a voice. I would be fine. Nodding, I turn to face her. She holds up her palm as if I can hand her my voice. And maybe I can; I mean, I've never been around this magic stuff before.

"All you have to do is tell the universe your voice is mine. It will be a verbal contract."

"Te- tell the universe?"

"Yes, *Anak.*" She calls me child, yet the problems I carry feel so adult. "Look up to the sky." The ceiling vanishes. It's as if the cave rose out of the ocean's depths just so I can speak to the stars. "Tell the universe you agree to this deal. That you relinquish your voice to me, Maguyaen, in exchange for a life in which you never made the mistake of dating that boy."

Looking up at the starry night, there are possibilities I haven't seen in a long time. The only thing I fear right now is losing this opportunity. "I relinquish my voice to Maguyaen so that she gives me a life in which I never dated Ian."

The cave shakes as if struck by lightning, and I fall to my knees as a fiery sensation consumes my throat. Auntie Maggie's smile stretches the skin on her wrinkled cheeks to reveal rotting scales littering her porous face. Her eyes gleam as if I've just gifted her the universe itself.

I try to speak, but my throat seems disconnected from the rest of my body.

"Looking for this?" Auntie Maggie points at her throat. Only she doesn't say it in her voice; she says it in mine. My eyes widen because some part of me didn't think this was possible. "Don't worry," Auntie Maggie says in her own voice. "I haven't forgotten my promise."

She grabs me by the hair, leaving all motherly pretenses behind, and pushes me toward the water wall. Since I haven't suddenly sprouted gills, I fight her with every step. She's surprisingly strong for someone so bone thin. She sings in some language that I'm sure isn't Tagalog. Perhaps the god's language? I'm half-submerged in the icy water wall, fighting to stay inside the cave.

"Listen to me." Auntie Maggie turns my head. "Hold your breath. Run through that forest of seaweed until you are in pitch blackness. And then, you will be free."

I can't tell if she's speaking metaphorically, and I don't get the chance to argue as I'm shoved out of the cave. I turn back to rush inside, but the wall is as solid as bulletproof glass. Bubbles from my shouting distort the sea witch. I pound on the barrier. Auntie Maggie blows a kiss, then cringes before pointing toward the crimson seaweed forest. In the distance, gargantuan creatures swim like monstrous shadows in and out of sight. I run because I only have a human's worth of breath in my lungs.

Running underwater here is not like running on land, but it's not like moving through water under ordinary circumstances. My feet hit the ground and stay there, though I'm not very swift. My hair streams behind me as I race through the forest toward the untethered creatures of the deep. Sooner than I imagine, darkness clouds the outside of my eyes. If the sea witch was being metaphorical, and I'm not supposed to die out here, then I've done something wrong. There is no pitch blackness out here.

Just my body dying.

Darkness.

And then...

The silhouette of a hand.

Peacock hues of light pulse to the slow rhythm of my heart.

I reach out, but the absence of light returns.

. . .

A hand in the blackness grabs my arm so tightly it hurts. Fingers dig deeply into my skin, yet my body relaxes—they're human. What a comfort they aren't snakelike. I drift away, so out of touch with life that I can't tell if I fade mentally or physically.

Someone is talking to me, but I'm so weak I can't respond. I can't even open my eyes. There's pressure against the back of my neck and then my side. Whoever it is lifts me, and the rocking sensation of my weight shifting from water to air makes my stomach turn.

Who is carrying me?

I force my heavy eyes open and push with all my might against a bare chest as I attempt to get down. My wet hands slip against equally damp skin, and I must be weaker than I thought because the guy hardly notices my efforts to push him away.

Get off. If he can hear me, he doesn't say a thing.

One of my legs is warm pressed against some impressive abs, while the other is chilly in this increasingly stormy weather despite my wetsuit. I wish I could see who was rushing me to the shore, but the sun broke through the stormy clouds behind him, casting his face in shadow while blinding me. Weakness overcomes me, and I drop my head back. My sense of touch seems on fire, though my mind lags far behind.

There was a witch ... I think ... and I was lost in a sea forest.

I'm set down in the soggy sand, my head laid back gingerly.

"Are you okay? Can you breathe? What am I saying, of course, you can breathe; you're conscious. Did you get hurt out there? What happened?" The guy leans over me, his head haloed in golden light.

Dense clouds pass over the sun, exposing every detail of his handsome, uneasy expression. His cedar brown eyes are deep, like the kind of forest I wouldn't mind getting lost in. I'm lost already. He's got one of those perfect noses, straight yet rounded at the tip. And when his plump lips pull to the side, there's a hint of a dimple.

My heart accelerates under his gaze, so I have to look away. The view of his hard, tan chest and arms is just as good and yet so much worse on my nerves.

Stop, I tell myself. *Think of something else.*

Is he Mexican or Filipino? Why? I don't know, so I can figure out what our babies would look like.

What is going on with me? It's like I can't get my hormones under control—like they've been dormant for a year and suddenly awakened. *You don't know him.* I'd slap myself if he weren't looking with those hypnotic eyes. His hair, thick and black, drips water onto my face. I flinch, and he swipes the water away.

"Sorry," he murmurs. His contact makes me hyper-aware that I'm alive.

I'm alive. I am not dead. Then I remember Ian. I have Ian.

I frantically try to sit up, remembering why I was out here in the first place. How long was I under? Long enough to dream about a sea witch.

"It's okay. It's okay." The guy holds his hands out, trying to keep me from sitting up but not stopping me when I do. My head sways, but his hand cups the back so I don't hit the sand. "Slowly," he says as I grip his forearm for support.

I lean into him, and he smells like mint—sharp and refreshing. Once I'm still long enough, he lets go.

"Are you okay?"

I nod, hugging my legs in embarrassment. He shivers in the cool breeze, and I grimace at the goosebumps cropping up on his arms because of me.

"I'm Salvador." He sits back on one foot but stays close enough as if he thinks I may need catching again.

Malaya, I try to say, but nothing comes out. My hands dart for my throat. I try again, but while my lips move, there's no sound. *Oh my god, it was real.* Ian. Getting caught in the riptide. The sea witch. Everything. I exchanged my voice for ...

I touch my chest, my heart.

"What's wrong?" Salvador's eyes widen, searching me.

Usually, the pain from my issues with Ian is so heavy that it's like a physical weight on my body, with my chest taking the worst of it. But there is no ache there. There is nothing. I can think of him, and I don't feel a thing. For the first time in a long time, I can think objectively. And damn, what a real jerk!

Does this mean the spell worked? I never dated Ian. I mean, it had to have worked. My limbs are so light with happiness that I throw my arms around this stranger. And I'm laughing, not that he or I can hear a thing.

"Okay, I don't know what's going on," Salvador says cautiously. "But maybe you should go to a hospital."

I pull back, smiling, and point to my mouth. *I can't speak.*

"You can't speak?" He reads my lips perfectly that time. "Could you speak before?"

Yes. I nod enthusiastically.

Salvador's brow furrows in confusion. "Okay, you have to go to the hospital. There's no way you should be happy about that."

Waving my hands, I try to convey that I don't need to see a doctor. After all, I know exactly what's going on with me, but Salvador misinterprets the waving as a request for help. He grabs both hands and pulls me up. I'm still weak from my exertion with the riptide and the sea witch, so I stumble into him. The heat radiating off his body causes my cheeks to burn.

"You okay?" He holds my shoulders until I'm stable, and I nod. "Look, I still think you need help, and I can ..." He stops at the sharp shake of my head.

I'm so good. I smile and don't even mind when Salvador's face scrunches like I'm weird.

"Good, I guess." He smiles a little. "Look, the only reason I saw you is because I took a video of you that could go viral."

Excuse me, what?

Salvador holds up a finger, scanning the sand around until he spots a black shirt. He pulls it on, then picks up a GoPro and blows away the grains of sand clinging to the screen.

"Check this out. You just appear out of nowhere." He holds the camera lower because I'm much shorter than him. At first, there's just wind scratching against the microphone as he points the camera at the waves. Then my limp body suddenly appears in the wall of a wave. "There. Did you see it? One minute nothing, and in a beat, you're there like a glitch in the matrix."

He's right. You don't even see me coming.

I break out in a cold sweat. What would honestly happen if Salvador put this video out there?

"It's wild, right?"

My cheek twitches as I attempt an amused smile of agreement. Should I ask him not to post it? Would that really stop him? I mean, we don't even know each other.

Then something odd happens. I decide it doesn't matter, and my entire body relaxes. I'm finally free of Ian, and nothing will ruin that. Even if Salvador had receipts to prove I wasn't out there before, I'm willing to bet people would come up with rational excuses for how I suddenly appeared. They would debunk his video even though it's one hundred percent authentic because that's what people do. I would be fine.

"I guess it's not as weird as I thought ..." he drops the camera at his side, his shoulders slumping as he seems to second guess himself.

I touch his arm, but only briefly because the shiver that runs up my spine from the contact is ethereal. *You should post that.*

Salvador squints at my mouth as I repeat *post it,* then he nods.

"You think?" I nod, eyebrows raised. "Cool, cool." He smiles, then adds. "Anyway, I'm gonna go now if you're okay." He jerks his thumb back toward the jetty.

My face falls. White water washes onto the empty jetties, and my pulse hammers in my throat. Gabrielle. Where is she? She would have found me by now unless ...

I race for the rocks, crawl up the jagged stones, and push myself up to stand atop the jetty. But my Mustang isn't among the trucks and cars parked along the dunes. There's no way Gabrielle would leave me. Did she jump into the water to save me? Did she race off to get help?

Running my hands through my hair, I try to figure out

what to do next. I don't have a way home, and I don't have a phone to call anyone.

I turn frantically to where I'd left Salvador. He saunters toward me, probably on his way to his vehicle.

I jump off the jetty to meet him, gesturing that my car is missing and miming with my hand for a phone. We're like Timmy and Lassie.

"You need to call someone," he confirms. I nod. "My phone is in my truck." Seeming to sense my urgency, he rushes to a black Ford. I follow closely behind, edging around a homeless guy asking for change.

I'm sorry, I have nothing.

"God bless," the man replies, understanding me perfectly —oddly. But I don't have time to think about how weird that is.

When Salvador hands me his phone, I pause. I don't have her number memorized. I don't have most numbers memorized because who does? I search for some kind of social media platform but find nothing. So desperately do I wish I could make a groaning sound as my eyes roll.

"What?" Salvador asks.

From the app store, I pull up a bunch of platforms and turn the screen toward him.

"Yeah ... I don't do social media." He shrugs like it's no big deal.

I open up the notes app and type:

What kind of person doesn't do social media?

"Social media is too mean. I don't subscribe to mean," he states unapologetically.

Again, he's got a good point.

As I download Facebook and sign in, Salvador guides me to his truck to escape the drizzle that's just hit the Island. My sister linked her number to her account, and although I told her not to, I'm grateful for her defiance. I hit call just as Salvador gets in.

Gabrielle's groggy voice says, "Hello?"

Gabrielle, I mouth then palm my forehead. I can't speak. What am I going to do?

Salvador takes the phone and turns it to speaker. "Uh, hey ... I have a girl here at the beach who knows you. She was drowning but seems okay now, except she can't speak."

"What?" Gabrielle's sleepy voice becomes an urgent tone, an octave higher. "Who?"

He looks me up and down like he's going to describe me, and heat moves from my neck to my ears. I mime surfing while saying, *Sister*.

Salvador mouths, *What?* Before saying uncertainly, "She surfs."

"Surfs? I don't know anyone who surfs," Gabrielle replies, the fear in her voice replaced with confusion. My eyes widen.

What? We were surfing together. Where are you? How could you leave me here if you weren't going to get help? You sound like you've been sleeping! Salvador squints at my lips but comes up with nothing for translation.

"Are you sure because she seems pretty upset?" Then Salvador leans over to my side of the cab, his hand brushing my arm as he reaches for his glovebox. My whole body floods with warmth—damn hormones. He pulls out a used envelope and a ballpoint pen from inside the glovebox like the kind dads steal from the bank.

After a deep exhale, I write:

I'm her sister, Malaya.

Salvador relays the information, but I don't hear the rest

of the conversation. Gabrielle never knew anyone who could surf? How is that possible? *I* learned to surf last summer ... Or maybe I didn't. I started lifeguarding because Ian was a lifeguard, and I learned how to surf from my co-workers. But if I never dated Ian, then maybe I was also never a lifeguard, which means I never learned to surf ...

My brain hurts, so I lean my head back against the headrest. Salvador must have ended the call because he says, "Listen, your sister said she just woke up and realized she and your brother missed school because you never came home from swim practice to pick her up."

My brow furrows. I guess I wake my siblings up in this life ...

"Anyway, I told her your car and phone are missing. She said it's not like you to go missing and asked if I could get you to a doctor while she got ahold of your mom. They'll meet you there."

Though I hadn't wanted to go to the doctor, it seems I don't have a choice.

I'm sorry. I'm sure this is not how you wanted to spend your morning. And thanks.

"No need for apologies. It's not a big deal."

I drop my head to the side, and a nightmarish version of me stares back through the window's reflection. Eyeliner runs down my cheeks, and my hair is a tangled, frizzy mess. My clothes look like the ocean beat them with barnacles, but my face ... it's as if it's *shining*. Though figuring out this new life is confusing, it's been so long since I was stress-free that I forgot what that looked like. How approachable I could appear when I wasn't carrying stress in the bags under my eyes or my forehead crease ...

Breathing in deeply, I rest my head against the cool window and look at the sliver of sun breaking through the mauve-gray storm clouds. This morning is magical. That ocean is magical. Even the homeless guy perched on the jetty with the creepy stare is magical. And though I'm not quite sure how I'll navigate this new path, I'm sure that nothing could ever feel this good again.

As Salvador drives us toward the main road, he clears his throat. "Do you remember what you were doing out there?"

A short, silent laugh comes out as a puff of air through my nose. Of course, I remember why I was out there—not that I would tell him. Instead, I shrug. It's reasonable that I might not remember everything after what I've been through, even though I do. Salvador doesn't catch my response as we approach the steep bridge that separates the Island from the mainland, so he taps the envelope he'd handed me earlier to write on.

The water-damaged paper waits for me to pen my story, but I'm unsure what that might be. The pen is also at a loss for words as it struggles to lay ink on the paper.

I went out for a run.

Salvador spares a glance at the envelope, his eyes glazing over. It suddenly reminds me of that homeless guy from the beach and his fixed stare. Then Salvador's face relaxes. "Out for a run in a wetsuit? Oh wait, let me guess, the water swept your shoes away."

Was my surfboard swept away? Or does it not exist in this life?

Ha. Ha. Despite my sarcastic response, lightness radiates through my entire body, so I just want to keep smiling. And I do, unconcerned about whether that makes me look cool or not. A smile plays on Salvador's lips as he turns the radio to some jams reminiscent of public pools in summer. It makes me crave a fizzy Sprite.

A rectangular, nylon case tumbles against my leg from the repetitive *thump thump thump* of the bridge. I set it back on what looks like film equipment with Texas A&M CC labels stacked on the floor next to my leg.

"Sorry about that." He leans over and rearranges a few things.

Film major?

I write.

"Yeah, well, sort of." He squeezes his steering wheel and then looks at me. "I'm undeclared."

How are you going to go viral if you have no social media?

I underline social media and smirk as he reads it. He snorts, looking back at the road.

"I'll make one eventually ..." I stare at him, waiting for more. He taps his steering wheel a few times, his eyes flickering toward me. Then he says, "Look, it's complicated."

Is it?

He groans. "It is ... You know that feeling when you're wasted at a party, and you pass out, and your douchey friends take pictures that make you go viral in the wrong way?"

Yeah ... I mean, no, but yeah. My hand gestures urge him to continue.

He exhales. "Well, hi," he offers me his hand. "I'm the Sleeping Pooper."

I take his hand hesitantly like it might be covered in poop, my nostrils flaring as I suppress a smile.

What the heck?

"Yep. I fell asleep on the toilet while, you know, going. And no, I wasn't actually pooping. I was stumbling drunk, so I sat down to pee and got too comfortable."

Oh my god! I laugh silently, pulling my legs up and wiping tears from my eyes.

He nods. "That was a lot of people's reactions."

I'm sorry. Laughing was not the most sensitive thing to do.

"Don't worry about it. I'm over it." He waves his hand dismissively. "But you can see why the next time I put myself out there on the internet, it has to be in a way that wipes out the Sleeping Pooper."

So whatever video you post has to wipe it as clean as a 4-ply?

"Oh, you've got jokes." He grabs the envelope and tosses it back at me. "Dorky jokes, but jokes." His laugh is warm, and I wish I still had a laugh that could meld with his.

There's an urgent care just off the Island, but Salvador keeps to the highway, heading for the hospital. When we arrive, he tells me to hold on while he digs through a gym bag in his backseat.

"Here." He hands me a pair of sweatpants. "Hospitals are cold, and you're probably still damp in that wetsuit. Promise they're clean."

Thanks. I smile, trying to pull the sweatpants on as smoothly as possible from a seated position. I'm about to thank Salvador for saving me and for the ride when he hops out of the truck.

"What?" he asks when I meet him in front of the pickup,

my forehead knitted. "You didn't think I would just drop you off here, did you?" He pulls on a black Seven Day Film Festival hoodie and turns toward the emergency room entrance.

I rush to catch up. *Well, yeah.*

Whether he can read my lips or not, he says, "Malaya, you drowned. You don't have a car or a phone. I told your sister I would wait with you until she and your mom get here, and I always keep my word. Besides, I'd feel less guilty posting that video of you if I knew I'd done what I could to help."

Right ... but his staying meant him seeing Mom scold me for causing everyone to miss school. I'd prefer to be the Sleeping Pooper right now. My fingernails crease the insides of my palms as I recall the last fight I had with Mom.

"We need to get out of the rain." Salvador turns me around and guides me to the cover of the building as water pours from the sky as if by the bucketful. His hands on my shoulders are fire, pulling me back to this new life—reminding me that the mom I'd left behind was someone infected by the *Aswang*, by the choices and mistakes I'd made. I wish I could tell her how right she'd been about Ian. Even though her way of going about things wasn't okay, I get why she did it.

Under the carport cover, I watch the rain wash leaves into the storm drains, surprised by my grief over my lost voice. Sure, I've gained a lot, but it hadn't occurred to me that I'd never get to talk to Mom again.

chapter nine

I'm still in the waiting room of the ER when Mom's silver SUV blasts through the parking lot like a bullet. One peek out of the noisy blinds, which crunch loudly enough to draw everyone's attention, shows Mom jumping out of the car, forgetting to turn it off, and then urging Gabrielle to grab the keys.

I release the blinds, which return to their original shape, unlike myself. I sink further into my chair. On the vinyl seat, just under my leg, is the envelope on which I'd written that Salvador didn't need to stay. He took it as a suggestion rather than a command to leave, misunderstanding that I don't want him to see Mom shout at me for drowning while she was supposed to be at work.

You can go now, I mouth to Salvador.

"Leave now? I'm sure your mom will have questions. At least, my mom would."

My lips press together in a grimace, which he overlooks because Mom finally catches sight of me and rushes over. She pushes her way through the air as if she's pushing through a crowd that doesn't exist. Gabrielle, finding it amusing, pretends to swim the rest of the way toward me.

I laugh, but nobody hears it.

"*Anak.*" She hugs me tightly before checking me out.

"What happened? Why did Gabrielle say you were out surfing? Don't you know you don't surf? And where did you get this thing?" She tries to pinch the wetsuit, but the fabric is made to be tight, so her fingers come up with nothing.

I ... uh ... Gabrielle and Salvador catch this inability to conjure an answer and exchange forehead-knitted looks. My chest tightens. Meanwhile, I'm prickly as I wait for Mom's anger at inconveniencing her to erupt and embarrass me.

But it doesn't come.

The high volume of her voice is not an indication of anger. That's just the register of her voice when she's anxious, or excited, or worried ... or happy. Perhaps there aren't as many things I've done to disappoint her in this life with Ian out of the picture, so maybe our relationship isn't built by inconveniences and disappointments. I hug her tightly, having missed this Mom more than I ever knew.

"So, it's true? You can't speak?" Gabrielle asks.

Mom pulls away, and all three examine me like a science experiment.

I open my mouth with no clue what to say, but it doesn't matter because Mom takes my indecisiveness as confirmation that I'm broken.

"Oh my god!" She grabs my face too tightly in her hands; my cheeks pinched in her fingers. "She will never be able to sing karaoke again!" If I could laugh, I would for the ridiculousness of that statement, which Mom said with absolute sincerity. She always did like my voice though it wasn't like I was going to be a professional or anything. Also, I find it humorous that she suddenly spoke about me in the third person, which suggests that she thinks I must not be able to hear just because I can't talk.

"Malaya?" A nurse with a clipboard calls out.

"Oh, good." Mom pushes me toward the nurse like I didn't hear her. "Malaya. You. Have. To. Go. In. Now."

I can hear you. I overemphasize my lip movements, using my hands to push the air down so Mom knows to lower her volume. She looks so confused.

"Mom." Gabrielle jumps in. "She can hear. You don't have to yell."

I nod, my eyebrows raised in amusement.

"Well, how was I supposed to know," Mom replies. "She didn't tell me."

I palm my face and then turn to Salvador. Suddenly, there's a feeling of urgency in my gut akin to the adrenaline I'd felt earlier caught in those riptides. Should I wave goodbye, or do I write him something? And if so, then what?

"Well," he says, "I'd text you later to see how all this went, but ..." He lifts his palms, and I take the phone from his hand. I hope my number is still the same in this version of my life as I type it in. "Thanks," he says when I hand him back his phone.

I shoot a finger-gun at him and then slap myself on the forehead when he turns to leave. I'll need to learn some much cooler hand gestures.

I want to say thank you, but he doesn't turn back around to look at me.

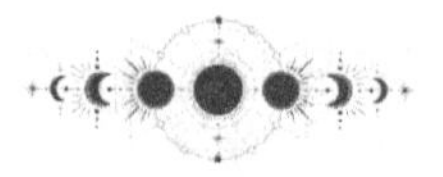

Mom addresses the doctor from the hallway in such a blaringly loud voice that I catch every word. She's insisting he run every test possible because she doesn't want to leave here with some vague answer to why I'm suddenly speechless. Too bad that's exactly what's going to happen. I tried to tell Mom that none of this was necessary, but you try telling a mom that their suddenly voiceless daughter doesn't need to be tested and see how reassured they feel.

Gabrielle slouches in a chair against the wall, and when she thinks I'm not looking, she shoots glances at me. I want to ask if I usually take her to school, but I stop myself because I don't want anyone to know about the deal I made with the sea witch. Then a memory—like a movie—takes over my third eye. Actually, it's two memories playing parallel to each other. One is a memory from my old life—the one where Mom only asked me to drive Gabrielle and Eric to school because she was trying to stop me from seeing Ian. The other from this life ghosts the first memory, in which I volunteered to take Gabrielle and Eric to school because Mom confided in me that she'd been stressed about a state inspection coming up at work.

The visions floor me. I guess that answers my question.

Mom pulls a chair up next to me, and a million questions fly out of her mouth. None of them are guilt-ridden or filled with suspicion. It's strange, and I want to chalk it up to the fact that I'm "hurt," but there's more to it. Memories from this life flash before my eyes, revealing I've rarely done anything wrong with Ian out of the picture—nothing that would sever her trust.

All the tests the doctors run take so long that I have visitors. They're people I haven't spoken to in a while or at all—at least, not in my old life. They're friends of Gabrielle's, people in my classes that sit across the room from me, and even the girl whose locker is next to mine. Memories return like movies as my mind recalls moments with these people I never got to experience in my last life, and the lightness in my chest makes me even more excited for this new existence. Turns out, the loss of my voice is a tragedy that breaks people's hearts. If only they knew I willingly gave it away to overcome my broken heart.

"Hey." A shaggy-haired guy peaks his head in at the door. "Have time for another visit?" It's Grant from history class—the one Hannah's obsessed with.

Sure, I mouth, waving him in. He sits by my bed and starts talking about what I missed in class and how he took over my part in a group project. Memories resurface of Grant and I laughing as we collaborate—which happens a lot because our history teacher is all about the group projects. In my old life, I normally partnered with Hannah, but it occurs to me now that neither she nor Stephanie visited me. My heart falters. Maybe we're not friends in this life. But if not, who am I close to?

"Mal," Gabrielle says while people start clearing out of the room. "Mal." Grant gets up and waves goodbye while I search the door. Who is she talking to? "Malaya!" Gabrielle raises her voice, and I jump. Her eyes narrow, annoyed. "Didn't you hear me calling you?"

My head jerks back. She must call me Mal here.

I'm sorry.

"It's fine, Malaya ..." she says pointedly, and I bite my lip. Then she hands me her phone for a video call. I'm surprised by another acquaintance from my history class. Anita, another half-Filipino girl whose mother is not part of my mom's circle of friends, so I rarely see her at the same Filipino parties, screams, "I cannot believe what happened to you! I just cannot even." The speaker on the phone distorts.

I try to stop my eyes from widening in shock and amusement. We're friends in this life? I love that! But why doesn't she come to the hospital? As if she can read my mind, or probably my questioning expression, she says, "My trip to the Philippines couldn't have come at a worse time. I can't believe you're going through this without me. And I'm so thoughtless, because I just realized you can't respond, but I just had to see you so you can text me while we chat." Anita talks a mile a minute, making her hard to follow.

I nod, and she goes on—asking me the same questions everyone else has already asked. And I send them through

Gabrielle's text threads to Anita, noticing that they chat like they're close as well. We must all be friends.

"I hate to say it, but I feel completely betrayed right now." Anita shakes her head good-naturedly, and her straight, black hair ripples.

Why?

"Well, remember when we went to H.E.B. camp back in eighth grade? We'd jumped off Blue Hole cliff together and gotten in trouble because it was only supposed to be one at a time."

I didn't remember because this wasn't a moment from my past life, but I twist my hair around my index finger, bright-eyed when I get to live through the memory that plays behind my eyes.

Yeah. It was worth it.

"Then you must remember how that night, in that too-small bunk that we insisted on sharing, we made a list of all the adventurous things we would do together, and surfing was on that list. How could you go out there without me? And was it amazing? Thrilling?"

My smile falters, but I lift my cheeks as I try to come up with a response that would make sense to this girl that I'm so close with yet don't know at all.

I know. I'm so sorry. I guess I just missed you and wanted to do something adventurous.

"Well, I am very missable, so I guess you're forgiven, Mal."

"Don't call her Mal," Gabrielle cups her hand as she

shouts from her seat. "She doesn't answer to it anymore, apparently."

"Oh, are we going by Malaya now?" Anita asks, shimming her shoulders. I laugh, then shake my head. But before I can type that "Mal" is fine, she says, "Malaya, it is."

After I get off the phone, I lean back against my bed. I'm so filled with warmth after talking to Anita like she's someone who just makes my soul happy. But as I relive the H.E.B. camp memory, something feels ... off.

I replay the memory in my head against my original memory of H.E.B. camp, but besides having bunks with an entirely different group of friends, I can't explain why there's something about this eighth-grade memory that's setting off little alarms in my head. Something about the memory feels ... off.

"You okay?" Gabrielle asks me as I stare at the TV without really seeing it.

Yeah, I reply, shaking my head. Maybe it's like forgetting something; it will come to me if I let it go.

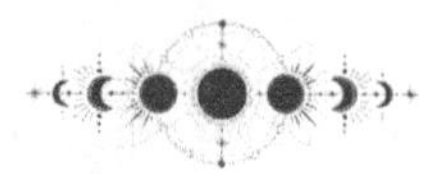

Later that day, Dad and Eric show up.

"Well, we found your car at the gym," Dad says, side-hugging me, but his eyes are on the TV, and his other arm reaches for the remote to switch it over to NASCAR.

"And your phone was inside, next to your car keys on the driver's seat," Eric says, his eyes on his phone as he finishes responding to a comment on one of his gaming videos. When I don't respond, he looks up. "Oh, right. You can't talk. Is that like a forever thing?" Gabrielle throws a balled-up napkin at his head, chiding him. He pulls my phone out of his pocket and tosses it to me.

Thanks, I mouth.

"If your car was at the gym, how did you end up at the beach ... in a wetsuit?" Gabrielle's eyes probe me as I turn my pink glitter case over.

I don't know. I shrug, dying to look through my phone but hesitant to do it with Gabrielle watching. What if my passcode is different, and I can't open it? What if Gabrielle can tell I don't recognize parts of this life? I shift my weight from one side to the other, and the hospital bed's plastic mattress groans. Gabrielle absently picks at the destroyed knee of her jeans, her gaze never leaving my phone, which seems to become heavier under her watchful glare.

Eric flops onto the edge of my bed, grabbing my half-eaten pudding for himself. Around a mouthful of food, he asks, "Why are you being weird?"

Mom, who I'd thought had been distracted with a puzzle game on her phone, smacks Eric on the back of the head. "*Bobo,* can you not see she is speechless?"

"What does that have to do with her being weird?" Eric ducks another smack, then follows Mom out of the room as he argues his point.

I drop my head back against the gray, plastic bar that's passing as a headboard.

God, even he sees it. Both he and Gabrielle can tell that I'm not like the Mal they're used to, and it's all because I'm hosting a whole other life of horrible experiences. Maybe I should have asked the sea witch to take those memories away.

"So, you can't remember anything? Nothing about who would take you surfing, or lend you a wetsuit that happens to fit you perfectly, or let you borrow a surfboard?" Gabrielle questions.

I scratch at an imaginary itch on my ear, guilt weighing down my limbs because I remember too much. I didn't want to taint this life with lies as I'd done in the last life, but this was unavoidable. I mean, I didn't want to come off as unstable.

I don't remember anything, I mouth.

She gestures to my phone. My fingers hover over the digital keypad of the lock screen, and I have to concentrate so they don't shake and give me away. I key in four digits and pause. The screen seems to hold its breath before finally turning to the home screen.

I exhale and then regret the action. Gabrielle's eyes narrow.

The background is a picture of Gabrielle and me on vacation in Florida three years ago. We look like twins in our similar black jackets and side ponytails. My heart skips a beat. I could've sworn we were in matching white jackets. Then I shake my head after a long blink. This was probably just one of the minor details that changed, much smaller than the drastic alteration of Gabrielle disappearing from the beach. I'm curious about what I'll find out about this life through my phone. Whose pictures will be in my gallery? Which friends will I have text threads with? Who's in my call log?

However, I don't have time for that now, with Gabrielle snapping jean fabric strands so viciously. Opening our text thread filled with funny memes and picture updates of daily occurrences like getting paper cuts from thirty-page English packets, I text:

> There are people on the swim team who surf… Maybe I went with one of them.

"Okay ... But who would leave you at the beach with no way home?"

I shrug.

I told you. I don't remember. But maybe they didn't leave me. Perhaps they went to get help.

"Hmmm ..." Gabrielle's lip curls. "And you're not keeping anything from me?" She's always accepted my stories before, whether she believed them or not. Why is she pushing for the truth now?

Suddenly, memories of Gabrielle and me resurface. My old memories of us are there, too, ghosting the other ones so I can see how different these two lives are. I'd sneak over to Ian's before first period in my old life. That memory seems to play in sync with the new memories of Gabrielle and me getting breakfast tacos and walking the school halls.

There are a lot of new memories like that. Memories of us sitting together at lunch, of me attending her volleyball games instead of JROTC competitions, and of her attending my art competitions. We binge-watch *Wizards of Waverly Place* episodes and get ice cream and pizza during study sessions. It's the sister relationship I never knew I wanted, and every memory is colored with feelings of happiness and love. We're not just sisters; we're friends.

"Malaya, are you okay?" Gabrielle is leaning forward in her chair, her forehead creased with concern. I face my best friend, seeing her for the first time. She looks back at me like she doesn't recognize me.

I'm fine.

"You're lying." Gabrielle's words make me freeze, and I'm trapped in her hard stare until she storms out. Her shoulders are so tense that if she's not careful, she'll end up with a migraine—something she's prone to when stressed.

Of course, she doesn't believe me. In this life, there is very little I keep from her.

Now that I'm alone, or mostly alone—Dad is still here,

but his mind is lost in the race on TV—I try to uncover as much about my new life as possible. In my gallery, I flip through pictures of me at events I'd never gone to because I was too busy making myself available to Ian for over a year. According to the app on my phone, I'm taking dual credit English at Del Mar instead of pre-ap English. There are also several contacts that I don't remember having and even a few flirty text threads from a couple of names I don't recognize.

My enthusiasm dulls minutely; Salvador hasn't messaged me. I slump into my flimsy hospital pillows, bummed but smiling as I stare up at the tiled ceiling. Even the sting of this small blow is tolerable, preferable, to the toxic emotions I'd traded my voice for. I'm free.

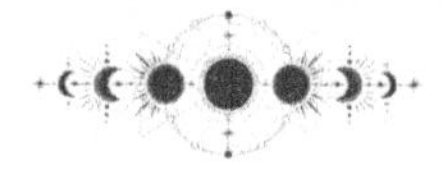

The doctors let me go home the next day, though not without several referrals to various specialists to appease Mom. The nurse insists I be wheeled out to the car, which is pointless because my legs are fine. However, since this ordeal is almost over, I sit while Dad rushes out to fetch the SUV. Gabrielle is looking through her TikTok for a funny video she saved to show me in person because she wanted to see my reaction. Meanwhile, Mom takes a lap around the main entrance while on the phone with Eric, asking if he remembered to take the chicken out of the fridge to thaw.

"I texted and called you." Mom throws her hands up like Eric can see her through the phone. "Now I have to stop at the grocery for meat because you don't do what I ask." Mom goes outside, probably wanting to continue the conversation at a louder volume but not wanting to disrupt the people in the lobby.

A blood-curdling scream rolls down the hall as if the

sound itself has a body. Everyone jerks, staring at the origin of the nerve-spiking noise, which seems to be coming from down the hall where the emergency room is. What could cause someone to cry out with that much terror in their voice?

Gabrielle and I race toward the ER, pushing open the swinging door that connects the hallway to the ER Lobby. There's a man on a gurney with several people trying to restrain him. In his adrenaline-riddled panic, he has superhuman strength as he shouts words that evoke nightmares.

"Giant beast. Giant spider-monster." He throws a punch, then points up. He's half-in, half-out of the sliding doors, so he seems to be gesturing to the ambulance or the rolling storm clouds—I can't tell. Crimson blood is smeared across his arms and face. His unblinking eyes bulge so intensely that you'd think a monster was waiting for him outside. One of the hospital staff grabs his arm and ties it to the gurney before rolling him toward the back.

I've got a clearer view of the emergency vehicle with its doors wide open, but it's empty. Then a grotesque woman with backward legs and arms, like a spider, materializes atop the ambulance. She is hissing at the doors the man is behind and pacing back and forth on her long, twisted limbs. That is until she shifts her vicious, scarlet gaze to me and clacks her sharp teeth together.

Instantly, I scream, and it's truly a nightmare that no one can hear me. I scream again, my body convulsing with terror that runs to my core. Gabrielle grips me tightly, her shaky voice asking, "Malaya, what's wrong?" I point at the monstrous woman, who leaps from the ambulance in one swift, inhuman feat. Gabrielle follows my trembling finger, but it's clear from her lack of terror that she doesn't see a thing.

I grip Gabrielle's sleeve and turn to run, tripping over her foot and collapsing onto the icy floor. Our parents race to our sides just as the monster stalks toward the sliding doors. They glide open with a swift *whoosh*, and the creature's clawed limbs click against the linoleum surface. Mom, shouting to know what's wrong, forces me to look at her.

Aswang. I stab a finger at the door, but when I look back, the creature of my nightmares is gone.

Perhaps the doctors *had* been wrong to release me so soon.

I want to tell people what I saw, but it was hard to know if I believed it once the creature disappeared. Only my recent, life-altering experience with the sea witch enforces my belief that the *Aswang* could be real.

Fortunately, the word "*Aswang*" is too hard to read on my lips, so when asked what I saw again, I have the time and forethought to lie my ass off. I text:

I didn't see anything.

That guy just scared me.

Mom looks at Dad helplessly, but he shrugs and takes me home.

I'm not sure what I expect when I arrive home, but for the most part, everything looks the same, minus a few things. My room is missing a picture of Ian and me in a frame I'd decorated with puffy paint. In its place is a ribbon corkboard filled with mementos from years of cultural festivals I danced in, Filipino debuts I'd gone to, and even concerts Mom hadn't let me go to because she'd thought I was lying about the events. I'm so much more fun in this life, which causes a rib-tightening pang of jealousy for not having been strong enough to take this path in the first place. A medal from running the Beach to Bay Relay Marathon hangs off the corner of my vanity mirror. I would never have done it with Ian because it would have taken too much time to train for, giving him too many opportunities to cheat. When I touch the heavy finisher award, flashes of me handing the baton to my sister return like an old movie.

Gabrielle walks into my room, heading assuredly to my dresser. I wait for her to tell me what she's doing, but she doesn't notice. Instead, she changes into pajamas and flops down on the edge of my bed, messing with her phone before plugging it into a purple charger on the bedside table.

Is she sleeping in here because she's worried about me? Maybe Mom and Dad made her do this ... Gabrielle gets under the covers and turns on the TV. On the opposite side of the bed is my pink phone charger. That's when it clicks. Gabrielle must regularly sleep in here with me, even though she has her own room.

Huh.

Crawling under the covers, I turn toward the TV as Gabrielle switches it to *Wizards of Waverly Place* reruns. I used to love this show but haven't seen it in so long.

When the character Alex is amazed at how spaghetti transforms in a boiling pot in just 8 minutes, Gabrielle and I burst into laughter—or at least she does. My body goes through the motions with my shoulders shaking and cheeks hurting, but no sound emits from me. Did the sea witch have to take my laughter too?

Gabrielle looks back at me, asking, "Why aren't you laughing—" but stops when she sees that I am. A grayness seems to wash over her features.

My face falls.

As the episode continues, I text any funny thoughts or

memes and respond to all of Gabrielle's commentary, but Gabrielle always has to pause the show to look down at her phone. Technically, she doesn't *have to* pause the show, but she doesn't like missing anything. This often results in issues like two-hour movies taking half a day to watch.

Though this episode is hilarious, of course, it's also part one of the two-part series finale we end up watching. The show's ending always makes me cry because Alex and Justin sacrifice their chances to be the family wizard to help each other out.

Those moments bring up memories in this life of Gabrielle and me being close in ways we never were in my last life. So many memories of us talking late into the night while watching this show returns to me. This is our thing, and the memories come with a side of giddiness, contentedness, blissfulness ... It feels so good.

I'm so glad things are different here.

However, I don't realize how different things are for Gabrielle until the episode ends, and she doesn't reset the show to season one. Instead, she turns onto her side to face me, her eyes swimming with tears.

"This isn't the same," she whispers.

I grip her hand. When I traded my voice, I'd never imagined other people would miss it—that she would miss it.

Of course, this isn't the same. Gabrielle can't make a funny comment and get an instant response back. She has to wait for me to type it out. I'm laughing with her as we watch TV, but she doesn't know that unless she glances back at me. I squeeze her hand and promise myself that I will make this better. I will find a way to make this the same for her.

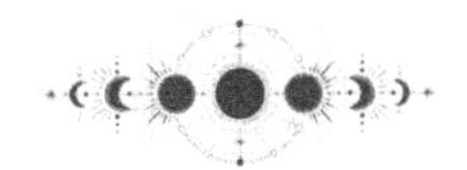

Nightmares of the *Aswang* wake me throughout the night, with the last so realistic that I jump violently.

"What's wrong? What happened?" Gabrielle grabs my arm, her features flickering in the light of the TV I always leave on while I sleep.

Nightmare.

"About what you saw at the hospital?" Gabrielle asks. I reach for my phone.

I didn't see anything at the hospital.

"I know when you're lying to me. And I don't understand why." Gabrielle is usually the peacemaker in the family, but right now, she shoves the covers off herself frustratedly.

My fingers hover over the keys; what could I tell her to make this go away? Do I want to lie to her again?

At the hospital, I saw...

The cursor blinks as Gabrielle looks over my shoulder.

"Saw what?" She nudges me.

An Aswang.

"No way! Did it look like a spider like that guy said?" Her voice shakes, but her question assures me that she doesn't think I'm just seeing things, so I describe what I saw.

"How come only you and that guy could see it?" she asks the question I'd been wondering myself. I shrug.

In the car, I looked for answers on my phone and found an article on "Psychology Today."

It said some people are more prone to witnessing the supernatural because they believe paranormal experiences are possible.

I've always been afraid of Aswangs, but they never bothered you. Maybe that guy at the hospital was haunted by something too.

My palms begin to sweat, and Gabrielle shudders as she pulls my dangling leg onto the bed.

"You know the rule," she reminds me,"as long as we're completely on the bed, nothing can get us." I smile, recalling the law we made when we were little to keep us safe against monsters. It must have been more of a game to her than to me.

Gabrielle pulls her phone close to her face, typing away. "So, we know *Aswangs* are shapeshifters, and their most common forms are dogs, crows, and black cats," Gabrielle says, passing me her phone. She's found a site, Fili-pedia Folklore, dedicated to Filipino mythology. "But they can take any shape *if there's enough fear* to power them. I think you're right about why you saw the monster and I didn't. You feared them already. Though, my stomach feels like it's full of rocks just thinking about them now ..."

Don't believe. I shake my head, but the way she's fidgeting with the blanket on her lap makes me think the next time an *Aswang* appears, she'll see it too because she believes me.

She exhales, taking the phone so she can read on. "It says the *Aswang* uses a proboscis," she stumbles on the word, "which is like the long sucker a mosquito has to suck out the hearts of their victims." A shiver rocks Gabrielle's spine. "Do you think it will come back?" She reminds me of five-year-old Gabrielle, who feared everything, and I can almost picture her chunky, dimpled cheeks.

After a silent sigh, I slump onto my bed. *I don't know.*

"Remember that time we built Fort City on the bed after Dad let us watch a *Chucky* marathon, and we'd decided the only way to stay safe was never to leave the bed again?"

Couch City? I jerk a thumb toward the living room.

"No ... Fort City. We had our grocery store on the far-left corner and our bank in the middle—" Gabrielle sits up on her knees, causing the bed to creak. My brow is furrowed as my memory of Couch City is replaced with Fort City. Gabrielle growls. "Look, I want to know what's going on, and I want you to stop keeping things from me."

My head tilts. I told her about the monster; what else could she want from me?

"Don't play dumb." She stabs a mauve-colored fingernail at me. "I woke up that morning to a call from an unknown number, from a guy you'd never met, telling me you were in a drowning accident. And it's messed you up because now you're seeing monsters. You've been lying to me, and I want to know why."

You're right.

My heart pounds so hard it makes my throat hurt. But I can't keep lying to Gabrielle—not if I hope to maintain our closeness in this new version of my life. Not if I'm going to make sure I don't fuck up this new chance at life like I did with the old one. So, I tell her about Ian and how Tita Blessica sent me to the sea witch. I tell her about the death wish.

"You traded your voice to a sea witch? That's why you're so different ..." Gabrielle rubs her temples as if her brain hurts from the information overload and its possible implications. Scrunching up my nose, I press on, explaining that the sea witch assured me that I couldn't go back to the past and redo my mistake. I could only have the choice altered and pick up my life where I'd left off.

"Okay, so I knew you were keeping something from me,

but this ... I can't even with how complicated this is. Who are you?"

I pause, confused but hyper-aware that something is off about this life, even if I can't put my finger on it. Gabrielle must sense that too, or she wouldn't have kept questioning my presence.

I'm Malaya. I smooth the blanket wrinkles out, the soft sheets rolling beneath my palms.

"Yes, but ... but are you *my* Malaya? Because you're different. My Mal wasn't in a relationship with anyone. She didn't need to make a death wish. How can you be my sister if we don't have the same memories? Like Fort City, for one. You called it Couch City."

I sit up straight, my skin prickling. My internal alarms have been buzzing since the hospital, but they're off the charts right now. I know now why Couch City, Anita's story about bunking together at H.E.B. camp, the picture of Gabrielle and I wearing black jackets instead of white ones in that Florida vacation picture, and even the years of mementos from cultural festivals have felt off. It's because all those changes happened pre-Ian ... They're all events from before I'd ever met him, which means they should never have changed.

When I'd agreed to the sea witch's terms, Auntie Maggie had led me to believe that she would only change my decision to date Ian, and I would continue living life knowing there would be some changes. Those changes, I'd assumed, would happen from that moment on. But what if she hadn't made a change to my past at all? What if I was placed in an alternate reality in which I'd never dated Ian, but I'd also never done a lot of other things either? That would explain why there are so many pre-Ian changes.

Then I realize what Gabrielle was really asking when she said, "Who are you?"

What if I'm not Gabrielle's version of her sister at all?

What if I took some innocent, fun Malaya's place? This "Mal" that never made mistakes ... That would mean I'm not living an altered version of my reality as promised but in an alternate timeline. It would also mean that Mal is stuck in my timeline, dealing with the consequences of my bad choices and probably even in danger at the hands of Ian. I can't rid myself of this gnawing sensation that Gabrielle is, in many ways, like a stranger.

"What?" Gabrielle's eyes are wide as she searches my jaw-dropped expression.

You might be right. I might not be your Mal.

If there's any chance I'm in an alternate reality rather than just my own altered reality, and I've sent the good Mal to live in my old, crappy life, then I can't stay here. This truth turns my insides. I press my hands against my stomach as a sickness infects my guts at the thought of returning to my old life —to Ian.

"How can we know for sure?" Gabrielle asks, chewing her lip anxiously and the dread within me builds.

I have to go back to the sea witch.

chapter eleven

The Mustang accelerates onto the highway leading to the Island.

"But Gabrielle's not a strong swimmer," Anita's voice blares through my car's speakers from the video call we're having. "Did you remind Gabrielle that she's not a strong swimmer, so if you drown again, nobody will save you? BECAUSE YOU'RE NOT A STRONG SWIMMER, GABRIELLE!" Anita shouts as if Gabrielle couldn't hear her from the driver's seat this whole time.

I know, I mouth at the camera, pulling at the snug collar of my wetsuit.

Gabrielle insisted on telling Anita everything, even if it meant waking her ass up in the middle of the night because she's still in the Philippines. When I asked if she would involve Bentley, who is her ride or die, she stiffened. Gabrielle's best friend flashed in my mind, but none of the memories were as recent in this life as in my old life. Did something happen to her? To them?

"Well, what is your plan if you drown again? You need another plan."

I palm my forehead.

We're already on the way there.

"I don't care if you're already standing waist-deep in the water, peeing on all the fishies; you need a backup plan."

I can't help laughing at that one and wish Anita were here, even though I don't know her that well. Mainly because I could use a real distraction from the way Gabrielle weaves around cars in these tight lanes ... in my old life, she wasn't even driving yet.

Gabrielle says, "Hey, what if we call that guy up who saved you the first time? Salvador."

My eyes stay trained on the road as I mouth, *No. Nope. We can't.*

"Awe, why not?" Anita asks. "He sounds dreamy."

My lips press together, and a blush creeps across my cheeks. Finally, I text:

> Because I don't have his number. He got mine, and he never texted me.

Anita reads the message aloud so Gabrielle can hear.

"Don't be embarrassed," Anita says, both calling me out and comforting me simultaneously.

I drop my head back.

"But *I* have his number," Gabrielle says. I slow turn to look at her, angling Anita's camera to face Gabrielle as well. "He called me from his phone when you drowned, remember?"

Oh yeah.

Before I can stop her, Gabrielle clicks on his number in her call log and turns on speaker. She's got her phone set up on a hands-free dock on the left side of the steering wheel, so I can't reach it or hang up. I can only embrace the jittery feeling crawling up and down my limbs.

"Hello?" Salvador's voice comes through the phone, and my heart leaps.

Anita's eyes are bright with excitement, but I bury my face in one of my hands.

"Hey, this is Malaya's sister Gabrielle. Remember Malaya? The girl who drowned?" I slap Gabrielle's arm and point threateningly at her, though we both know I won't do anything.

"Oh yeah, what's up? Is Malaya calling me for a date?" He asks in a teasing voice.

Anita bursts into a fit of giggles, and Gabrielle joins her. I want to disappear right now. Perhaps the sea witch can drop me into yet another timeline because, clearly, this one is ruined.

"Whoa, is that her? Is her voice back?" Salvador asks. "Because the answer is yes."

"No, that's not her. That's our friend Anita, who's on video chat with Malaya," Gabrielle explains. "Anyway, we're calling because we could use your life-saving abilities again."

"And what do I get out of this?"

"Besides my sister's company? What do you want?"

"I'm scouting locations for a movie I'm working on. It would help if I had a model to block the scene with me."

Me? I stab a finger at my chest.

Anita laughs at the gesture. "Damn. I could hear that 'no' from here."

"What's that?" Salvador asks.

"She said she'd love to," Gabrielle chirps. "She's just dying to help. She can't wait."

I lunge for the phone but back off when Gabrielle swerves a little.

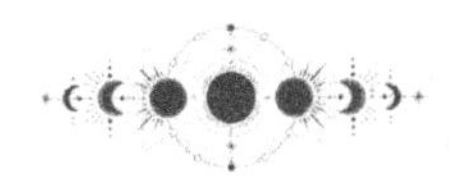

Considering Salvador's coming from the university, it doesn't take him long to meet us at the beach. While Gabrielle had him on the phone, I'd waved wildly, forming large Xs with my arms as I silently begged her not to fill him in on the sea witch and the death wish.

It's no surprise when his first words are, "Why are you here?"

I open up my notes app where I'd prewritten:

I lost a necklace my Auntie Jeslyn gave me, and Gabrielle is paranoid about me going back into the water even though I'm on the swim team ...

I don't know why I feel the need to re-emphasize to him that I'm on the team rather than just saying I can swim, but after reading it, he looks at me doubtfully. "Swim team? Right."

Gabrielle pulls Salvador's hand down to see what I wrote, then says, "Plus, the riptides are still bad." She throws up fists in fake frustration but winks at me when Salvador isn't looking. I shake my head warningly.

"You want to go back in there?" Salvador points at the sea. "To look for a necklace? I highly doubt you'll find it because the ocean is like a black hole. But I'm in." He gestures to the jetties for me to lead the way.

I hesitate, eyeing Salvador's camera slung over his shoulder. If I go first and the sea witch sends me back, I won't have fulfilled my end of the deal that Gabrielle made for me when she promised I would help Salvador block a scene.

You first. I gesture to the camera.

"You sure?" The lift of his eyebrows and purse of his lips makes me feel like I'm staring at a male model looking out at me from a magazine cover. Is he doing that on purpose, or could he actually be unaware of what that expression is doing to my insides?

I blink, shaking my head as I scroll through the notes in my phone.

What's blocking a scene mean?

He leans over, his arm brushing mine as he reads. "Oh, it's like choreographing a dance, except for actors. The director I'm working with is filming a K-drama-style movie. One of the classic tropes is the girlfriend no one knew about showing up partway through the drama to add conflict to the budding relationship."

But I can't speak. I point to my mouth.

He only stares at my lips so he can read them, but every time he does, it feels ... intimate. More intimate than when anyone else does it. Thank God I can't speak, or my nervousness would be so obvious by the shaking of my voice.

"Oh, you don't have to. I'm just going to show you where to stand or direct you on how to move as I film a few shots. No acting necessary."

"Thank goodness, because acting is not her strong suit," Gabrielle says. "Wait, it's not, right?"

My eyes widen as I press my lips at her in warning. Luckily, Salvador doesn't seem to pick up on how odd that statement is. She's right, though. I'm not an actress.

"The premise is like *The Legend of the Blue Sea.* Have you seen it?"

It's only my favorite K-drama.

"Ugh. Mi-Sun made me watch it before she would let me on set." Salvador leans in, wafting me with his minty scent. "Don't tell anyone, but it's my favorite too."

Gabrielle heard, I mouth, half-smiling as I point over my shoulder at Gabrielle pretending to text when she's actually taking pictures of us for Anita. I know because I'm in the group chat and have to keep swiping the messages away before Salvador sees them.

"What?" He waves a hand dismissively. "No. She couldn't have heard."

"Yes, I did." Gabrielle laughs, lifting her eyes briefly to meet mine.

Told you! I clutch my stomach with silent laughter.

"Damn." He rubs the back of his neck.

I can't believe you watch K-dramas. And don't try to deny it because you can't have a favorite unless you've seen more than one.

"Fine, you got me. My last girlfriend was Korean."

I hold my smile in place, though I recognize a familiar tightness in my chest. Is Mi-Sun the ex he's talking about? The one he's currently working with on this project? I step back—away from him. Something within me shuts down at the recognition of jealousy—no matter how slight that jealousy may be. I'm so familiar with that ugly emotion because of Ian that I instantly reject what might or could be happening here. I *never* want to feel that way again.

"Whoa, what happened?" Salvador asks, gesturing to the space between us.

Nothing. My hand cuts through the air, and I manage a real smile after a beat.

Salvador's mouth opens, but I gesture to his camera. He hesitates, then nods.

"Right ... You will be a mermaid turned human, emerging from the sea. I just need a couple of angles of you walking out of the water. Maybe a few shots of you walking up to me if Gabrielle is willing to hold up the camera."

"Hey, how did I get roped into working?"

"Technically, you are the one who called," Anita's voice rings out over speaker phone, and Gabrielle's expression turns to feigned shock.

"Anita, how long have you been on the phone? I must have accidentally butt-dialed you." She shrugs at us. "I swear, I'm not at all letting her spy on the conversation happening before us."

I glance at Salvador to smile shyly, looking away.

Though I would have been incredibly embarrassed by something like this in my old life, my chest fills with relief. I breathe more easily because of their lightness, and I can think more clearly. Salvador isn't mine. We don't know each other. There's no reason why this can't just be a lot of fun—especially since I don't know if it's the last time I'll have fun in case I have to leave.

Salvador lies on the ground to get a shot of me walking out of the water. It's amazing how something I've been doing almost my whole life can feel so awkward when a camera is pointed at me. Then Gabrielle has entirely too much fun directing us on the stylistic, long-lingering glances of K-dramas. I can't look at Salvador, covered in sand from chin to legs, without laughing.

"What is so funny?" Though his eyes are bright with amusement, he runs a hand through his hair. Is he a little self-conscious?

Fearlessly, effortlessly, I brush the sand from his jaw.

He becomes still, and his eyes dart from my hand to my eyes. I shiver.

"You must be freezing from that water." He rubs my arms one quick time and rushes off to get me a towel from his truck.

Would these crush-like feelings feel like cheating if I had to return to my old life this instant? Would I even remember how this feels if the intensity of my love and hatred for Ian returned?

chapter twelve

Wind tosses my hair from side to side as if trying to blind me as I approach the place where I'd exited my old life and entered this new one. Though I'm determined to speak to the sea witch, I'm not sure this will work without having a death wish.

The sky darkens, almost magically, as the clouds move fast for the dunes.

"You ready?" Gabrielle asks, holding my phone and car keys for me.

I take a deep breath and plunge forward.

Each step into the water is bone-chillingly cold on my bare feet, though the rest of me is protected by the wetsuit. One wave passes me, then another. I dive into the smooth, curved base of a wave, completely submerging myself. The shock of icy water over my head and neck causes my mind to freeze and my body to stiffen. I try to swim, but my muscles don't flex in this temperature the way I need them to. It's as if a magical force is lowering the ocean temperature dramatically, rendering my wetsuit useless. I use this to my advantage and focus on staying under while waiting to be dragged to the witch's cave.

I wait until there's almost no air left in me before I surface again. On the beach, Gabrielle and Salvador stare as if waiting for a signal from me. Feeling a little more warmed up, I go under again, swimming low until I graze the ocean floor with my palms. I swim toward the horizon, feeling the ocean waves thrash above me but find nothing else—no serpentine limbs coming to drag me away.

When I surface again, I'm gasping for air—having stayed under as long as my lungs allow. I try repeatedly, even swimming out to the end of the jetties, but Auntie Maggie isn't coming for me.

As I drag my legs through the water headed back to shore, a weight falls heavy over me. What will I do if I can't get to Auntie Maggie?

Gabrielle crouches, chewing on a fingernail. Is she wondering the same thing?

Salvador meets me at the water's edge and throws a towel over my shoulders. His arm lingers on my shoulder for a moment, fiery even beneath the thick terry cloth.

"I'm guessing by those big, sad anime eyes that you didn't find it."

I shake my head, and Gabrielle buries her face in her hands. We both expected more from this trip, and the disappointment makes my stomach clench.

"What are we going to do?" Gabrielle swallows hard. "Is there another way?"

I don't know. Full moon? I make a circle with my hands and hold it up to the sky. Salvador's squints up at the sky and back down to me in confusion.

"We just had a full moon. Like the night before you drowned. Ugh!" Gabrielle slams both fists on the ground, then pushes herself up in the next move.

I jump, having never seen her this angry before.

"Okay, let's all just breathe." Salvador holds his hands up to put space between us. "Gabrielle, I keep an extra hoodie in my truck. Would you mind getting it for Malaya because she's already soaked through this towel?" He gestures to my fingers, which are blueish. "I never imagined it would be going to the same girl I last lent clothes to, but sometimes a guy just gets lucky." He winks at me, and a fire within my chest warms my entire body.

"Fine, I guess." Gabrielle passes me my phone while holding her hand out for Salvador's keys.

When she's gone, he peers at me from the corner of his eye with a smirk. I want to smile back, but I'm still too frustrated that I couldn't get to the sea witch. I just wanted to hear that I hadn't taken another Malaya's place to ease Gabrielle's mind and get back to enjoying this new life. But now my insides are infected with this icky feeling, like when I have a big project due soon, but I haven't started yet. How can I finish this task when my only option is unavailable?

"What clothes do you want me to pack for next time?" The glint in Salvador's eyes makes my limbs weak. "You have my sweatpants and soon a hoodie. How about some t-shirts? I have a tux from a *quince* I went to back when I was fifteen. It won't fit me anymore, but it might work on your small frame."

Ha. I shake my head sardonically.

"This necklace from your Auntie ... is it an heirloom? Because you and Gabrielle seem pretty upset over it."

Though the necklace isn't real, this attempt to talk to the sea witch was, so when I mouth, *It was important,* the significance of what I was doing out in the ocean resonates.

"Then I'm sorry you didn't find what you were looking for."

I cross my arms, and Salvador moves to block the wind

from hitting me. Then his eyes glaze over just as they'd done in the truck that first day we met, and his voice is more serious as he asks, "Are you sure you weren't out there for another reason?"

I shake my head, feeling as if I'm talking to someone else entirely. But before I can question it, sand crunches and Gabrielle crests the jetty. Her head tilts when she first sees us, and she's empty-handed.

"Couldn't find it?" Salvador must notice she's not carrying the hoodie too. His voice is light and carefree again.

"Uh, no." Gabrielle eyes me stiffly, still needing more time to calm down.

"Well, let's go together. Malaya was going to tell us if there was another reason she was out in the ocean." He climbs the jagged rocks of the jetty first before offering his hands to help me up the stony ridge.

"Was she now?" Gabrielle's annoyance is cutting as she glares at me.

With a fast shake of my head, I try to convey that I wasn't, but Salvador's deep brown eyes entrance me. At Gabrielle's exhale, I fumble to pull out my phone.

I wasn't going to tell you anything.

I hold the phone up to Salvador's face, then make sure Gabrielle sees it too, so she knows I wasn't just about to tell him my big secret when I'd only just shared it with her this morning. The old me would do that, and I'll never make that mistake with a guy again.

Gabrielle is unusually quiet, her nod jerky and unnatural. It may take time for her to calm down, even if she's accepted my gesture as an apology of sorts.

We'll figure it out, I mouth, trying to assure her that I'm not giving up.

Her hands are sunk deep in her hoodie pockets as if she's trying to look casual, but there's one problem. She never walks that way.

To my surprise, Salvador grabs my phone from my hands and begins typing. It seems pointless since he can speak, but whatever.

"There. Now you can text me."

When he hands my phone back, my eyes narrow at him.

Hey there, hot stuff. It's Malaya. Now you have my number.

It's followed by a winky face. I stifle a laugh, one eyebrow raised. *Hot stuff?*

"Hey, you gotta have something to call your hero."

My hero ...

You could've texted me since you had my number, I mouth, closing out the app.

"Yeah, but I was too shy." He shrugs sheepishly. It startles me that he understood my soundless lips. I glance at him, and he's staring at my mouth, so he doesn't miss a thing.

Did you ever upload that video of me?

"Not yet," Salvador says, rubbing the back of his head.

He doesn't offer more information. Maybe he's not as "over" the Sleeping Pooper thing as he says he is.

At Salvador's truck, he opens the passenger side and passes me the hoodie. I motion for him to turn by circling my finger. He winks before facing his vehicle. I reach for the back driver's side door of my Mustang, which isn't closed all the way. As I tug the wetsuit down to my hips, I spot Gabrielle's phone on the backseat. I pull the black Quiksilver hoodie over me and reach for the sandy device, which is unlocked and opened to the Fili-pedia Folklore webpage on weapons to fight off *Aswangs*. There's a picture of some whips. I don't remember Gabrielle looking through this before I got out of the car, especially since she was in the front with me.

The phone is slippery as if it fell on the muddy shoreline, but Gabrielle isn't wet, so I can't figure out what could have caused it. I lean further into the car, and my foot brushes against something stiff and damp. I immediately jump back, my mind flashing a picture of a crab as a warning. Instead, there's a long tail haphazardly kicked just under my car. I pick it up as a chilling breeze presses against my cheek. One good whiff tells me this whip-like object is from the ocean. Then I fumble it. It's part of a dead animal—a stingray's tail.

The end looks ripped like someone found a dead carcass on the beach and yanked the tail right off its body. It certainly isn't fresh. Is Gabrielle trying to make a whip out of this thing to fight off *Aswangs*? I gag from the smell, dropping the thing again at my feet and bumping into Salvador as I jump back to avoid touching it. Salvador laughs when he sees me shaking my hands like I touched a roach.

"Be careful with that," Gabrielle warns from the car's passenger side.

I gesture to the ground, eyebrows raised, waiting for an explanation. Gabrielle must have brought it here or at least picked it up since the inside of my car is damp and sandy.

But something is wrong. Gabrielle's eyes are bloodshot as if she's been up all night crying. And for some reason, my reflection in her deathly stare is upside down.

She is not Gabrielle.

Gabrielle's clone seems to realize I've figured it out the second the thought enters my mind because she lunges up and over the car at me with inhuman gravity. A deep and guttural growl emits from the depths of her diaphragm, unlike any earthly sound my sister could make.

Ducking, I reach for the stingray whip, holding it above my head as the only weapon I can find. When fake Gabrielle lands on us, she shrieks in pain as the stingray whip grazes her arm. The place where it scratches her oozes a thick, moss-like goo.

"What the—" Salvador begins as Gabrielle's features shapeshift into the *Aswang* from the hospital. She no longer looks or sounds like my sister as she becomes the creature from my nightmares. She gnaws at the injured limb until she rips it from her body and slings it across the beach with her bare teeth.

I push with all my might to get her off me, but at least three of her backward limbs pin me and Salvador against the ground and my vehicle's open door. Salvador yells out as the *Aswang* slashes at his deltoid, spattering blood across the white sand. I flick my wrist repeatedly, trying to strike the *Aswang* with the stingray tail any way I can, but she reinforces her grip with yet another backward limb—a grotesquely deformed foot.

Most of her focus is on me, giving Salvador the advantage he needs to push himself out from under her grip. With incredible strength, he bends one of the *Aswang*'s limbs behind her back, straddling the spidery beast as he braces his legs against my car to pull her away from me.

It frees my arm just enough to lunge forward and stab the monstrous woman in the heart with the barbed part of the stingray tail. Her bloodshot eyes widen, then go sightless as her body collapses limply to the sand.

I fall to my knees, my breathing violently out of control.

"What happened to your sister?" Salvador fought the *Aswang* to avoid being killed, but now he's pointing from the jetties to the other side of the car where the fake Gabrielle had been standing to the place where the creature lay dead in the sand and squeezing his face.

It's hard to get him to focus on me while he's trying to make sense of what he's seen, but I pull his face to mine and force him to look at my lips as I mouth, *That's not my sister.*

chapter thirteen

Gabrielle's scream pierces the air emanating from the dunes.

I step on the *Aswang*'s chest and rip out the stingray tail. This disgusting weapon is coming with me. I race toward the dunes, but Salvador is quicker—practically jumping up the dunes and disappearing over the crest before I even reach the base.

"Malaya," Gabrielle screams my name this time. I pinpoint it to one of the dunes just to my left and wrap the stingray tail like Indian Jones's whip before scaling the slick, soft sand of the dune on all fours. But when I reach the top, I'm alone. Where is Salvador? My heartbeat thrashes in my ears. What if Salvador is another *Aswang*? Did I just send him after my sister?

I spit the gritty sand out of my teeth, searching for Gabrielle's red hoodie as my breaths become shallower, raspier.

Gabrielle screams again, and I charge toward another sandy hill. I use the plant life as ropes to pull myself up this dune, and then I spot Salvador. My hands go clammy seeing him bent over Gabrielle, who is trapped under woven beachgrass.

He yanks the grass backward, his muscles flexing, and any fears of him being a monster dissipate. He's trying to free Gabrielle. I check the perimeter, just as Dad taught me to do when we would scout the swamplands of my grandfather's property for gators. There are no monsters, but I try to stay more aware of my surroundings now that I know Salvador is taking care of Gabrielle.

What happened? I mouth, kneeling next to Gabrielle.

"It's got me," her voice quivers, and then she fights to loosen the beachgrass by thrashing her entire body. The beachgrass tightens its hold on Gabrielle, and she cries out in panic. Having always been claustrophobic, this must be a real-life nightmare for her.

"Malaya, help." Gabrielle squeezes my fingers. I roll the stingray tail off my shoulder and try to slice at the grass with the barb. It doesn't do much, so I yank at the grass instead. It tightens under my fingers, turning my hands purple as they become stuck against Gabrielle's forearm.

Salvador sits up suddenly, feeling his pockets, and pulls out his keys, revealing a pocketknife on the silver ring. The woven beach grass is as tightly sewn as a *sulingkat* basket, but he saws at the blades near my fingers, and it loosens just enough to free my hands. "Ow," Salvador pulls his hand back to rub his knuckles.

What?

"Every time I cut it, the plant snaps at me like it's biting back." He tries again, and I witness the plant slap him on the knuckles. I grab the plant with two hands as it rears back to bite again.

Cut the roots!

Blades of beachgrass I hadn't managed to catch whip at my forearms and thighs. Luckily, I'm pretty covered, so it doesn't hurt unless it strikes the tops of my hands. Salvador cuts through the roots, and whatever magic the plant contains dies down. Gabrielle rolls herself out of the trap and stands. I throw my arms around her, my chest rising and falling as she hugs me back.

"Malaya." Gabrielle's tearful. "After I left you guys, this weird homeless man tried to give me a stingray tail. He kept saying I needed to protect myself, and I thought he would attack me, so I ran." She shutters, and I urge her to go on by nodding. "I dropped my phone, but I kept racing for the car instead of going back to get it because he was so close. When I got to the car, he was standing there with the stingray tail and my phone."

"Was he that shapeshifting monster?" Salvador gestures beyond the dunes.

"The *Aswang*? Definitely not," Gabrielle says. "The man opened my internet browser to that website we were looking at about the *Aswangs* and held the screen up to show me the part about how to defeat an *Aswang* with a stingray tail. Then his eyes got wide as they trailed up to something above the car roof, and he pushed me into the backseat before he disappeared in an instant."

In my notes app, I type:

Did the *Aswang* get him?

"I don't think so. The homeless man must have just ... teleported somehow. Then the car shifted to the right as the *Aswang* hung off the side to look at me through the window. I thought I was safe inside, but she started pulling the window out, her long claws inching inside the car like she was trying to hit the unlock button. I opened the door where the man had been and stumbled on the stingray tail and my phone. I picked them up, but the *Aswang* got me before I could do anything. Then I woke up, out here, alone. I was so scared you wouldn't find me."

I'm here. It's okay. I wrap my arms around Gabrielle again and squeeze her tightly.

But it's not okay. If I hadn't told Gabrielle I'd seen the *Aswang*, she wouldn't have started believing in it, and she wouldn't have seen it.

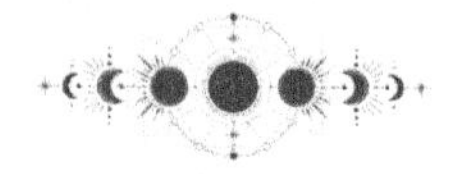

By the time we descend from the dunes, I'm so shaken up that even my knees wobble. I'm unsure how I'll drive; I almost take up Salvador's offer to bring us home. But then he groans in pain when the wound on his deltoid gushes blood.

"I thought it stopped bleeding." He rips his shredded sleeve away to get a better look, and his eyes widen. "It's gone."

My brow furrows as I look at the wound on his arm. It is most certainly not gone. What the hell was he talking about?

"It still hurts, though." His hand crushes the place where the wound is, covering his fingers in blood, and I gag. "What?"

It's still there.

"Huh?"

I avert my eyes from the jagged cut, my gaze falling over the monstrous half-beast lying dead on the ground as I reach my car. Even through the crowd of people surrounding her as they take pictures with their phones, her blank, bloodshot eyes penetrate me. A shiver rocks my body.

"She took your shape after she tied you up," Salvador fills in Gabrielle, his voice still incredulous. "I thought she was you. I still don't know how Malaya figured it out."

The eyes, I mouth, tapping the spot just below my bottom lash line.

"Weird," Salvador says, a lift of curiosity in his voice. Normally, I wouldn't mind answering questions, but at the moment, I just want to get the hell off this beach.

At first, it seems everyone in the crowd can see the *Aswang*, but before I close my car door, I overhear something unusual.

"It's right there. It's a creature with long limbs and sharp teeth. How can you not see it?" A freckled lady points within an inch of the *Aswang's* face.

"Because there's nothing there," the bony man says, his hand cutting right through the *Aswang* as if cutting through the air. Greenish *Aswang* blood glistens on his fingers, but he doesn't seem to see or feel a thing.

"Okay, you need to wash your hands," Freckles says, stepping back.

I approach the couple, passing Freckles my phone with the note:

Excuse me, but do either of you believe in the paranormal?

"I do," Freckles says. Then she jerks her thumb at the bony man next to her. "But this guy doesn't believe in anything."

"I'm sorry, but it's nonsense." He waves his bloody hand around. "Just like telling me there's a monster right here when there's literally nothing is nonsense."

Salvador gets out of his truck, and I show him the same message.

"I don't know. Sometimes, I do. My grandfather visited me the night he died. But I second guess myself a lot." Salvador inhales sharply through his teeth, gripping his arm again. "The cut is back," he says through clenched teeth. "How is this even possible?"

I want to wrap his arm up, but if his injury is coming and going based on his belief, then the best thing I can do for him is convince him it's not real.

There's no cut on your arm. None of this is real, and you're not hurt.

"What are you talking about? Of course, it's real. I can see the blood."

My cheeks puff. How can I explain that if he wants to heal, he can't believe in any of this without him inevitably believing?

But it wasn't there before. Pretend it's not there now.

"That's a little hard to do, sweetheart." He holds up his bloody hand.

I press my lips together, trying to get my expression to say, *Just try.*

"Fine." He closes his eyes, and when he opens them, he says, "It's gone."

I sigh. It's not gone for me, but at least it worked for him. There's a chance he might be saved yet, as long as I don't drag him into any more of this. I don't know if he gets the sense of finality in my goodbye, but when he tells me he'll call me, I don't hold my breath. Who would want to after all this?

I get into the Mustang, and Gabrielle grabs my arm.

"Malaya, that's him. That's the guy who gave me the stingray tail." She points out a man I've definitely seen before —the homeless guy I'd noticed that day on the beach when I'd first met Salvador. He's sitting cross-legged on the shore, and I'm about to get out of the car and ask him who he is, but when he looks in my direction, my skin prickles. I shift the car into reverse, cutting the wheel, but his gaze never leaves the Mustang or me.

We need monster protection in case there are any more *Aswangs*, and I only know one person who might have the tools and knowledge we need. I also need another way to reach the sea witch since my way failed. Who better to ask than the woman who knows her: Tita Blessica?

Every time I tried to call her over the next couple of days, it goes to voicemail. I casually ask Mom what Tita Blessica is up to these days and if she changed her number or perhaps left town, but Mom shakes her head dismissively.

"Of course not. Blessica is just at home, as usual." Mom doesn't look up from her Filipino novellas, so she doesn't notice my deep slouch.

I'm starting to feel like Auntie is avoiding my calls because she knows something when Salvador texts me.

SALVADOR

The cut is back. I tried to go to the hospital, but a lot of the doctors and nurses couldn't see it.

> The one doctor who could, put in stitches which immediately fell out the next time the wound disappeared. But the worst part is, doctors say one woman died of a heart attack, but she had an open chest wound. They couldn't see her injury, so they didn't know to treat it. Don't know what to do.

My heart seems to disappear from my chest. Someone is dead? I can't push past the feeling that the *Aswang*, the monster from my nightmares, is here because of me. Which means she's dead because of me. I want to save Salvador from all of this, but perhaps he's doomed to see the supernatural whether I infect his life or not. So, I break the news about my belief theory.

> Looks like you're stuck with this injury. You're going to need a Mangkukulam to heal it.

Fortunately, I know just the *Mangkukulam* to see.

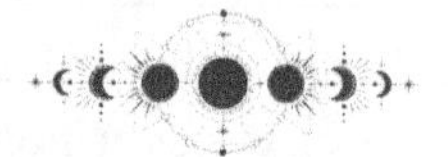

I pull up in front of Tita Blessica's house and parallel park along the street because her driveway is cramped with cars. The road is so crowded it's as if she's having a Filipino party, though she can't be because Mom's car is nowhere in sight.

We get out and wait for Salvador at the front door because he has to turn around up the street to find a spot. Except when he comes around the corner ... Is this really him? I shove him against the wall and look deep into his eyes. Are they bloodshot? Is my reflection upside-down in them the way they were when the *Aswang* impersonated Gabrielle? Or is my reflection turned in any other direction that it shouldn't be, for that matter?

No. All that's there is the crazed look of my face reflected at me in Salvador's soulful, worried eyes. His gaze makes my blood pump faster, sending a tingling sensation all over my skin. I jerk my hand away from him.

Sorry, I mouth. *I had to check.*

I turn to open the front door of Tita Blessica's house, but Salvador reaches for my arm. "Wait," he says gently. "You've got to tell me what's going on. An Asw-whatever ... shapeshifter attacked us a couple days ago and people are dying from invisible injuries. Why don't you seem as shocked? How did you know how to kill it?"

Salvador's questions cause Gabrielle to clench the stinky, stingray tail in her other fist more tightly, looking over her shoulder as she takes cover in the alcove.

I gesture for Salvador's phone and pull up my new favorite website: Fili-pedia Folklore. I show him all the tabs he should click on, including the diagram of how to make a whip out of a stingray tail, called a *buntot pagi*, as the best defense against the *Aswang*.

"That's nice, but how does this explain—"

I point more firmly at the screen. Salvador might as well read up on the subject before I get to the hard task of explaining myself.

"Okay, I'll read it when we're inside."

When I open Tita Blessica's door, *patis* (fish sauce) and cooking rice, which oddly enough smells like popcorn, assault my nose. It reminds me of the night Tita Blessica read my fortune about the sea witch, and I get that same uneasiness I'd felt that night as if I'm walking toward danger when I should be running away.

"It'll be about an hour and a half wait," a redhead in sea-green joggers says from her seated position on the couch.

I exchange confused looks with Gabrielle before shrugging.

Tita Blessica reads fortunes for pocket money, while her husband covers the bills with his work as a civilian on base with Dad. However, she's never had this much business before. A line of people sit on the living room couch, browsing the makeshift store of candles and pendants that take up half the dining table in the open-concept space. The standard incense burns, making the air feel thick—or maybe that's just the tension in the room. Everyone here seems made of shifty glances and shaky fingers. One man's posture is so rigid he jerks at every slight noise. Two of the women are rocking as they pray the rosary.

Business is booming.

A door clicks before swinging open as a towering man with busy, blue hair exits Tita Blessica's office/storage room. I hope to see Auntie before she gets back to work, but she doesn't come out. Instead, like clockwork, the next person walks in, and everyone seated on the couch or standing against the wall shuffles down one space.

As I stand next to the couch, some people who seem to be getting restless begin to talk.

"... attacked in my backyard," one woman with a boho headband says.

"Well, one of them stalked me in the parking garage at the mall," a middle-aged lady sitting on the loveseat across from the first woman replies.

"This town's gone to hell. A literal hell," a blonde woman in leggings responds with exaggerated head nods. "My neighbors have already listed their house for sale."

"Why bother?" a guy with a man bun interjects as he leans against the dead fireplace. "If it's like this here, it's got to be like this everywhere."

"Just a matter of time …" The redhead purses her lips in agreement.

"That's why I'm here," Headband Woman adds. "I need protection."

I tug vigorously on Gabrielle's hoodie sleeve.

Ask them, I mouth. Gabrielle looks confused, but Salvador's been paying attention and holds up a hand that says I-got-this.

"Excuse me, but what are you guys talking about?" he asks in a low voice as if this conversation is a secret. Maybe it is if they are talking about what I think they are talking about. The people look at each other as if for confidence before turning back to us.

"The monsters. Have you seen them too?" the middle-aged woman asks in whisper tones.

Salvador, Gabrielle, and I exchange tense glances. The room got extra quiet as they wait for our answer. I nod, and the space erupts in whisper-shouts as everyone seems to unite because they have yet another confirmation that they are not ridiculous for fearing these previously non-existent creatures. No wonder Tita Blessica's witch doctor business is doing so well. We're all here for monster protection.

Something else about the room is making my intuition flare the way it did when I'd realized that my pre-Ian memories had also changed, but as my gaze moves over these frightened people, I can't figure it out.

An hour goes by as we move little by little across the room. More people come in after us, so the space remains hot and crowded. Eventually, my head nods with sleep as I'm sandwiched on the couch between Salvador and Gabrielle.

While he reads through the website, well past the *Aswang* entry, I shake the sleep out of my head and open the notepad on my phone. I have questions for Tita Blessica and things I know I'll be asked, so I write. I write for so long that my thumbs hurt. I write until my hand cramps, and then I write some more. My eyelids are so heavy, but they snap open when the door to Tita Blessica's office opens once again. This time, Tita Blessica's loud voice seeps out before she emerges.

"The next person can wait in the office while I use the restroom." She gestures to the door. I stand up immediately, shouting her name, though no sound emerges. Will I ever get used to this? The lack of sound doesn't matter, though, because my sudden movement puts everyone on edge and catches Auntie's attention.

"Malaya. Gabrielle. What are you doing here?" She employs her chiding auntie tone. "Shouldn't you be resting?" She looks pointedly at me. It is just like an auntie to hear that someone's been hurt and bypass all concern for scolding. She hadn't come to see me in the hospital, but I'm sure Mom filled her in on everything.

"Tita, we need to talk to you." Gabrielle stands by my side, and Salvador follows.

Tita Blessica looks around at her customers. Quite a few more have come, all with the same problems; people who have seen monsters on the news or in their own lives, who believe and want to ward them away. I don't know if there's anything that Tita Blessica can do for these people, but I still hope there is.

"As you can see, I'm very busy—"

"It won't take long," Salvador speaks up. Something is commanding about his voice, though it remains entirely polite.

She examines him, her eyes looking down her nose though she is very much the shorter of the two. "Fine." Her accent thickens with annoyance.

The balding man next in line glowers, and I give him my best apologetic expression. He tosses his flannel shirt backward like a dress as he retakes his seat.

Tita Blessica's face tightens as Gabrielle, Salvador, and I walk past her into the office. Then she turns to the guy who is next in line and bows her head slightly. "I'm sorry, huh? Family business."

I sit nervously at the wood and glass table she uses for her readings.

"Make this quick. As you can see, business is going well." Tita Blessica reaches for her cigarettes but seems to think better of lighting one in this enclosed space. That's out of character for her—or at least my version of her.

The prewritten questions and responses I'd compiled for Tita Blessica while sitting in the waiting room will help this go faster. I open the digital notepad and pass the phone.

Do you remember sending me to the sea witch?

Tita Blessica pulls the plum reading glasses out of her curly bangs and squints so hard her eyes nearly shut as she stares at the bright screen.

"Sea witch?" Her nose shoots into the air as she looks up at me. "*Ano ba?* I never sent you to the sea witch."

"Tita!" Gabrielle gasps. "You know who the sea witch is? How are you involved in all this?"

Salvador, still in the dark about everything besides the *Aswang's* existence, gets up and goes to Tita Blessica's side of the desk to read over her shoulder. Gabrielle joins him, though she already knows my story and is probably doing it to put more pressure on our auntie. I'm aware of how isolated I am on my side of the table, their shadows casting over me from the lamp behind them.

"I don't know a sea witch!" Tita Blessica adjusts her wording, her tone becoming shorter with Gabrielle than usual. She smooths the glass table like a tablecloth, then turns to me. "I don't know what to tell you, Malaya. I remember reading for you recently, but I told you that you will become a TV star if you go to the Philippines. Your dance moves could use some work, but you have a wonderful voice."

My shoulders fall.

Misinterpreting my expression, she adds, "I'm sorry. *Had* a wonderful voice," she corrects herself. She thinks she's being nice, but a lot of our aunties' comments can come off a little bitchy. Then again, the compliment does warm me.

"But Tita," Gabrielle says, "You just said I never sent you to the sea witch. Like you know her."

"Fine. I know the sea witch. But I did not send you to her. I was forbidden to."

That was not a response I'd anticipated. I open a new page in my notes.

You were forbidden to send me to the sea witch? Who forbid you?

And if someone forbade Tita Blessica from sending me to the witch, why didn't they do the same for me? Or did they, but she went through with it anyway? All of this only makes me more scared there is actually another Malaya that belongs in this timeline, and I didn't just have a moment in my past change. My insides twist.

"Don't be angry." Tita Blessica's voice contains none of the strength I'm used to. "But I was just so aggravated about the way Filipinos are treated. The way I'm treated. I wanted to prove that Filipinos have culture. That we are important and needed."

My mind flashes to the night when Tita Blessica got particularly drunk and shouted about how people think we have no culture.

"That was the last straw for me," Tita Blessica explains. "I went to the sea witch to make Filipino lives better." And it must have worked because with all those people sitting in her living room, her business is flourishing as people flock to her for help.

"Are you saying that you asked the ... sea witch for *Aswangs*?" Salvador says, his pronunciation perfect.

"No." Tita Blessica looks up at him, insulted. "I asked for a change. But the sea witch turned me down."

What? That's not what I was expecting at all.

"If she turned you down, then why has everything, including Malaya, changed?" Gabrielle asked.

"The sea witch said I wasn't desperate enough to fulfill the death wish's requirements. She told me to bring her someone so desperate for a change they'd make this wish and never look back."

I squeeze my phone so tightly that the cheap screen protector cracks.

You set me up? Though not a sound emits from me, every word is heard.

Tita Blessica holds her hands up as if defending herself from my energy. "No, honey—"

"She couldn't have used my Mal because Mal's life was perfect," Gabrielle interjects. "She didn't have an abusive, cheating boyfriend or fight with Mom all the time like this Malaya."

Salvador's eyes flicker to mine, and I can't hold his gaze. A cold sweat rushes through me as Gabrielle explains our theory that I'm not the Mal that belongs in this timeline.

"I don't know what you're talking about with this Mal or that Malaya, boyfriends or fighting with Floribeth ... But Mal's life was not perfect. She was not happy, and I'm surprised you, of all people, couldn't see that," Tita Blessica says to Gabrielle. "The girl was miserable. She felt like she had to be perfect all the time; perfect grades, perfect sister, perfect daughter ... she was afraid to make a mistake."

Gabrielle shakes her head, but she doesn't see the new memories flooding my mind—washed in fear of failing. Set on this path of achievement with everything geared toward a nursing career she didn't want. Longing to be loved by someone but always worried about if Mom and Dad would approve. The expectations were a crushing weight.

Gabrielle's eyes are flooding with tears of denial as I type:

Why didn't you go through with it?

"I couldn't. Before I could even propose the idea to you, two men appeared in my house—in my safe space." Now that she's said it, I notice there are twice the *agimats*, Filipino amulets, to ward off evil and three times the protective candlelight than usual. She must have been really shaken. "They said the sea witch had been imprisoned for crimes against them. She incited a war that nearly destroyed the Earth and that if I did anything to set her free, they would kill me and anyone else involved."

I can't breathe. I lean over, pressing my forehead against the cold glass table, trying to catch my breath, but they only become shallower. Gabrielle comes to my side, and Salvador tells me to sit up straight.

"What's wrong?" Tita Blessica asks. "They're not coming after you. I told you I didn't go through with it."

"Then how do you explain the *Aswangs* walking all over the place?" Gabrielle asks.

Tita Blessica fumbles. I drag my phone across the table and type:

You may not have sent me to the sea witch, but another version of yourself did.

There's no denying it anymore, no matter how much I may want to. I'm not the Malaya that belongs in this timeline. I didn't just change a moment in my past. I robbed another Mal who'd made good choices and sent her off to deal with my bad ones—my dangerous ones.

Listen, I tried to see the sea witch again today to get some answers, but it didn't work because I no longer have a death wish. If I'm going to get Mal back to her life and return to my timeline, I'll need to get the sea witch to undo the wish. How can I get to her?

The light from the phone casts hard shadows on everyone's faces which look more menacing as I wait for them to finish reading.

"I doubt she'll undo it," Tita Blessica shakes her head, "but did you try submerging yourself during the full moon at the witching hour?"

Gabrielle chimes in, "The next full moon is more than three weeks away." Gabrielle and I know because Anita posed a similar question that morning when I filled her in on how I was going to throw myself back into the ocean and hope Auntie Maggie came to get me again.

Tita Blessica sighs. "I was strictly forbidden to talk to her by those men. We could all lose our lives."

Then we need to contact those men. Let them know I'm not trying to help the sea witch; that I'm trying to fix things. Maybe they can even help me get to her.

Trembling, Tita Blessica nods.

Pakiusap naman, we need protection, weapons, anything you can give.

Also, we need protection, weapons, anything you can give us, *pakiusap*.

Salvador clears his throat. "If an *Aswang* hadn't just attacked me, I would ask if you're joking. But after the last two days, and all the stories I heard from the people out there ..." His mouth opens and closes as the sentence remains incomplete.

Tita Blessica fills plastic grocery bags with *agimats*, candles, books, and even a Visayan knife. "Do not tell your mom where you got this, huh?" Tita holds the knife menacingly, which would have rendered me speechless if I wasn't already. I'm guessing I'm safe from Tita Blessica telling Mom why I came here to see her, which is a relief. Meanwhile, in another bag, she includes a salve for Salvador's wound and instructions on how to care for it.

"Thank you, Auntie." Gabrielle wraps her arms around Tita Blessica's small frame.

Tita pinches Gabrielle's one dimple, then slaps her cheek like she's slapping a baby's cute bottom before she says, "You're welcome, honey. But reaching those men will take some time to figure out. They came to me before, and I know very little about them besides that they are gods."

Gods? My eyebrows raise.

Tita Blessica doesn't notice my exclamation, but Gabrielle meets my widened eyes. "Now I'm so busy making herbs and pendants to ward off many monsters. I put several different kinds in one of the bags for you, labeled with instructions. Follow carefully and go now. It's best not to keep these people waiting any longer."

"Wait, there are more monsters than just *Aswangs*?" Gabrielle asks.

Tita Blessica stands. "Yes, yes, honey. Watch the news." She ushers us to the door.

As we're walking out of Tita Blessica's house with a room full of irritated eyes on us for taking so long, I figure out what caused my intuition to flare earlier. None of Tita Blessica's customers are Filipino.

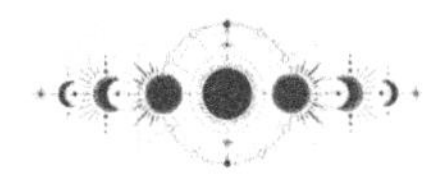

Once outside, I run my hands through my tangled hair. There are more than just *Aswangs* running around the world, I have no clue how to reach the sea witch, and I might have gods coming to kill me. But if they wanted to kill me, they would have by now, right? I'm hopeful for a moment but not pacified. I haven't been in this timeline for very long—maybe they're just plotting the best way to get me. I'm sure they're just busy doing a bunch of god-things.

I place a hand on Gabrielle's arm. *I'm sorry.*

But she jerks away from me. And I don't blame her; I altered her entire reality and fixing this feels insurmountably hopeless. Salvador places a comforting hand on my shoulder. It's everything I need at this moment and nothing I deserve.

A loud bray fills the air, which seems to still. At the far end of this old neighborhood, a gigantic, humanoid figure rocks a Silverado back and forth from its perch atop the roof.

A man watering his lawn a couple of houses down, closer to the beast than I am, pulls an earphone out as he spares a curious glance at the truck after all four tires return to the ground and then goes back to his roses. Non-believer. Meanwhile, a couple checking their mailbox screams, running into their house. Believers.

"Keys," Gabrielle says, searching her pockets. "Keys!" She holds her hand out to me.

As if the very thought of escaping summons the gigantic figure, the monster turns its orange orbs for eyes at us. Instead of a human head, he has the skull and mane of a horse. A demonic neigh, rolling at such a low pitch, emanates from his throat, reverberating against the asphalt road and bouncing around my car.

I yank the keys out of my hoodie pocket and toss them at Gabrielle. We race to my car, piling in as quickly as possible.

Go, go, go, I mouth, slapping Gabrielle's shoulder with each word.

"Does that thing have hooves?" Salvador asks from my messy backseat.

"Yep," Gabrielle confirms, fumbling the car keys and struggling to pick them up off the floor. "And if it's what I think it is, it's also got spines running down its mane."

I lean over the center console, grab the keys from the floor, and shove it into the ignition. The car roars to life.

"And what do you think it is?" Salvador's fingers dig deep into the leather of the driver's seat as Gabrielle throws the car in reverse and slams on the gas.

The beast's eyes roll in my direction, and his horsey lips smirk before he leaps from the truck. The thunderous cracking of cement is nearly as loud as his wicked bray as his hooves hit the ground. A gasp gets caught in my throat as the creature races toward us.

"A *Tikbalang*," Gabrielle says, hand on the passenger seat as she looks over her shoulder to avoid hitting any parked cars. "Like a werehorse."

I grab my phone, open up the Filipino monster lexicon and click the "T" section. Then I turn the screen around to show him a similar image of the monster, like a reverse centaur.

"Hey, look," Salvador says dryly, pointing at a passage. "If we can tame it, we get a wish."

The beast neighs again, and it's so close the strength of it rattles my car on its frame. I get a real sense of just how big the horse beast is as it takes exceptionally few running leaps on all fours to be right in front of us.

Faster. I grip Gabrielle's shoulder and shake it with full force. Then the *Tikbalang's* hooves scrape along the roof of my car as it misjudges its speed and distance, leaping over us.

"Brake," Salvador shouts.

I jerk forward as the car comes to an abrupt halt.

Salvador throws himself over the center console, yelling, "Drive," as he shoves the shifter into gear. Gabrielle smashes her foot on the gas, and we're launched forward. In the side-view mirror, the beast chases us, and I swear his gaze targets me. Gabrielle cuts the wheel sharply, and the car turns a corner.

Tires screech against the pavement before finding traction and launching us forward. The vehicle seems to jump with each thunderous stomp of the *Tikbalang's* hooves on the pavement, as if he's creating an earthquake. I scream soundlessly as Gabrielle flies toward the main road with no indication of obeying the stop sign.

"Hold on tight," she shouts, taking a sharp right. The back

tires skid from her turn and another car's horn blares as it swerves into the next lane to avoid colliding with us.

Breathing heavily, I turn to see if the werehorse will follow us to the freeway. But the dark figure pauses at the corner, clenching and unclenching its fists. It recedes into the shadows of the street from which we'd escaped.

Only one car slams on its brakes before pulling into the median as if they see the *Tikbalang* too. A long-haired man leans out of his open window with his phone poised. Maybe he'll be social media famous later as people debate whether there is anything on the video or not. I almost suggest that Salvador do the same, considering his need to go viral and erase his embarrassing internet footprint, but his tightly clenched arms and stiff posture tells me now is not the time.

It's not until Gabrielle has weaved through several main streets and enters the freeway that I realize Salvador's truck is back at Tita Blessica's. Despite the bright Texas sun, I'm afraid to go back for the vehicle like it's the witching hour.

Salvador must feel the same because he says, "You can drop me off at my dorm. I'll have one of my friends drive me to get it later."

My head whips toward the back seat, my eyes wide with alarm.

"Don't worry; we'll wait till tomorrow. Maybe that Tik-monster will be gone by then."

"*Tikbalang*," Gabrielle corrects.

Slumping low into my seat, I press my hands over my ears, wishing I could block the guilty thoughts running through my head the way I'm blocking out the noisy wind rushing past the car. I fucked up my life before, but now I'm fucking with everyone else's. Salvador nudges me and does one of those what's-up nods, his brow furrowed. I sigh soundlessly, shaking my head.

"We'll figure things out," he promises.

As Gabrielle pulls up to the university, Salvador directs her to a set of buildings on campus. She parks near some tall, stone dorms, and I glance back at Salvador. I don't know about Gabrielle, but I'm filled with a devastating emptiness that he's leaving.

"You guys want to come in?" Salvador asks.

Instantly, I want to say yes, but there's hesitation in the creases of Gabrielle's forehead.

"I'm so tired from all of this," Gabrielle says, her hand making a circular motion. "But you can go in if you want."

My breath catches in my throat. I have this strong urge to go with Salvador, but my head shakes. Annoying, smart head acting before I can make the wrong decision. It knows before my heart does that hanging out alone with Salvador would be something the old me would do. It's safer on my heart to have Gabrielle with me, so I don't make bad choices because the fact is, I don't trust me anymore.

I may be imagining it, but Salvador's shoulders slump infinitesimally.

"At least walk him out." Gabrielle's gaze shifts from him to me. "I, uh, need a moment to breathe. But don't walk out of my sight. And take the *buntot pagi* just in case."

Okay. I grab the stingray tail before I get out of the car.

Salvador waits for me on the sidewalk with his hands shoved into his pockets. My palms sweat more than they did when the *Tikbalang* chased us, which I hope Salvador doesn't notice when I take the hand he offers.

Electric waves pulse through my body, causing my breath to hitch.

"I was going to hold the stingray tail—" he says.

Oh god, no. I did not just make this mistake. Immediately, I try to pull my hand away, a flush of heat making my insides die, but he holds on tightly. "No, don't. This is nice." A small smile forms on Salvador's supple lips as he takes the *buntot pagi* in his other hand.

"I'm just up here." He gestures to the left.

I walk up a slope of grass, and when I reach another sidewalk, he lets go of my hand. I'm filled with an awful, buzzing energy as I wish so hard that I was brave enough to hug him like I did that first time at the beach. But my arms are dead weights at my sides, refusing to move.

"Sal," a girl's voice calls from the balcony.

Both of us turn toward the melodic call, and my heart drops at the beautifully tanned girl with long, dark hair looking down at us. A breeze moves gently through her perfectly curled locks like she's an animated princess, while it seems to shift my wavy hair like a brick wall blocking my face.

"Hey, Olivia!" Salvador says. "What's up?"

"Just wondering if you're coming to the Theta party tonight."

"If Wes and Miguel are going, then yeah." Salvador smiles at me sheepishly before turning back to Olivia. I try to suppress any facial expression that would make me appear sullen, but inside I'm pulsing with sickening jealousy. Salvador was going to party with this amazingly hot girl. It didn't even matter that his two buddies would be there too because there would surely be other gorgeous college girls. Meanwhile, I'm just some high school kid who's seeing monsters.

"This is Malaya," Salvador introduces us.

I wave, smiling as genuinely as possible through the pain. It's not her fault she's divine.

"Nice to meet you." Olivia waves easily, confidently. "I love your hair!"

Great ... she's nice too. My smile is a little easier now as I mouth, *Thank you.*

Olivia's face scrunches up adorably before Salvador explains, "She can't talk."

"Oh," Olivia mouths before adding, "you *would* find a girl who couldn't call you on your bullshit." They laugh, then

Olivia heads into one of the dorm rooms. Is it Salvador's dorm?

He turns back to me, shaking his head. Her last comment should've eased my mind, but I can't help wondering if she's an option. Is he dating Olivia? Then I ask myself, does it matter? We've only known each other for a few days. All I want to care about is the fact that flirting with him is the most fun I've had with a guy in a year. I have to quantify that statement with the "with a guy" part because, truthfully, the most fun I've had in a year was with Gabrielle and Anita in the car the morning of the *Aswang* attack.

My shoulders slump when I remember how angry Gabrielle is with me.

"You okay?" Salvador touches my arm, and my insides flutter. God, he looks so good in this light it hurts. Even though I'm no longer in pain from my time with Ian, it's as if my body remembers the trauma. What was it that the witch had said? That I would remember everything, but it would be as if time had passed? Even though I no longer long for Ian, and those wounds he inflicted are no longer fresh, they left scars. And those scars want me to run as far from Salvador as I can before he's even got the chance to hurt me.

But Salvador pulls me close to him. It's so unexpected that I don't even have time to open my arms. They're trapped between me and his chest. The tightness of his embrace and the scent of his minty shampoo make my knees weak. What does this mean? Is he trying to reassure me that he's interested? Or is he like Ian, pretending to show a preference for me, so I'll stick around?

I lay my head on his chest, feeling safe and conflicted. I don't think I'll ever trust myself to know the difference again. When he lets go, I pull out my phone and open our text thread. The flirty message he typed from me is still visible, so different in tone from what I type now.

> Now that we're out of your hair, the monsters should probably leave you alone.

His pocket chimes, and he smiles crookedly as he pulls out his phone.

My heart thumps loudly in my chest, pressing against the cavity as if it's going to burst. There's no other reason for Salvador to stay after this unless I run off with his salve. He glances up at me through his thick, dark lashes. "Like it's that easy to leave ... you two," he tacks on at the end.

Air catches in my throat at the first part of his sentence, but the second half brings me back to this reality. Though I think we've flirted, I still can't tell if I'm misreading his easy nature. Some people can click with everyone, and Salvador might be some people. I turn to go before I can do anything I'll regret.

"Malaya?"

Yeah, I mouth when I look back at him.

"You might want this," he says, holding out the stingray tail. As I take it from him, his fingers linger on mine. Fire radiates from my hand throughout my body. Then he adds, "I can't imagine who would ever want to make you sad enough to leave your old life behind—to run. But I'm glad you're here."

We smile at each other before going our separate ways—me back to Gabrielle and him into the dorm that Olivia went in.

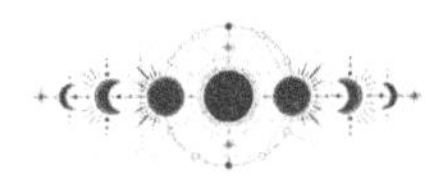

Mom paces the sidewalk in front of our pepper-gray brick home with her Filipino broom over her shoulder like it's a battle ax. The thing may be half the size of American brooms, but the way Mom wields it at dirt and pests, it's clear she channels her work stress into every wood and dry grass fiber.

Of the things my mind is currently fixated on:

- Daydreaming about Salvador
- Obsessing over what he and Olivia are doing in that dorm together
- Gabrielle's deeply troubled scowl
- And now Mom's frantic shuffle as she yanks open the car door

I'm just a multi-tasking ball of emotions.

"You were gone too long, huh? Where did you go?" Her shrill voice is demanding and concerned at the same time. She waves her broom over our heads like she's swatting away giant-sized flies as she hurries us into the house. Once the door is closed, Mom starts smudging us with the burning sage she left on the entryway console.

Gabrielle coughs from the wispy yet potent smoke. "Ugh, Mom, stop. We were just out shopping, not summoning demons."

"That is not funny." Mom lifts the broom like she's going to strike, though she's never hit us with it. "You are too busy gallivanting with friends to notice the world is over?"

Though Tita Blessica doesn't want Mom to know anything about what she did, I'm still surprised Mom doesn't already know where we were. It isn't in Tita Blessica's nature to keep anything from her. But the news blaring from the living room pulls me toward the voice of a reporter who's gone live at the beach where the *Aswang* made headlines.

A confused journalist gestures to a video posted on the internet. "Several Filipinos on social media have identified the first creature as an *Aswang*, part of Filipino mythology. However, there is an ongoing debate as to whether there is a monster in the video footage, sparking a feud that rivals the great 2015 gold or blue dress controversy. Now there are reports of a horse-like beast in town. Whether or not you can see these creatures, the city has advised locals to stay clear of the beaches and stay inside after curfew until further notice."

As the reporter signs off, I gaze at Gabrielle. We're lucky we're not on that footage, or Mom would have grounded us for six months.

"First, the *Aswangs* are all over the news, and now a *Tikbalang*. I told your father, but he doesn't believe. Look with your eyes." She gestures to the screen though he's in their room with the door closed.

"Mom, can you see it?" Gabrielle asks hesitantly.

"What do you mean, can I see it? Of course, I can see it. I have eyes." Mom is indignant, her house slippers scratching the tile as she makes her way into the kitchen. Clearly, she's a believer, and Dad isn't. Huh.

While pulling bowls from the cabinet, I side-eye Mom. Has she connected this *Aswang* to the creature the man described at the hospital?

"The whole town is infested." Mom takes a bowl from my hand, dumping a scoop of rice into the center before handing it to Gabrielle, who pours a ladle of *nilaga* inside. "There's a video of a *Berberoka* on the walking trail near the University and some *Lampongs*. It's making the national news. All the creatures are Filipino, and people blame us. We're not safe from the monsters, and nobody likes Filipinos right now," Mom says, pulling out a handful of spoons.

"What? That can't be true." Gabrielle sets two bowls down on the dining table, eyeing me with alarm when Mom turns her back to yell for Eric and Dad that, "the food is cook." Filipino monsters are making the national news, and one is stalking the refuge near the University. Salvador lives there, and he's going out partying. Will he be safe? Suddenly, I'm too sick to eat.

"*Anak*, if you don't believe me, look at the social media," Mom says, adding more patis to the steaming bowl of soup.

I grab a grocery list Mom was working on and a pen:

> *Do you think we should leave town? Find somewhere safe?*

I still need to reach the sea witch, but I have a feeling her cave isn't near Corpus anyway. I turn the paper over to Mom.

"Go somewhere?" Mom rolls her eyes. "But I just cooked dinner."

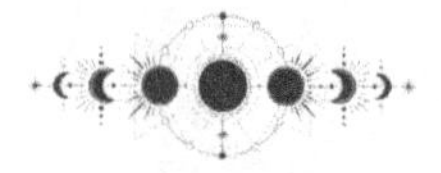

After I eat, I find Gabrielle in her mint-colored room instead of mine. I don't know why she bothers sleeping with me when she's created this masterpiece. She claims to not be artistic but loves living in aesthetic spaces. Her back is to her cushioned headboard, framed in fairy lights, as she browses her rose gold computer. Soft lighting illuminates her features, giving her that silky skin look.

"Tita Blessica texted. She tried to leave her house to send that message to the gods, but apparently, the spell can only be performed from the highest place in Corpus, and she can't leave her house because of the *Tikbalang*."

I drop my face into my hands. I'm not surprised—we barely got out of there, and we move much quicker than Tita Blessica.

"The monsters are everywhere." Gabrielle turns her screen, and there's evidence of these once mythological creatures on at least a dozen tabs. I crawl onto her coral Sherpa bedspread, leaning in to watch a video of some *Lampong* traipsing around Duke Ranch. A composition book jabs my side, and I find scrawled notes, bookmarked with a pen, about each monster and its current location. As I'm running down the list of places in Corpus where there have been monster sightings, I recognize an address and text Gabrielle:

> Isn't this Bentley's street? Did you call her already?

Gabrielle exhales. "Yep. I texted her. She knows."

I twist a freshly washed strand of hair between my fingers.

> Is something wrong?

Gabrielle bites down on her tongue before asking, "What do you remember about my friendship with Bentley?"

> You two are inseparable. Down to duet any Ariana song on karaoke. Linked at the hip at every Filipino party.

Gabrielle squeezes her temples, probably summoning that unbelievable patience I've come to expect from her my entire life.

"While you were walking Salvador to his dorm, I looked up gaslighting because the things that happened to you with your ex sounded *so* familiar. The abuser isolates the victim. But it's also a kind of emotional abuse where the other person makes you feel like you're crazy. They might pretend that the bad things they did never happened, even though you know they did. Or they do annoying crap like move your stuff around, so you start questioning yourself. Does that sound familiar?"

My lips purse to the side. At first, I want to say no, but then I start to see my memories through this new lens. Ian used to move my car keys around and then act like I was absurd, even if I caught him doing it. He used to make plans with me, and instead of telling me he needed to change the time and date, he'd act like I misremembered what we'd planned.

Gabrielle continues. "Bentley's ex would do stuff like that too. Things she didn't have the strength to tell me about." Gabrielle's eyelashes flicker as she meets my gaze, and I go unnaturally still. It must hurt to have someone close to her not confide in her. It only occurs to me just now that I did the same thing to my version of my sister—but we weren't that close.

She turns her stare to the ceiling, her eyes shifting side to side as she watches the blades of her ceiling fan slowly spin. "I only found out about Bentley because I saw the bruises. I flipped the fuck out and made her go to the guidance counselor. Bentley was so mad at me ... That was the turning point for you and me—well, Mal and me; the moment we started spending more time together because Bentley didn't want to hang out anymore."

What happened to the guy?

"When her brother found out, he fought the jerk. But Michael got his butt kicked. Bentley's dad had her boyfriend arrested for assault on a minor for Michael and statutory rape for Bentley. He got two years in prison since he's eighteen, but he might be getting out early. His absence made her stronger again. I have to hope that she's still strong when he gets out. But our friendship isn't the same."

I don't know why I can't remember any of this. I'm sorry.

Gabrielle sets the computer down, the screen wobbling like her voice. "I'm glad you figured out a way to escape."

Me too.

Gabrielle's mouth opens, but no words come out.

What?

"Are you happier now?"

More than you could ever know. My ex made me need to be with him even when I didn't love being around him. I was addicted. I never want to feel that way again.

"Not even for Salvador?" Her voice is teasing and light.

Not for anyone. My head shakes with each word.

"Well, Salvador's in danger of feeling that way about you." She nudges me playfully, trying to lighten the mood. Heat burns my cheeks, and I bury my face into her Pusheen cat pillow. "OooOoo, you like him."

I lift my head and then kick her. *You're five.*

We giggle, though my voice doesn't meld with hers like it does in my memories.

"What? He's cute," Gabrielle says. "But I don't think Grant is going to like it."

What? I sit up straighter. Grant from history class? Hannah's Grant? What does he have to do with anything?

A second later, a flood of images returns to me of shaggy-haired Grant. He'd once caught me when I'd started to fall from my desk after a sleepless night of studying, and it had led to me falling for him.

"He's the guy you're—Mal's talking to," Gabrielle shrugs. "I thought you knew that when he visited you in the hospital."

Mal's in a relationship with someone, and you let me walk off with Salvador?

"Mal doesn't get in relationships with people." She shakes her head. "She was just dating Grant, as in sometimes she would go on dates." Her nostrils flare, and after a beat, she says, "I can't believe she was so miserable, and I knew nothing."

Maybe she wasn't miserable. Tita Blessica wouldn't know her better than you.

"Except she did with you and the other version of me, right? The other Gabrielle didn't know you were in an abusive relationship."

The last time I saw my Gabrielle standing on the jetty, shouting encouraging words to me to fight the riptides comes to mind.

No. She had no clue.

Gabrielle sinks lower into the bed. "Look, I know you didn't plan to sweep my sister off to your world, but I want to be alone tonight. I'm going to stay up late and find more information on this sea witch and the gods.

I get up, and at the door, Gabrielle says, "You should probably brush up on your non-relationship with Grant since tomorrow will be your first day back at school. If you want to know more about it, then reread your messages. I'm sure there's a text thread with his name somewhere."

I close the door, lingering in the empty hallway that separates our rooms. Though I hadn't been used to Gabrielle's presence in my previous life, her absence now is acute. What did I expect? I'm not the sister she's close to.

In my room, I sit at the antique sewing desk that functions

as my study nook. I pull one knee up, reading through the messages on my phone when something Salvador said earlier returns to me. If you can tame a *Tikbalang*, you get a wish. My brain goes a mile a minute as I search the internet for *Tikbalang* folklore. It takes me at least an hour to compile a list of possible weapons and hours more to plot how to tame the monster. Still, I fight to keep my lids open because if I can tame the beast, I can wish for it to take me to the sea witch.

chapter seventeen

By the time I have to get ready for school, I've had zero sleep, but I have a plan. As Gabrielle pulls up to the junior high drop-off, I turn to wave goodbye at Eric, and he eyes me like I'm a zombie.

"Okay, what is going on with you two?" he asks.

My brow furrows at Gabrielle, and then I notice she's got bags under her eyes.

"We were up late playing *Villainous.*" Gabrielle dabs concealer on her bags.

"Without me? Again?" Eric exhales and gets out of the car without a goodbye.

I type:

We'll have to make that up to him, even if we didn't play without him.

"Maybe after all this is over." Gabrielle starts driving, not connecting that I won't be here anymore when all this is over. Will she miss me like I'll miss her?

As she parks at the high school, I hand her my phone, explaining how I can tame the *Tikbalang* for a wish which I can use to get to the sea witch and free Tita Blessica to reach out to the gods to make sure I'm not on their hit list.

Gabrielle looks at the phone, the tendons standing out in her neck. "That *Aswang* was after us—tracking us since you saw it at the hospital, and it took a lot to defeat it. Now you want to go chasing another monster? No."

I sink into my seat, not surprised by Gabrielle's response. She was attacked and held hostage by the *Aswang*. But it's more than that—both versions of my sister are afraid of trying things—even if they seem fun. When we were little, Gabrielle refused to go on a trampoline because one of the big kids double-jumped one of the smaller ones, and that was just a little too much for Gabrielle.

A puff of air escapes my lips. I don't want to sneak out at night to do this alone, but I will. Things are so much scarier in the dark, and the *Tikbalang* already makes the hairs on my arms stand on end, but she isn't giving me a choice. I pull the backpack up from the floor between my legs and open the car door.

Gabrielle catches up as I pass the library, headed for the side entrance. "Wait." I stop when I reach the sidewalk, conscious of people eyeing me as they pass by. Gabrielle folds and unfolds her arms.

"You didn't fight that *Aswang* alone. If Salvador wasn't there, things could have gone a completely different way." She exhales. "Maybe ... if we ask him for help, we can do it."

My heart stills. I hadn't planned for Salvador to be part of this—not with everything so up in the air. Not when I couldn't trust myself to act like a normal person when it comes to dating. Until I could be more like Mal, who knows how to date without losing her entire self, I shouldn't be around people I'm attracted to. But ...

All of me hates the idea of Gabrielle being in danger. The memory of her trapped under that dune grass causes physical pangs in my chest. Still, the thought of having Salvador along to help with the fight does quell the nervous energy buzzing through me. I'm not thrilled at coming face to face with this demonic horse alone on a darkened street, so I nod.

"Good. Just text Salvador that we need to meet up with him."

She starts walking, and my gaze moves to the creamy stone building. I'd been so busy last night coming up with my plan to defeat the *Tikbalang* I forgot to be nervous about going to school. Now that I'm here, I'm a ball of anxious energy. Gabrielle turns, waving for me to come with her. I bite my lip, walking slower than before.

It's not like it's my first day, but it kind of is. Usually, I would go to Stephanie or Hannah's locker, and we'd walk the halls until first period. But neither of them visited me in the hospital, and I can't find any text threads connecting us. Anita was supposed to be on a flight home right after we video-chatted yesterday, but she's probably too jet-lagged to come to school today.

Gabrielle loops her arm in mine. "Come on. We'll go to our locker, and then I'll walk you to class."

Like her room and notebooks, Gabrielle's locker is a Pinterest board aesthetic of pinks, soft golds, and various-sized storage bins, which causes me organization envy. It's decorated with pictures of her and Mal dancing the *Sayaw sa Bangko*, singing karaoke, and hanging out with several other Filipino friends I used to think of as just her friends. At the bottom of the locker, I pick up a pre-Calc book.

Yours? I ask, my forehead creasing in confusion.

"Uh, no," Gabrielle says, laughing. "You know I hate math."

Then whose? My gaze clouds over as I try to activate a memory that will reveal if we share this locker with anyone else. It is one of the few sections of the school that houses full-sized lockers, after all.

"*Yours.*" Gabrielle laughs. When my head jerks, shocked

that I'm taking Pre-Calc. She laughs even harder. "That's exactly how Mal looked when she got her schedule at registration."

Oh. I want to laugh, but the worrier in me wonders how I'll make it through the day if I don't even know my schedule. I swap the book for my chemistry text and know I've chosen right when Gabrielle doesn't bat an eye.

We get to chemistry, which seems to contain the same people. Hannah is already there, and I raise my hand to say hi before dropping it quickly as her eyes pass over me. She doesn't know me, so who do I sit with in this class?

Gabrielle grabs my shoulders.

"I have to go, or I'll be late." She pokes at one of my fists tightly gripped around my textbook, and when I loosen it, the bones in my fingers ache. "Relax."

The bell rings right as I pass the threshold of the door to my chemistry class. A lot of people stare, and the majority welcome me back. I raise my hand in an awkward hello, then head for my favorite seat on the far side of the room. As I slide onto a narrow blue stool and drop my backpack on the black tabletop, I'm startled by Mr. Winer's appearance. He's tall and lanky like Slenderman and has to lean over to talk quietly to me.

"Hey, Malaya," he says in a somber voice. It's the voice you use when someone dies. "I just wanted to check in and see if you're okay. Your mother has spoken with the school about accommodations for your inability to speak but let me know if there is anything else I can do to make this transition easier."

My nose crinkles, but I smooth it quickly. Mr. Winer didn't like me much in my previous life. He was also one of those teachers who made the association that if a student gets bad grades, they must not be a good person. From the report cards I'd found stashed in the desk in Mal's room, she's an A student. No wonder he's so concerned. I'm filled with this conflicting need not to disappoint him and simultaneously not give a crap about what he thinks. It's weird how teachers have that effect on us. The pressure to do well weighs heavy on me. How will I ever live up to the standards Mal set? I think about what Tita Blessica said about Mal being miserable. Do I even want to?

By the time third period rolls around, I'm drained. It's hard to figure out who I know and how well I know them when my brain flashes memories from both lives at me. Why can't my mind color code these things like Gabrielle color codes all her notes? It's hard not having my regular friends to vent to and shoot the shit with between periods. And then there's Grant.

I walk into class and bump into him right at the door.

"Hey." He smiles, and it's different from the polite smiles I've gotten all morning. It feels like we're something more than friends, even though I hadn't picked up on that at the hospital.

Hey. I hug Grant as I would never have in my previous life.

When I pull away, his gaze is intense. Crap. Did I come on too strong? A memory from our most recent date returns. We're sitting on his living room floor, having an indoor picnic, when he leans over and kisses me. Though he and Mal have been on dates, Mal seems to have a more laid-back approach to dating than me—she's hardly contacted him since then, according to the text threads in my phone. From that memory, I get the sense that she didn't really feel sparks between them. I smile sheepishly, and he rubs the back of his neck as his face reddens so brightly it accentuates his constellation of freckles.

I take a seat, and Grant sits next to me. Hannah glares at me from across the room. I'd suspected we're not friends in this life ... but are we enemies? Maybe she's crushing on Grant. Even if Hannah and I are not friends, I'd never want to hurt her. Besides, if I'm being honest, I'm much more interested in Salvador.

Anita rushes into the room, looking around madly. "Oh, my gosh. Oh, my gosh. Oh, my gosh," she shouts, taking the seat behind me. Then she throws her arms around my neck. "I couldn't wait to see you. Mom wasn't going to let me come to school today because of how late we got in, but I insisted that I could at least do a half day when I woke up. I just had to see you after everything that happened." She lets go, and I turn around to face her. I write in her notebook:

You remember I'm Malaya, right? Not Mal.

Luckily, Grant can't see what I've written from here.

"Of course, but I'm still so excited to meet, uh, *see* you." She winks very obviously. "I still can't believe everything that's happened. It's like coming back to a new life where my best friend isn't speaking to me anymore. So very K-drama," she practically screams, and my eyes widen. Please don't say anything about the death wish, or the sea witch, or even the monsters. Despite those fears, my smile is uncontained at her infectious energy.

Anita talks about how her mother wouldn't let her see me when they got in last night because of the monsters lurking. I nod like I'm following, though it's hard, then nod like I sympathize with her plight. The two nods are different because the nod of sympathy is slower with a head tilt.

Lucky for me, Mrs. Cortes starts her lesson, and it's mostly note-taking. It doesn't require a lot of verbal interaction, which is good even though my eyes wanted to roll back in my head out of sheer boredom. My phone flashes a notification halfway through the lesson, and my heart races a little faster when I see the name.

SALVADOR

Hey, are you free later?

I smile, turning my phone over quickly because Mrs. Cortes is the type of teacher who reads messages of any kind aloud. From my periphery, I catch Grant looking at my phone. We smile stiffly at each other. I guess I didn't turn the phone over fast enough.

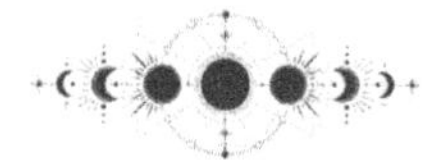

After school, Gabrielle and I park in front of our house, with Anita pulling up right behind us. Salvador waits outside, leaning against the garage door. I sit up straighter, smiling involuntarily as he lifts his hand in a wave. He looks so handsome in his fitted black tee and jeans that Gabrielle has to wave a hand in front of my face to get my attention. She shakes her head amusedly.

"So much for Grant," she murmurs. I push her playfully, then get out of the car.

Anita rushes up to me. "Oh, my G, is that him?" She is a better whisperer than Gabrielle, but her energy is so loud aliens in space could figure out what we're talking about. We look like a pack of junior high girls afraid to approach a crush.

Yes. Be cool. I close my eyes and shake my head.

"Yeah, Anita," Gabrielle whisper-shouts. "We wouldn't want him finding out she likes him." I open my eyes, giving Gabrielle the death stare. Anita doesn't seem to notice.

"Right. Right. We'll dish later because I'm dying to tell you about this girl I met in the Philippines." Now I'm smiling widely, thinking about comparing notes on our crushes later. Gabrielle and Anita are ... everything I never knew I wanted in friends. They are embarrassing, and supportive, and happy ... My old friends were fun, but we tended to bond through misery. I never realized before how contagiously heavy those bonds were until now.

I introduce Anita to Salvador, and she gives me a thumbs up from behind his back.

"Malaya messaged me about the plan to catch the *Tikbalang* but didn't go into details. I forgot you were in school."

For the briefest moment, I am a child. The one-year age difference seems like nothing one second and then everything when I compare how much freedom he has versus myself. I never worried about that when Ian graduated, but it occurs to me now that it might be because not much changed after he walked that stage. He didn't go off to college. He didn't go into the workforce. He just kept living off his dad and partying with the same old people.

Salvador does one of those playful head nods at me, and that feeling of inadequacy disappears. I drop my gaze sheepishly, then glance around. When I'd first texted him, I worried that asking him to be a part of this plan was too much.

> You don't have to say yes, but I thought you could film the whole thing and maybe use the footage to help you in school or on the internet.

It must have worked because here he is.

Where's your truck? I mouth.

"I ... have not gone to get it yet. I could have had a friend drop me off, but honestly, I was not ready to see the *Tikbalang* again."

Gabrielle cringes. "I don't blame you. But little miss adventure over here is ready for a second date."

"Is she?" Salvador says in a teasing tone.

With the monster, I mouth. *She means with the beast.* It's too many words, but my face blazes, causing all three of them to laugh, and it gets my meaning across.

Gabrielle fills Anita and Salvador in on Tita Blessica's mission to reach the gods being thwarted because she's trapped in her home. Then she moves on to our plan to tame the *Tikbalang,* so we can gain the wish that will get me back to the sea witch to reverse the deal I made.

Salvador claps his hands together. "Sounds good. You guys want to go inside and map this thing out?"

I laugh as memories of Mom's strictness about boys in the house when she is not home parallel play in my mind from both my lives.

No. My hand slices the air with finality.

"Uh yeah," Gabrielle chimes in, "it would be best if we just stayed out here while Mom is at work. If you meet her later, she might invite you in."

Until then, you're a vampire.

"Huh?" His confused eyes turn from me to Gabrielle. "Did she say vampire?"

"Did she? Oh my god, that's perfect!" Anita laughs while opening the garage door. "Because until Tita Floribeth invites you into the house, you can't cross the threshold."

"I see." Salvador shakes his head playfully. "You all have a monster thing going on. I didn't expect that."

Gabrielle, Anita, and I smirk at each other because, according to my memories, while you could say we have a K-drama thing or a karaoke thing, not once would I have ever claimed we have a monster thing.

The garage is not one of those wide-open spaces you see in movies where there's a neatly kept workshop off to the side and plenty of room to park the cars. It's a car virgin. Storage boxes line the walls and invade the spaces where one might park. Piles of random clothes from forgotten laundry marathons are placed atop discarded office paper boxes that Mom is afraid to throw away because, "If someone finds them, they will steal the information, and I will get sued."

I weave my way around lawn equipment like weed eaters and leaf blowers, then hop over an old AC window unit to get to a forgotten desk that leans to the side because Eric climbed on top of it once to hang a poster and the flimsy metal bent under his weight.

While Anita and Gabrielle look for makeshift stools we can sit on, I drop my backpack on the ground and dig around in it. Inside are my plans, including a crudely drawn map of Tita Blessica's neighborhood and possible weapon options I'd sketched out from the internet searches I'd done.

On the hand-drawn map, I'd written:

Stingray tails are good for fighting off Aswangs, but they won't work on the Tikbalang.

"I like your handwriting," Salvador says in a low voice as if it's a secret. I cock my head in disbelief, and he smiles.

Rifling through my sketchbook, I flip to a page on which I'd drawn several cords and ropes with various knots I wouldn't even know how to make. I diagramed different types of rope materials in each picture and circled the one to the far left that seemed to match what I need most.

Weapons, I mouth, pointing to the sheet.

"A syngrass rope?" Salvador reads while Gabrielle and Anita return with two buckets, a laundry basket, and a questionable beanbag to sit on.

I pull up a pre-written note in my phone:

It's treated with a unique blend of oils. Because of that, it will be more pliable to other infusions. I can infuse it with herbs that ward off evil to strengthen the rope.

"Like what?" Gabrielle asks.

I circle a list of plants I'd written down to ward off evil, such as dill, oregano, and parsley.

"This looks like a recipe for spaghetti." Anita smirks.

"All we need are the hotdogs," Gabrielle says, and we high-five.

"You ... you put hotdogs in your spaghetti?" Salvador's lips press together.

"What good Filipino doesn't?" Anita says jokingly like it's common knowledge.

"I'm confused. How can we use this as a weapon?" Gabrielle turns the paper with a flick of her wrist, so it's facing her.

I mime roping the beast and pulling the rope tight.

"But won't that just capture the werehorse?" Anita asks. "What then?"

I suppress silent laughter as I flip to another page in the sketchbook. Despite my drawing abilities, I'd sketched an elaborate plan that included me as a stick figure.

1. I wait in a nearby tree.
2. I rope the Tikbalang.
3. I ride the beast until it gives up from exhaustion.

"Is that ... Are you wearing cowboy boots in this picture?" Gabrielle's voice is thick with amusement. My brows wiggle as I nod enthusiastically.

The gesture sends Gabrielle and Anita into a fit of giggles as Anita points out the wildly exaggerated expressions of sneakiness, panic, and triumph drawn on my figure's face. I fall into soundless, breathless laughter when Gabrielle falls back into a pile of boxes and laundry behind her. Even Salvador's eyes are wet from laughter, though I suspect it's more from our reactions to my drawings than the hilarity of me in cowboy boots.

Finally, I suck in a deep breath, grip Gabrielle's forearms, and pull her up.

She says, "Okay, let's say you're riding this thing until it's exhausted. Then what?"

I pull out my phone and open my internet browser to the page that explains how after the beast is exhausted, you can rip out one of the three most prominent spines on its back and use it as a talisman to control the werehorse.

While they read, I write:

Once I have the spine, I'll wish to see the sea witch.

Gabrielle exhales.

What? I rub my arm.

She shakes her head. "I know you're doing this to get Mal back, but I want you to be safe. You can't jump on some monster's back like a cowboy riding a bucking bull. You could get thrown."

"I could do it." Salvador volunteers.

No. I slash my hands through the air like an X.

"Why not?" Anita asks.

I write:

From what I'd gathered from the lore, it's

the rider who tames the Tikbalang who has the right to pull a spine from the werehorse and receive the wish. If Salvador does it, I won't be able to make the wish.

Gabrielle says, "I'm sure he would make the wish for you."

"Of course, I would." His gaze makes my ears burn.

I shift from the guilt gnawing at me for letting him do this, but I can't deny the weight lifted off me.

Salvador pulls out his phone. "According to this website, the *Tikbalang* is great at misdirection but just as easily confused when it's done to him. So instead of just luring it straight to my hiding spot in the tree, what if we each hide throughout the neighborhood and lure him to several places with animal calls? If we confused him enough, tire him out ahead of time, it would make the job easier by the time I jump on his back."

Salvador leans over the hand-drawn map of the neighborhood, pointing out spots that might be good places to hide from the *Tikbalang* while we're confusing him. Gabrielle is picking her nail polish off as she eyes the spots.

"Who will take the spot on Tita Blessica's porch?" Anita asks. "I'm sure she's got wards, so while it seems open, it's probably one of the safest spots."

"I'll do it." Gabrielle's hand shakes as she raises it.

I grab her arm. *Don't do this.*

"I have to. For Mal."

I reach for my notes app and type:

She wouldn't want you to put yourself through this.

"What's going on?" Salvador asks.

Anita explains, "This kind of thing scares Gabrielle. It's really out of her comfort zone to do anything risky."

"I'm a big coward." Gabrielle tosses her hands up, frustrated. "I can't even go down the water slide at the base pool. I freeze up when I'm scared. How do you think the *Aswang* got me so easily."

You can't judge yourself for how you acted when facing the *Aswang*. You were alone.

Salvador says, "Any of us could have been captured by that thing. That's why we're stronger together. But I am worried about you putting yourself in a situation that scares you like that. You could get killed if you freeze up in front of the Tikbalang, and we're too far to help."

"I'm just going to be useless?" Gabrielle's voice is small.

"No, not useless." Anita jumps in while I shake my head. "We could still use you as our getaway driver if things go wrong."

I type:

And we still need to get the rope ready. Without it, Salvador can't tame the *Tikbalang*.

"Alright, I guess," Gabrielle says, looking up the syngrass rope on her phone while Anita finishes blocking out the rest of the plan. I pick a date that gives us time to practice, so our actions are second nature. Then Gabrielle says to Salvador, "We'll get the stuff we need and text you when it's ready."

Gabrielle starts redrawing the plan in pearly ink on graphing paper in one of her digital planners while Anita pretends she's busy clearing the garage of our plans so that I can wait with Salvador for his ride to pick him up.

We sit on my lawn, leaning against an Ash tree. I text:

I still haven't found that video of me magically appearing in the ocean anywhere on the internet. What's up with that?

"Yeah, I just haven't gotten around to it."

Now is the time. So many of these monster videos are going viral. That could be you. I thought it was important to create a new identity.

Salvador sighs. "Yeah, it is. But ..."

But ... I mouth, nudging Salvador's shoulder.

He laughs, then says, "When I was little, I told my mom I wanted to be an astronaut. And she said, well if you want to be an astronaut, you have to be good at math. Sometime after that, I said I wanted to be a doctor. And her response was if you want to be a doctor, you have to be good at science. For years, these types of conversations would go on in which I'd reveal a dream, and she would lay out the reality." He sighs, and his voice shakes a little. "I started to question myself. Am I not good at these things? Should I choose something else? What will make her say, I bet you'd make a great ... fill in the blank ..."

I wrap my arm around his and squeeze it. His cheeks lift, but it's not a smile.

"So, I ask myself, if I want to be a film major, what do I have to be good at for her to accept it? If I post viral videos, gain a lot of followers, make money as a content creator ... if I can pay for my classes with clout, will that be enough for her to believe in me?" His eyes drop to his hands.

That's why you haven't posted ... Because you're second-guessing yourself?

"I can't tell if it's good enough. If any of the videos I've done since coming to school here are enough." He lacks confidence in himself, in his abilities, in a way that crushingly resonates with me because it was caused by someone he trusted.

> You'll never know if you don't put yourself out there. You have to try or risk being something reliable like an accountant forever.

"Yeah, I guess you're right. Besides, with all the monsters running around, there's a high chance that no one thinks much of the video."

> Exactly. This is a good way to test the waters. It's not high risk, but it could reap a lot of rewards.

"Well, in that case ..."

I make him pull up the video of me he'd been keeping on draft, and together, we hit post.

He lets out an exaggerated sigh of relief, but there is a lightness to his shoulders as he drops his head back to look at the sky.

"I did have a favor to ask when I texted you if you were busy earlier."

Oh crap. I totally took over that conversation.

"Mi-Sun loved those test shots we blocked, and she wanted to know if you could shoot a few scenes as the girlfriend who comes back."

Ha! I fake laugh until I notice the serious set of his eyes. *No, I can't.*

"Don't you think you owe me after the week you put me through? I saved you from drowning and got injured fighting an *Aswang* with you." He gestures to his injured bicep wrapped in gauze. "I'm joking, of course, but she really would love to have you."

I can't speak.

"I told her that," he holds his hands up in a don't-shoot-the-messenger way, "but she actually loved that angle even more. I mean, my girl is changing the whole movie for you."

At "my girl," my heart sinks. But I remind myself that I might not be here for much longer, so I should enjoy this apparently platonic male friendship for what it is—something fun and free. And I might as well take all the advantages of being Mal while I can.

Okay. I'll do it.

"That's what I want to hear," Salvador says, holding up his hand for a high five.

A white Mazda pulls up then, and I'm relieved to see that Salvador's ride is a guy.

Salvador nudges me with his elbow. I meet his gaze, which he uses to point down at his palm. In his hand is the first note I'd written him after he'd picked me up out of the ocean. My lips part in shock that he still has it, let alone is carrying it around with him.

As he slips it into his pocket, he says, "Told you I like your handwriting." The low hum of his voice is like leaves rustling on a cool autumn day—not at all platonic.

For the next few days, whenever I'm not in school, I'm on a set filled with people discussing scenes, holding up boom mics, and white balancing cameras—all things I learn about from Salvador as he talks passionately about each aspect. His eyes are bright even when he's doing things that seem insignificant, like adjusting how someone is holding a reflector so that the shadows under our chins are less harsh. I never realized how many little things had to be just right to take something from amateur quality to professional. He's in his element and watching him like this is ... hot.

Ian never had ambition, and I never realized how much that matters.

This job couldn't have come at a better time. I don't have many scenes, so I have the perfect excuse to sneak off to get things for our *Tikbalang* plan, like flashlights and a backpack. Some of the time, I'm just browsing hunting equipment because I'm not sure what we might actually need, but most of the time, I go over the plan alone because I'm desperate not to mess this up.

I don't think Salvador even notices I'm missing, especially when he's working so closely with Mi-Sun and her perfect glass-like skin, but as I walk up on the last evening of my character's scenes, he says, "Where do you keep disappearing to? You got a secret boyfriend?"

Ha!

"Why is that so funny? You could have one." He peers around like he's looking for someone, and I follow his gaze to Mi-Sun ... his girl.

Pressing my lips together, I pull out my phone.

> After what I've been through, I'm a little done with boyfriends for now.

"Oh," his voice sounds ... funny. "That makes sense, buddy."

My forehead knits because I cannot read this guy or navigate this situation. Is he disappointed? I thought college students didn't like labels. I thought they wanted to date but keep things casual. I thought he had Mi-Sun and maybe even Olivia too. My stomach hardens.

Salvador pulls out his script, flipping through it though he doesn't quite seem to be looking at it. I try to think of something to say. Anything that will rewind or erase the awkwardness between us so we can go back to how things have been the last few days.

Thankfully, Mi-Sun pulls me away for another scene, and I let myself be distracted by the sheer number of people it takes to shoot a measly scene of me emerging from the water. It's the golden hour, so the sun over the ocean waves makes the sea glitter. The water is still too cold, but I suck it up as I get in deep enough to submerge myself.

I'm not sure how waterproof this makeup is, so I aim to get this right in one shot. But as I close my eyes and go under, Tita Blessica's voice reverberates around me.

"*Ang* true love *mo* is coming ..."

My eyes shoot open, burning the instant they come in

contact with the salt water. But it's all murky darkness. I kick off the floor, but the water's surface is like impenetrable rubber.

Tita's hushed voice continues, "He won't see you coming."

Tita? Soundless bubbles escape my lips.

"He will make you believe in magic because you will create magic together."

That's when I realize it's not Tita Blessica talking to me now but the memory of her from over a year ago—predicting my true love.

"He sounds dreamy," Auntie Maggie whispers into my ear, but when I jerk back, there's no one here. "He looks dreamy too. Shirtless the first time you met, and he didn't see you coming when you just appeared in those waves. I wonder what magic you two could create together."

Auntie Maggie, I have to talk to you. Soundless, useless bubbles. *Auntie Maggie?*

Darkness that had been present since the moment I entered the water dissipates—allowing the sun to penetrate the ocean's surface. Her voice is gone, and so is the barrier. I burst through the water, inhaling like it's the first time I've ever breathed, and search the shoreline.

The dying light of the sun illuminates Salvador, and I'm magnetized to him.

When I reach the shoreline, whatever spell he's cast on me grows stronger. His stare is hypnotic and only broken by the leading man, Aaron, entering my eye line. I look up at him, confused, and the director yells, "Cut."

I'm a horrible actress, but Mi-Sun praises my improvising. I'd completely forgotten I was doing a scene. Thankfully, I don't have to explain that. She doesn't wait for a response as she turns to the crew to shout, "Time to get a shot of Malaya kissing Aaron, and then that's a wrap for our little mermaid here."

My eyes bulge, searching for Salvador's immediately.

"Are you okay? You were under for so long. I almost ran in there."

I want to tell him ... not everything but at least the part about hearing Auntie Maggie, but I'm stuck on the last thing Mi-Sun said. I point at the director. *She wants me to do what?*

Somehow, he gets all that because he says, "She wants you to kiss him."

A huff of air escapes my nostrils. I haven't kissed anyone since I started dating Ian, and now I have to do it in front of all these people. This is much more than just walking around or gazing longingly. Salvador touches my forearm, stopping me from the pacing I didn't even realize I was doing.

"Hey, if you don't want to do this, you don't have to. I could drive you home right now."

I look around at all the people I'd witnessed working their butts off for days. I knew how much work they'd put into this. If I backed out now, even if I wasn't in that many scenes, they would still have to reshoot everything we'd already finished together. I couldn't do that to them.

No, I'm okay.

Salvador drops his face to my level. "Are you sure?"

Yeah.

I'm in a daze the entire walk over to Aaron, twisting my drenched dress until someone from costumes steps in to stop me. I smile, but it falters.

Salvador stands near the director, biting his lip. But I nod to let him know I'm okay.

When Mi-Sun yells action, I slam my eyes shut and purse my lips, hoping this ends quickly. She immediately calls cut.

"Okay ... Okay. Malaya, let's try again. But this time, try to relax. Remember, you're in love with him."

I nod, exhaling slowly. But when I look at Aaron, I am so far from relaxed. I'm cold from the water and the constant wind, and honestly, he's a little bit douchey. This kiss should mean nothing because it's not like I have feelings for him. But Mi-Sun has to call cut two more times.

"This isn't working," Mi-Sun says in a low voice to Salvador. "She was so good when she came out of the water. This is not that."

"Let me talk to her," he whispers.

Before he can say anything, I'm already running my hands through my wet hair.

"You're uncomfortable. You want to tell me what's going on?"

I haven't kissed anyone besides my ex in so long.

"Oh. I am so dumb. Of course, you haven't. Look, I'm sorry." He presses his lips together, then leaves to talk to Mi-Sun again. I'm not sure what he says, but whatever it is, she nods begrudgingly.

I bite the inside of my cheek as he approaches.

"Okay, since this is supposed to be K-drama style, Mi-Sun has agreed to do a freeze-frame kiss. So instead of actually kissing, you'll just hover near his lips, and Mi-Sun will shout cut. She's letting Aaron know right now."

I inhale through my nose, nodding. *Thank you.*

"But she does want me to coach you a bit."

Coach me? On kissing? My face flushes.

"Don't get me wrong. I'm sure you're great at kissing, but... Okay, when was the last time you watched a K-drama?"

I shrug. *Last night.*

"Good. Imagine the last kissing scene you saw."

My eyes get far as I picture the two young actors leaning

into each other with the music rising and the slow-motion effect. The K-dramas I watch usually have such clean, sweet romances—which is one of the reasons I love them. Salvador reaches for my face, and I pull back.

"May I?" His hand hovers inches from my skin. I nod. "Kissing in pictures or film is not the same as a kiss you might give in real life." He squeezes my lips between his fingers, so they pucker, then mirrors it with his own lips. I laugh, and his eyes brighten. "We don't pucker our lips like this in pictures," he demonstrates, kissing the air in front of me, "because puckered lips don't translate to that intensely intimate kiss on film or even in couples' photos."

I glance away, this moment probably feeling more intimate to me than it does to him.

"Look at me, sweetheart," he says, and I peer up at him through my lashes. He's close, slipping his hand around my waist when I start to back away. "Instead of puckering, you'll just part your lips and lean in." He leans, looking from my lips to my eyes. "Hold my gaze, and don't close your eyes until my nose brushes yours." His nose brushes mine, and I inhale shakily as my lids close involuntarily. For an immeasurable amount of time, I wait for him, feeling the heat of his breath against my lips.

Then the air becomes chilly as he pulls away.

"You got it?"

I nod, though I can't meet his eyes. I'm afraid of what my eyes will betray—like how I thought he was going to kiss me.

"That was perfect, Malaya." Mi-Sun pats me on the back, and my face reddens as I remember we're on a set, surrounded by people watching, and all of this is fake.

I don't know if I'm angry at myself for letting my guard down or at Salvador for being so good at lowering my defenses, but it's the kick I need to suck it up and get this over with. After all, it wouldn't be a real kiss.

Aaron is already on his mark when I arrive, his expression pinched. I ignore it because, after this scene, I'm done.

When Mi-Sun calls action, nothing is as slow as when Salvador directed me. But I remember his instructions, letting my eyes close only when Aaron's nose brushes mine. I wait for Mi-Sun to yell cut, but it is taking forever. Then, just as I am about to open my eyes, Aaron's lips come crashing down onto mine.

I'm so stunned, I can't even think to move or push him off. I just keep waiting for the cut. Instead, my eyes open just as Salvador grabs Aaron's shoulder, jerks him backward, and punches him in the face.

"What the hell are you doing?" he shouts as Aaron backs away, gripping his nose. "You were supposed to freeze-frame the kiss."

"What are you talking about? No one told me to freeze anything."

Salvador turns on Mi-Sun. "You were supposed to take care of this?"

"What is the big deal?" Mi-Sun asks.

"I told you she wasn't ready," Salvador says, pulling Mi-Sun to the side. She starts shouting about the days of waiting they would have to do now that her lead actor has a black eye.

I don't want to hear the rest of what is said. I feel like I'm constantly stuck in this in-between space—in-between Salvador and Mi-Sun, in-between cultures, in-between Mom and Ian, in-between Gabrielle and Mal, in-between my attraction for Salvador and the idea that I don't belong here, so how could it ever amount to anything? And here I am in-between deciding whether this is no big deal because it was just a kiss or if it's a very big deal because it was a kiss. The anger and confusion are too much. I head for the truck, determined to call Gabrielle to pick me up.

"Malaya," Salvador calls, catching up to me. But I don't stop walking. "Malaya, I'm sorry. Talk to me."

I whirl around on him, and he stops abruptly, his head jerking back.

You knew about that scene. You had to know ahead of time because you have the goddamn script. I yank the script from Salvador's hand and throw it as hard as I can. *How could you not warn me? How could you let that happen?*

He can't possibly understand me, but in this moment, he seems to get every word—magic.

"I know. I didn't think. I forgot you just got out of a relationship—"

I didn't just get out; I escaped it. I escaped. My chest heaves with each word, and he dares to come closer—despite the explosiveness of my anger. *I escaped it. But I still feel like I'm running.* Instead of being angry that I'm mad, he wraps his arms around me, and I sob. *I feel like I'm still running.*

Though the hug is nice, it can't be this easy for him because I'm still angry. I push him away.

Why? Why did you do that?

"I don't know. I was dumb. You kept sneaking off set, so I thought you must be meeting someone. Maybe even someone you met on the cast. You were so secretive, and I thought I didn't care, but it backfired on me."

What backfired on him? His face is crimson, but before I can ask, he says, "I'm sorry."

Tears keep sliding down my face, despite how often I swipe them away. Then his hand runs from my cheek to my neck as he pulls me to him. "I am so sorry." But I'm not crying because I need to hear him say sorry. I'm crying because it's such a relief that I could get so mad at him, and he'd still hold me like this. And isn't that just so fucked up?

chapter nineteen

It's Saturday, and Mom, Gabrielle, and I are doubled over in laughter, tears swimming in our eyes because we were in Target for a full ten minutes before we realized we'd forgotten Eric in the back of the car. Mom never took the child locks off the backseats, and Eric was too dense to break out from the front seat after we'd walked off. Also, possibly, he wanted to nail this joke, and he did. Instead of coming after us, we found him, nose kissed against the glass, staring at us with overly dramatic, sad eyes.

A bittersweet sadness strikes me like the last sunset of summer.

When Gabrielle first said I should get Mom to take us shopping because we have to get the rope anyway, I questioned her sanity. I used to hate these shopping trips back in my old life. Mom would say she needed to get rice from the Asian Market or buy new shoes at the mall. Whatever the reason, that one store would turn into another store and another until I'd spent all Saturday out with her. I couldn't do anything else with anyone else because she'd taken up all my time on purpose, and it was exhausting. By the end of the day, I was so grumpy that we'd fight. And this is the part I always felt bad about: Mom would inevitably feel unappreciated because she always bought us something while we were out. Her love language is gifting.

When flashes of these days in this life present themselves without the same exhausted, tense coloring, it reveals two things: one, that Gabrielle and I both love these days, and not just because Mom buys us things, and two, that I'm an asshole because I was the one who was making shopping days so miserable in my other life.

Experiencing it now for myself, I love this. I love how we are at this moment, and it makes me sad to think this may be the last time I feel this way. Tonight, Gabrielle and I will prepare the cords Salvador needs to tame the *Tikbalang*, and then we're off to face the werehorse. I read they like to eat humans that try to conquer them. Any one of us could die. But even if I survive, I'll be making a wish to see the sea witch.

If everything goes right, this will be the last time I hang out with this version of Mom that I didn't ruin for a boy. That also means this is the last time I get to hang out with this version of Gabrielle and Eric.

I wish I could stay.

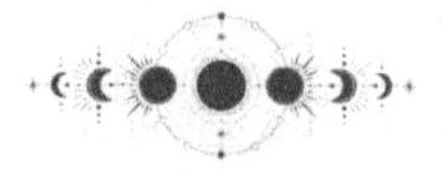

I pull into Tita Blessica's neighborhood on a different side from how we escaped the last time we were here. A demonic neighing reverberates off the suburban houses as I remind everyone to turn their shirts inside out. Anita researched that it was the best countermeasure for the mind tricks that *Tikbalangs* like to play on travelers so that they get lost.

The night air seems stiller as we head for the corner of Tita Blessica's street. It's like walking in the woods and realizing sound is absent. You know there's something big out there, but you don't know exactly where it is.

A clanking noise emanates from behind us, and I jump-spin around.

"What was that?" Gabrielle holds up her fists like an old-timey fighter.

I grab Salvador's arms so tight my fingers dig into his skin. All of us are statue-still as I strain to see if the *Tikbalang* has found us before I can sneak up on him. But the street seems to become still.

After several long beats, my posture relaxes, though my chest continues to rise and fall.

"Something probably just fell over in your trunk." Salvador touches my hand.

"That thing is full of crap," Anita says. My jaw drops in feigned insult.

I let go of Salvador's arm, but he catches my hand, giving it one tight squeeze. I don't want to think about how I'll miss my heart skipping around him.

I tug his arm so he faces me, his expression alert. Then I type:

> Your camera. You were going to film this, remember?

It was the only incentive I had to entice him with when I'd asked him to join us besides the promise of helping him get his truck back.

"Do you really think that's the only reason I'm here?" His expression is hurt, and when I reach for his arm to apologize, it's too easy for him to pretend he doesn't see and keep walking.

Every shift in the night, every creaking door, every vehicle driving in the distance, and every rustle of leaves is amplified. I hadn't realized how scared I was until I'd thought the *Tikbalang* was behind me. How am I going to execute this plan once it's time?

The beast is nowhere in sight, but there's an awful tearing sound bouncing off the hollow spaces of Tita Blessica's street. I sneak forward, yard by yard until the *Tikbalang* silhouette comes into view. It's bigger than I remember—bigger than the werehorse in my nightmares. Unzipping my backpack one tooth at a time, I pass flashlights to everyone—meant to distract the *Tikbalang* visually in addition to the animal noises we're making.

I hand Salvador the rope I made him. As a precaution, Gabrielle made a backup cord that will stay with me. It's not as long or strong because we started running out of supplies, but it's unlikely that Salvador's will break. I keep that one in my backpack because I need my hands free to climb the tree I'll be hiding in. I have no clue how Gabrielle turned this boring cord into something Wonder Woman would envy, but it glistens iridescently. I clutch the black backpack, worried now that I'm sizing up the horse-beast, that even Salvador's rope is too short.

With two fingers, Salvador signals for us to move into position. He darts for the carport farthest from everyone, exposing himself to the most danger as the *Tikbalang* could see him before he ever reaches its cover. Anita hides in Tita Blessica's front yard, which Auntie assured us has additional wards in place. And Gabrielle, who'd walked us to the corner, is already sneaking back to the car to reposition it closer to the exit when she notices that my hiding spot in the tree is already occupied by the *Tikbalang* as he lounges against the mesquite's low curled trunk. We are a conversation built of shaking heads, pressed lips, and widened eyes as I try to figure out what to do. I need a new spot—something high up.

There's a ridiculously tall, white truck ahead of me; it's the kind used for mudding—the tires caked with crusty, brown splashes. I grip the top of the tailgate and pull myself up as quietly as I can, but it creaks. I freeze.

Without moving any other muscles, I glance at the *Tikbalang*.

He, too, is frozen. Only his ears flicker as he listens for the source of the sound. Then his head snaps in my direction as he takes in my entire, exposed presence.

Too late to hide, I launch myself into the truck bed. I shake my shoulders violently as I try to get the backpack off my back. Panic seems to speed up time while simultaneously slowing down all my actions. When the bag hits the ground, I turn on my knee and rip the zipper open. The *Tikbalang* gallops toward me, his hindlegs *clop clopping* against the asphalt while his two gnarled human hands pad the ground.

I reach for the rope and yank to get it out of the small bag opening, but it catches once before I get it free. The monster is so close that its long shadow nearly touches me, so I don't have time to unravel this rope to get it around the *Tikbalang's* neck.

As the werehorse runs full force into the truck, I clumsily grab the edge of the bed and hold on tight with all my might. Sweaty palms and a hand full of rope causes my right hand to slip. My chest slams against the metal bed, sending a shooting pain throughout my torso. Luckily, the *Tikbalang* backs up, dropping the truck to the ground.

I jump to my feet and launch myself at his neck as his arms swipe the air to grab me. His horsey frontal vision must not be great because he misses. I hit his side with all my body weight, causing him to grunt. One foot digs into his mid-back, and I clench my muscles as I try to mount him. The *Tikbalang* swings around, banging me into the side of the truck.

Pain bursts through my leg and up my back, but it's not as bad as it could have been if he could see me properly. I loop the rope around the *Tikbalang's* neck and yank myself into a seated position on his back just in time to see Salvador standing in the street, flashing his light at the *Tikbalang* and howling like a wolf.

Run! I point in the opposite direction.

Salvador shouts, "No!" But the *Tikbalang's* thunderously deep neigh covers most of it. The beast huffs, and his sticky breath whips around toward me as he spins on the spot. Then he starts bucking.

Somewhere in the distance, Anita is screaming, but I can't make out a word.

We're spinning and bucking in circles so fast that the night, the street, the trees are a swirling palette of receding colors. Then the *Tikbalang* runs. He races up and down the road, trying to scrape me off on tree trunks and mailboxes. I shift my body weight, lifting my legs to avoid the objects when I can, but hot blood pours from my arms and legs as my skin is ripped open from the shrapnel.

I don't know how much longer I can last, but I grip the monster with my knees as tight as I can and remind myself that there won't be a do-over if I die. The muscles in my hands cramp from gripping the rope so tightly. Suddenly, the werehorse throws its head back and rears up on its hind legs. I lose my balance, and the world slows as the rope slips from my grasp.

I clutch the *Tikbalang's* spiny mane, and there's white-hot pain as he comes back down on all fours. Blood pours out of my left hand as I'm impaled through the palm. I cry out, but not even the strength of this pain is heard from my silenced throat.

Gabrielle shrieks from the yard nearest me, "Malaya, car," and points behind me. An engine roars, and I lift my legs in time to see the Mustang fly by, narrowly missing the *Tikbalang*—who slides sideways onto the asphalt to avoid being hit—trapping my leg under his giant body. The crushing weight sends a stabbing sensation through me.

Salvador and Anita are flanking the beast, trying to distract it so I can get away, while Gabrielle is darting behind bushes, flashing her light at us, so who the hell is driving the car?

"Get out of there," Gabrielle shouts. "We'll try something else." Her fearful eyes connect with mine, and I point with my lips at my impaled palm—afraid to let go of the beast's mane with my other hand. Gabrielle races toward me and then runs back into the yard. I shake my head furiously so she stays away, but the *Tikbalang* starts to rise.

Gabrielle races full speed toward us.

Lifting one of its long humanoid arms, the *Tikbalang* swipes at Salvador, who knocks the werehorse's muscular arm out of the way like he's swatting at a fly. Salvador's face is triumphant for a split second before the *Tikbalang's* other arm swings at him, knocking him to the ground. His head hits the pavement, and he goes still.

No! With my free hand, I grip the spine trapping me to the werehorse and rip it out in one swift movement. Though the *Tikbalang* neighs demonically, it's not enough to distract him from Gabrielle's running war cry.

As she comes into the werehorse's reach, he swipes at her, nicking her face. She ducks to avoid his long, jabbing arm sliding against the gravel with only her jeans to protect her and grabs the rope. Gravity doesn't exist the way she swings onto the beast's back just as he stands. Anita crosses the *Tikbalang* path, pulling his attention away from us as he chases her back into the street.

The Mustang slams into reverse, groaning as it heads for us again. The *Tikbalang* paws the ground, dipping his head like a bull as he runs for the vehicle.

"We need to jump," Gabrielle yells, and maybe we should.

How much more of this can I take? The lights become blindingly bright, and then my name is whispered, not into the world but within my mind.

"Malaya... I yield."

How does the *Tikbalang* know my name? I lean into the beast's neck as it retracts its spines. My face grazes his soft, brown coat.

Take me to the sea witch. I accentuate every word on my silent lips, projecting my intention with my thoughts, and hope that something translates into a wish.

A flare of luminescent light, different from the red of the brake lights, flashes as a portal opens before us. We pass through it, seawater pelting my skin, and then the street is gone.

The portal is a vortex of light and space that passes through the underwater forest. Swirling ocean water forms the walls, so the smell of fish is potent, and the roar of rushing water is deafening. As the water wall of Auntie Maggie's cave is fast approaching, the *Tikbalang* seems to speed up rather than slow down.

It's just ahead. I warn the beast, projecting my thoughts.

Lifting off the muddy seafloor in a giant leap, the *Tikbalang* bursts through the water wall into the cave, skidding to a miraculously messy halt.

Somehow, he finds purchase against the wet rock and stands upright.

"Malaya!" Auntie Maggie opens her arms like she's waiting for a warm embrace, but her face shifts just as quickly as a snake striking. "Why are you here, child? Barging into my home on this beast without invitation. Go outside, Felipe." She commands the *Tikbalang* with disdain. Felipe eyes me but doesn't budge.

Auntie Maggie's nostrils flare. Perhaps she can't control him since I tamed him ... The way her hunched back tenses, I expect her to throw something or rage at me. But Auntie Maggie turns back toward us, her face composed.

"Come, come, Malaya and ...." She looks at Gabrielle as if

she expects her to introduce herself, but the girl is all stiff muscles and flustered noises. "You must be the sister." Auntie Maggie's lip curls, unimpressed. She gestures to two rocks as seats though they're backless and uncomfortably roundish. Gabrielle inches closer to me, and I pull out my phone to type, but it's dead. I could have sworn it had a full charge.

"It won't work down here, child." Auntie Maggie waves her hand dismissively.

Great. I conquered a *Tikbalang* like a freakin' badass for nothing. There's no paper down here that I can see, Gabrielle is practically comatose, and my phone is zapped of power. Is there enough mud on the ground to trace out words?

"Well? What do you want now?"

I point to my silent mouth and shrug.

"Oh, fine." Her hand shoots out like she's commanding me to stop and sparks fizzle from her palm.

Shielding myself with my arms, I shout, "What the hell?"

Gabrielle and I both jump because the words "what the hell" come out of me, though not from my vocal cords. It's a warbling, reverberating sound that emanates from my body as if seeping out of my pores. Though it is not quite how my voice sounds, the words are mine. It's how I always imagined mermaids would sound underwater.

"Better?" Her stiff jaw clenches like an Auntie providing an inconvenient favor. You had better say yes.

"Yes, thank you po." The way my bodyless voice bounces around the cavernous space makes me shiver. Thank goodness only the words I would want to say aloud are produced because my thoughts about being back in this stink hole aren't polite.

"No, they're not," Auntie Maggie's voice is low, growling. I'd forgotten she can read my thoughts. This voice trick must be for Gabrielle's sake.

Auntie Maggie hunches over wet fish bones, sorting

through them with some system I can't fathom. "I suppose you're not here to talk about how perfect your life is. How perfect your true love is?" she says pointedly. Gabrielle glances at my profile because I can't meet her eyes.

"Did I take another Malaya's place in this life?" Though I'm reasonably sure, I want confirmation.

"Of course not." Auntie Maggie picks at the dirt under her blackened nails with a skinny fishbone.

"That can't be right." Gabrielle seems to find her voice. "This is not my sister. No offense," she turns to me, "but I know my sister. My Mal is my best friend, and she's someone who can read my thoughts. This isn't her."

I've never known Gabrielle to talk to an adult like that. Despite her bravery, her fingers are trembling.

"Okay, fine." Auntie Maggie exposes her blackened gums as she grins, closing the space between her and Gabrielle. "Maybe I dropped this Malaya into an alternate timeline. Your timeline."

My breath catches in my throat, eyes unblinking. "But—that's not what you said you were doing. I would never have agreed to put someone else in my own hell."

"Well, I lied." Auntie Maggie is dry, unapologetic.

"But why? If you couldn't undo my mistake, why promise it? And how could you think I wouldn't notice?" I rip the disgusting bone out of her hand and toss it across the room. Its size doesn't create a giant impact, but I have the sea witch's full attention.

Auntie Maggie presses a reeking finger against my nose. "One, I didn't say I couldn't do what you asked. I just *didn't* do what you asked. And two," her dirt-crusted nail pokes both my cheeks, "I simply didn't care if you noticed."

Gabrielle turns Auntie Maggie with a jerk of her arm and slaps her so hard that the sound echoes throughout the cave. Auntie Maggie's head turns deathly slow toward Gabrielle, and in a flash, she grabs her by the arm and holds Gabrielle over the cavernous watering hole. "Do that again, and I will damn you to the blackest pit of eternity."

I race toward them, yanking Gabrielle out of the sea witch's grasp.

"Don't touch her again." My ethereal voice commands, bouncing off the water at a higher volume.

"If we're done here, you can show yourselves out." Auntie Maggie gestures behind her to the water wall.

"We're not done here," Gabrielle says, following the sea witch. Auntie Maggie's skirt of serpents snaps at Gabrielle's ankles, causing her to gasp. Though my blood is rushing with adrenaline at the thought of returning to my old life, I need to do this to bring Mal back to Gabrielle, to this amazing life she created.

"You have to switch us back." I limp after Auntie Maggie, my leg stiffening with time.

Auntie Maggie's eel-like limbs swish as she turns to face me. "I have to do no such thing."

"But you broke our contract." A huff of air escapes my nostrils.

"No, I didn't. You gave me your voice in exchange for a life in which you never dated that boy. I gave you that life." My ears ring as the witch projects my own contractual words aloud for us to hear. I shake my head, searching for the words that would right this.

"But I had no clue there were alternate universes for you to switch me to."

"That hardly matters." Auntie Maggie waves a fish around. "I did my part."

"Can't you just undo it?" Gabrielle asks pleadingly. "Give Malaya her voice back and make the exchange?"

"This is not the return center at Walmart. Even if I wanted to, which I don't, there are more things at work here."

The *Tikbalang's* clopping hooves remind me of the monsters. "All of the creatures ... You released them into the world? And ... you used my voice to do it?" I ask.

Auntie Maggie sits on a makeshift rock throne. "Not just your voice, dear. I used your willing exchange as a sacrifice to open the portal and your voice to command the monster's release into the worlds."

"They're in both worlds?" Gabrielle paces back and forth. Auntie Maggie nods.

"But why me? And why the monsters?"

"Look around at my kingdom, dear," Auntie Maggie's voice rises to a thunderous volume. "A goddess in an underwater kingdom of one. My magic is nothing down here. My voice speaks spells that fall flat like spilled coconut milk rather than mixing with the recipes of life. I create sparks in this prison—parlor tricks when I want explosions. And then someone came along with a wish."

I hang my head, staring at my injured palm. "Me."

"No, dear. Not you."

"Who—" Gabrielle asks, confused. "Because Tita Blessica already said she didn't do it."

"Maybe your Tita Blessica wouldn't," Auntie Maggie says pointedly. "But hers ..." She points at me with her lips.

"But if she wanted a change, why didn't you use her sacrifice and voice? Why get me involved?"

"Because she couldn't give me what I needed. You see, she wasn't asking for monsters. She wasn't even sure what she wanted. She just wanted a change. I knew if I used her to open the portals, she would return to me and want the spells to reverse. I've come to learn that humans so often regret their mistakes. No, I needed someone who couldn't reverse the spell. I asked her to find me someone desperate for a change—someone whose life was so bad, they would take this deal and never look back."

"Well, she failed because I'm here, telling you to reverse it." I hold my chin up, hoping it will inspire the confidence I'm lacking.

Auntie Maggie pinches her lips together in a suppressed smile, looking at me like a precious toddler. "Yes, you are. And I'll tell you how to break the spell, but you'll never be able to do it. That's why I chose you."

"How?" I try to sound daring, despite the sinking feeling in my stomach.

Auntie Maggie picks at her rock throne, flicking a pebble at my wet feet. "To switch places with Mal, all you have to do is truly want that old life back."

"That's it?" Gabrielle asks, eyeing the witch suspiciously.

The sea witch laughs, and it echoes back at me until a symphony of maniacal laughter surrounds me. "You truly don't know what Malaya has been through. You haven't grasped the depth of her pain as I did when I saw the wreck she was."

I wince under her words, becoming small.

"You see, while she remembers the pain, she doesn't feel it like she did before this spell. The second she's back in her universe, all those excruciating emotions will return in full force, and as easy as it feels right now not to want that boy, it will not be as easy once she's back. She will return the weak little human under his control. It might even kill her." Auntie Maggie claps like she's watching the riveting climax of a play.

"Don't listen to her, Malaya." But Gabrielle avoids my gaze.

"Don't worry about me. I'll be okay." *Will I?*

Gabrielle wipes her face with her forearm. I've never seen her look so guilty in her life when I'm the one who put her in this no-win situation.

I close my eyes, wishing with all my heart to undo this deal. Telling myself that I want to go back. Telling myself that

I'll be stronger this time. But when I open my eyes to see if it worked, Auntie Maggie breaks out in convulsive belly laughs.

"You see! I knew you were the one. The moment I saw your sunken eyes, I knew that in your heart of hearts, you would never want to return to that old life. Blessica knew too. That's why she chose you. You can't want it back partway. You have to want that life back all the way, huh? And a part of you never wants to go back."

Gabrielle breaks out in sobs, and I dig my nails into my palms as a sharp pain sears the back of my throat. *Don't cry. It's not over yet.*

"You and Blessica got what you asked for. And soon, I'll get what I want too."

"And what's that?" My gaze trails Gabrielle, who makes her way back to Felipe.

"Freedom, my child. The freedom to leave this cave. The freedom to exact my revenge on the gods who put me here."

I try to think of some way to fix this, but I need more information.

"Why *my* voice after you've been imprisoned all this time? Why couldn't you get your freedom earlier? There had to have been other miserable people in the world."

"Your mind is quick." Auntie Maggie wags a finger at me like I'm a clever, naughty child. "Yes, I have been trapped here for a long time because I couldn't use any voice. I was searching for the right voice. I needed the voice of an *Albularyo*, a healer."

"But I am not a healer. Otherwise, I wouldn't be limping around your cave, covered in cuts and bruises from Felipe."

Auntie Maggie grabs my injured hand, pressing my other hand over it. The tendons pull together, the skin stretching until it is moderately, though not entirely better. I suspect she imbues her magic with whatever is in me to do it.

"Your magic is there but dormant." Her lips purse.

"Practicing *Albularyos* are few and far between. Luckily, your lineage contains many *Albularyos*, or I would not have been able to break the barrier keeping the monsters within the underwater realm."

"But how could you tell I had *Albularyo* lineage? My mom didn't even know—Tita Blessica only claimed Mom was because she's got hot hands."

"The mark of an *Albularyo* is in your hands."

I look at my palms. "Here," the witch says, her fishy breath intruding into my personal bubble as she points to a place just under my pinky. "You see these lines that look like a pyre of wood?" I nod. "That is the mark. It's as clear as the water separating the Philippine Islands. You were the one I waited centuries for. The perfect mixture of healer who cannot heal herself, of *Albularyo* and broken."

My stomach rolls. How many others have come through this cave, and what has Auntie Maggie done with the ones she'd had no use for? The black water pit seems as thick as graveyard dirt. I pull my hand away from the sea witch's pinching grasp.

"I'm going to keep wishing. I'll fix this, and then you won't have anything."

"Unless you can change your mind before the next full moon, your wish won't mean a thing." Her onyx eyes sparkle like stars in the night.

"What's happening at the next full moon?"

Auntie Maggie's plump lips purse as her gaze sizes me up. I must not be a threat to her plan because she says, "Every day that I grow stronger, I use your voice to release more monsters into the worlds. As the creatures roam both worlds, I gather the power of those who believe in what had once been considered mythological. Their belief in magic is the gasoline that fuels my magic."

My heart stops. I'd turned Gabrielle from nonbeliever to

believer simply by describing what I saw. It had been that easy —that horribly easy.

"When the next full moon is high enough in the sky, I will use that energy to release the *Bakunawa*. That winged dragon will eat the moon and cast the night into permanent darkness. Only then will I be released from this prison to walk all the universes as the free goddess I am."

"Can't you reverse the spell after you have what you want? And let us be with our families?" Gabrielle chimes in.

The sea witch makes *tsk tsk* sounds with her tongue. "That will not work. As long as I keep this Malaya in this world, her voice cannot be restored. And as long as her voice is not restored, I do not have to worry about her sending my monsters back to the underwater realm. I may have my magic once I return to the drylands, but powerful gods still imprisoned me. The only thing I have on my side is the allegiance of the beasts they'd imprisoned. With them fighting by my side, I stand a chance at not being banished once again."

"Then send me back to the other universe without my voice," I suggest, reaching for any option—anything that will return Mal to Gabrielle and her family.

"I cannot," Auntie Maggie screams, frustration boiling over. "I can't change some aspect of the deal, like picking flowers for a bouquet. Conditions were set once the spell was cast. Once I've released the monsters, I will lock your voice away in the underwater realm so no one, especially not the Gods, can use it to send my precious babies back." She eyes Felipe, a hint of loss in the flicker of her lashes.

Gabrielle's chest caves in.

"If you're going to lock my voice away, then I'll stop the *Bakunawa*."

"How? You can't possibly stop every monster in this world from being seen, and you certainly can't stop any of the monsters in the other world."

"But I bet the other Mal can." My ethereal voice is cutting.

Auntie Maggie's amusement dissipates. I've struck a nerve.

"I'm right, aren't I? Mal is out there in my universe, fighting these beasts too." Felipe grunts. "Sorry, Felipe. Creatures ..."

Gabrielle is alert at the mention of her sister.

"I bet there's a loophole because you took her without *her* willing sacrifice."

"You and Mal are the same person. I never needed her permission if I had yours." Auntie Maggie's voice rises in volume but lacks her usual steely confidence. "It doesn't matter because you still have to want to reverse the deal. And there's no way you'll be able to do that." Auntie Maggie throws a bowl against the rock wall, and it shatters.

"Yeah, we'll see about that."

I mount the *Tikbalang*, ordering him to take us home. Auntie Maggie erupts, destroying the precious items she's collected from the ocean floor. I try to find confidence in her anger, telling myself it's a sign I can fix this. But how can I convince myself to return to a life I hated?

chapter twenty-one

The journey back through the water portal seems faster this time. Every gallop fills me with this warmth and elation that makes me want to punch the air or whoop, even though I can't because the second I leave the cave, my ability to project my thoughts evaporates.

When the portal opens to Tita Blessica's street, I practically jump off Felipe's back and leap into Salvador's arms. He's okay. We're all okay. I conquered the *Tikbalang*. I found a way to break the deal with the witch, and she's threatened. Today, at this moment, I won. I can do anything.

I run my fingers through tufts of Salvador's hair, pulling him against me. An electric current pulses, and my entire body aches as he looks at me like the sun looks on the Earth when the day breaks. I lower my face to press my lips against his but—

"UGH UM," someone clears their throat, breaking my euphoria. Gabrielle's arms are crossed, and Anita's peeking out through her fingers pressed against her face. Salvador's hands slide from my hips to my waist as he sets me down. When we break eye contact, my heart sinks.

"Why are you so happy?" Gabrielle asks, taking the rope off Felipe's neck. He walks away, untethered.

I pull out my phone, which is fully powered again, and the world slows as I return to reality.

> Look at what we just did. Never in my life did I think I could do something like that.

"You know who could have? Who is? My Malaya. Mal is doing all of that. She's fighting these monsters off in your world because of your death wish, and she's in danger because of you. Yet here you are, bouncing around like you fixed things. You didn't fix anything. You failed to reverse the death wish because you don't want to."

My eyes sting because while she's right, and I want to be mad at her for bringing me down, I can't.

> And I'm sorry. I swear, I'm going to fix this. I've just never felt so self-possessed before. I'm not trying to take anything away from you.

"You're not? Because it seems to me like the happier you are in this life," she glances pointedly at Salvador, then back at me, "the less likely you are to want to leave." I step away from Salvador, who must be confused because he has no idea what we've been through.

The street rings with Gabrielle's voice, and as blinds shift down under spying eyes, Salvador says, "We should probably go before the cops get here."

I have no words, and Gabrielle is pretty done as she turns to get in the Mustang. I follow, watching her heels, but she says, "Eric? What are you doing here?"

Eric leans against the back of the Mustang. My jaw drops. I forgot that someone was driving the car during the fight. Then I remember the noise from the trunk when I thought the *Tikbalang* was stalking us. Eric had been in there all that time.

"Why didn't you tell me we were hunting monsters?" Eric asks, his hands up in a shrug. "You had me sneaking into the back of this thing like a stowaway."

"We aren't hunting monsters." Gabrielle's finger circles around the group. "*We* are hunting monsters," Gabrielle emphasizes that the four of us are the monster hunters, and he is not included.

"Like hell," Eric retorts. "I saved your butts. Me and my sweet driving skills."

I point a stabbing finger at him. *Watch your language.*

"Okay, okay," he flinches as if the volume of my voice can be heard through alternate universes.

"Damn," Anita says. "Maybe we should have just sent you two out to scold the *Tikbalang*. Would have been an easier fight." Anita manages to tease me and Gabrielle and welcome Eric into the group all at once.

"By the way," Salvador asks, "what do we do with that thing?" He jabs a thumb over his shoulder at the beast sleeping like an exhausted toddler under the mesquite tree.

"His name is Felipe," Gabrielle says.

I got it. With Felipe's spine as a talisman, I bend down over the sleeping creature and touch its hand. He shifts his head to the side to look at me. *Listen, you can't attack anyone anymore. It might be better to go back to where you came from because I also can't have you seen by anyone. It will give the sea witch too much power.*

A gentle snort emanates from the beast, and he rises.

"You want to ride with me," Salvador asks, pulling out his truck keys. I'd forgotten this was also a retrieval mission for his truck.

"No." Gabrielle takes my arm, dragging me to the car.

As I drive Anita, Gabrielle, and Eric to our home, all is

silent. I'd like to imagine that it's a contemplative silence, but since Eric leans his head against the window, Anita fell asleep, and Gabrielle scrolls through social media, most of it is exhaustion. The rhythmic passing of shadows over the vehicle makes my eyelids heavy. It reminds me of the nights I'd wasted sneaking out to see Ian and all the times I feared the *Aswang* because, deep down, I knew I was doing something wrong.

I could have died so many times under these same shadows that pass over me now as I park outside our house, and all for a boy. I reach for Gabrielle to apologize, but she leaves me in her dust as she sneaks back into the house through my bedroom window and beelines for her room. Eric's mouth stretches in one of those stiff smiles like I effed up, then peaces out. I'm not sure it occurs to him to have questions ...

"I'll talk to her," Anita says, disappearing into the hallway to join Gabrielle.

As I collapse onto my bed, grateful that tomorrow is not a school day, my phone chimes. My spirits lift at Salvador's name in the notification box.

SALVADOR

Hey, so that was intense. You want to talk about it?

I don't even know how to begin.

Start with what happened after you plunged through that magic portal. What was Gabrielle talking about, and what does it have to do with me?

I pause; my insides are a rung-out rag as I try to think of what to say. I've got nothing. I sigh, scared to type.

You still there?

Yeah...Uh...

Tears slide down my cheeks and into my ears.

While visiting the witch, we confirmed another Mal belongs in this world. I have to want to go back to my old life to switch places. But when I tried to undo the wish, it wouldn't work...

Why is Gabrielle acting like that has something to do with me?

Well... because she thinks that if I'm happy in this life, I won't be able to get her sister back.

And I make you happy?

I smile and turn onto my stomach. Then drop my face onto the screen, my feelings warring within me. Salvador makes me feel alive. But I don't know what that happiness means. And I'm repelled by the idea that I'm in too deep with yet another guy after the crap I went through with Ian. I can't be trusted to know what's right, so instead of answering his question, I type:

Gabrielle is scared she may never see Mal again, and I don't blame her for that.

I think you belong in this world.

Thanks, but the truth is I don't. And you saying that is a problem because I want to believe it.

Why?

Why? I don't know why. Would I be this confused if any other person had dragged me out of the ocean that fateful morning, or is it Salvador that makes this confusing? Would I be so conflicted about this issue if my rescuer had been someone else because I was so desperately in need of saving, or am I confused because I'm attracted to him? I found it impossible to notice other guys when I was with Ian. Would I have noticed him if I'd met Salvador in that life?

Because Gabrielle's right. I can't afford to let anything in this life get in the way of setting things right. I messed up so much in my last life. I can't do that again… not here.

Otherwise, I'm just being selfish.

Oh… What do we do?

We do nothing.

My cursor blinks as if asking me if I want to go through with this, but I hit send.

You've been so helpful, but maybe this is where it ends.

Tears blind me, piling one on top of the other at a loss I didn't realize I would experience.

We just stop? After what almost happened?

We have to.

Then I downplay everything with a lie.

After all, it was just a hug.

I wait for him to ask me to do something I know I shouldn't: to feed the *Aswang* by going behind my family's backs. I wait for him to remove the other arm so that panic forces me to comply in its absence. But he's not Ian.

K. I'm here if you need me.

Three dots appear on our message thread like he's going to say more, but then they disappear and don't return. I turn onto my back, letting myself sob until my stomach seizes. The mistakes I made in my past are not as easily wiped away as I'd thought.

A gasp startles me.

I turn my head, and I'm lying on the bed next to me. But it's not me; it's Mal, looking as petrified as I feel. I toss my hand toward her, and she takes it eagerly.

A portal, built of a swirling whirlwind of warped curtains and furniture, divides my bed and connects our two worlds. It's not made of water like the last portal, and it's not traveling us to a new location. We occupy the same space as the air between us churns like a fast-forming tornado.

Don't let go. I try to pull Mal with all my strength to my side of the portal, but the pressure on our linked hands is so weighted I can barely move.

"I won't," she responds—my jaw drops.

She has her voice. Our voice. Does she know she might be able to send the monsters back by simply commanding them with our voice? That would thwart Auntie Maggie's plans.

Tell the monsters to go back, I mouth.

Her forehead wrinkles.

"What?"

She isn't used to reading my lips like Gabrielle has come to understand. I grip her hand with my other hand and attempt to sit up on my knees. I wish I could scream for Gabrielle's help, but since I can't, I kick the closet doors with all my might. I repeatedly kick, hoping Gabrielle didn't fall asleep yet. All the while, I mouth over and over again, *Send the monsters away.*

"Send? I don't understand," Mal says, trying to army crawl through my portal. However, every time she gains an inch of space, gravity seems to increase in weight as if to flatten me into the Earth. "I don't think we can be in the same universe. We have to switch evenly."

I shove my hand through the portal to mirror how far her hand is to mine. The universes seem to want an even trade because it's slightly more accessible.

Mal shouts, "Gabby!"

Is she calling my sister or hers?

Anita, who must have been coming in to check on me, screams, "Mal," and jumps onto the bed beside me, pulling Mal's arm. I didn't hear her come in because of the ever-growing windstorm. "Gabrielle, get in here," Anita shouts.

A second later, both Gabrielles join us.

"Don't let go," the Gabrielle next to me shouts.

Mal explains that the harder she's pulled through the portal without pushing me forward, the harder it is to get her through the portal, but it's so loud here that I'm not sure they get it. I try to show both Gabrielles by getting up on my knees, but it feels like a three-hundred-pound man is sitting on my back.

A blur jumps over our heads, crashing into the windows and causing them to rattle. Mal lets go, yelling, "Damn, Duwendes," and then the portal shuts.

chapter twenty-two

Anita flies into the window seat while Gabrielle and I hit the floor from all the pressure built up from the portal vanishing instantly.

I tried, I tell Gabrielle, *I tried.* But she can't hear me and won't look at me. She beats the floor in furious sobs.

"What is going on?" Mom says.

I turn, startled. How long was Mom there?

Mom points a shaky finger at the space where Mal was, then at me, repeating her question.

Gabrielle flings herself onto Mom. Her shoulders wrack with sobs. I, ever on the outside, pull my knees up to my chest and bury my head into my arms. Anita hugs me while hard sobs roll through me. I've failed Gabrielle again.

In the comfort of Mom's arms, Gabrielle quiets enough for Mom to tell her to wait in her room. I watch Gabrielle leave, her face red and swollen. Anita excuses herself as well. Mom closes the door behind them and gestures for me to sit on the bed next to her.

She grabs my shoulders and pulls my head against her while I cry.

"Alright, *Anak,*" Mom says, wiping one of my cheeks. "Now tell me."

I sit up, wiping the other cheek, and grab my phone. Mom

pulls the glasses from their home on top of her head and puts them on so that she can read as I write.

I am not your Malaya.

"You're not?" Mom glances to the other side of the bed where her Mal was. So she had caught at least the end of our struggle with the portal. "Then who are you?"

I am from a parallel world. In that life, things were bad.

I pull out the explanations I'd written to Gabrielle, Anita, Salvador, and Tita Blessica since I've been here. Meanwhile, I write in my sketchbook about what happened tonight with the sea witch. My hand cramps with the pain of writing for so long, but I view it as a punishment for my crimes.

Mom takes my writing hand and rubs my aching palm when she finishes. At least I don't write with my impaled hand. "So instead of fixing things in your life, the sea witch swapped you for my Mal?" Mom confirms. "Isn't that just like a sea witch to not follow through with her word? Or so I assume, from the legends."

I nod, my gaze blurring with tears as I write:

I promise I'm trying to fix it, and I almost did just now when you saw Mal, but it's hard. For me to go back, I have to want to go back, but the problem is—

"You don't want to go back," Mom finishes for me.

I don't want to confirm the worst. She nods, then pulls me in close. I hug her, trying to convey how sorry I am. And she kisses my head like I'm hers.

"I can see why Gabrielle has been so upset since your accident. Mal is not just her sister; she's her best friend, her twin flame."

I lift my head, shocked that she picked up on that. Gabrielle had been so careful to maintain her cheerful self, even around me and especially around everyone else. That's her way. But somehow, Mom always knows. Why didn't she demand to know what was going on earlier? That's what my version of mom would have done.

My lips quiver as I write:

> *I'm so sorry. I messed everything up. And I'm not sure I can fix it. I'm sure you hate me now too.*

"*Anak*," Mom sighs. "You know why I call you *Anak*?"

It means child.

"Because you are my child, no matter what universe you come from. You are mine. There is nothing between us in any life that cannot be fixed. If I never get my Mal back, of course, I will feel sad. But she is not dead. She is right here," she holds my chin. "She just has different experiences."

> *But Gabrielle—*

"Gabrielle is right to feel sad and angry. And you are right to feel scared. To want to run. Just know you are my *Anak* in this life and the next. No matter what happens, you are mine."

Fresh, hot tears roll down my cheeks.

"Now tell me. What is it that you want? Do you want to go back, or are you just trying to make Gabrielle happy?"

I sit up straight, combing my hair back with my fingers. I'm so confused by Mom's question. It hadn't occurred to me to think of my reasons like that. I figured it was the right thing to do. *I don't know.*

"That's the problem. You cannot do things just to make other people happy."

Except everything I did in my last life was to make myself happy. I chose to be with that guy over everything else and look where it got me. I thought that, for once, I should do things differently.

"Maybe you don't see yourself in your life clearly enough. Maybe you thought you were choosing him, but he was choosing you."

I scoff. Considering how many other girls Ian chose at the same time as me, I constantly felt like I was the one choosing us. Like my need to hold onto the relationship was the only reason there was a relationship.

"You don't believe me? From what you told me, the relationship was bad."

Yes, I mouth.

"But by the end of it, you felt stuck. How did it get that way? How did he get you to feel like you couldn't leave?"

I think about everything I'd learned about gaslighting. Even knowing how someone can make you question your sanity, make you feel like you have no one else, it still hadn't occurred to me that I was with him because *he* chose *me*. But when Mom says it like that, I can see it. I can see how I was a thing he wanted to possess, even if his actions had convinced me that I was lucky he kept me around. He'd chosen me, and then he'd made sure to keep me by pulling me away from everyone.

"So maybe you weren't just doing it to make yourself happy. Maybe you pulled away from your family and friends to make him happy. And it was a mistake, of course," guilt runs through my veins, "but it was also a trick. What if he'd just came up to you one day and told you to stop having a good relationship with your family, huh?"

I would have told him no.

My eyes widen as I stare at the words. If Ian had said that, I would have told him no. But he didn't say that. Ian just prodded at the weaknesses in my relationship with Mom, with everyone, so I felt like our connections weren't good until one day, they just weren't. And then he was there to pick up the pieces he'd help break. A gust of air falls from my lips.

But I still did things to make my mom mad and disappoint her. And Gabrielle and I weren't close.

"You weren't close yet. That doesn't mean you would never have been close. And yes, I would have been mad to see my daughter sneaking out and lying. But none of those are things we couldn't get past."

I shake my head.

The you in my other life is different from

the you in this life. We're constantly fighting. I don't remember the last time we talked. She doesn't hear me. She's as different from you as I am from Mal.

"You have to stop talking about us like we are not one and the same. Maybe the things we experience make us respond differently to each other, but love is still there. You ran away because you thought you would never have my love again; that is proof that love is still there for your mother. We love you."

She sighs, pulling a strand of my hair straight and watching the wave bounce back.

"Whether you stay here, or go there, just know there is nothing you can do that will break our love."

I nod, and Mom gets up, sliding her slippers on.

"I will talk to Gabrielle. Together, we will figure out how to make this work. No matter what you decide."

My lips press together as I nod. When Mom leaves, I curl onto my bed, wondering if my mom knows I'm gone and if she misses me.

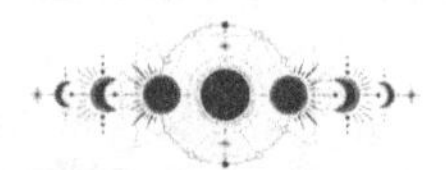

I hate this toxic feeling of messing everything up and not knowing what's next. However, Mom in both universes is a doer. When something is messed up, she doesn't wallow. I get that from her, which is why I'm not surprised when I wake the following day to find Mom sitting at the dining table with a yellow legal pad of thoughts and plans.

"Well, it never should have happened in the first place,"

Mom's raised voice forces its way out through her gritted teeth before she hangs up the phone.

"Who was that?" Gabrielle asks from behind me. I didn't even hear her leave her room.

"Tita Blessica," Mom says. "I just spent an hour giving her a piece of my mind."

I peer at Gabrielle, realizing she must have filled Mom in on Tita Blessica's role in all this, but she doesn't meet my gaze. I'm sure she explained that it was *my* Tita Blessica and not *their* Tita Blessica who is responsible, but the way Mom seethes over her coffee, I'm not sure she sees the rational side of all this.

"Get your brother." Mom points with her lips. "We have things to discuss."

Gabrielle is gone before I can even finish turning toward his room. Anita stumbles out of my room, rubbing her eyes. Then Eric emerges, half asleep, and moves toward the dining room table like a zombie. I'm not sure how he manages to even get there with his eyes practically closed, but he does.

Mom slaps the table. "Open your eyes, huh? We have work to do."

"Mom, what is this all about?" Gabrielle sounds defeated as she sits down next to her.

I lean against the back of a dining chair across from Mom to see everything she's written.

"We need to figure out what we're going to do next, but before we do, let me make something clear. If this Malaya wants to stay here, my home is always open. She is my daughter, and that is final."

Mom's words cause the whole house to silence as if it, too, were a living being. I glance at Eric, who shrugs. "I guess that's cool."

"I'd love that, too," Anita adds, stealing Mom's coffee.

Turn your head. Turn your head. I try to convince myself

to look at Gabrielle, but fire builds within her, radiating off her skin. Finally, my gaze darts to hers for a quick second and then back down to the dining table again. She is staring daggers at the wall across the room, her arms folded so tightly it's like she's trying to crush something between them.

"Okay. Now that that's settled, we need a plan to get Mal back too."

Impossible. I gesture to my mouth to get everyone's attention.

"Impossible?" Mom huffs. "Why?"

I lean forward quickly, pushing the dining chair out of the way as I reach for the yellow pad.

Because when I tried to pull her to this side of the universe, I kept getting weighed down. It's like the universe wouldn't accept both of us on one side. We had to swap places evenly.

"Oh," Gabrielle says, and she must finally realize what Mal was trying to explain over the loud wind portal. "I just thought you weren't trying as hard to pull her through."

I shake my head, placing a hand on her arm. *I tried so hard.*

Gabrielle yanks her arm away, and I become a ball, gripping my knees to my chest.

Mom interjects, "Then we will figure it out. The point is, you are not getting kicked out of this house if you don't want to leave."

I nod, but that reassurance doesn't stop me from dropping my head against my knees from the weight of the guilt.

"So last night, Gabrielle explained more about the sea

witch. By the way, you're all grounded because I never said you could see a sea witch without me."

"What? No way!" Eric sits up, fully awake now. "I didn't go see a sea witch."

"Did you go help your sisters see a sea witch?" Mom's hand comes down on the table, slapping it as sharply as her narrowed eyes.

"Yes, *Nanay*." Eric drops his head, his morning hair flopping as if it, too, is defeated.

"Okay, then grounded," Mom says, settling that business.

I laugh soundlessly, which Gabrielle catches from her periphery. She shoots me a warning glance, but I can't help it. Mom from my universe is known for doing group groundings, even if we weren't involved. If one person messed up, we all messed up because it is our duty to look after each other. It was her way of getting us to police each other and a blanket excuse to keep us all home rather than letting us go out. As good as Mal's relationship is with this version of Mom, this characteristic of hers is the same.

Mom's eyes are not curious for an explanation. They simply warn me to stop, and I shut my silent mouth.

Anita raises her hand. "Um, could we not tell my mom about the whole sea witch thing? It's just that I don't think she'll let me help get Mal back if she knows."

Keeping a secret from another mom goes against everything Mom stands for, so my shoulders perk up when Mom hesitates. "Maybe I won't tell your mom but you cannot help with these monsters anymore, or I will tell her."

"No!" Anita crumbles.

"I'm sorry, Anita." Mom pats her, then continues. "The sea witch will escape from the ocean floor prison on the next full moon?"

Yes.

Mom pulls out a calendar with chunky babies sleeping in

chunky blankets.

"Look here," Mom points to a date further in the month. "The next full moon is in two weeks. That is how much time we have to stop the witch from escaping."

"Why?" Eric rubs his eyes like he's finally awake and realizing that what's going on is not normal. I forgot that he knows virtually nothing. How is he even following this conversation?

"Don't question me, huh?"

Gabrielle exhales. "Mom, he snuck out to see what we were up to last night. We didn't tell him what was going on."

"*Anak*," Mom says more gently, trying to brush down his unruly hair with her fingers. "If we do not stop the witch from leaving her prison, your other sister will be trapped in another dimension forever. Right now, the sea witch needs the monsters to gain power to get out. After she gets out, her full power will be restored, and she will not need Malaya's voice anymore." She gestures to me, so he knows which one of us she's talking about. "If she succeeds, she will put Malaya's voice in the underwater jail, and that will be it."

She washes her hands in the air. I wait for Gabrielle to laugh or make a joke, but she concentrates on ripping a corner of the yellow paper.

Eric looks so confused, and I don't blame him. It's a lot to take in.

"We need a plan to stop people from seeing the monsters because she gets more power when they see them."

"Oh, it's like Magipunk," Eric says, nodding.

Mom's brow furrows.

"This is not a video game, huh? It's real life."

"I know, but in the game, the more people you can get to believe in your abilities, the stronger you are. The sea witch needs confidence points to have power."

"I never thought I would see the day when the video

games are helpful but yes." Mom massages her temples as she flips her yellow legal pad to a new, blank page.

"Okay, so how do we—you guys stop the sea witch from gaining ... confidence points?" Anita asks. Eric smiles encouragingly.

I raise my hand, having thought about this all night. After all, I am my mother's daughter, obsessive about finding solutions.

Mom passes me her legal pad, which acts as our playbook.

We need to neutralize the monsters out there, like paranormal hunters. However, we also need to debunk the monsters because they're such a hot topic that they've made national news.

Anita takes the pad and reads it aloud so that no one has to get up.

"Debunk?" Mom takes the legal pad, pulling the paper so close to her face that her nose has to be touching it. "*Ano?* Debunk?"

Gabrielle picks up the pen, tapping against the table as she says, "It means we prove they are not real."

"But they are real, and that's the problem," Mom says, like she's missing something.

"Yeah, but it's like those ghost hunter shows." Gabrielle sits up straighter, more enthusiastic as she sees where I'm going. "People will swear a place is haunted and share their experiences with a haunted house or object. If it gets famous enough, a team of ghost hunters like the ones on those shows I watch will come out and try to prove if the ghosts are real or not."

"Oh, I get it," Eric says. "We'll be the monster hunters. Only instead of trying to prove the monsters are real, we disprove them. That will take away the witch's confidence points."

"How can we do that when everyone has videos?" Mom lifts her phone. She probably has a dozen tabs open with the videos herself.

I type in my notes app:

Yes, everyone has videos. But people are more willing to accept that something does not exist than it does. We need to make videos showing how the monsters are hoaxes.

At this, Gabrielle slumps.

What's wrong? Where did her enthusiasm go?

"I only know one person who might be skilled enough to debunk monster videos."

"Who?" Mom and Eric ask together. Before she even says the name, I know who she's talking about. I, too, only know one person who may be tech-savvy enough to pull this off.

"Salvador." The dread in her voice is evident.

"Who?" Mom asks again.

"The boy Malaya likes," Anita says, making my face go as red as a warning light.

"He's a film major at the university," Gabrielle explains.

"Why is this bad?" Mom looks from Gabrielle to me, reading the tension in the room like the subtitles of our favorite K-drama.

When Gabrielle refuses to answer, I type:

Because the happier I am in this life, the less likely you will all see Mal again.

chapter twenty-three

Gabrielle and I agree on one thing: Salvador doesn't need to be involved in our mess anymore. But while Gabrielle's doing it to protect Mal, I'm doing it to protect him. He'd only gotten caught up in this mess because he'd pulled me out of the ocean, and his truck was trapped in *Tikbalang* territory. Now that Felipe is no longer an issue, he has no reason to be involved.

Eric, Anita, and Gabrielle leave to research film stuff in her room, trying to see if they can figure it out on their own. Meanwhile, just in case they can't figure it out, I promised to track down another film person who can help us. Mom stops me.

"You're not going to win her over by letting her have whatever she wants."

I sigh, sitting back down on the hard dining room chair. *What do you mean?*

"Were you close to your Gabrielle the way Mal is close to mine?" Mom dunks a *pandesal* roll into her coffee.

Not really. I press my eyes into my palms, feeling a headache coming on.

"Then you haven't figured either one of them out yet." Mom looks at me the way she does when analyzing movie plots. She always knows how a movie will end in the first act.

"You won't become close to someone by always giving in to them." Mom's coffee mug clinks against the glass as she sets it down. "Let me tell you about my older sister."

I pull the yellow legal pad toward me and write:

The one in Libya? What about her?

From what I recall, they aren't close ... Well, they weren't in my old life. Images of phone calls and visits during the holidays surface in this life.

"When I was little, I lived with my mom and dad, while Mari lived with my grandparents. I'd been my father's favorite, which is why I'd gotten to stay with him. This caused my sister to hate me."

That same resentment I felt for Gabrielle always being my mom's favorite returns like water boiling over. I clench the pen in my fist but keep my face neutral so Mom doesn't notice. I'd always thought my mom was the biggest hypocrite for telling this story in which she was her dad's favorite but claiming that Gabrielle wasn't hers.

Meanwhile, her sister looked like the villain, just as I'd always felt like the villain.

I'd never understood how Mom could let me go through that. And I'd never forgiven her for all the times she made me feel ridiculous for saying Gabrielle was her favorite. The fact that she didn't see how damaging it is for someone to know their parent has a favorite, well, that's the lie my mom always chose to believe. And I never could figure out whether she didn't think she was letting her daughter hurt or if she let me go through it because she never saw it as that big a deal.

I push my chair back, scraping the tile floors. I don't want to hear this story again, but then Mom says, "One day, my sister caught me riding a motorcycle with a boy, two things I was not allowed to do. She dragged me off the motorcycle and beat the crap out of me in the street." Mom's tale takes a turn I'd never heard before. Mainly because what happened to her never happened to *my mom*.

"I remember looking up at her wild eyes through my arms that I held up to shield myself. Years of resentment coursed through her fists. When she was done, she left me crying in front of everyone. I was shaking with fear. Mom would do worse to me, and Dad? I would not be his favorite after this." Mom shakes her head; then, her eyes widen in amazement. "But Mari never told anyone ... She could have taken everything from me, things she wanted ... but she didn't. I didn't know why she didn't do it, but from that moment on, having experienced the dread of losing my father's favor, I understood why she'd hated me so much for being his favorite."

Something clicks. This is one of those moments where my two mom's paths diverge. Her sister's choice to not ruin her relationship with grandpa made her realize how valuable that relationship to a parent is. *My mom* isn't close with her older sister. Maybe if she were, she would have understood me better. But my mom's older sister told grandpa about the boy and the motorcycle rather than beating her up. And Mom's punishment was to be shipped to America, as far away from that boy as possible.

"As you know, it took another decade, but we are close now. But it didn't happen because Mari gave me everything I wanted or took everything away from me either. Mari knew that taking my father from me would hurt way worse than anything she could do with her fists. She knew the line drawn in the sand and didn't cross it. It was the gesture I eventually learned to appreciate after my fat lip and bruises healed." Mom offers me some *pandesal*, but I wave her away. "It's like I said. You'll never be close to Gabrielle by always giving in to what she wants. But you might get close to her if you figure out what she needs."

I give Mom a curt nod and write one more thing. This time, it's a note for Gabrielle that I drop onto her bed before grabbing *my* car keys from her dresser. It says:

I'm going to get Salvador. Because whether you want to admit it or not, he's our best chance to save Mal.

I don't wait for Gabrielle to respond, and I'm almost at my car when someone calls my name.

"Wait up!" Anita races after me.

Going home?

"Yeah, I guess." Anita's lips pull to the side. "But just because Tita Floribeth won't let me be part of the monster-hunting show doesn't mean I can't help behind the scenes, right?"

Absolutely. Anita throws her arms around me, and my eyes sting. At least she doesn't hate me for not getting Mal back.

"Listen, I took pictures of the stuff Tita Blessica gave you so I can see how to use them to their full potential when I get home. But I grabbed this *agimat* out of the bag for you to try out." She holds a triangle-shaped amulet necklace. "That girl I met on vacation, Sinta, had one like this, and she said it made her invisible. I mean, not literally invisible, but Sinta said she wore it when she needed to be unnoticeable—like when she'd sneak out to see me." Anita smiles, and I push her shoulder.

Then I text:

> You're not going to leave me for the Philippines, are you?

"I mean, if you saw the way Sinta dances ..." Anita spins

before getting serious again. "Anyway, if this one works the same, you or Gabrielle can wear it when you're monster hunting so they don't notice you."

Sounds good. And thanks.

Anita dances off to her car while I put on the *agimat*.

When I get in the car, I message Salvador to meet me on the roof of the tallest building in Corpus Christi: One Shoreline Plaza. Then I pick up Tita Blessica, who does not love that I show up without calling first. I will give her credit, though; she has the spell to contact the gods ready. I can kill two birds with one stone by meeting with the gods to let them know I'm trying to fix my mistakes while asking Salvador if he can be part of our team. And meeting him there with Tita Blessica present ensures I won't let anything happen between us that will mess things up for operation rescue Mal.

Now that I'm driving downtown, the bravery propelling my impulsive decision to get Salvador is waning. I park next to the seawall while uncomfortable heat-flashes flush my system. His truck is already here, but he's not in it. He must be on the roof already.

"Grab the lantern, Malaya," Tita Blessica says while she picks up a tote of candles and other concoctions.

"*Opo.*" I grab the sky lantern with the spell Tita Blessica had written on it in Tagalog, but then I catch sight of a man whose very presence makes the hair on the back of my neck rise. It's the hysterical man from the hospital, and he's lingering near the seawall. I grab my phone to call Salvador.

A roaring *TIK TIK* rattles the car windows. My gaze darts back to where I'd seen the hospital man, but he's gone.

Shapeshifter.

"Malaya." Tita Blessica is trying to reach for me, but her eyes are searching the street, looking for the source of the roar.

TIK TIK. It's like I'm back on that dark road to Ian's house, the way my skin crawls. Why is this *Aswang* making that warning noise when the other didn't? Then I remember that *Tiktiks* are a *type* of *Aswang*: a shapeshifter whose only warning is the noise it makes before it kills. Is this *Aswang* taking the shape of the hospital man? Has it been stalking me all along?

Run. I grab Tita Blessica's arm and pull her across the street toward the plaza—an asymmetrical H-shaped building where the North and South towers are connected by the center building that bridges them.

TIK TIK. It's loud, so it's far. Somehow, that knowledge doesn't console me. We race past a fountain and fling the glass doors open. A few people stare, but nobody says a thing. Maybe they're all nonbelievers, and none of them hear the booming *TIK TIK.*

The elevators. I grab Tita Blessica's tote, so she has less to carry and race into the first open elevator. Tita's slower, but the monstrous *TIK Tik* lights a fire under her, and her slippers slap against the brown granite as she rushes inside.

I exhale, leaning against the glass walls when the doors close with us safely inside, but Tita Blessica grabs my arm.

"*As—aswang!*" She shouts, pointing downward out the window. The *Aswang* climbs the glass panes outside our elevator, eyeing us like it can't wait to rip into our skin.

My gaze darts for the floor levels—sixth, seventh, eighth ... There are only nine floors in this part of the building. Can it break through the glass before we can get out? It meets my eye level and pulls its fist back just as our doors open. We stumble out and race toward the South Tower. A shiver rocks my shoulders as if the beast's eyes are on me, but there's no glass shattering explosion. Just silence after the elevator doors close. It must have headed to the South Tower from the outside, and if Salvador is already up there ... I shouldn't have told Salvador to meet me here. I've put him in danger.

At the next set of elevators, we race to the highest floor.

From there, I drag Tita Blessica up the stairs to the roof, *Tik Tik,* but she's slowing me down. I'm so afraid I'll find the shapeshifter feasting on Salvador that I pull ahead of Tita Blessica, bursting onto the roof.

Salvador grabs me by the arm and yanks me into a shadowy nook.

"Where is your aunt?"

Has he forgotten I can't answer him? I pull out my phone, but he pushes it down, and the *tik tik* gets softer.

"It's going away," Salvador whispers. I shake my head furiously, pushing against him. *We have to run.* But he holds me in place because he doesn't know what I know: that the beast is only getting closer as it gets quieter.

tik tik.

I stand still, gripping Salvador close to me. A giant shadow flies over us, darkening Salvador's features for a moment. I have to call the gods. Right now. I'm not sure how the summoning works, but I have all the stuff, and the spell is already written.

I unfold the lantern and scoop air into it. Then I light the fuel pad and wait. *tik tik. tik tik.*

The lantern shakes from my trembling fingers as I hold it by the base, waiting for it to fill up enough to float.

Come on. Come on. Come on.

The *Tiktik* lands on the roof, its footfalls crunching against the rooftop gravel. It comes around the corner, and I'm no longer breathing.

It rips the roof access door from its hinges, and Tita Blessica screams. She must have just reached the top, and the *Tiktik* heard her. It grabs her by the head and slams her into the steel door, where she collapses. She appears to still be breathing but doesn't get back up.

Salvador races toward her and the *Tiktik* with the stingray tail lifted high before the creature can fly off with her. The winged creature knocks Salvador to the ground. I push the lantern into the air, no longer caring whether it works. I speed past the *Tiktik* as if unnoticed and make a mental note to thank Anita for grabbing this *agimat* for me. Frantically, I search for the *buntot pagi* that went flying out of Salvador's hand.

"To the left," Salvador yells. I grab the stingray tail, whipping the *Tiktik*. Its skin sears, and it twists around, lifting Salvador high into the air. I whip it once on its leg, but the *Tiktik* pulls its long proboscis back and stabs Salvador right through the chest. I scream soundlessly as blood spatters everywhere. Then the beast's black eyes widen. It and Salvador fall to the ground, crushing me.

chapter twenty-four

I'm trapped beneath Salvador's lifeless, breathless body, the beast's immobile face staring blankly just inches from mine.

Then two shadows fall over me—neither one looks like Tita Blessica.

My heart pounds furiously in my chest as I try, with all my might, to push the bodies off me, but I can't. A hand waves over us, and the *Tiktik* disintegrates into pearly black dust. I cough as the ashes filter through the air, then gently roll Salvador over.

A man in liquid, sapphire robes pulls me away from Salvador with magic, while the other one, dressed in a white cape that billows as if there's wind in this dead space, kneels next to him.

In a language that makes my body prickle for its similar cadence to the one Auntie Maggie spoke, the man in white waves his palm over Salvador's wound. I try to throw myself onto Salvador to protect him, but when I reach to rip the Sapphire man's hand off me, there's nothing there. His hand grips the air near my arm as if he's holding me in place even though he isn't touching me.

How—

Salvador coughs, drawing in air as if his entire body had

emptied of it, his eyes flickering open. White Cape backs away, and Sapphire releases me. I rush to Salvador, and he clings to my arms with his feeble grip. But when I rip the remaining shreds of his shirt to check his wound, there's no longer a puncture. It's just a healing red circle smeared crimson with blood. What kind of magic can bring a guy back from the dead?

Thank you, I mouth to the men. Then I stumble backward, digging my heels into the ground. I'm face to face with the homeless guy from the beach who'd tried to give Gabrielle the stingray tail, only he's cleaner now in his white robes and wood-carved chest plate. I grab the very same *buntot pagi* he'd given her off the ground, my only weapon, and hold it up.

Who are you? What do you want?

"We're here because you summoned us." White Cape points at the lantern in the sky, then raises an eyebrow at Sapphire, who I recognize as the hysterical man from the hospital. The one who'd been at the seawall downstairs. My mind tries to connect how the hysterical man is also the *Tiktik* that just disintegrated before my eyes, before I realize he never was.

I grip the whip in my hand tighter, ready to strike.

Why have you been following me?

Sapphire uncurls his hand before me, and a gust of wind hits me in the chest. Salvador, with the bit of strength he has, tries to shield me. "Stop." His voice is weak but commanding.

"Speak now." Sapphire stares at me.

"Who are you?" My voice is a bodiless, warbling sound that emanates from my thoughts rather than my lips, just like when Auntie Maggie cast that spell on me in the cave. I'm instantly grateful and weary that their magic and language are similar to hers. Salvador, who hadn't been in the cave, stares at my mouth, his face ashen. "Are you with Auntie Maggie?"

"Auntie Maggie." Sapphire harrumphs.

"I'm Kaptan, god of the sky," the man in the white cape says. "And this is my brother, Maguayan, god of the sea. But you can call him Yanny." He gestures to Sapphire. "And you are the girl working for my wife, Maguyaen." Kaptan looks me up and down with deadpan eyes.

"Working for? I'm not working for her." I scoff. Gods or not, I won't be aligned with Auntie Maggie.

"So, you didn't give her what she needs to escape the underwater prison we banished her to?" Yanny folds his arms over his chest, the hint of tribal tattoos peeking out through the edges of his robe.

"Why would you banish your wife?"

Kaptan's colorful headband flutters as if caught in a breeze. "We sentenced her for eternity under the sea after discovering that she was trying to ignite an eons-old war between us. She allowed us to nearly destroy the Earth and each other to assume power over the sky and water."

"If you're gods, then you can undo everything, right? Send the monsters back?"

A huff of air escapes the wind god's lips, chilling the atmosphere. "Hardly," Kaptan says.

"As long as she has your voice, she can keep releasing the beasts." Yanny stirs the air, pulling droplets from a nearby ac unit and swirling them like a small tornado. "When we realized what you'd done, the power you'd given her, we knew there was little we could do to stop her."

"But you're gods," Salvador croaks.

"That may be so, but she is dabbling in human magic to regain control," Kaptan says. "We can't touch human magic without losing our godhood. That was the mistake that my wife, Maguyaen, made. The corruption of human magic consumed her."

So that's why he wasn't touching me when he pulled me

away from Salvador because I have *Albularyo* lineage. "But the monsters? Didn't you banish them to the underworld once? Couldn't you do it again?" I sit on my knees, but Salvador grips my hand like he doesn't want me to leave.

"We used our powers as gods to create their prison, but humans banished them. These monsters are born of human magic. That is one of the reasons not everyone sees them in this science-based time. You have to believe in magic to see them. Even the smallest belief, like the suspension of disbelief that people experience when they watch movies, is enough to catch a glimmer of that world. Only a human can undo this."

"Then why did you yell *Aswang* at the hospital, Yanny? You could have started a whole epidemic."

"I did not yell *Aswang*. I described the monster as a spider, and I was testing to see your intentions. If you were on her side, you'd want to awaken everyone in the lobby—to infect them with belief. But your reaction was off ... it confused us—made us pause."

"If you think I'm working for Auntie Maggie, why are you helping me?"

"We're not helping you. We are helping our champion." Yanny gestures to Salvador, whose back goes rigid.

"Me?" He points at his chest, then shakes his head like they have the wrong guy.

Kaptan stares at Salvador, his grave expression making me gasp. If Salvador is their champion, that means they've been here since the second I entered this world.

"Me and Salvador meeting wasn't an accident, was it?"

Kaptan strokes his silver-streaked beard. "We chose Salvador to be our champion the moment your body washed up in a different timeline." Under his expressionless eyes, guilt causes my shoulders to draw into me.

It makes sense now.

Salvador rubs the back of his neck. "It was never a

coincidence that I happened to be in the right place to save Malaya? That explains why I randomly decided to go to the beach ... Well, I guess it wasn't random. I hate the beach," Salvador murmurs. "But why me?"

"We needed someone whose tapestry of life was never meant to weave with Malaya's—either version of her. That way, fate is not disrupted when both worlds are righted."

"We were never meant to meet?" Even though my voice possesses that ethereal quality, my sadness is undeniable. There's a sickening feeling in realizing that Salvador was never meant for me in either world.

The two gods' expressions are like the thunderous sky and stormy sea meeting the land. "We wanted to kill you." Kaptan's voice claps like thunder. "However, we weren't sure if that would relinquish your voice from Maguyaen or ensure that your voice remains hers forever."

Yanny pulls water from the ocean to create thrones for him and Kaptan, which cast rainbows onto the rooftop. "Since we couldn't be sure, we sent our champion on a reconnaissance mission." Yanny gestures to Salvador.

I slow-turn toward him, but he shakes his head. "I had no clue. I swear."

"He didn't," Kaptan says. "He was just a lens to examine you and a microphone to hear you ... At first."

"That moment in the car when he first asked me why I was at the beach?" I remember how Salvador's stare eerily reminded me of the homeless man ... who turned out to be Kaptan.

"Yes," Kaptan confirms. "We were listening. But we didn't truly doubt your allegiance to Maguyaen until the first time you killed one of them, an *Aswang*. That's when we decided to use our champion to help you out."

I remember how Salvador pulled the *Aswang's* limb behind its back with incredible strength. It hadn't occurred to me that that strength might have been godlike. Then there was the way he swatted the *Tikbalang's* arm away like it was nothing during the taming. Yanny confirms these as instances when they intervened. "We remained close to Salvador, aiding him when he needed a little ... luck ..."

It seems like more than just luck to me until Salvador asks, "Then why did you let me die just now?" He gestures to the *Aswang* dust covering both of us.

"We were testing the girl. After she revisited Maguyaen, we became suspicious once again. Humans so often do things that confuse us, but this one ..." Yanny's sapphire robes roll like waves as he sweeps his hand at me. I shift uncomfortably, and the pearly black dust clinging to my clothes swirls into the air.

"You don't have to worry about me. I came here to assure you that my family and I created a plan to stop Maguyaen from gaining the power she needs before the next full moon." I explain our monster debunking plan to the gods and Salvador.

I cannot tell, even a little bit, if Kaptan and Yanny like the plan or think it will work. But I turn to Salvador and say, "I know you probably don't want to be around me after ... yesterday ... but this show could be big if you help us, and you could be big because of the show. It could be everything you need."

Salvador scoffs. "Is that all you think I want?"

I take his hand. "Of course not. But it's all I can give you."

Salvador nods, and he feels so far from me. But when he looks back, he smiles ... a little.

Kaptan clears his throat. "We'll give you a chance to fight off the monsters so we don't risk our godhood unnecessarily. But if you don't stop Maguyaen, we will use our champion against you."

“I would never fight her,” Salvador says, his shoulders back.

“I don’t think you would have a choice.” I squeeze Salvador’s fingers. “One of them is willing to sacrifice their godhood to stop her, even if that means possessing a human to kill me.” I raise my eyebrows at Kaptan and Yanny for confirmation, but their silence is confirmation enough.

Which one will peer through Salvador’s eyes if it comes down to that?

chapter twenty-five

Salvador and I have small, stiff smiles as I drive Tita Blessica back home. She doesn't like hospitals, so she wouldn't even entertain the idea of getting the bump on her head examined. Once she's gone, my chest aches with this urge to fix things between Salvador and me. There's so much I want to say, but the moment the gods vanished, so did my ability to project my voice.

Damn them.

As we park our vehicles outside my house, I touch his forearm to stop him before going inside.

Are you sure you want to help?

"I'm not giving up on you yet." His smile isn't as full of life as usual, but his eyes blaze. How can he say that, knowing we were never meant for each other?

Salvador and Mom hit it off over a bowl of *tinola* and rice. Actually, Salvador had three bowls because he'd never had Filipino food before, and, like many before him, he lost his damn mind.

While Mom and Salvador wash dishes, because neither one of them would relinquish control over the chore, Mom asks questions about Salvador's parents.

"Dad's an Electrician and had a hand in wiring or repairing half the houses in our small town. And Mom, well, she's a dental hygienist working in the public service space."

I pretend to wipe down the breakfast bar, but it's clear I'm just here to listen to him.

"They're community servers. That's good. My Mal is going to be a nurse." Mom passes him a bowl to rinse, her chest rising as if filled with pride.

She has no clue how miserable Mal is ...

"Yeah, my parents work hard." His head tilts, one cheek pulling to the side to reveal a dimple. I imagine Mal making that face as well when people tell her how great it is that she already knows what she wants to do with her life.

Mom holds a soapy wooden spoon up, and the bubbles slide like slime down the handle. "Why did you say yes to helping us? Your parents sound like very responsible people. They probably would not want you taking this risk. You might die."

Salvador's chest rises as he sucks in a deep breath. Do I tell them what happened with the gods? Will it change anything to worry them with this new threat?

Salvador's eyes flicker to mine, his gaze a wildfire that spreads through me. "I want to be a filmmaker, and Malaya has taught me that that means diving into experiences that might scare me and putting myself out there in a way that exposes me." He bites his lower lip, looking back down at the dish he's rinsing, then a smile forms. "Monster hunting was not on the docket before ... because it didn't exist," he suppresses a smile, not looking at me. I duck my head. "But I've seen what your girls are capable of, so I know hunting these creatures will not be an opportunity I'll experience in the future with these two saving the world."

Mom tosses him a rag to dry his hands, examining us before looking at Gabrielle's sullen expression as she leans against the island. “I’m making you *pancit*,” she says, which is the gold standard of Filipino party food, and the highest honor she can bestow on him.

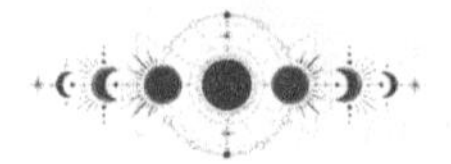

One shopping trip to the Asian Market later, and we’re all standing in the living room in minimal clothing as Mom insists that we get cleansed before we do any monster hunting because, “How can the herbs protect if you’re covered in negative energy?”

Eric watches one of the many paranormal hunter TV shows that Gabrielle loves. His following as a gamer and his penchant for making ridiculous lip-syncing videos makes him the ideal host for a social media show.

“What was that?” Eric repeats a line from the show, mimicking the actor’s startled way of ducking his head into his shoulders.

“Stand still.” Mom nearly drops the egg that she’s running down his dodgy forehead.

“What? I’m practicing.” Eric takes on the role of the token skeptic looking for the cause of the noise that sent the cast running. “Gabrielle’s gonna be the scaredy-cat one, right? The one that believes everything is real?”

“Uh, yeah. Do what comes naturally.” Gabrielle tosses her hand as if to imply the word ‘duh,’ then bites her lip as she takes a seat on the couch, eyes riveted to the show.

I roll my eyes, amused. Everybody has their role. Of course, outside of the show, we’re all hunters trying to rid the area of monsters. But within the show, Gabrielle and Eric are the main players because both have big personalities and, this is critical, both can talk. My production job is to film the areas where the most popular videos circulating the internet have been shot, while Salvador is the person who will use his knowledge of film tricks to debunk the monsters. Finally, Mom is the advisor and authority on Filipino mythological creatures, which will give the show more credibility as she points out things in the folklore that don't match what is being seen in public, even though technically it does.

To put it bluntly, she'll have to lie her ass off—something she cannot stand any of us doing in either timeline.

Still ... Eric thinks that people won't believe Mom as an authority because so many videos of the monsters stalking the Coastal Bend show what these creatures are like. That sparks a huge argument because mythology doesn't always match the stories, even though these monsters are real. For example, in *Tikbalang* legend, the creatures can turn invisible. However, that wasn't part of our experience.

Gabrielle argues that's exactly the reason we need Mom to reference the mythology. "If we match what we know from the legends to what people see in the videos, we can say that these videos are fabrications because these monsters aren't behaving as the folklore says."

The whole thing goes a little over Eric's head, but he doesn't care as long as the videos get him views. We all argue that Mom can do her job from the safety of home, and she immediately chastises us for acting like she's some ancient *Lola* who can't wipe her butt. Needless to say, she's coming on every hunt to protect her children, which includes Salvador. I'm not sure if that makes her a liability or an asset.

"Here," Mom hands me an egg covered in coconut oil. "Gabrielle, get up, *Anak*."

I follow Mom's instructions moving clockwise from top to bottom on Gabrielle while she finishes up on Eric. Though Gabrielle and I are still not okay, she asks to sit with me tonight as I try to open the portal between the worlds again.

Of course, I mouth with as much conviction as my silently moving lips will convey.

"Okay," Mom slaps Eric on the chest and hands him the egg. "Destroy this, *Anak*."

Eric walks to the kitchen while Mom takes the egg from my hand to finish Gabrielle. She might be forcing us together in small bursts, hoping we'll get over the tension with teeny pushes. "Here." Mom hands me another egg, and my mouth opens and shuts in confusion. She can't mean ...

"Start on him." Mom gestures to Salvador.

I shift weight from one foot to the next, peering at Salvador nervously, then at Gabrielle, who forces a huff of air through her nose.

Salvador stands, and I have to tell my hand to stop shaking for the love of God. It doesn't listen to me, and as I squeeze the egg more tightly and lift it to his forehead, I wonder what would be more embarrassing: him knowing I'm nervous being this close to him or me accidentally breaking this egg over his face.

"Clockwise," Mom instructs. She must think my hesitation is because I've forgotten what to do. She's not entirely wrong. Looking at Salvador does seem to have that effect on me ...

I run the egg over his forehead and down the side of his face. The outside of my hand grazes his soft, thick hair, and our eyes meet. Fire burns through me as I long to explore the thing between us that shouldn't exist. Though we've communicated, we haven't really talked about the last time we messaged each other. Those words "we do nothing" are like questions in his eyes. How can I do nothing when so much between us buzzes electric? How can I do anything knowing we were never meant to be anything to each other?

"Mom," Eric calls from the kitchen.

"*Ano*?" Mom is squatting at Gabrielle's legs, a shiny streak of coconut oil glistening on Gabrielle's shin from her work.

"Where's the salt?"

"It's in the cabinet," Mom replies, brow knitted in concentration.

Gabrielle and I look at each other with narrowed eyes that turn wide.

No, I mouth, so in sync with Gabrielle that it's as if her gasped word comes from my mouth.

"What?" Mom looks up, startled.

"He cooked it." Salvador slaps his hand on his forehead. "I'm not Filipino, and even I know you're not supposed to cook it, bro," he calls into the kitchen.

"Eric Kent!" Mom uses the full force of his first and middle name. "You better not have cooked that egg." She gets up immediately, handing Gabrielle her egg. Mom's slippers scrape the floor all the way into the kitchen, and I stand on tiptoes to see over the breakfast bar as Eric bites a forkful of scrambled egg. "*Hay naku,* Eric! What are you doing, huh?"

"I'm destroying this egg," Eric says, waving both hands as he would if demolishing a pizza. "You told me to."

"No, destroy it. *Destroy.* Not eat. I didn't say eat. *Gago,* you put the bad energy back into your body."

Gabrielle goes in there to explain what destroying a plate of food means, bringing the last egg that was meant for me with her because she knows Mom will have to do Eric's cleansing again.

"You're lucky the Asian Market was out of *balut.*" Mom cleanses Eric again while Gabrielle prepares the oil and herbs needed to make my egg.

At the mere mention of *balut*, Eric pretends to gag. If he's like me, he's probably reliving our childhood trauma of a not-real uncle chasing us around a Filipino party with a half-peeled *balut*. I will never not gag when I recall the dead body of an underdeveloped duckling encircled in a half-peeled eggshell.

Salvador grazes my wrist with the edge of his finger, and I gaze at the place where we connect before looking up to meet his eyes. I'd been rubbing the egg over his neck as the drama unfolded, and his neck was now thoroughly shiny.

Sorry, I mouth, pulling the egg away from him.

He smirks, and my insides flutter. I'm more alive when he's near.

I wave my arms dramatically at Mom, so she can finish the job on Salvador, even bang on the breakfast counter—the ring on my finger clacking against the laminate, but nobody notices me amid their arguing. This is another one of those moments when having a voice would be nice.

"I don't mind if you do it." Salvador's voice is a soft breeze grazing wildflowers.

He reaches over his head, grabs his shirt from the back of his neck, and yanks it off. My jaw drops as he tosses the shirt onto the couch next to Eric's. Every muscle in his back ripples with the most minute of movement, and when he turns to face me, my head darts back toward the kitchen as if he hadn't just caught me looking. *Breathe*, I remind myself, trying to recall what that means. I've seen him with his shirt off before, touched him before, but ever since that almost kiss ...

A slow smile builds on his face revealing the deepest dimples. He knows exactly what he's doing to me. The egg loosens in my hand as if my body is boneless. He lifts my wrist, placing the palmed egg on his chest. The heat radiating between his hard muscles and my trembling hand is nothing compared to the fire blazing in his eyes. I find myself leaning forward as if hypnotized by his soft lips.

I swallow, forcing myself to concentrate on the small circular cleansing motions. At any moment, my family could look over from the kitchen and see us. They could walk into the living room and find us ... doing what?

Cleansing?

I mean, that's all it is, right? Except ... as my knuckles brush his abs, I know that it doesn't matter if he and I are not doing anything because the flush of my skin, the part of my lips; there is no denying my attraction to Salvador.

I move down his leg, and he offers me his hand as I shift to his backside and stand. His breathing stops as I move the egg across his back. His hungry eyes meet mine as I drag the egg down the other side of his back and up his chest again.

He brushes a fallen curl off my face, his hand lingering behind my ear as he tucks the strand. For the longest moment, I am transported to another world—a world in which I don't have to deny my impulses or worry about making the wrong decisions—a world in which we were made for each other.

If only such a world existed.

If only there were a place where my choices didn't have monumental consequences. Why could some people be impulsive and carefree, but I ruined lives when I tried to be?

I take Salvador's hand from my face and place the egg in it. I'm careful not to look at his eyes, or I may make an unfixable mistake.

chapter twenty-six

Planning our first debunking and monster removal operation takes another two days, which causes me to lose sleep. Salvador assures us, as his eyes scan over the cluttered kitchen table, that the others should move much quicker once this first episode is complete. I hope he's right because I feel this deadline like a student assembling a diorama into the early morning hours of the day it's due.

It had rained heavier this year, causing the water levels in the wildlife refuge near the university to be extra high. However, while the wetlands should be easily visible from the pier extending through the park, many researchers from the university report that something, as of late, has caused the water to run dry.

Though there were several videos of a giant, hulking silhouette erupting out of nowhere, sending the birds scattering across the skies, no one had subdued the creature. Mom watched the videos repeatedly, even consulting Tita Mari about the best way to approach a *Berberoka*.

Gabrielle passes her phone with a hand-drawn image of the creature. It looks like a mound of dirt suddenly sprouted arms and legs. Vegetation seems to grow straight out of the beast's back like a turtle's shell.

Mom holds her tablet with the monster lexicon pulled up,

though she doesn't read from it as she says, "The *Berberoka* will suck up all the water from ponds and rivers, creating a dam with its body, so you think, 'oh, there is no more water, let me get the fish.'" Mom pretends to pick fish up from the floor. "Then, when you are in the middle of the dry pond, it releases the water to knock you off your feet. Of course, *Berberoka* is a good swimmer. He will eat you while you are," she flails her arms like a drowning victim, letting the action complete her sentence.

"What in the—who the heck wants to eat dead fish?" Eric leans back, waving his hands at the imaginary dish in disgust.

"Who the heck wants to eat the bad juju egg, huh?" Mom says, raising her hand like she's going to slap my brother. We all laugh as she pats his face instead.

How do we stop it? I gesture stop like Diana Ross, knowledgeable of the oldie because of karaoke.

"With crabs," Mom replies. Eric stares at her, jaw dropped as if waiting for the punchline. "*Ano*?" Her head tilts, a warning flashing across her face.

"Does someone else want to take this one before I get hit?" Eric suppresses a smile.

"Mom!" Gabrielle giggles, her carefree self shining through. "He's waiting for you to say you're joking because of the egg, and the fish, and the ... crabs."

"I'm not joking. *Berberoka* don't like that the crabs pinch."

"I might be a *Berberoka*," Salvador chimes in, "I don't like getting pinched either."

Surprisingly, this breaks Gabrielle from her Grumpy Cat phase as she bursts into laughter. It's good to see that she isn't treating him differently despite how much she hates bringing him back into the group.

I grab our yellow legal pad of monster debunking plans.

Across the top is our show's name *Debunking the Aswang* in bold sharpie. I find a blank corner and write:

How are we supposed to fight with crabs?

Mom counts us the way one counts their party when a hostess asks how many will be dining at a restaurant. In theory, you know how many people you came with, but you still count anyway.

"Five ..." Mom says, thinking to herself. "*Anak*, come help." Mom gets up, and Gabrielle and Eric gesture to each other like they don't know who she's talking to. I get up and follow her to the backdoor.

"No, you're too short," Mom says when she looks back and sees me.

Eric shrugs like, 'I guess she means me,' and follows her outside.

They come back with four bamboo lanterns from the porch. Sitting on the arm of the couch, I open the door on the side of the oval-shaped lantern. Mom regretted this purchase because the solar-powered lights never gave off a useful amount of light. I remember telling my version of mom that they're romantic, but she didn't like that explanation. The bottom of the lantern was just big enough to fit a small crab.

"We'll go down the docks and buy fresh crabs when it is time to go," Mom explains.

Will the *Berberoka* still be scared if they are in the cages?

"How should I know? I never asked him," Mom says. "But what else can we do?"

"Could you show us how to pick them up?" Salvador asks.

"Why? You want him to bite you?" she asks, meaning the crab.

Salvador laughs. "No, just in case the *Berberoka* is not afraid of a crab in a cage, I want to use it as a weapon."

"Can the crabs be dead?" Eric interrupts before Mom has a chance to say anything.

"*Hayop ka*!" Mom says, getting frustrated with Eric.

"How am I an animal?" Eric gets up to avoid her swing. It likely wouldn't have hurt a giant preteen like him, but Filipino Mom slaps are emotional wounds too.

"You want to kill an animal that is not hurting anyone?" Mom gives him a glassy stare.

"You just want to cook them when we're done." Eric's mouth lifts in a half-smile.

"Well, it's my money."

I laugh soundlessly, and Mom shakes her head, smiling too. I guarantee that any crabs not hurled at the *Berberoka* will be made into a victory dinner.

When we've stopped chuckling, Mom shows us the correct way to pick up a crab from the back while using a rolled sock. Now I have to hope the pinchers are not facing me when I reach into its cage.

Eric sets his pretend crab sock in his lantern cage, then does a pseudo karate kick that he, no doubt, picked up from *Cobra Kai* which he's been using as his sleepy-time show. So restful. Gabrielle gets up, pretending to be the monster, and swipes at him while he reaches into his crab cage. His hand gets stuck on the little door, and he finally tosses the crate at her, screaming in a high falsetto.

Dad walks in through the front door, pausing as he looks at the lanterns strewn about next to rolled-up socks. I try to shove a stingray tail back into the black backpack at my feet as quickly as possible, but Dad eyes it before looking at Mom, who's in the center of it all, having just shouted, "Point the pinchers!"

"You know what?" He lifts his hands like he's stopping traffic. "I don't even want to know."

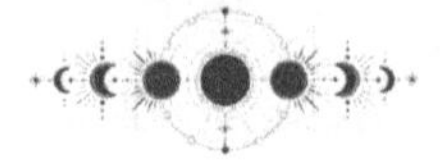

The next day, in the small parking lot at the entrance of the wildlife refuge, we file out of Mom's SUV. I sat in the front so Gabrielle wouldn't be tense and distracted by interactions between me and Salvador. But while everyone else is getting their crabs out of the trunk, Salvador approaches.

"Here." He hands me a *buntot pagi*. Then he whispers, "Anita messaged me about how to treat it so that the skin becomes a soft leather that doesn't reek of fish."

It also had a handle, which he'd carved with the Filipino star. My jaw drops because the Filipino star is not easy to draw, let alone carve.

It's beautiful. I slip it through a leather utility belt I'd dug up in the garage.

I pull his backpack open to look at the other whips, but they aren't as intricate. He shifts, giving me a small smile.

"Do you think we can talk later?" He fidgets with a handheld tripod.

My head whips around to look for Gabrielle, but she's busy practicing some opening lines that she and Eric cooked up for the entrance into the refuge.

I shake my head. It was best to stay away.

"You chose to be here," he says in the softest tone, slipping the lasso Gabrielle and I'd made when hunting the *Tikbalang* through his arm. "You gave up a whole other life to have this one. Don't you think you should be living it?" Salvador walks away backward, his palms up like he could be part of the life I should be living though we both know it wasn't meant to be.

I drop my head back on my shoulders and look up at the

evening sky. There are still a couple of hours before actual nightfall, but the sun is already getting closer to the tops of the trees as it slowly descends. *Focus on this.* I tell myself. *Worry about that later.*

I suck in a deep breath and head over to where Salvador is directing Eric and Gabrielle. They are absolute naturals as they talk about Filipino legend, and you would have thought they were pros on the subject. And, of course, Mom is adorable as she leans in from the side to wave to the camera before launching into the many guesses people made as to what they believed the creature was: a *Berberoka*, a *Kapre*, and even a *Tiktik*.

"In the videos," Mom says, glancing at Gabrielle and me for encouragement, then looking completely awkward talking to the camera by the way her eyes shift all over the place. "We see a large figure moving through the forest ... uh ...like a giant."

I stand directly behind Salvador and gesture for mom to look at me.

Say it to me. I point dramatically at myself because she's still not great at reading my lips. However, she seems relieved to have someone to look at as she's talking, and she's much stiller. Salvador points at Gabrielle, directing her to prompt Mom as she seems to have forgotten her point.

"Mom, people on social media say it's a *Kapre* or even a *Tiktik* because of the oversized silhouettes captured on video. What are your thoughts on that?"

We'd decided to indulge the idea that the monster is a *Kapre* rather than the *Berberoka* that I expect to find because it's easier to debunk the things that a *Kapre* is not, such as the way the *Kapre* is a giant while the *Berberoka* can change in sizes, or the fact that *Kapre*'s smell heavily of smoke because they enjoy a nice hand-wrapped cigar, while we'll claim the woods are clear of those smells.

"If it is a *Kapre*, then we have nothing to worry about. The *Kapre* likes to make friends and plays jokes to trick you into coming back and playing with him. It will be giant like the ones in the video, but they are not jumping out of trees as we see in the recordings. They don't like the exercise."

"Is it your opinion that we will see a *Kapre* on the trails today?" Eric asks.

"No." Mom waves her hand like he's being ridiculous. That part of their relationship comes so naturally that she doesn't appear so nervous anymore.

"What do you think we will find?" Salvador asks.

"Maybe a bear. Maybe a person faking the monsters to get famous."

"A bear sighting seems a little far-fetched for Corpus Christi," Gabrielle chimes in, smiling out of nervousness.

"But someone trying to get famous?" Eric shrugs his shoulders. "Now that's an interesting angle. So, Mom, you don't think there are Filipino monsters out there at all?" Eric asks, to be clear about her side in the matter.

"No," Mom says again in the harsh, not-actually-harsh way a Filipina responds to something she thinks is absurd. "People want to be famous and want to make fun of Filipino culture."

"Why do you think that?" Salvador asks.

Even the cicadas seem to quiet as I wait for Mom's answer because the conversation had taken an unrehearsed direction.

Mom sighs. "Like many people of color, Asians experience prejudice, discrimination ... *pero*, the difference is that many of us take it in silence. This makes it seem like we do not mind. Or we think we deserve it." My shoulders go back as Mom pauses. "So, if someone wants to create chaos and they want someone to blame, they blame the Asians. And this time, the Filipinos. These monsters people say they see, why Filipino? Don't the Spanish have Duwendes too? The one on the beach that look like a spider woman—aren't there shapeshifters and *bampira* in every culture? Why are the monsters Filipino? Because people say they are Filipino. There is no proof. Many people don't see anything when they see the videos because there is nothing there."

"So, it's like hysteria?" Salvador asks.

"I don't know." Mom throws her hands up. Her chest rises and falls as she tries to keep her voice steady. It never occurred to me that these monsters could be creatures from other cultures with different names. And everything else she said? Well, Tita Blessica's complaints from that card reading night at the Filipino party are echoing in my head about people saying the Philippines has no culture. That we steal from other people's cultures. I just never realized Mom might feel that way too. The difference is, she is one of the suffer-in-silence types she just mentioned. Perhaps she and I have more in common than I thought. I'd suffered in silence with Ian.

Salvador gestures to Gabrielle after several beats.

"Well, having seen many videos and followed these stories on social media and the news avidly, I'm leaning toward thinking there is some kind of monster out there, Filipino or not." Gabrielle plays her role as the believer well and brings the theme of paranormal hunting back around. "What about you, Eric?"

"Nah, I'm with Mom on this one," Eric says, throwing his arm over Mom like the good son he is.

"And cut." Salvador drops the camera to his side. "It was different than I thought it would be, but good. Authentic."

"Maybe we should not put what I said." Mom swallows, doubting herself.

No. I cross my arms in an X. *Don't silence yourself.*

I hope that knowing a thing or two about silencing myself helps her understand why she shouldn't.

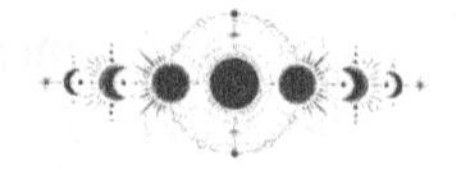

Deep in the refuge, we find a waterless pit next to a pier. Salvador has one camera with night vision, which he sets up high in a tree, pointing it at the pier. Gabrielle and I set up an iPhone on a tripod at the end of the dock, trying to be as light of foot as possible though every creak under our feet makes me feel like we're a 5-ton weight on the rickety boards. Mom and Eric set up two more phones at the ground level near the edge of the dried-up water embankment.

From the pier, it's easy to tell how this area usually contains water. The tall, brown grass on the edges of the wetlands is still damp and darker in color halfway down the stem where the water had been.

I don't see dead fish. I put my hand to my forehead to emphasize searching, beginning to wonder if we'd come to the right place or if fish were even a necessity in this mythology. Then something silver flops just in my periphery.

The mud glitters as fish flop in the sunlight.

Gabrielle looks at me hesitantly, her lips twitching as she asks, "Do we just go?"

Eric signals her forward, but I put my arm out to stop her. I scan the landscape. With the water gone, the brush seems as tall as trees. It would be easy to get swept up, even if the water wasn't that deep. But where was the large mound that was damming the water? Where was the *Berberoka*?

Then my gaze finds a leafy mound that seems to spasm, not like wind passing through leaves, but like slow, steady breathing.

I point. *That's it,* then glance at Mom. She's frozen, her fingers having gripped Eric's arm. If this monster can change sizes, it has chosen one of its largest forms. Mom's head shakes, and while she seems incapable of speaking, her actions are clear. No one is to go out there.

She turns around, attempting to push all of us back, but Gabrielle stops her.

"This is for Mal," Gabrielle says through her teeth. Mom's eyes flicker to my face; then, she realizes Gabrielle is not talking about me. Not all her children are here to save.

I step out onto the slippery mud before Mom can change her mind, holding my arms out for Gabrielle to help her down. My crab cage is clutched tightly at my side as I trudge forward slowly. Gabrielle's fingers shake, and rather than use her free hand for balance, she's got it hovering near the door of her crab cage.

Though we'd gotten down first, all of us make it to a fish near the large mound at about the same time. The mounds breathing is ominous and low, like air blown into a bottle. I squat, reaching for a fish, and the second I touch the small, slippery creature, the floodgates open.

The beast stands, and mounds of mud and vegetation that are not part of his body, slip back to the Earth as he rises slowly. The water, however, is fast-moving, and it knocks Mom down. I scoop her up. She'd never learned to swim, but she swore the *Berberoka* would not show unless it thought it could trap everybody.

The water sweeps me off my feet, but I don't let go of Mom as I crash into thick, tall grass. Mom grips the roots of the grass with all her might; her neck muscles tense as she tries to keep her head above the rising water.

Gabrielle screams, and my heart stutters.

Gabrielle! She's trapped in the *Berberoka's* fist. Salvador makes it to the water's edge closest to the *Berberoka* and whips the giant ogre with his stingray tail. Smoke rises from his skin, which sizzles on contact, though the *Berberoka* doesn't have the deathly reaction to it that the *Aswang* did. The giant swats

Salvador away with one hand, and as his whole body swings with the force of his heavy arm, Gabrielle swings forward, too, like a small doll.

Salvador lands in a thick patch of low grass, turning over slowly like it's hard to get his footing. The beast opens his mouth and raises Gabrielle like her head is a grape to pluck from a vine.

Though the water is still rushing strongly, nearly paralyzing my body with its power, I yank myself up onto the grass, then pull Mom up with inhuman strength. Are the gods helping me out as well? I yank a cattail sticking out of the ground and toss it at the monster, knowing it won't hurt it but hoping to distract him just long enough.

The cattail smacks him in the face, and he must think Gabrielle slapped him because he roars deeply in her face, spittle flying everywhere. The brush near his feet quivers, and Eric emerges. He must have crawled out of the water and snuck through the tall grass to come up behind the *Berberoka*. He discreetly tries to tie the *buntot pagi* around the *Berberoka*'s ankle, but it's way too short.

The beast notices the stinging and swipes at Eric, but Eric dodges him easily. Roaring, the brush flattens. Then the *Berberoka* shrinks to the size of a tall basketball player—though much thicker. He seems to forget that he's holding Gabrielle because her head hits the muddy ground.

With Mom on my heels, I race toward the monster, and the *Berberoka's* eyes go wide. He stomps forward, almost stepping on Gabrielle to get to us. I push myself until my lungs burn, hoping to stop him in place before he accidentally crushes her. With my lantern clutched to my chest, I yank my crab out. It's backward and almost pinches me, but I quickly fix it. My hands shake as I'm within the *Berberoka's* reach.

The *Berberoka* stumbles on the spot when he notices the crab's pinching arms. I try so hard not to let the live thing go, though holding it is quickly becoming a new, squeamish fear of mine. The *Berberoka* lets Gabrielle go, and she immediately crawl-runs to Mom, devoid of all weapons. I yank the *buntot pagi* from my utility belt and toss it back to her without taking my gaze off the beast.

Salvador pulls the lasso from his chest to capture one of the beast's fists. The *Berberoka* swings at him, but Salvador lifts the crab in his other hand.

"*Umupo ka,*" Mom commands, pointing her finger downward.

The *Berberoka* drops into a seated position at once, looking like a fearful child as Salvador, Eric, and I surround him with crabs.

"What now?" Eric asks. "He's not dead, so what do we do?"

Salvador looks at me. Like the *Aswang*, this thing was trying to kill us. But killing it while it can't defend itself seems wrong. And I didn't have this problem with the *Tikbalang* ... Then I remember the gods telling us that humans banished the monsters to the underwater prison long ago.

I reach for the *Tikbalang*'s spine dangling around my neck and mouth, *Felipe.*

From the direction of the sea, water begins to swirl. A portal opens, and Mom gasps as the *Tikbalang* comes charging through. He stops near me, and I touch his neck.

Take him back to the underwater realm, I command, though I have no clue whether he can do that or how considering the *Berberoka* is bigger than him.

Felipe circles the beast several times as I back away. The beast's eyes roll as the *Tikbalang* seems to be using his ability to get travelers lost on the *Berberoka*. The giant ogre gets up, his stomping feet causing the ground to tremble as he walks straight into the portal with Felipe trailing behind him.

chapter twenty-seven

By Monday, our video has circulated so that when Gabrielle and I drop Eric off at school, he's got a crowd of people waiting for him like he's a movie star. Even when we'd viewed the movie together and the title *Debunking the Aswang* flashed across the screen, I felt the need to get everyone's autographs. It looked like a legit web series rather than the amateur point-and-shoot video I thought we were making. And I must admit that while I found Salvador's talent sexy, his vulnerability as he needed my support to publish his post was irresistible.

I'd wondered how Gabrielle would be perceived at school, considering that she'd lost at the end of the video in the round of real versus fake. However, when I pull up, people even ask *me* questions about the trails in the wildlife refuge and complimented my acting abilities, which they felt were so real when I'd yanked the crab from its cage. We'd used the footage of us fighting the *Berberoka* to show how one would fight off this mythical creature if it existed, then Salvador used his movie magic skills to erase the creature from the scene.

Since I can't speak, I wasn't a main player in the video, akin to an extra or support crew whose name is not said or known until season two. Yet, even friends from my old life, like Stephanie, come to ask me questions.

"How could you go into the refuge not knowing if the monsters were real? Did you guys check it out before filming? Or did you jump right in?" Stephanie asks eagerly.

I've missed this enthusiasm from her. She was always a bit of a thrill-seeker, which is part of why we were friends ... back in my old life.

I want to engage in this conversation badly, but I wasn't prepared for anyone to talk to *me*, so my head nods and shakes quickly become a disappointment. Stephanie's face falls as I gesture to my mouth.

"Right, I forgot," her voice falling. Before I know it, Stephanie's blending in with the crowd, returning to Hannah, who sneers at me from her locker just as Grant approaches.

"Cool video," he says. "A family of paranormal hunters. That's impressive."

I cross my fingers together to form an X.

No monsters. I qualify.

"No paranormal creatures yet," Gabrielle interjects, pretending to sound disappointed that she lost even though that's what we want. We'd discussed that she'd need to maintain her character as a believer despite her loss.

Before Grant can reply, a shrill scream emanates from the science wing. A stampede of people come running around the corner. Students around us run on instinct, despite nothing being visible, while others shout for explanations. "What is it? What's going on?" A few people freeze, only moving as teachers and friends grab them by the elbow and pull them toward us.

Mr. Winer is one of the many shouting for students to clear the hallways, a severe panic darkening his eyes as a lack of recall for school drills may be overwhelming him.

Gabrielle and I look at each other. *There's no way,* I mouth.

"One of them must have gotten into the school."

I guess the sea witch didn't like our little internet debunking stunt and is sending a message.

Gabrielle and I race against the crowd as door after door slams shut and locks click. More than one teacher tries to grab me, stop me, but I duck and dodge them. A stocky woman with short brown hair, known for her fearless ability to jump between two students fighting, catches me by the arm, but I yank free from her. Everyone is too afraid to come after us.

I skid to a halt at the corner and peer down the hall. At the end of the science wing is a creature built like a miniature kangaroo with the head of a hornless goat. It snaps its teeth warningly, and the noise has an unearthly echo to it. But my heart doesn't freeze in fear until it turns, charging toward us backward. It looks unreal, like something seen in a horror movie whose movements seem to defy gravity and speed. Its every movement is stilted the way claymation is stilted. Gabrielle yanks the backpack off my shoulders, which snaps me out of my frozen state though it doesn't erase the fear.

As it gets ever closer, the creature's claws click against the ground like the drumming of angry fingernails.

"Malaya, help," Gabrielle says as if she's already asked me a million times. And maybe she has. Squatting next to her, I grab my stingray whip and a pencil. What is she looking for? I pull everything out of my bag, hoping one of the items will be what wants.

She pulls up the webpage on Fili-pedia Folklore. She must be trying to figure out what the creature is to defeat it, but I have no time for that. I pick my backpack up and throw it at the monster, who slides to the side to avoid being hit.

Clutching Gabrielle, I pull her up as I ditch my stuff. I race back up the hauntingly empty hall, the monster on our heels. It runs just as fast backward as I imagine a dog can run forward.

Gabrielle stumbles, and I fall over her legs. I flip over,

expecting the kangaroo-goat to lunge, but it stops abruptly. It's about five feet away, and its head looks back to bare its fangs menacingly. It stalks toward us, putting its long snout to the ground. The creature's yellow eyes never leave mine, and then it strikes at the air above the ground.

Though he's not near me, there's a searing pain in my right leg. I scream, grabbing my thigh and seeing bite marks. The monster moves forward and strikes again. Though he's not physically touching my leg, the corresponding pain and ripped flesh are his doing.

"Your shadow!" Gabrielle gasps, pointing to the shadow of my leg near the beast's mouth. The beast snaps at my shadow, and its bite is deeper this time. Blood is squirting out of my leg, and my head spins. Only the sound of slippers slapping loudly against linoleum keeps my eyes from closing.

I grip Gabrielle's sleeve. She seems to be shouting directives at someone, but her voice is so faint. She gets up, but I don't want her to leave me. Then I'm dragged backward, my shadow just out of the kangaroo-goat's reach before he can strike again. There's a flash of long, silky black hair and a figure standing in front of me.

Anita?

She throws her hand out to block the beast, and I tell her to run, but I can't be sure if my lips form the word correctly.

"Go," Anita shouts at the kangaroo-goat, though in my ears, it's muffled. The beast immediately starts running backward down the hall. His head becomes smaller the further he gets until he twists around, jumps against the bar of the exit handle to let himself out, and disappears outside.

Seeing that we're safe now, Gabrielle comes down to my level, covering the bleeding wounds with her panicky hands before Anita takes off her sweater to help her wrap it.

Wind presses my hair into my face as a portal opens beside

me. On the other side, Mal lies on the ground, a near mirror image of me, except passed out.

Gabrielle screams, trying to scare off the kangaroo-goat creature from our side of the portal while it tears into Mal's leg and my Gabby's defending arm.

The Gabrielle on my side of the portal starts yelling at the beast the way Anita did, but it isn't fazed. I keep waiting for the other Anita to burst into the scene, but then I remember that I'm not friends with Anita in that life. She probably isn't coming.

Shaking Gabrielle's arm with all my strength, I mouth, *Anita,* and point viciously at the beast.

"Anita, help Mal!" Gabrielle jabs a finger at the portal. Anita jumps to action, commanding the beast to go. It, too, hightails it out of there—obeying her command when no one else's would work.

The wind portal is open wide, but Gabby has to drag Mal's unconscious body to the opening.

How did it open? I've been trying every night to forge the connection, but I hadn't gotten so much as a breeze.

"What?" Gabby asks. There's so much blood she's forced to stop and wrap Mal's leg like mine.

Gabrielle says, "She wants to know how she got the portal to open. She's been trying to open it ever since the last time." I crawl toward the portal's edge, waiting to make an even switch.

"You have?" Gabby's arms pull the sleeves of her hoodie tight around Mal's thigh before she picks her up beneath her armpits again.

"Yes, Malaya's been meditating every night. So why now?"

Gabby hesitates, catching her breath. Her injured arm dripping crimson. "I'm guessing it hasn't worked because of this one." She points with her lips at Mal's still form. Gabrielle stands right next to the portal, wiping sweat from her brow.

What do you mean? I try to ignore the sickening spark of intuition in my gut.

Then Gabby says something I didn't even know I should fear.

"She likes your boyfriend."

chapter twenty-eight

How? How could confident, perfect Mal fall for Ian? And how is there any hope for me when I return?

Mal starts stirring, and the portal begins to shut.

There seems to be some link between her consciously not wanting to return to this life and her actual consciousness. We need to switch places now before she's fully awake.

Switch. Switch. I gesture wildly between the two of us.

But the second Gabby yanks at Mal's body harder, she rouses. Too soon, the portal shrinks, but I'm at its barrier, banging on the invisible line that divides our world as I can't pass through without Mal.

Tell her he's dangerous, I mouth to Gabrielle, forgetting that Gabby never knew the truth about how bad Ian was.

Gabrielle glances at me, then back at Mal. "Uh, uh ..." She scrambles to make her brain work, but she's not fast under pressure. "You have to get Mal away from him. He's abu—"

Before Gabrielle can even complete the word "abusive" the portal warps, distorting her voice.

"What?" Gabby's brow wrinkles, her voice twisting and warbling so that she's barely comprehensible.

Auntie Maggie laughs, and the distortion of it through the portal echoes down the hallway.

I beat on the barrier, urging Gabby to hurry with my waving arms. But Mal's eyes are open, and she's defiantly struggling to break free of Gabby's grasp.

"I won't go," she shouts, slamming the portal shut.

I lunge at the space like if I can grab her, I can stop it from shutting, but instead fall to the ground, pounding the floor.

Gabrielle paces back and forth.

"We have to open it back up again. You have to get her," Gabrielle says.

I open up my notes app and type:

I can't. This whole time, I thought it was just me. That it was only my fault, but it's not. Mal is keeping the portal closed because she doesn't want to come back.

When Gabrielle doesn't fight back or give me that accusatory look I've come to expect, I know she knows it's true.

"What the hell?" Anita startles both of us. "Why wouldn't she want to come back?"

Gabrielle shakes her head, but I think I know.

She likes the life I fucked up because it's giving her permission to make mistakes. Mistakes like Ian. Tita Blessica said she was miserable here with all those expectations. Nobody expects a goddamn thing when you mess up as often as I do. In a way, she's free.

Gabrielle punches a locker, and it echoes through the empty halls.

"Okay, but I have a super serious question." Anita's head

bobbles with attitude. "Why didn't I see my other self on that side?"

Because you and I, I mouth each word slowly, *are not friends on that side.*

"Oh. Sad." She elongates the last word.

I laugh one short time. *It is sad.*

Classroom noise becomes louder as they sense it's over, but the doors stay locked just like they do during lockdowns. Then the sound of heels and dress shoes slap against the floor as the principal, assistant principal, and security speed walk toward us.

"Get up," Assistant Principal Johnson says before she's even reached us. "Come with us to the office, now."

Despite our injuries, Anita, Gabrielle, and I stand as quickly as possible. None of us have ever been sent to the front office before. With each heavy step, a ball of anxiety seems to barrel over my guts.

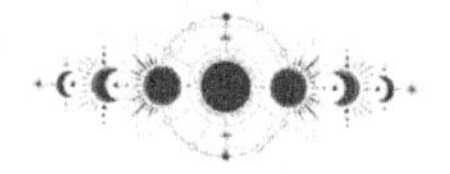

Though the principal was grateful for us removing the monster, he made it pretty clear that we were not to monster hunt on campus again. He then proceeded to call our parents. Unfortunately for us, Dad was the one who answered. Meanwhile, Anita's mom was raging.

The second Mom found out, she called Auntie Perlah to come over to fill her in. They're close in the way our race bonds all Filipinos, but they don't often frequent the same Filipino parties. Anita is instructed via text to follow us home, and before long, we're all gathered in the living room, where Dad and Perlah are told everything.

"All I did," Anita says, explaining her role in the fight, "was tell the creature to leave, and it did. Both creatures because there was one in the other world too. But when Gabrielle tried, it wouldn't. Why did it listen to me?" I sit in silence, hoping someone else has an answer.

Mom clears her throat. "What did you say the creature looked like?"

Gabrielle describes it again.

"Hmm, that sounds like a *Sigbin*," Perlah offers.

Mom agrees. "Malaya, can you look it up on Fili-pedia Folklore?"

Dad shifts in his seat when Mom addresses me by his daughter's name. He's trying not to look at me like I'm an alien, but I'm an alien. I try to find the page as quickly as possible, but my hands fumble over digital buttons.

"It says here that there are families called *Sigbinan* who possess the power to control these creatures. To contain them, a *Sigbinan* can keep the *Sigbin* in a jar."

Perlah shakes her head. "I don't know what that is. I came to America when I was practically a baby."

"So, no family history of being a *Sigbinan*?" Gabrielle asks.

"If there is, no one told me." Perlah throws her hands up like she's going to have words with her mother.

"Well, if all it takes is a jar, I can put the creature in there. But it'll have to be a big jar. That thing was like a mid-sized dog." Anita uses her hand to show how tall the creature is.

"Mmm, mmm, no." Perlah wags her finger as she gathers her purse and her daughter in one arm. "You are not going around those ... those things again. Look at Malaya's leg."

Dad flinches again, and I strongly suspect it's at the use of my name and not the heavily bandaged wound on my leg that's seeping blood. I can't be the only one who notices.

"But Mom, I'm the only one who can command it. Unless you want to give it a try."

"Nobody has to command it. Let the government deal with it." She starts cussing in Filipino, and even Mom flinches.

Perlah and Anita are nearly to the door, arguing the whole way when Mom stands.

"Perlah. I understand why you would not want to put your daughter in danger. I do not want to put my kids in danger either. *Pero* ... my Mal is on the other side, fighting these creatures without me. And I'm only trying to get her back. I know this is a lot to ask for. But the more creatures we can keep from the public, the less power the sea witch has to complete her plan."

"Floribeth," Perlah says, shaking her head. Both women have tears in their eyes because the burden of asking for a favor and refusing a favor in the name of someone's child is too significant. And yet Perlah nods once, sniffling.

Mom thanks her as she walks them out. However, when she returns, Dad is up and pacing. Whatever he's thinking, it's not good.

Mom tells us to leave, but I still catch the front end of it as he says, "How could you ask her to do something like that for a stranger?"

And who is that stranger? Why, it's me, forever the stranger in this house.

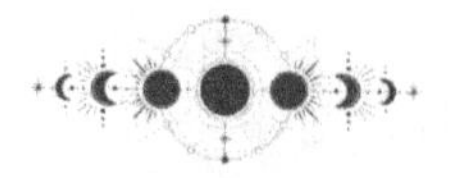

Salvador pulls up outside of the house later that night. I let Mom know he's here and promise we're not going anywhere. I just need the company of someone who is not family ... or whatever I have in this house.

We sit in the driveway, soaking in the truck's coconut-scented A.C. and some *Matt and Kim* jams. I'd never heard of them before, but it's happy music, which I need right now.

"The other Mal and your ex?" he asks as if picking up in the middle of a conversation I'd thought we'd finished.

Yep. One side of my mouth lifts in disbelief.

"Are you jealous?"

I don't even have to think about it. *Not even a little.* Honestly, if anything, I'm scared for her.

He nods, his expression distant.

"I almost lost you today." Salvador's hand twitches like he wants to reach for me but restrains himself.

I didn't die. I prop my injured leg up on the dashboard. Extra gauze from my poor wrapping job flaps in the A.C. Salvador turns the vents to a lower setting.

"No, I mean, to the other side."

He looks at me through thick, bone-straight eyelashes with uncertainty I've never seen before. He's usually so self-assured, and it makes me want to smooth his frown lines.

Oh … yeah …

"You were just going to leave without saying goodbye?"

It's not like I can open the portal at will.
When the time comes, I'll have to take it.

"I hate that." He grips the phone in his fist, his eyes meeting mine.

Why?

"Don't act like you don't know why," Salvador says, disappointed. "At any moment, you're just going to leave, and I'll never see you again. You know why I hate that."

My heart races because he's saying a lot without really saying much. I find myself hoping he means that he'll miss me as more than just a friend, but I'm not confident enough to jump to that conclusion as the gods' words about our fates never being meant to cross paths replay in my head.

"Would you hate it too?" he asks.

I nod, my body tense.

"Then … don't leave." His words low, hesitant.

I have to. I turn to face the windshield and slump in my seat. Thinking of how Mal and I can't exist in the same timeline. Of how she deserves this life—not me. Of how I have to save her from Ian before it's too late.

"I know." He grips the steering wheel because he had to know that would be my answer.

"I'm torn between kissing you every day like it's our last day until you're gone or just leaving this alone."

His expression is grief and hunger as his eyes search mine.

"Both will hurt, but I can't tell which will hurt more."

I get that. I could kiss Salvador every day until it's our last, never knowing if our last kiss is the last one until I'm gone. Or I could never know what it's like to be with him and always ache with wonder.

"What are you thinking?"

I recall our conversation by the SUV before we went to fight the *Berberoka* when he asked me why I wasn't living the life I chose. That question has played like an anthem in my head ever since. I'd been so happy when I'd first gotten here, but there was never a moment in which I wasn't also worried or wondered if I'd made a mistake. I tread lightly in this life, but it doesn't seem to matter because I'm still not quite part of it. I don't know the right answer, but I take his hand and place it over my heart, so he can feel how it beats as quick as lightning.

Our eyes connect, and there's possibility. The risk of making this mistake seems worth all the consequences that could come later. Maybe he sees that in my gaze because he grips the hand I'd pressed over his and pulls me close, pressing his soft lips against mine.

It's a slow, soft kiss. The kind that asks for permission without words.

I lean into him, aching for more, and he matches my urgency. He pulls me to his side of the car like I weigh nothing. I straddle him, breathing deeper as he runs his fingers through my hair. The tank top strap slides off my shoulder as his warm hands run down my arms and up my spine.

This kiss is everything. It's more than I ever thought I could have or need. And it hurts to know I never would have found this in my world because he was never supposed to be mine—that I had to do the impossible to be with even the promise of him. He shouldn't belong to me, yet here he is ... mine.

But before the car windows completely fog over, my guilt-ridden brain starts taking over my heart.

Don't do anything to break this world.

Don't do anything to mess up the plan.

Don't be the reason Mal can't return.

I grip the door handle and pull it open, letting the humid night air hit us.

Though I pull away from Salvador, he draws me in for another kiss. His lips soft and slow. It's hard to let him go. I kiss him back, harder this time, and somehow manage to get off his lap. He's out of the truck with me, pressing me against the door in a series of urgent kisses.

"Not yet," he says when I try to leave.

This is our last kiss, I tell myself, as if I could be leaving tomorrow. I pull Salvador in one last time before letting him go. Then I race into the house.

chapter twenty-nine

With Anita's help, we trap the *Sigbin*, which turned to clay when I herded it into the jar. We also capture and remove a *Pugot*, which nearly snapped Salvador's hand off with its mouth stump, a *Kadu-Kadu*, which Gabrielle wanted to keep as a pet for its adorably tiny body and pointed ears, two *Kapres*, and an infestation of Duwendes in a mansion on Ocean Drive.

I'm pretty tired, but as our views grow, the number of sightings and attacks in the city decreases so significantly that, after the first week, I finally watched an entire newscast that didn't once feature monster sightings. We celebrate with a *cassava* cake.

Perlah is our weapons dealer. As far as she was concerned, her daughter would not face a *Sigbin* with a mere jar in hand. Since they own the city's most popular Filipino restaurant, Anita is a genius with a knife. Her mom procured a *balarao* forged in the Philippines and sold at the Trade Center. After that, acquiring weapons became her obsession, especially after explaining that we were never quite sure what would work on a monster.

"I wish I'd known we would need some authentic Filipino weapons while we were in the Philppines," Anita says. "But

Sinta is sending us a *balikbayan* box full of weapons. I only hope they get here on time."

Mom prefers *Kali,* which is the art of stick fighting. Apparently, she used to practice it when she was younger. My instinct is to believe this is one of those harmless lies Mom tells, like never wave at another car. But she wields the bamboo sticks the way she aggressively handles her Filipino broom. Eric, unable to pick up on any of the training Salvador provided with the *buntot pagi*, quickly swaps the stingray whip out for a *karambit*. It only appeals to him because Perlah described it as curved like a tiger claw.

While heading for our last classes of the day in the math hallway, Anita says, "Mom is looking for something for you and Gabrielle, but weapons are scarce since people believe the monsters are Filipino."

"I can help with that," Grant's voice intrudes from behind us.

Gabrielle jumps, turning instantly on the spot. "Jeez, dude. Make a noise."

"Sorry. I'm pretty light on my feet. Also, it's hard to be any louder in a hallway as noisy as this one." He has a good point. I feel so comfortable talking about this in public because little is heard in a crowd.

"What do you have?" Anita asks, holding both straps of her backpack.

"What do you need? We have knives, spears, swords, and even those little dart things. My dad bought anything remotely Asian within city limits the second the *Aswang* aired on the news."

"*Bagakay*?" Anita asks, and I picture the ten-inch bamboo darts. Anita and her mom have thrown themselves into this.

"Uh, yeah. I guess." He looks at me, his brow raised. "Anyway, it's cool what you guys are doing, taking back the city."

From what? I ask because this is not the first time someone has tried to trick us into admitting that the monsters are real.

"We haven't found anything ... yet," Gabrielle adds, pretending to be annoyed.

"Right," he says, like he's in on it, even though we haven't confirmed anything. It makes me uneasy.

I open the spiral notebook in my arms and write:

The monsters aren't real, but the authentic weapons give the show more credibility.

"Right," he says again. "Anyway, if you need anything, we probably have it. My dad has been charging people a fortune for these weapons, but I bet I could sneak one away for *you*." How he looks at me leaves no doubt that he means me specifically and not the group collectively.

Thanks. I turn to Anita and Gabrielle for clues about how I should respond. I can't believe he'd give us a weapon for nothing.

"What sort of weapon are you looking for?"

"What we could use are *agimats*," Gabrielle explains how I'd been looking for more of these Filipino amulets so obsessively for the last 48 hours, and she's not exaggerating. The second I saw the different kinds on Auntie Perlah's list, I felt in my gut that there would be one that I'd need to win this battle—I just needed to find it. Being with Ian destroyed my abitity to trust my instincts, but the way my blood buzzed when I read about this, I knew it was something I had to have. I nod vigorously, shaking Gabrielle's arm.

"What are those?" Grant's brow raises, amused.

"Like amulets," Anita explains. "They might be on necklaces or just pendants. Sometimes they're clothes ... Oh, and they might—"

"Got it," Grant says. "And yes, we have those."

I jump around, crashing into Anita. Grant laughs, gripping my arm to steady me even though Anita is far worse off.

Agimats are said to give the possessor unnatural power, but the ones I have from Tita Blessica work on a small scale. I've been speculating that these amulets would be incredibly useful if I could get my hands on the right one—not that I know exactly what the right one is yet. When Perlah checked the trade center, Tita Carmen said they were all bought by the same person. I guess I know who that was now.

"I can swipe one for you," Grant says, looking at me.

"But only if it's from Filipino soil," Anita rushes to add. Perlah was very clear about the talisman's potency against mythological creatures if it is from the homeland.

"Gotcha," Grant says, turning back to me. A blush creeps over my cheeks.

I can give you money. I do the universal fingers-rubbing-together sign to signal cash in case he can't follow. Honestly, I'd love to buy several, but Grant waves his hand dismissively.

"Nah, it's cool. I overheard we're forming groups in English tomorrow. Let's team up, and you can pick the object up at my house later."

I want to ask him if I could just come over today since school is almost over, but he says he's busy before I can finish.

"Are you sure we can't just buy it from you?" Gabrielle asks. She looks uncomfortable ... like she doesn't like whatever's going on. Is her intuition flaring, or is it just that she still doesn't want me to form any attachments that might prevent the switch?

"No," Grant says a little harshly before clearing his throat. "I mean, it's fine."

Grant winks at me before he walks away, and the bell rings. Anita rushes off because she doesn't want to give her mom an excuse to pull her from monster hunting. I turn toward my class as well, but Gabrielle stops me.

"I don't like this," she says, ignoring her teacher calling for her to get to class.

Pulling my spiral away from my chest, I jot down:

I know Mal was dating him, but I don't like him like that.

Salvador's kisses are still hot on my lips—kisses behind closed doors, stolen in small moments of seclusion, swift pecks, and long make-out sessions. Gabrielle misinterprets my flushed cheeks.

"That's not really what I'm talking about. This just feels ... weird."

I nod.

I got that feeling too.

My gut says I could use an *agimat,* even if there's just one.

"Gabrielle," her teacher calls again.

"I'm coming, I swear." Gabrielle flashes her teacher one of those winning smiles. "Malaya's just telling me how to solve for x."

"That's not—" Gabrielle's teacher starts but rolls her eyes as she realizes Gabrielle's joking. "I'm marking you tardy." Then she closes the door. My math teacher is calling attendance, and I'm sure my name is coming up.

It will be fine, I say, using Grant's words as I grip Gabrielle's shoulders. Then I rush to class just as my teacher calls my name a second time.

Though we did group up in English class the next day, Grant makes no plans to meet up at his house, even though Anita and I suggest it. Instead, our little team ends up researching in the library. It feels like a waste of time to our entire hunting party—all except the moms, of course, who expect our grades not to fall despite our new extracurricular activity.

Isn't that just like an Asian mom?

The pressure of time weighs more heavily on us when a dragon-like bird called a *Minokawa* appears on the news later that night, prompting a surge for weapon-related posts on social media. I start to worry that people will buy up all the weapons in Grant's father's arsenal before I ever meet up at his house. Of course, he doesn't know our deadline, which is less than a week away now.

I attempt to gently prod him about the *agimat* when we're in class together or when he randomly shows up at my locker throughout the day to walk me to classes, but he doesn't seem to get the urgency.

"You're dating," Gabrielle says when she joins me at the lunch table.

What? I drop my fork, fumbling wildly to catch it before

it comes crashing down onto my tray with a loud *clang*. Had she seen Salvador and me kissing during training?

"You and Grant," Gabrielle says, opening her milk carton.

"You are?" Anita's eyes are wide. "Because I thought you and S—"

I drop my fork loudly again, this time on purpose. Then shake my head wildly at Gabrielle. *I'm not.*

"Well, he thinks so." Gabrielle stabs the air with her fork.

I scoff. No, Grant couldn't possibly think we were dating. We hadn't even gone out on a date ... Well, he and I hadn't, but he and Mal had. Ah, crap. I recall how he waited for me in the library parking lot this morning to walk me into school and touched a strand of my hair before heading off to class last period. I slap a hand over my forehead.

Oh my god, he thinks we're dating.

"I told you."

What do I do?

Anita laughs while Gabrielle says, "Hell, if I know. I can't get a boyfriend to save my life."

That's not true. Plenty of boys like her, but the only boys brave enough to approach her were boys she didn't like back.

"Dump him," Gabrielle says. "We don't need the *agimat* anyway; the ones we have are fine. Auntie Perlah just found us two *kris* swords. We can wield them like twin warriors." I smile at the idea of her pairing us up that way.

"Your mom has us scheduled to clear several *Lampongs* disguised as white deer out at Duke Ranch tonight." Anita stabs a piece of wet broccoli with a spork. "They don't attack, but when they feel threatened, they might cause illnesses. The *Lampongs* might be less intimidated by the *agimat* than traditional weapons, though no weapons are probably ideal. However, the moms also have us scheduled to take down the *Minokawa* on Saturday, so it's probably best to be as equipped as possible."

I count the days we have left on my fingers.

"That's only two days before the full moon." Gabrielle reads me correctly. "That doesn't give us much time to defeat the dragon bird, so we have to be prepared. Like overly prepared. A weapon in each hand prepared." I laugh at the dramatic way her voice rises with each "prepared."

"The *Minokawa* has been sleeping on top of buildings downtown. It's like a spotlight the way its feathers glow at night." Anita twists the bracelet around her wrist. "That sea witch is pulling out all the stops..."

Okay, I'll ask Grant for the *agimat* again.

"Good." Anita nods, her bangs bouncing against her forehead.

"Fine." Gabrielle stabs at her Frito pie.

"What is up, chica?" Anita asks with lightness in her voice, an effort to keep the peace. Gabrielle sighs while she avoids answering.

She's suspicious of Grant. Also, she doesn't want me dating.

"Seems a little selfish," Anita says, causing Gabrielle to flinch. "That can't be true."

"It's not selfish. Selfish is taking someone else's life and putting them in danger. Putting them in the path of a dangerous person to save themselves."

Unblinking, I lower my gaze.

"Well, that's not fair," Anita says. "You know Malaya didn't do that on purpose. She had no clue—"

"Well, she has a clue now, and she's still doing things that could prevent her from switching back." Gabrielle snaps at Anita before turning to me. "You weren't close to your other family. You stopped identifying yourself by them when you started identifying yourself by that guy. And here you are again, identifying yourself by the guys in your life. You don't know how to be happy without them."

I slam my fork down, and Gabrielle starts. *Enough.*

I've been killing myself trying to fix my mistakes. I've done everything to get your sister back, but she has to want to come back here too. That's why the portal won't open. You know that, but you keep blaming me.

I jab at the send button in our group chat, so both Anita and Gabrielle's phones chime, then continue furiously tapping at the screen, my teeth grinding.

And that's fine. But don't you dare talk to me about how I can't be happy without a guy in my life. I could have been happy in this life with you. But you've rejected me since you found out I wasn't Mal. You are making me unhappy.

Gabrielle's eyes move back and forth over her screen; then she grabs her bag and leaves. My hands shake uncontrollably, so I have to let my phone tumble onto the cafeteria table. I'm breathing so heavily that my nostrils hurt from the cold air of the lunchroom.

"Man, she is wound tightly lately."

Yeah. Will happy-go-lucky Gabrielle ever be the same, even if her sister returns? Or is this one of those things that alters you in the wrong way forever?

"I pictured you with Salvador, myself." Anita swirls the spaghetti and hotdogs her mom packed for her in worn-out Tupperware. It's all about the leftovers today.

I swat at her playfully, making sure Gabrielle is far from hearing or seeing anything.

"Oh my god, I knew it. How long? This whole time?"

The excitement on her face is contagious. How could she possibly know? Salvador and I hadn't spent any more time together. We barely stand next to each other, though I long for those moments when our arms brush.

"The tension is obvious, of course," Anita explains her suspicions. "You may not be my Mal, but you still read like her. I can tell you she never felt as strongly about any guy in this world as you do about him."

My face falls.

I guess Gabrielle has a right to be angry. I shouldn't have gone off like that.

"Oh, she needed to hear that. She's been pretty hard on you. Anyone can see how bad you feel."

I shrug.

I feel guilty because I've been kissing Salvador, and that could mess everything up for Mal's return.

Anita's hands slam on the table, but her eyes sparkle. "Oh my gosh, how was it?"

I blush.

"Okay, okay, don't tell me here." She looks around like anyone could hear us when it's unlikely that anyone can even hear themselves with how loud it is.

"But as for messing things up, I mean ... that's a tough one. I want Mal back too, but not at the expense of making you unhappy. You need help too."

I smile, but it doesn't reach my eyes.

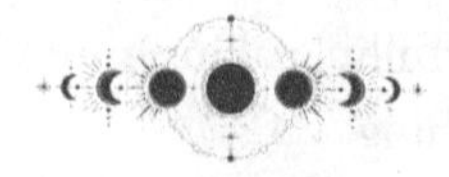

As I suspected, Grant meets me at my locker after school to walk me to my car.

"Ready?" he asks as I mouth a hello.

Yeah. I smile stiffly, feeling like I'm cheating on Salvador even if we aren't officially anything. It doesn't help that I'm nervous about asking Grant again if I can get the amulet.

I hold up my spiral in which I'd pre-written:

Can I come by your house today to buy the agimat?

"I already told you that you don't have to buy it." He focuses on my politeness, ignoring the request.

I turn the page and hold up a different message.

I don't mind paying. I just need it.

He opens the side exit, and I walk through the library parking lot. I don't see Gabrielle anywhere, and she usually beats me here because her class is right beside the exit.

"Don't worry. I'm not going to sell it. We're just swamped right now," he says, leaning against the Mustang.

I want to write "busy with what," but I don't want to be rude to someone who's doing us a favor.

"In the meantime, I can protect you from the monsters." He kisses me on the cheek, and my head jerks back in surprise, pushing him away. I wasn't expecting it, and though I'd felt some attraction to him at one point, I'm more shocked at how I feel nothing at all now. It's like being kissed by my brother.

He turns before I can tell him I don't feel that way about him, but that doesn't stop me from trying to get his attention to set him straight. I grab his arm but let go when Salvador and Gabrielle stand frozen mid-street. Gabrielle's expression is one of fury, and Salvador's ... well, I don't think I've ever felt so much hurt at causing someone else's pain.

In that moment, I've lost them both.

chapter thirty-one

As Gabrielle drives us home to prepare for tonight's filming, I wrack my brain for ways to get through to Salvador. What he saw was me letting Grant kiss me.

I didn't know he was going to do that.

Salvador doesn't meet my eyes from the back seat.

SALVADOR

Are you going to keep seeing him?

I'm not seeing him. I'm just trying to get an agimat. His dad's got all the ones left in the city.

I don't understand why you're suddenly so obsessed with this thing. We've been doing fine with the ones we have.

I have this feeling that I need a different one to defeat the sea witch.

I'm not sure what I need, but my gut tells me I'll know when I see it. I haven't trusted my instincts for a long time, but something tells me not to ignore this feeling.

Well, my gut tells me not to trust this guy. Does that matter?

Of course, it matters. And I don't trust him either. But it's not about him. This is about defeating the sea witch.

He stops messaging me after that, and I'm left with this twisting guilt in my chest that I'm struggling to make sense of. He and Gabrielle are right about Grant. They're worried that I'm trusting him like I trusted Ian and think I'll make those same mistakes. I guess I can't blame them, but I'm also frustrated.

The death wish ensured that I'm not in post-breakup mode with Ian. It gave me instant relief and perspective about my abusive situation that I couldn't see before—perspective on the curse. And yet, the echoes of trauma from that time are still present, because even though it never happened in this life, it did happen.

When I was with Ian, I regularly felt alone ... but I'm not alone anymore. I'm with people I should easily be able to trust. But I'm also trying to figure out who I am, and how much I can trust myself. I'm unsure how to do both ... or if I can. And I can't figure out how to explain this need to trust my gut about the *agimat,* other than to say that to my core, I know I'm right.

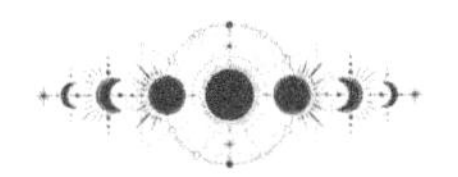

Several unanswered texts later, we walk through Duke Ranch toward the places the ranchers told us the Lampongs were rumored to be last. Eric talks Salvador's ear off about viewers commenting on all the debunking, so I can't talk to him about the Grant situation anymore. Despite my glances, Salvador won't look at me.

"I mean, we're losing people who want to see something real," Eric says, his eyes far away, though I doubt his mind is.

"Isn't that what you want?" Dad asks, holding his shotgun at his side. He had to come out with us because Mom had to work late, but he doesn't have much input unless I wield a weapon wrong. Otherwise, he hangs back to make sure we don't die.

We don't want them believing. I mouth at Dad, but he pretends not to see even though he has to look past me to see Eric as he says, "Yeah, but not at the risk of people going back to the other videos."

He's yet another person who's not talking to me, and I wish I could turn around right now and disappear into the portal. But no matter how hard I try, I can't get it to open. If Gabrielle is working her butt off to get Mal away from Ian, it must not be working.

I touch Eric's arm so he looks at my mouth. *What should we do?*

"I don't know, show something. Leave the episode with a question mark." He shrugs.

"We could let Gabrielle win one." Anita pulls her knees up high as she walks through the tall grass, stickers catching around the ankles of her jeans.

Gabrielle starts to argue, and I'm surprised when Salvador says, "Yeah. We're never going to stop the sea witch if we let people think the monsters are real."

A sharp pain stabs at my heart. Even he wants me to leave now.

"I'm not saying give them proof, exactly. I can still deny it. But flashes of something real would give the show the appearance that Gabrielle is a believer. They're starting to think no one is."

Salvador nods. "I guess we can do that."

The *Lampongs* are some of the easiest and most reasonable mytho-creatures I send back to the underwater realm. They're protectors of wildlife, but they seem to realize fairly quickly that we don't want to hurt the animals on the ranch, either. It is tougher to convince Gabrielle that I need to get rid of them because she's an animal lover, and she knows the *Lampongs* are only trying to save deer from being shot.

Salvador got several shots of the creatures chasing the deer off as we approached. I peek at the shot from over his shoulder, but he shuts the camera off.

"Do you think this episode is going to be too short?" Eric asks. He had a good point because finding these creatures didn't take long.

"Yeah, we'll probably have to combine it with another hunting."

"Why don't we shoot something out here while we're here? We can pretend to see another shapeshifter and hunt for it, but it can turn out to be ... I don't know ... just a raccoon or whatever wildlife we see out here."

"Uh, yeah," Salvador says. He's usually so agreeable, but he's a million miles away. Still, he rallies for the team, consulting Mom on the phone about what creatures lurk in wooded areas as he looks over at some patches of forest in the distance.

My role today has been reduced to crap holder. I pull up the monster website on my phone and pass it to Gabrielle, who mutters thanks. Anita rolls her eyes but doesn't know what happened with Grant. She only knows there's a weird vibe.

"What about the *Nono*," Gabrielle says.

"*Nuno*," Anita corrects her pronunciation.

"Sorry." Gabrielle grins sheepishly, a lightness in her voice reserved for anyone but me.

"Okay, what are they?" Salvador asks like he's in a hurry. He pulls out his phone, texting someone, and the burning sensation of jealousy hardens my insides when my phone doesn't vibrate with a response.

"A *Nuno* is an elderly spirit living in forests, usually in mounds of dirt like a giant anthill. They cause physical illness to trespassers."

"Great, let's go." Salvador tucks his phone in his pocket, rushing like he's got places to be.

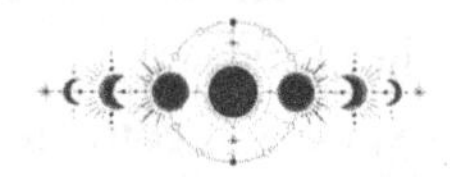

When filming is over, I walk back through the field. We're less like a team than we were before the team was even a thing. There's a disconnection that even the fireflies between us can't draw lines to.

The ride home is silent, with Anita and Eric eyeing everyone.

I address Anita's questioning eyes with a shrug as she looks back at me from her place next to Salvador in the middle row. Again, I can see him messaging, and it's not to me.

Will you talk to me, please?

SALVADOR

...

I care about your family, but I don't think I can be around you, so I can't come to hunts anymore. I've trained you well enough to shoot the footage. Have Eric send it to me, and I'll still work with him in post to get everything edited and uploaded.

My stomach drops as I read the words, and a sickness spreads throughout my body. I reread the message to make sure I didn't misread things, and it's torture all over again. I try to get Salvador to look at me, but he's like a statue, cold and unmoving.

When Dad parks at Salvador's dorm, I reach for my seat belt, determined to talk to Salvador somehow, but he's out of the van and jogging toward his place before I can move.

Olivia waves at him from the sidewalk, and he drapes his arm around her shoulders as they head up to his place. It feels like I've swallowed whole boulders as Dad pulls away.

chapter thirty-two

The next day Grant comes by my locker. I'm alone, of course, because Gabrielle has figured out a way to access her locker around my schedule so that I rarely see her. The sight of Grant makes me sick, and I try to ignore him as he talks to me, hoping he gets the hint that I'm not interested.

If he notices my lack of interest, he doesn't let on. Later, in English, he tells the group we should meet at his house. Anita taps me with her pencil to see if I've heard because I'm just staring straight ahead. I nod, and Grant leans over. "I set aside the *balarao* for you."

My gaze narrows because I know he can't seriously think I want a *balarao* after all this time. *Agimat,* I mouth.

Anita, listening in, gently nudges. "I think she needed the *agimat*."

"Right. Yeah, I set that aside."

Was he kidding right now? He didn't even remember what I'd been offering to pay for? And here I was, ruining relationships for this.

I get a very Ian-like feeling about the whole situation.

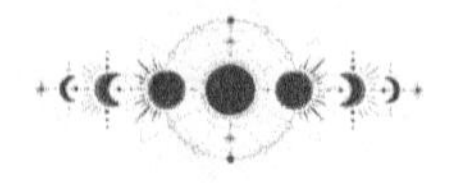

Grant's house is located in one of the nicest neighborhoods in the city, far from Laguna Shores' school district. He must pay tuition to go to our school.

I brought money for the *agimat*, even though he doesn't need it by the looks of his McMansion. Still, I intend to give it to him to clarify where I stand on this non-relationship. And if he doesn't take it, I'm going to stash the money somewhere and text him its location after I've left.

Gabrielle drops me off before rushing to bring Eric to a gaming session at his friend's house. He needs to make sure his first following as a gamer isn't lost just because he'd been caught up in our web series. And Anita has to help her mom with the dinner rush at the restaurant, but she swore she'd be here as soon as possible. When Grant answers the door, he goes in for a hug. I put my arms up between us, but he laughs.

"You're so awkward." He tousles my hair in what I think he imagines is cute, but my wavy hair doesn't move gracefully. It tangles.

He guides me in, giving me a tour of his house, but I quickly notice that none of our other group members are here. His mom, Karen, is cooking in the kitchen. When she sees me, she looks away, taking two large gulps of her wine.

Only after she sets down the empty glass, does she wipe her hands to say hello.

I immediately sense that she disapproves of me, though I cannot pinpoint why. I'm not dressed in any way that's too revealing or loud. Mom in every life has never liked that. I smile and respond to her questions as politely as possible.

There's an exhale of impatience as I long-hand some of my responses, but I tell myself that maybe it has nothing to do with me, even though my mind wants to go to negative places. Karen is still wearing office attire, so perhaps she's tired from a long day at work.

Then Grant's father, Ken, walks in, setting his leather

work bag down. He nods a greeting to me, and they share a wide-eyed *look-at-this-one* glance. They seem to be under the impression that just because I can't speak, I can't interpret the head-tilt in my direction.

What the hell?

"We better hurry up and eat," Karen says, grabbing two plates and carrying them to the dining table. "We don't have enough for all your little friends."

I try my best to shut my dropped jaw though my thoughts uncontrollably ask, "Are you kidding me?"

I'd never heard of people rushing to eat so they didn't have to feed guests. My mom would never do that if company was coming over. If she didn't have enough of the food she was making, she would start making another dish. Or she would order food from somewhere. That was just a thing I thought everyone did, but this seemed like a regular thing as Grant doesn't bat an eye. He grabs his dish and starts scooping generous portions of food onto his plate before heading to the dining room. Having not expected to eat, I try to mouth, *It's okay. I'm not hungry.*

If they needed to save food, I wasn't going to take it from them. Karen stares at my mouth like I'm a simple-minded person she's tolerating. I can't help but wonder if it's my voicelessness or something else about me that bothers her.

"Don't be silly." She hands me a plate.

I eat quickly, which is not something I'm used to. I'm a notoriously slow eater. However, I do what I'm told.

What time had Grant told everyone else to come? Why was I the only one here when he said come over at five? I want to ask him, but I don't know how in front of his parents. Finally, someone rings the doorbell, and Karen gets up to clear everyone's plates while Grant gets up to answer the door. It's 5:45. A whole 45 minutes after Grant told me to be here.

Karen clears her throat, looking at me. I'd picked up my

plate to clear, but she smiles stiffly, looking at Grant's plate. She's grabbed her husband's dishes, and she expects me to grab Grant's. Of course, as a guest, I don't mind helping out. But it's the serving-a-man expectation that makes my nostrils flare. I turn back to get the plate and help clear the dining table for our group project.

I work for another hour and a half. Anita is the last to arrive but stipulates that she's only thirty minutes late. He must have rescheduled the time behind my back so that I could have dinner with his family. Obviously, he hadn't told his mom, which might be why she seems to hate me. It doesn't matter, though because I'm not trying to be a part of another family that doesn't like me. I'd gotten enough of that with Ian's family.

My phone chimes, and then my pulse quickens. Gabrielle and Salvador are on their way to pick us up. It must be bad if he's coming. There's a mess of *Wakwak*s fighting for territory with the *Minokawa* as they circle the buildings downtown. And a rumor that they're scooping up victims as they flee from the bird-like creatures. Anita packs up quickly, rushing home to gather weapons to meet up as soon as possible. The monsters are becoming more public, and I can't help but think the witch is sending out the worst to pump up her power for the big night. It's a relief that I will soon be out of this luxuriously oppressive atmosphere.

Heading for the door, I pass the living room and overhear, "How can we let him traipse around with one of them?" Karen's voice carries into the foyer. "They're the reason the city's gone to s.h.i.t."

The conversation is so audible it seems meant for me to hear. Grant's parents don't dislike me because I bombarded on their family dinner. They dislike me because I'm Filipina.

"How can we let him traipse around with *one of them*?"

Karen's voice carries into the foyer. "They're the reason the city's gone to s.h.i.t."

"I'll talk to him," Ken assures her.

I pull my backpack higher on my shoulder as I stand at the entryway. I look around as obviously as possible because I don't see the *agimat* anywhere. If Grant hears a thing, he certainly doesn't act like it. He ushers me outside and closes the door behind him. It's like we've just ended a date I never agreed to, and he's standing there waiting for his goodnight kiss or something.

I mime putting on a necklace, mouthing, *agimat?*

"Seriously?" Grant says, shaking his head. "Is that all you want from me?"

Yes, feels like the wrong answer, even though it's the right one.

"Wow. I can't believe you were using me to get something."

My jaw drops. *Are you kidding?* My head shakes with every word. I pull out my phone, typing furiously fast.

You were the one who offered it to me. I didn't come looking for you to get it. I even offered to pay. If you didn't want to give it to me, you should have just said.

Grant scoffs as he reads my message. "I thought you were better than that."

Oh my god. Am I a magnet for these crazies? What is happening right now?

Headlights come around the corner, flashing us in the eyes before pulling up alongside the street. Salvador is looking straight ahead, gripping the steering wheel. Meanwhile, Gabrielle is waving for me to hurry.

"Is that your boyfriend? Is that the guy you want to be with, but you just strung me along to get a weapon?"

I shake my head, incredulous.

> I spent days waiting on you to bring that agimat. My life and the lives of my family are in danger because people like you hoard things and then lord it over everyone.

"Oh, is that right? Because I thought you were proving there are no monsters."

You know what? Just forget it. I fold my arms across my chest and start for my ride.

Grant calls out, "She told me you would do this. That you would choose him, and you were just using me."

I face him, my skin prickling. *Who?*

"This lady who's been messaging me—Maggie. She's even sent me something to prove you've been lying to everyone." He pulls out a small wooden whistle and blows.

A screech pierces the night sky, and a bird-like creature, similar to what Gabrielle described as the *Wakwak* in her message earlier, appears in the sky above the front yard as if traveling through an invisible portal. It swoops down, and I duck, narrowly avoiding its talons which camouflage almost perfectly to the night sky.

Grant falls back into his front door, his eyes searching the sky as the *Wakwak* circles around. Salvador, having looked over, notices the panic on my face as I try to pull my backpack off. I need something to fight the *Wakwak*, but what?

"I knew y'all were lying. I knew *Debunking the Aswang* was a cover-up, and now I have proof."

I want to punch him in the face if only to get him to shut up, but when I turn around, he's pointing to the security camera outside of his front door.

"Anyone who sees that video of you ducking from that bird demon will know you can see it. They're all going to wonder how someone like me caught a video of a paranormal creature when hunters like you are out there with your fancy equipment can't catch a damn thing."

I grab the front of his shirt, mouthing threatening nothings, but he pushes me off him just as his eyes widen at the sky. The *Wakwak* swoops down, narrowly missing me and clawing at Grant, who twists his door handle, falls inside, and kicks the door shut, leaving me alone with the monster circling above me again.

It swoops down faster this time, but the audible click of Grant's front door lock seems louder than the *Wakwak's* screech. I cover my head with my arms, ready to be swept away, but warm arms scoop me up.

Salvador must have raced across the yard, endangering himself to get to me. The bird-like creature's wings beat wind against our heads, but Gabrielle is shooting darts at it from the passenger side window of Salvador's truck.

Gabrielle is reloading, so she doesn't see the *Wakwak* coming up behind her.

Duck! I stab a finger downward, and she slides back into the truck.

Salvador throws me into the front seat, and Gabrielle yanks me to her. The truck speeds out of the neighborhood in reverse, and though we don't lose the *Wakwak*, eventually, it gives up—for now.

"We can't go out there with a swarm like this. There are too many of them," Gabrielle says as Salvador cuts a corner through a fancy yard.

"They seem to be increasing with nightfall. It may be better to search for a nest during daylight. We need to ask your mom to let us skip school," Salvador says, including himself in that permission.

Gabrielle gasps playfully, knowing Mom would never allow something like that.

"How could that guy just leave you out there?" Salvador asks, then turns to Gabrielle. "He locked the door on her."

Gabrielle nudges me, and I meet her with a tear-filled gaze.

"Hey, what's wrong? Did it get you?" Her eyes are concerned as she searches for scratches, but I've come away completely unharmed from the *Wakwak*.

What's happened is much worse than any physical wound.

Grant had a video of me acknowledging a *Wakwak*. The creatures fill the night sky, and each sighting gives the sea witch the strength to multiply them. After days of fighting against Auntie Maggie, fighting monsters, planning attacks, building a following, I'd undone it all in one video. A video that Grant would surely put up because I'd hurt his pride. And when he does, everything we've worked to accomplish will be undone.

I pull my legs up and bury my head in my arms, blocking out this world.

chapter thirty-three

Salvador drives us, not home, but to Bob Hall pier. It's not *our* beach. The dock is so long that the end is shrouded in fog. I sit in the cab of the truck parked in the parking lot and cry.

Gabrielle pulls me to her side, stroking my hair.

"I'm just going to step out and give you two a moment," Salvador says.

I peer up through the windshield, looking for *Wakwaks*, but the skies are clear. They seem to be loving the downtown scene where all of the spectators are.

"Why don't we take a walk instead," Gabrielle says, poking at my balled up legs. "Before Malaya gets stuck like this, and we have to roll her into battle."

When we get out, Salvador hands me every weapon in the truck and even buckles my utility belt to my hips. I head to the shoreline, where the water touches my toes, and drop the weapons at my side.

When I'd told them what happened in the truck, Gabrielle kept refreshing her social media apps until she'd found Grant's video posted with the title "Monster Hunters Debunked." I'd expected her to explode, to tell me I'd ruined everything, but she just looked out the window at the starry sky like she was trying to work out math problems using the stars.

You were right about Grant.

"Here's the thing." Gabrielle hugs her knees. There's something very different about her now. She's somber, but there's a lightness in her watery eyes. "This increase in *Wakwaks* cannot possibly be your fault. At the rate these monsters were multiplying before this video posted, it's clear the sea witch's powers are only on the incline."

"But the show. How can we go back and say these monsters don't exist?"

Gabrielle shrugs. "Maybe we don't." She lies back in the sand, her fingers laced behind her head. "I'm so exhausted from fighting this. And we did so much. But the truth is, even if we debunk all the monsters and stop the witch from entering the drylands, Mal has to want to return. You can't even open the portal unless she's knocked unconscious, and for some reason trying to get her in her sleep isn't working."

What are you saying? Should we give up?

Gabrielle sighs.

"I'll never give up on Mal." Gabrielle pulls me down into the sand, and I turn on my side to face her, my hands in prayer as I lay on them. She seems to like being the big sister. Meanwhile, I'm small and exhausted.

"Bentley was killed today." Gabrielle turns into the sand, her body convulsing with sobs. I sit up, throwing my arms over her, and she cries into my knees. "It was that damn boyfriend of hers. He got out of jail early, but none of us knew."

My lungs constrict as I try not to drip tears over Gabrielle's face.

Eventually, she sits up, a calmness washing over her though she's pulled herself into a ball. "I just realized how ridiculous

I've been. How selfish. All you wanted was a fresh start. And I took away your chance to figure that out here. I wasn't the sister you needed."

I place a hand on her back, and she stops rocking. Forcefully, I shake my head, trying to get her to understand that she doesn't need to feel that guilt, but her eyes are far away.

She sniffles. "I should have been encouraging you to explore other relationships here so that maybe you wouldn't fear going back and trying again. I was just so afraid that you would be too happy here that I didn't see how much you were doing for me until you were attacked in front of Grant's house. You could have died too." Her voice breaks, and she sobs again so that I barely understand her as she says, "He shut that door on you and left you alone, but so had I."

Tears fall down my face, but I wipe them quickly before the wind blows sand into my eyes.

"I'm so sorry," Gabrielle says. "And I don't want to stand in the way of you living your life anymore. We never know how long we have."

One more day. I point at the moon, a silver orb above the ocean.

"I hope. But I'll figure out a way to be okay if not." I forgot she has no clue the gods are coming after me if I fail.

She gets up, dusting herself off above me, so I have to cover my face. I sit up when sand stops pelting me, only to see her running to Salvador. He gets out of the truck like there's a monster, and I stand quickly, looking around.

She gets in the truck, and he walks toward me, his hands in his pockets. He stands close, looking down at me with those beautiful cedar eyes. "Is it true you were never dating him?"

I nod, and he pulls me to his chest, but I hold him at a distance.

Olivia?

"She's dating my buddy. I just saw an opportunity to make you jealous. Childish, I know." He apologizes. "Do you think you can forgive me?"

It was childish but not unforgivable—especially considering the time I have left here, whether I fail or succeed. Our days together are numbered. I pull him closer. A mess of sand flies off me, and I laugh.

"I wish I could hear you laugh." I touch his face, and he leans into my hand. "I wanna be yours," he says.

Then he presses his soft lips against mine, and the whole world feels like it belongs to me.

chapter thirty-four

It's late by the time I get home, but Salvador still comes in with us because tomorrow is the full moon: the night we face the witch.

Muffled talking and weapons clinking alert me that the whole house is awake and congregating. I drop Salvador's hand at who's waiting in the living room: Tita Blessica.

Mom's arms cross, and her lips purse. This isn't *their* Tita Blessica. It's *mine.* I gasp, taking a step back. And then, though it doesn't make sense, and though I should be severely angry with her, I'm so happy to see someone from my world that I hug her.

To my surprise, Tita Blessica cries.

I pull back to look at her, and she sits me down on the giant ottoman next to her.

A lot of guilt pours from her lips, as well as heartache and the determination to make things right. She briefly explains how she and the Tita Blessica from this world exchanged places for her to be here, though she doesn't discuss what it cost her.

"I just wanted people to see that we have culture. We are more than ... well, it doesn't matter now. Everybody knows about our culture now, and they still hate us."

"I don't hate you guys," Salvador says, organizing the equipment we'll need for tomorrow.

How is my family? I ask.

"They are so mad at me. But otherwise, good. I want you to know how sorry I am for the danger I put you in. I thought the sea witch would take your voice and fix your life. I thought she would break the curse and make you happy, and I would get what I wanted too. I never thought ..."

Her eyes well up again.

"Anyway, I brought you something from the other side. Something you can use to help you fight the witch."

Tita Blessica holds up a polished rock.

"It's a rose quartz *agimat* from the Philippines. The Tita Blessica here explained that you were looking for amulets, and this one was calling out to me. It is supposed to be more powerful if it passes down a family line. You know, I always thought of you like family."

Wow. I hold it in my hand while Gabrielle comes to get a closer look. In my gut, it feels like the *agimat* I've been looking for.

"Did you bring me one too?" Gabrielle asks, laying on a thick layer of guilt.

"No, I'm sorry," Tita Blessica says. "But Mal is wearing a matching one."

"So she's still fighting the monsters?" Gabrielle asks, a note of hope in her voice.

What about Ian? I cringe, having only said his name one other time since entering this world because of the knife-like stabbing it causes throughout my body.

"Your mother is about to kill that boy," Tita Blessica says, shaking her head with disapproval. "She suspects that he is sabotaging their hunts, but Mal loves him. The curse has gotten her as well. She doesn't want to believe Ian would do anything to hurt her."

"You tell her to get her butt home." Mom sits forward so fast.

Then she and Tita Blessica argue in Tagalog. Gabrielle and I look uneasily at each other.

"Wait?" Gabrielle gasps. "What did you say his name is?"

"Ian," Tita Blessica says for me.

"Nooo," Gabrielle cries, standing immediately and pulling out her phone. "Is it this Ian? Tell me it's not him."

She holds up a picture of a mug shot, and my heart stops. I had pretended that Ian didn't exist in this world. And it was easy when I didn't see him anywhere. Now, here he was on Gabrielle's phone. A cold sweat flushes my body.

"Yes, that is him. Didn't Malaya tell you?" Tita Blessica tries to hand me the phone, but I cringe away from it.

"She told us about him, but she never said who it was," Mom explains. "We didn't need to know. Why?"

"Because Mom," Gabrielle says, "This is Bentley's boyfriend. This is her killer."

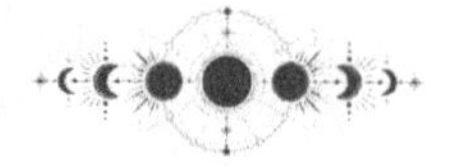

Everyone decides to sleep in the living room as if simply being in each other's presence will make us stronger. But it's more like a sleepover the way we lay across the couches watching movies and snacking on popcorn and pickles.

I'm dangling the soft, pink *agimat* along the ridge of my nose when Salvador pulls it out of my hand.

"Let's see why this thing was such a big deal," he says, pulling me up. He sweeps my hair aside, and the way my cheeks flush makes me embarrassed to meet anyone's eyes. After he puts the *agimat* on me, I wait expectantly for something to happen. The clock's tick-ticking is the loudest thing in the room until I break into silent laughter when nothing happens. Everyone joins me.

Anita shrugs. "I could stab you."

Auntie Perlah gasps then hits her daughter on the knee.

"What? The gift might be protection from bullets and knives," Anita reasons, a playful glint in her eyes.

"What do you say?" Gabrielle reaches for Anita's *balarao* on the coffee table. "Want to find out?"

No, thanks.

"If we had ever caught a *Dalaketnon*, they would be able to tell you exactly what the *agimat* can do for you," Mom explains. "They only need to see you paired with it."

"A *Dalaketnon*?" Gabrielle says, reaching for her phone to pull up Fili-pedia Folklore.

"Don't bother." Eric puts his hand out to stop her. "Anita will tell us about it even if we don't want to hear it."

Anita grabs a throw pillow and pummels him with it.

I want to know. I mouth to Anita, who's laughing good-humoredly.

Anita clears her throat like Mr. Winer calling for the class's attention. "*Dalaketnons* are elf-like creatures with leaf-shaped ears, but they're evil as fu—," Anita stops dead mid-word and looks at her mother, who has taken off her slipper. "Fudge... evil as fudge to ... a ... dieter ..." Amid laughter, I take the slipper out of Auntie's hand and put it back on the floor. "Yep, they're so high up the evil *engkanto* chain that they can control *Aswangs*, *Tiyanaks*, and even *Manananaggal*."

"Dang ... And you want Malaya to talk to one of those. I thought you liked her," Eric says.

"They are perfectly capable of talking to some humans without feasting on them and making them slaves," Mom replies, though she looks sheepish.

Too bad we haven't seen any. I emphasize every word, my eyes rolling, so Anita picks up the sarcasm.

"Don't make me throw a pillow at you," Mom says, reaching for one on the couch. "All I'm saying is it would be easier to figure out your gift if someone could just tell us."

I nod, eyebrows raised.

"What other things can *agimats* do besides protect?" Eric asks, having already admitted that he's jealous and would take it off my hands if I didn't want it.

"Some are used for removing hexes or gaining love," Tita Blessica explains.

"Well, she doesn't need that," Anita says, noticing how Salvador plays with my hair.

Her eager expression says she's dying to know what's changed and that I'll be spilling my guts the second we're alone. My chest is light with the need to divulge everything while also not leaving Salvador's side.

Tita Blessica continues, "But the ones like this, the ones that give a gift, can be as simple as giving luck or as big as invisibility, elemental powers, or healing."

I pretend to shoot fire from my hands, and Eric falls onto the couch. Then, as if in rewind, he's up again and falls to the sofa once more. I tilt my head, confused and amused by his joke.

He gets up, his face scrunched.

"Don't worry," he touches his chest. "You didn't shoot me with elemental magic. I'm just that good an actor."

I know, I mouth, shaking my head. My intuition sparks again, but I can't place why.

All I know is, if there is any magic in this amulet, I hope it presents itself in time for tomorrow's battle.

chapter thirty-five

The sun breaks through the windows before any of us pass out. When I wake again, it's afternoon. Mom is up first, putting the weapons into totes like she's organizing stuff for a road trip. I peek inside one of the totes and see a green bag of garlic cracker nuts—one of my favorite snacks. Mom used to get them for me because I once commented how Ian wouldn't kiss me if I ate them.

I sneak them out of the bag and toss a few into my mouth.

Salvador, the unsuspecting fool, wakes up when I sit down next to him and kisses me full on the mouth.

"What the—?"

I shake the bag at him.

"Hmmm, gross." Then he kisses me again. At least I know he's not a *bampiro*.

As the sun moves across the sky, I go over the plan repeatedly. Checking and rechecking that we have our chosen weapons, that all of us are wearing our shirts inside out, and practicing our pronunciation of *tabi tabi po*, in case we need to be in any mythological creature's favor.

Mom still thinks it's best to prevent as many people as possible from seeing the monsters and giving the sea witch more power despite the overnight spike in believers.

"If we can't open the portal, fine. But we can try to stall

the witch from releasing the *Bakunawa* in this moon cycle if she doesn't have enough power. That will give us another month." It's not a bad plan, hoping for the future. And I don't want to take that hope away, but Salvador had to go and spill the beans about the gods.

"Yeah, except if we don't succeed, then we have the sky and sea gods to contend with," Salvador says like everyone already knows.

"What?" Mom's voice is sharp. "What are you talking about?"

Salvador's face scrunches. "You didn't tell them?" I shake my head. "All this time, I thought you told them."

Salvador quickly explains what happened the day the gods came to talk to us.

"That's why you were so obsessed with getting the *agimat*," Gabrielle says, shaking her head as she looks at the ceiling. "To protect yourself with human magic because they won't touch the stuff."

Yeah, but they pretty much guaranteed that one of them would sacrifice themselves to kill me, so it won't do much good unless it's a protection amulet.

"We better win this thing so we don't have to find out." Gabrielle squeezes my fingers, eyeing the necklace.

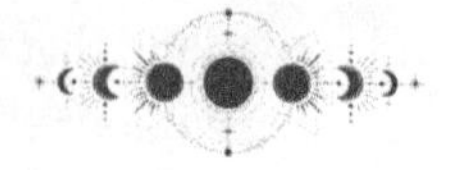

As I pull up to the jetties, the sun is low in the sky. I cross to the far side, where I'd had a death wish. But instead of reminding me of the day I'd felt like I'd lost everything, I'll forever think of it as the place where Salvador pulled me out of the water into this new world I adore and can't imagine leaving.

Everyone hugs, like we're saying goodbye, even though I don't want this to be goodbye. But it is. If this goes the most right, I will open the portal and switch lives with Mal. As far as Tita Blessica is concerned, that is the plan on that side as well. Apparently, I'm missed—something that equally makes my heart ache.

Light glints off Gabrielle's *kris*, and we clink our swords. Salvador squeezes my hand and then pulls me in for a kiss.

"I wanted to do that the first time I saw you, but you know ... that would have been a creep move."

Yeah, I mouth. *But me too.*

He lets go of my hand, gripping his stingray whip and making sure the crab secured to his belt is covered so the thing can't pinch him.

Eric musses my hair, and Dad presses his hands on my shoulders.

"You're alright, kid," he says. I know it's tough for him to express because ... feelings, but he did it anyway.

Auntie Perlah hugs me tight, and Anita cries on my shoulder.

Finally, it's Mom's turn.

"If you could figure out a way to stay," her voice breaks. "If I could have you both."

Tears are streaming down my face. I wish I could stay so badly, and I don't even feel guilty for it this time because it's possible to want both. Just like I'd learned from Ian that it's possible to love someone and not want them. I'd learned that it's possible to want to be somewhere and still want to leave. Because you know it's what's best for everyone. Because you know it's what's best for you too.

I love you too.

We stand on the shore, not unlike surfers in a line. I have

Gabrielle and Mom on one side and Salvador on the other. Tita Blessica stands behind me and points to the water.

"There." Her finger shakes, but I still follow it to a dark spot in the waves.

I walk to the water and see the sea witch beneath its surface. She bangs on the water like it's bullet-proof glass. She can't get out yet, but she's close.

Laughter erupts from the ocean. She's positively gleeful at how close she is to what she wants.

"Malaya. Come to welcome me to the drylands!"

Golden water bursts through the surface and hits me in the chest, soaking my front side.

"What the—"

My thoughts project from me in that ethereal voice that is not my own. Several of my people gasp, having not experienced it before.

"Just give up, *Anak*," Auntie Maggie says. "Save your family and friends before it's too late."

"And how many people will get hurt once you're on the drylands?" I ask.

"I'll make you another deal. Go home now, let me be, and I'll spare all your friends and family. *All* of them."

By emphasizing "all," she's including Mal.

This can't just be my choice, so I turn to my people. But they shake their heads no, telling me not to listen to her. And I know that even if we're safe, I'll never be able to live with myself when other people die at her hands.

"Suit yourselves," the sea witch says, not waiting for my response.

The water seems to vibrate, and I take several steps back as dark figures, large and small, appear in its depths.

As the first beasts emerge from the water, I get in a fighter's stance.

A *Kapre*, usually known as a gentle giant, is ordered to attack us. Salvador, Dad, and Eric all charge forward, trying to contain the monster before he's even made it to land because they know he's weaker in the water. A horde of *Duwendes* burst from the sea and race toward Mom, who starts chanting *tabi tabi po*, before scooping them up into empty rice sacks. They snap at her fingers, and more than a few Filipino curses fly out of her mouth. Perlah and Anita hang back as they fire slingshots of fiery salt rocks at the *Wakwaks* circling low above us. Gabrielle and Tita Blessica throw short spears at the *Sirenas* when they emerge from the water singing their hypnotic song.

"Plug your ears," I shout to everyone, grabbing the earplugs from my pockets and shoving them into my ear canals. My knees are still a little weakened from the *Sirenas'* song, but I stand straight as a *Tiktik* crawls out of the ocean, dripping black liquid.

It seems fitting that the *Tiktik*, which I so feared in my other life, would be the *Aswang* I face in this one. It taps into my nightmares as we link eyes, forming the humanoid bird-like creature I've always dreaded.

It shakes the glistening saltwater from its black wings as it makes a clear path toward me. I'm hypnotized by the beast whose eyes seem to be telling me to stand still. That this would all be over soon. *TIK TIK*, its voice booms.

I sheath my sword, pulling the *buntot pagi* from my utility belt and whipping it open. But as I race toward the tall drink of nightmare, it turns to attack Salvador and Eric, who are preoccupied with the *Kapre*.

The *Tiktik* swipes at Dad, who'd knelt to pull the lasso he used to rope the *Kapre* tight. He flies across the beach, lying on his back and groaning in pain. Eric grabs the lasso, dodging the *Tiktik* before it can hit him too.

"Felipe, come." The *Tikbalang* emerges from the ocean's

depths, galloping across the water and scooping me up from the beach as I run him toward the *Tiktik*.

Tik Tik. The noise softens on our approach, but the beast still doesn't turn toward me, bee-lining for Salvador. I race around the *Kapre* and the *Tik Tik*, and I whip it with my *buntot pagi*. It hollers in searing pain but rises from its knees two seconds later.

As the *Kapre* untangles itself from the rope, it makes its way fast for the road leading to town. Salvador gets on the *Tikbalang's* back, and the *Tiktik* takes off after us as I try to contain the *Kapre*.

I fly by Mom, who's covered in little bite marks. She's roped off several rice sacks and left them in the sand to join Gabrielle and Tita Blessica as they fight off the *Sirenas*. But the scaly women keep throwing the spears right back at them. A spear strikes Gabrielle's arm, and she cries out in pain. The *Tiktik* grabs Auntie Perlah with its long backward limbs and smashes her into the ground.

"We have to get the *Tiktik* to chase us instead." I turn us around, forgetting the *Kapre* as I whip the beast again. It leaves Auntie Perlah, and Anita drops the slingshot to grab her mom.

TIK TIK. Tik Tik. tik tik.

"Don't look it in the eyes. It will hypnotize you."

"Okay, then how will we know if it's following us?" Salvador darts a *Pugot* who'd burrowed past the shoreline and come up with a mouthful of sand.

"If the sound is loud, that means it's far away, and if its sound is quiet, that means it's close by," I shout.

"What the hell? How can we escape a monster that wars with my instinct to run from scary sounds?"

"By denying our usual instincts." I try to convey that I understand this is weird, but we have to do it. However, I'm unsure if the message lands because I'm suddenly aware of the absence of noise. It's as if the beast has canceled out the noise of the waves, the weapons clashing, and my family and friends screaming. I strain my eyes while listening for the direction I should run toward.

"Do you hear anything?" My heart beats wildly.

"No," he whispers. Even the sound of his word seems to lack life.

I grab the *Tikbalang's* mane and turn right into the face of a gruesome, winged human, keeping my gaze down. Its putrid breath smells of decaying flesh, and its drool consists of human blood and bile. Each bone in its spine cracks as it slowly stands to its full height.

Tik tik.

Felipe rears up, and Salvador and I fall backward onto the sand. I try to get up, to push myself away, but I can't seem to get traction.

"Run!" I shout at Salvador and Felipe as the bird-footed monster shuffles forward.

"Not without you!" Salvador picks me up from behind, pulling me to my feet.

I race back toward the water, jumping over driftwood, and slipping on thick pockets of soft sand, all in an attempt to be at the height of the monster's *TIK TIK* as it booms so I know we've put enough distance between the beast and us.

Lightning flashes and the winged creature glides above us. When it lands in front of us, it doesn't strike me. It reaches over my head to Salvador, lifting him high into the air and threatening to pierce him with its proboscis. I grab the barbed part of my stingray whip and stab the beast in the chest. It drops Salvador at my feet, writhing in the frothy ocean foam on the shoreline before collapsing into a motionless heap.

I kneel beside Salvador, bleeding from his side, then look at everyone on the beach, injured and hurt. Everyone is in pain, though they are still fighting—everyone but me.

"Stop," I shout, turning to the ocean. "Stop!"

But the fight doesn't come to some grinding halt. The battle goes on around me, and beasts come traipsing out of the ocean right past me as if I'm nothing. But I'm not nothing. Why are they attacking everyone but me?

"They can't kill me, can they?" I yell across the waves to the sea witch, who peers at me as if through a window.

She doesn't answer. Growing suspiciously still.

I laugh.

"This whole time these monsters were attacking, they were never going to hurt me. They couldn't because if they killed me, you would lose my voice. You would lose the ability to release them. You hear that, Yanny? Kaptan? If you want this to end, all you have to do is kill me."

Atop the dunes, Kaptan and Yanny appear, their clothes billowing in the breeze. Salvador and I look at each other, and he throws his weapons far from his body, preparing to make it as hard as possible for the gods to kill me if they possess him.

Salvador falls to his knees, and I collapse as he groans in pain.

"What's happening?"

Salvador squeezes his head. "Yanny is trying to influence me to do his will," he says through clenched teeth. When Salvador meets my eyes, they flicker like a tv screen, changing to Yanny's sea green color, then back to Salvador's warm cedar.

"Why are you fighting them?" Back when they'd possessed him to question me, it had been so easy for them. Is it hard now because Salvador is aware and fighting?

"Don't put me through this."

I don't know if he's talking to Yanny or me, but I press my forehead to his, and together we make magic. Gold light flashes between us, and Salvador falls to the sand, breathing but free from the fight. Kaptan grabs Yanny, who almost topples off the dune, and I'm sure they can hear me when I whisper, "Of course, I couldn't let him live with this nightmare, with this kind of regret."

But maybe they don't have to kill me at all. Perhaps I just have to do it.

A *Wakwak* dives for Gabrielle, and I race after her, throwing myself over her body. Its sharp claws pierce my back.

"Nooo," the sea witch cries. The monster struggles to shake itself free, but its claws are embedded deeply into me. I cough up blood, and somewhere behind me, I'm aware of Eric slicing the monster's legs clean off. The beastly bird falls dead at my side.

Then the world goes black.

But it's not blackness that comes from unconsciousness. No, the blackness comes from a giant beast, a beast too big for this world, erupting from the ocean and filling the sky—the *Bakunawa*.

"How?"

I roll over to look up as the beast rises and swallows the moon—darkness ripples over us like a thick blanket. Auntie Maggie laughs joyfully, breaking the sea's surface like she's shattered glass. As she rises, ocean water pours off her like a waterfall.

Salvador stands in front of me, raising my kris sword. Everyone blocks her from me though they're all weak and covered in wounds.

"It's too late," the sea witch says, using her magic to fling them aside as if they were nothing more than toy soldiers. She kneels in front of me.

"You liked this life better. I can tell. You'll be happy here if you live through this."

I try to stand, but she makes a sit-down motion with her hand, and I'm stuck.

"Oh, that looks like it hurts," she says, peering at my back. "Let me get those." She uses her magic to rip the *Wakwak* feet and claws out of my back, and I scream so hard my head becomes hot with blood.

"How?" I project again, crying into the sand.

"Well, I was worried for a second that you would be able to stop me when you threw yourself onto your sister. I had to use most of my collected magic to pull the beast back before it could do irreparable damage."

"If you used all your magic, how did you have enough to release the *Bakunawa*?"

"Oh, I got a boost. The boost I needed when all your biggest fans showed up to watch your live feed."

"What live feed?"

I followed her hand to the jetties, where a large crowd stood, watching us die.

"Recognize the little shit in red?" she asks.

I squint. "Grant."

I grind my teeth. He must have followed us out here and started live-streaming when the fight began. And as many people as he got to follow him out here, there were so many more on the other side of their cameras, seeing proof of the monsters, feeding the sea witch her power.

She positively glistens with magic, the vibrations of it moving up and down her limbs like an electric current.

"And now, there's nothing left to do but lock your voice away and take my revenge."

She throws her hand in the air as if searching for something on a high shelf, and lightning strikes the ocean so close my hair crackles with static.

Then she shoots a bolt of lightning forward, striking Grant down.

chapter thirty-six

People on the jetty scatter like roaches when Grant falls. His lifeless body slides down the rocks leaving no doubt that he is a goner.

"No!" I scream, holding out my hand. Though he's a total douche, I couldn't stand to see him die. For a second, he stands back up again, and people turn to look back at him, but there's something odd about the way he moves. It's stiff, like when you scrub the timeline of a video to rewind it. Grant falls again, and this time, he stays down.

My breathing is heavy because this feels important, but I don't quite understand why. It also seems familiar, though I can't explain how.

"That's enough," Auntie Maggie snaps at me, turning so quickly that her torso seems disconnected from her serpent legs. What's surreal about it, what makes me and my family step back, is that she says it in my voice. "*Tinatawag ko ang mga halimaw mula sa kaharian sa ilalim ng tubig.*" Her hand gestures to the sea and monsters erupt from the boiling water. Thousands upon thousands of heads break the water's surface like zombies digging their way out of their graves.

My breath catches in my throat as I hyperventilate. Then something in me snaps, and I launch myself at the sea witch.

"You're a monster. No wonder the gods locked you up."

I'm clawing at her face and chest like I can somehow get my voice out of her throat. But the psychopath laughs before flinging me off. I'm propelled high into the air, landing on several little elf-like creatures with leaf ears, *Dalaketnons.*

They push me up with their tiny hands, and I pass a large staff to the one closest to me. "I'm sorry, po."

"Time," the being whispers, wiping his nose to cover his mouth. His dark hair and eyes turn white and then fade back to their original color.

"What?" I whisper back.

"Get away from her." The sea witch shoots her palm out furiously, and lightning erupts out of her hands. The elf-like being stiffens before falling over—another casualty.

I glare at the witch as the other monsters give my team and me a wide birth. The fight is over for them. Their sole mission is to find new homes on this Earth.

But I don't accept that it's over until the sea witch croaks out a spell in an old Filipino tongue. Her entire body illuminates from the inside. A golden light moves up her throat, and the witch chokes as the orb exits her mouth. I race toward it, not knowing for sure but assuming it's my voice. My fingers are inches away when the treasured light flashes like a UFO in a sci-fi movie. My gaze follows the light as it journeys into the ocean until the depths of the sea conceal it. Though I haven't had my voice in what feels like ages, the sight of it disappearing as it's locked away feels as if I've lost a part of my soul. I'm utterly motionless.

Hands grip my arms, and Mom's face moves into my line of sight.

"Honey? *Anak*?"

I blink hard, looking around.

I lost. I'm unable to feel my face. My thoughts aren't projecting like they were. *The witch is free. My voice is locked away in the depths of the ocean. I failed everyone.*

"Yes, you did." Auntie Maggie swipes upward, opening a portal of sand. As it whips outward, the swirling vortex stings.

On the other side of the portal, my family battles the monsters, but there are too many of them. My family is killing themselves to keep up, though there's no point. We've lost. Still, they must not know that.

On the jetties in the distance, that same line of people watch and record the battle. But in the center, instead of that prick Grant, it's Ian. Ian is standing there, staring at the war, holding up a phone to record it. On that side, *he* betrayed them, not Grant.

Auntie Maggie steps through the portal, and I race after her, determined to kill him. But the portal is just a window for me, as unmovable as the night I tried to pull Mal to my side. It takes both of us, but she's too busy whipping an *Aswang* to see us.

Auntie Maggie looks at me with a fake sad face, her lower lip protruding. "That lover boy of yours just can't be trusted. He'd even sacrifice Mal to get to you. I wonder where he got an idea like that." My nostrils flare as my mind tries to make sense of how he could stoop so low. I thought he loved Mal. "Don't worry," the sea witch says in a simpering voice. "I'll take care of him."

She throws her hand out, and lightning hits Ian with such force he's blasted backward off the jetty wall. I can't even see where he falls. But his little roaches scatter just as they'd done with Grant.

Gabrielle, Eric, and Mal's parents all beat on the portal window as well, trying to get Mal's attention. Mal looks up, her eyes finding us the way you can find that one person staring at you in a crowd of people. She smiles, her flyaways crossing over her face. Then Auntie Maggie stabs her in the chest with only her fist, and Mal falls.

No! I scream soundlessly as Gabrielle and Mom fall to their knees.

All of my family on that side of the portal break away from their fight, and life seems to move in slow motion as they race toward Mal. I killed the one that everyone in both worlds loves. I killed her by letting this all happen because

I.

Am.

Poison.

And it should have been me.

I wish I could take it back.

A ringing in my ear grows, becoming deafening as I stare at Auntie Maggie laughing over Mal's lifeless form. No one can touch her because she seems to know everyone's every move before they attack.

Everyone moves in reverse, and Mal stands, looking at us, then turns back to the monster she was fighting.

Auntie Maggie blinks, then hits Mal with her fist again. Mal collapses like a toy that's run out of charge.

Mal's Eric and dad beat the windowed portal with a rage that could put the gods to shame. My family throws themselves angrily at the sea witch. Dad flies through the air. Magical wind holds back my Eric. My mom's arms are bound behind her back. My eyes water as I stare unblinking through the portal, fighting the urge to press my hand against the ringing growing in my ears.

My Eric runs backward toward the *Tiyanaks* he was fighting before Mal fell. My mom backswings a rice sack full of *Duwendes* at a *Sirena* that has pulled herself to shore.

Mal stands, alive once again as she turns back to the *Aswang*.

"No!" Auntie Maggie walks furiously toward the portal, screaming at me. "Stop doing that! Stop messing with time."

My entire family and Mal all hear her scream, noticing her

and the portal as if for the first time. The sea witch reaches through the portal to choke me as she tries to rip the *agimat* off my neck. Mal's family pulls me out of the witch's grasp while Mal and my family race to attack the sea witch. Auntie Maggie whips around to face them, shooting fireballs from her fingertips that strike both Mal and Gabby down this time.

I leap forward, like I can do anything to stop it, and hit the sand as the portal closes.

Gabrielle, Eric, Mom, and Dad scream just like it's the first time.

chapter thirty-seven

Salvador is holding Mom, who is crying so hard that none of her words are words. They're just anguished moans that fall out of her like pieces of her soul leaking from her body. Eric is comatose. Anita and Perlah are holding Dad back because he looks like he will kill me. I want to tell them to let him go. I deserve whatever it is he wants to do.

Tita Blessica is struggling with Gabrielle, but she's not strong enough. Gabrielle pulls loose and grips me, grips my face.

"What were you doing? What were you doing with time that Maguyaen wanted to stop?" Gabrielle asks, digging her nails into my cheeks and neck.

I shake my head, confused.

I gesture to the place where the portal had been. *You saw.* Everyone saw. Everyone had to have seen Mal die again and again. How could anyone not recognize that nightmare for what it was?

"TALK!" Gabrielle screams so loudly her voice is hoarse.

Mal kept dying. Tears stream down my face as I relive the image.

Gabrielle reaches in her back pocket and hurls her phone at me.

It hits me in the wrist, and I pick it up. I explain the

ringing noise, explain the way time moved backward. As I type, I realize this happened with Eric in the living room the other day, getting up and falling back down again. How odd his movements had seemed. How unnatural.

It's the agimat. It let me reverse time. I saved her three times before the witch came after me. But she killed Mal anyway. She killed my Gabby.

I fall to the ground, letting the phone slip from my grasp. Gabrielle grabs it, murmuring with Mom, Dad, and Eric, trying to piece together what has happened. Not that any of it matters now.

Salvador picks me up, laying my head in his lap.

"There's blood coming out of your ears. And your neck." He touches my throat gingerly, but I swat his hand away, turning onto my side.

"Can you do it again?" Gabrielle asks from behind me.

I lift my head. I don't know if I can do it again. I don't know if I need to see the other side to control what happened over there. I don't know anything. But I *want* to know.

I'll try anything. I stand.

"Now wait," Tita Blessica says. "Wait, this is dangerous. You're talking about reversing time. You could get lost in time or hurt. And the witch still exists in both worlds. She could easily stop it again."

Not if I go all the way back.

"Go all the way back to before the death wish?" Salvador's voice cracks as he must have realized what going back to before any of this means. It means we will have never met.

Yes, I say, placing my hand on his face. He kisses my palm, shaking his head.

"You can't. We won't know each other. We won't even have the memory of each other."

I know. I drop my head onto his chest.

Nobody is struggling against anyone else any longer as they all stand around us.

"Maybe it won't be like that," Gabrielle says. "You remembered everything from both lives. Maybe we will too." She sounds like she wants to believe that but doesn't.

I shake my head. None of them experienced Mal's death over and over again. They only saw when the witch told me to stop and then killed Mal and Gabby. Nobody saw Eric playfully fall onto the couch twice—just me.

I'll remember you. I tell Gabrielle, squeezing Salvador's fingers. Of course, I don't know if that's true, but they can't hear the weakness in my voice because that voice only exists in my head now.

"Bring her back to us," Mom says, coming over to squeeze me. Eric joins her, and to my surprise, Dad comes over too.

"It's not that we don't love you too," Dad's voice cracks.

I stop him because I get it.

I get all of it now.

It's possible to love someone and want someone else. It's possible to want to stay in the same place forever and still need to see the world.

I hadn't understood that when I was with Ian. I hadn't understood how it was possible to love someone and know that you can't be with them because they're no good for you. It took a death wish for me to get that life isn't about making perfect decisions. It's just about trying to have the best intentions and dealing with the consequences, whatever they may be.

I kiss Salvador one last time. His lips press against mine, making my knees weaken, almost convincing me to stay.

Then I turn to face Gabrielle, realizing that as much as I'd come to care for Salvador, I would miss her the most.

I will fix this.

"I know," she says, throwing her arms around me and squeezing me so tight I can feel how much she'll miss me too. I pull away, not looking any of them in the eyes as my whole heart yearns to return to my old life, ready to fix all the wrongs.

The portal opens as easily as a light switching on. And on the other side, Mom, Dad, and Eric cry over Mal and Gabby's bodies.

Dad picks Mal up, walking her to the portal. Then he clumsily places her in my hands. I'm strong, but I still stumble over her weight. Luckily, my other family is there to support us. I turn our bodies with everyone's help, and once they have their Mal, I'm free to let her go.

The second I'm back in my world, all the suffocating agony I'd battled because of the way I'd loved Ian returns. I collapse under the weight of it, but my family is there to catch me. They hold me up.

It's so much worse than it was before because now it's coupled with the weight of losing Salvador and Gabrielle. I try to keep my face from contorting, but I'm helpless against the overwhelming gravity that the emotions of two lives encompass.

Anita and Perlah wave a last goodbye from the other side, and Anita looks like she wants to help hold me up. I'm determined to befriend her in this life, knowing she's got to be spectacular in every universe. Salvador pushes his way to the portal, his hand pressed against its surface.

My breath is shaky as I lift my hand to meet his. I can't feel him physically, but his energy matches mine perfectly—like two souls meant to know one another, though we were never meant for each other at all. And even if I found him in this life, he wouldn't be my Salvador.

I take a backward step away, then another. Finally, turning from him.

Mom, Dad, and Eric embrace me, crying into my hair, and onto my shoulder.

I'd failed them. Killed their favorite daughter, and they still cling to me like they love me. Other Tita Blessica approaches us, touching my shoulder. Then she walks to the portal. I dare to look back, though I'm afraid that another glance at my other family, at my people, will shatter me before I can even fix this.

My Tita Blessica approaches the portal as well. She nods once at my family, then trades places with her doppelgänger. The second she steps over to our side, she drops dead.

I gasp, reaching for her.

The other Tita Blessica looks down at her twin's lifeless body. As I stare at her with questions in my gaze, she says, "This was the sacrifice she had to make to fix her mistake."

I gulp, knowing it's my turn.

I grip the *Tikbalang's* spine around my neck and reach out to Felipe in my mind. He charges through the portal and into my world. I touch the soft part of his mane, communicating my intentions about traveling through time.

He kneels, and I jump on his back.

My mom yells, "Where are you going, *Anak*? We just got you back."

"She's going to fix this," Gabrielle says to her through the portal. Mom looks at Gabrielle's mirror image and practically falls apart again. She's divided between stopping me, looking at the lifeless form of Gabby on the ground near her feet, and seeing the living, breathing Gabrielle in the other life.

Before anyone can say another word, I turn Felipe, and he races into the water.

Icy liquid drenches my legs, and air swipes the freezing tears streaming down my face as the ringing in my ears grows to a deafening roar. Then I plunge into the darkness of the raging sea.

Somewhere in the distance, amid the water thrashing against my ears, the sea witch screams.

chapter thirty-eight

Time feels strange when you're moving through it. I can't tell if I've been under the water long, but I know exactly the moment the death wish is undone when the weight of my love and hatred for Ian finishes spreading throughout my limbs like fresh poison. It is a crushing pressure that I'm only distracted from momentarily as the tightness from lack of oxygen in my lungs takes priority.

When my surfboard strap connects to my ankle, completely unbroken, I know I'm back in my world and that time has reversed. The last time I was submerged in this surf, I'd been pulled away by what I'd thought was a creature. This time, I feel a creature, the *Tikbalang*, letting me go.

My throat tightens as I reach out in the dark water for Felipe, but he's gone.

"Thank you." I hope even though my voice is garbled, he understands how much I appreciate him. I hope he remembers me because no one else will.

My foot hits the bottom of the sand, squishing between my toes, and I kick myself upward with all my might. I'm much deeper than I'd thought, and I have to swim faster before I run out of air. The second I break the surface, thunder cracks. Light spots zigzag before my eyes as lightning rips across the sky viciously. I'd forgotten about the stormy weather—having assumed it was the witch wielding her magic over the heavens to drag me to her hell.

Grabbing the side of my board, it's hauled forward to shore and then back to the horizon, a pendulum ticking away the seconds of my life. Rather than breaking on top of me, a swell passes under as I gasp for as much air as possible. Last time, my lungs had been so deprived I couldn't get enough. I don't want to have that same problem again, so I take every opportunity to breathe.

The clouds move supernaturally fast overhead, accumulating so that darkness veils this world, my world, unnaturally quick. I get the very real sense that the sea witch is near me. I'd thwarted her plan. I'd undone the death wish, so Auntie Maggie should be confined to her underwater prison. But that doesn't mean she isn't waiting just below the surface to grab me. My hands tremble from this unending nightmare, and I kick harder than necessary as I tread.

This is not how I die.

"You've got this, Malaya, keep swimming," Gabby shouts from the platform the way she does during swim meets. My gaze snaps to hers.

Gabby.

She's alive. She's here. I blink away tears to keep her in my sight. This is all real. I'd done it. I just needed to get to the beach to see her. I needed to survive this so my parents wouldn't have to know what it means to lose a child. I never want to cause that haunted, hollow look on their faces ever again.

But at the base of the jetties, a group of people gathers to watch me die. Flashes of Grant and Ian and their crew of followers overlap this image. It's like they're there to haunt me, to remind me that life isn't all better just because I fixed one mistake. A distant cackle whizzes by my ears. Auntie Maggie is enjoying this.

Growling, I turn my board forcefully against the furious swells and dig my arms deep into the water, trying to summon anger as strength. Whenever the waves try to turn my surfboard to their will, I recall every fight I'd had with my parents since I started dating Ian. Petty arguments that were seemingly not about him, like using the microwave at night or leaving my towel on the floor in my room, were just residual anger directed at me about him. I let that anger fuel my arms to work. Every time the mighty ocean threatens to turn me over, I imagine Ian telling me I'm the only one in his bed. I claw the water with fury. I kick my legs violently, remembering every time my mother preferred my sister's company over mine because she was "easier."

But nothing I did pushed me closer to the life I wanted back or the life I'd left behind because I've changed. I'm not angry about those things anymore, even though there was lingering hurt from their memories. I'd let that deep, resenting anger go when I'd let my other life go.

I know what I have to do.

The muscles in my throbbing arms twitch when I drop them by my sides, exhaustion from the battle catching up to me. I turn my board toward the storm, facing my nightmare the way I should face all my problems—head-on. Because maybe if I let the sea take me out past the jetties, I might be able to surf with the waves instead of against them. I might be able to return home to Mom and tell her to just say she hates Ian instead of picking fights about the way I do dishes. I might be able to tell her that maybe Gabby is easier because my mother spent my entire life asking me why I couldn't be more fun like her. And that was just a little too hard for a five-year-old to comprehend. If I could go home, maybe I'd stop at my boyfriend's house on the way and tell him I wasn't here for his bullshit anymore.

All I know is I can match these waves rage for rage until I die, or I can let them wash over me.

The waves deepen from this perspective, and the water gets choppier as I'm sucked inward. I allow myself to be enveloped by these black mirrors, wondering if the dim light before the darkness would be the last thing I see. Bubbles ripple over my face and down my body, but there is no magical land on the other side. There are just more waves. After the first two, it's easier to dive through the waves than fight the current. With each dive, I'm able to get further away from the jetties, and while that's a relief, I still shiver at how far I've gotten from everyone—not just the people on the beach but the people in my life. I find a rhythm in breathing deeply and letting myself go as I duck each towering, opaque wall, hoping I'm making the right decision but knowing I won't know if it's right until I'm either safe at the shore or it's too late.

Outside of the rip current, well past the jetties, the beach, and the onlookers, my troubles seem small. The water is not without swells, but it's calmer here. It's more manageable. I'm even able to sit up and rub my aching shoulders.

For a long time, I paddle perpendicular to shore before I'm ready to try surfing in again. The surf, billowing and robust, is not quite so scary. It pulls me back as I paddle forward. Then I am a bird gliding just above the sparkling water. It carries me to shore, sweet as the day we met. This ride is everything the ocean promises me, and yet ...

As I trudge through the water, my legs surprisingly as exhausted as my arms, my adrenaline disappears. I drop my board, unable to hold even its lightweight any longer, and collapse onto the wet ground where the water meets the sand. The sea pats my leg, and the wind whispers that it's going to be okay.

Will it?

I turn my head away from the jetties, my face contorting as

I sob one hard time for Gabrielle and for Salvador. I missed them so acutely, and they would never be able to miss me back because I'd erased our time together. Another sob forces its way out of my throat as my love and pain for Ian are just as strong as the day I'd left it all behind. I'm back where I started, yet somehow things are worse because I'm living with the heartache of two lifetimes. My hand presses against my stomach to stop me from curling in on myself. No one can see me cry. I suck in a deep breath and face the sky. Hot tears slide down my cheeks, but they can't be seen from here. I take a shaky breath.

Still panting, I turn my head toward the jetties, where Gabby is making her way toward me. The pedestrians are still standing there, staring at me. They hadn't called for help. They weren't coming to see if I was okay. We didn't know each other. Yet, I still cared what they thought. I dreaded walking past them. I would have to muster all my strength to hold my board at my side in one arm like it's not about to fall off. My head would need to be up to meet their eyes. I would only give myself a few more minutes of rest here before I stood, despite how much my body hurts, despite not being able to catch my breath.

I didn't come out here wondering whether I wanted to live or die. I'd been dying for over a year. I wanted an escape, yet I'm back, forced to confront many of my issues. My life was as stagnant as I was caught in that riptide. Before the death wish, I'd been alive but not living. Now that I knew who I could be, now that I had fixed things and am no longer in danger, would I face my issues in this life head-on like I thought I would? Was I strong enough?

Maybe not quite yet.

Rain falls gently, cleansing me of the ocean's damage, and I only know a few things for sure. I didn't want Ian anymore, but I wasn't strong enough to break it off yet. Salvador was firmly in my heart but coming back to this place in time meant that Ian's spot in my heart is as solid as it had ever been. It would take time to distance myself, but the breakup was coming as sure as this storm would make landfall.

I didn't want to fight with Mom about anything besides the things she and I were really angry about, but since I wasn't quite sure where to start or how to talk to her, maybe I'd begin by letting a few things roll over my shoulders like I let those waves roll over me. Perhaps I could let go of my resentment of her preference for my sister. These changes weren't going to happen all at once. I'm positive. I'd have to fight to live differently, find a way to approach things even if they scared me, and dive into those issues one stroke at a time.

chapter thirty-nine

The second Gabby and I enter the house, I rush her to shower and grab her pajamas for a *Wizards of Waverly Place* marathon.

"Jeez, you are so weird today." Gabby laughs before disappearing into the bathroom.

"Get used to the weird." I pull seaweed out of my stringy hair and toss it at her. Her laughter, so alive, causes my chest to pang. I'd almost lost this.

"Malaya," Mom shouts from the living room, a question in her voice.

I race over to her, throwing my arms around her. She pats me like I'm a stranger, and it's not the warm embrace I'd imagined or hoped for. But how can it be? She doesn't remember what these past few weeks have been like. I'm still just her screw-up daughter.

I try to ignore the layers of hurt and confusion swirling inside me.

"What is going on? Was that your sister?" Mom's eyebrows rise, causing rows of wrinkles on her brow.

"Oh." My shoulders tense. I forgot we'd skipped school to go surfing. I'm still wearing my wetsuit and reek of ocean water.

"You want to lie to me about where you were?" Mom

crosses her arms over her chest.

"No," I say in a small voice. It was so strange to have my voice back. To be able to say as much as I like. I keep my answers short like I'm only granted so many words before people can't understand me anymore. "I skipped school, and I made Gabby come with me."

I hang my head, waiting for her wrath.

"Honestly, Malaya. I don't know what to do with you anymore." She starts to go into everything I've done wrong; everything she harps on me about that she feels goes in one ear and out the other.

I touch her arm, and she stops.

"I'm sorry." I think for a second about everything I felt on the beach. Everything I wanted to say to her about how we communicate; everything I'd done to get us to where we are now.

But she interrupts me.

"I don't want to hear it, Malaya. I am so tired of getting phone calls from the school about you. I'm tired of your attitude. I'm just tired. And now you're dragging your sister into your mess?"

I look at Mom, and though I know all my faults in this relationship, she has faults here too. It's something deeper than me. Something I'm not sure I will ever be able to fix. She's not the mom from my other life. But maybe I wasn't the only thing that broke her. I'd never considered that *this* version of my mom may have made very different decisions in her life that got her to the place she is now, just like Mal and I made very different decisions.

I hug her again, long and hard, until her arms circle around me. I could get angry all over again for the way she isn't hearing me. But one of us has to step down if we're ever going to get better.

That person has to be me.

chapter forty

Mom intended to go back to work after lunch, but as she grabs her car keys on the entryway table and slips on her heels, she pauses.

"What's wrong?" I ask, leaning against the wall in my pajamas after a hot, tearful shower. My eyes are still puffy, but I'm not sure she notices.

"I know I said you don't have to go to school since it's already halfway over, but ..." She drops her hand by her side, the car keys clinking together. Is she conflicted about leaving me home alone? Maybe she thinks I'll invite Ian over. Old me would have.

"Then don't go." My voice is small. It's hard to request things from her when I've gone it alone for so long. It's like I'm reverting to a child in most ways.

There's a tightness in Mom's eyes. I hadn't said don't go with the attitude she's used to, but with the tone of a child needing her mom. Maybe she's trying to figure out what my angle is.

"Maybe," I say, pressing one foot against my calf, "maybe if I can drag Gabby away from the charcuterie board of snacks she's assembling in the kitchen, we can go have a shopping day instead. I've already convinced Gabby to skip. Can I convince you too?"

Mom's head shakes infinitesimally as if she can't believe what she's hearing. Too early to joke about being a bad influence?

"You don't want to stay home by yourself?" Mom's purse strap slips from her shoulders.

I shake my head.

"And you're not trying to see that boy?" Mom asks. This is one of those things that would have set me off before, and it nearly does now because I'm trying here. But I take a beat and breathe in a deep breath.

"No. Trust me I didn't skip school today to see him." This is the most truthful thing I've said to her in a while, and I wish I could have done it without my voice shaking.

"Are you ... Did you break up?"

I laugh but humorlessly. "No."

She nods one quick time like she doesn't trust herself to understand what's going on here, what's going on with me. I don't trust myself either because even though I said I don't want to see Ian, I do.

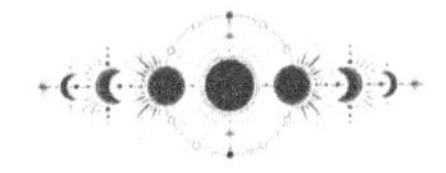

Mom stays home with us, though she says it wouldn't be a punishment if she took us out shopping. They sit with me on the couch, eating leftover *sinigang* and watching a Filipino novela about *Sirena*s.

I point at the TV with my fork, saying around a mouthful of rice, "The actresses in their mermaid costumes are so much more beautiful than real *Sirena*s with their veiny, scaley fish bodies." I'd missed her food even though my other Mom cooked the same way.

"Real *Sirena*s?" Mom blows on a steaming spoon of soup.

My eyes widen as I slow-turn to her. "Uh ... yeah. Like the kind in the Filipino mythologies."

Gabby giggles at the reddening of my face.

"Huh," Mom says, one side of her mouth lifting. "I didn't know you liked that stuff."

"I wouldn't say I'm into it. Just that I'm familiar with it." I set my bowl aside, and my insides sink. What are my other family and my other friends doing right now?

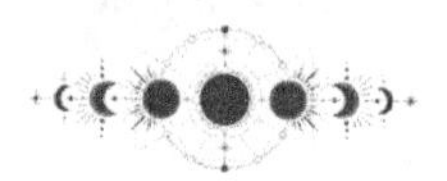

After skipping school, it is no surprise that I'm so grounded. What was surprising was how I couldn't stop myself from smiling when Mom and Dad said it.

"Are you giving me attitude?" Mom asks, though there is a smaller bite to her words than usual. Is she calming down?

"I swear, I'm not." I cover my mouth to hide the relief. It's just that I'd been so filled with anxiety about having to see Ian that the moment she grounded me, I felt the pressure removed.

Still, that doesn't stop the thread of text messages from him asking me when I'm coming to see him, if I was ever going to speak to him again, how I could still be angry when he apologized already, and then a series of apologies scattered in between. A more confident Mal might actually believe he's struggling to regain power over me. But I'm not that confident yet, as I try to answer his questions without inciting too much anger.

Then Mom does something that shocks me. After merely days of me staying at home, sitting in the living room with her, and making Gabby watch *Wizards of Waverly Place* reruns with me at night, Mom walks into my room her eyes narrowed at me.

"What are you doing?" she asks us both.

Gabby and I are wearing matching pajamas that I'd made her get at Target on the way home, and we're eating chips and dip on the bed over a towel.

"We're having a sleepover," Gabby says.

"It's Tuesday," Mom replies.

"Malaya says it's a permanent sleepover." Gabby smiles.

I pull open a drawer to show Mom how Gabby moved her clothes into my room.

Mom sits on the bed as her eyes alight with what I can only assume is amazement. "I was thinking. You've been pretty good, and Dad doesn't think I should be so harsh on you, so if you want to see your boyfriend tomorrow *after school,* that would be alright."

A forced smile is planted on my face as I thank her. She and Gabby both exchange curious looks that they think I don't see as I glance at my phone. Ian's most recent text that I should sneak out flashes across the screen. It's been hard to say no. That's one of the reasons I'd had Gabby move into my room ... so I wouldn't be tempted.

Now I have no choice but to face him, and the thought of seeing him tomorrow evening makes my heart race uncomfortably.

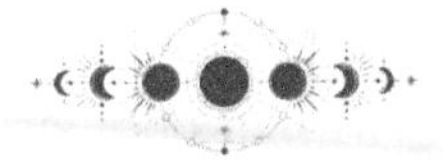

Though I'm not grounded from my car, I let Gabby drive me to Ian's house. She's shocked I let her drive the Mustang since I was so "stingy" about it before. When she says that, I pull the keys out of her grasp, causing her face to become gravely still. It's the same face she made in past fights right before I'd blown my top. I laugh, and she relaxes as I toss her the keys. When she pulls up to Ian's house, I sit there. Do I tell her to come in with me? Do I have her wait out here? Am I trying to break up with him? *Just break up with him!*

I can't.

Ian opens the door, and it's like I haven't seen him in weeks, even though it's only been days in this time. My heart hammers, but not the way it had ever felt around Salvador. Even though that was a completely different lifetime, I feel like a cheater.

"Just ... ugh ... Just go hang out at Bentley's and come back in thirty minutes."

"Thirty minutes? Are you sure?" The rise of her voice makes it sound like she's questioning my sanity.

"Yeah. Why? Is that too short?"

"Considering you were dying to live at his house like last week, uh yeah." She takes her foot off the brake and puts the car in park. "What is going on?" There's that mom intuition she's got. Or should I say that Gabrielle intuition?

I never told her about my other life. There was no point since, technically, that life didn't exist anymore. Every day it becomes harder to remember the details. They aren't as sharp and vivid as they'd first been. Those memories have faded edges like the memories of my childhood.

I tear up a little, trying hard to remember Salvador while looking over at Ian, waving for me to hurry up. But Salvador is like a dream quickly slipping away—his edges are fuzzy, but his voice is not as I recall him once saying, "You gave up a whole other life to have this one. Don't you think you should be living it?" Though he meant that I'd given up this life to have that one, I can't help but think the sentiment applies here too.

"Malaya?" Gabby shakes me.

I wipe away a tear. "Huh?"

"I said, what's going on?"

"Nothing. I'm just not feeling like myself."

I get out of the car, closing the door quickly behind me so I can't hear her ask me anything else. Sucking in a deep breath, I exhale as I navigate the broken walkway to Ian's house.

"Where have you been?" He picks me up by my ass and pulls me inside.

He presses his lips hard against mine, shutting the door behind him and all outside light.

tik tik. tik tik. tik tik.

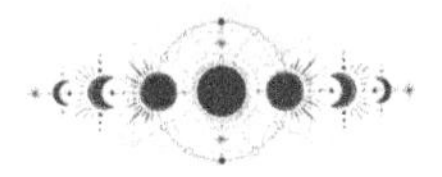

I'm lying on Ian's bed, looking up at his popcorn ceiling, and listening to the ticking of his radio alarm clock—which he only keeps because he thinks of himself as retro. I used to think it was cool, but now the room is all evidence of a baby hoarder. He can't say no to junk, like the record player missing its needle, so it never played music, or the original Nintendo he swiped from a pawn shop a year ago but never plays because he prefers his PlayStation. These things cultivate an image for him, and he only pays attention to the junk when he's showing them off.

Am I like that for him as he sits on the floor before his TV tray rolling a joint and completely ignoring me? I'd barely spoken to him since I'd gotten back, and he'd called and texted non-stop, but now that I'm here, I'm just another thing occupying this room.

"Why are you so quiet?"

I shrug. "I guess I just have nothing to say."

He looks back at me, and I shift to look at him, not caring if it causes a double chin. The sea witch was so wrong about so much, but she was insightful as hell. She'd been right when she'd said that coming back might kill me. The flood of emotions, like the thrashing waves of my homecoming storm, pounded against my chest the moment I entered this world. Only the need to survive the sea saved me from the crushing weight of betrayal, love, rejection, fear ... Still, as I look at Ian now, my eyes well up.

"What's wrong?" he reaches for my hand and pulls on me until I sit up. Once I do, he tugs on my arm again so that I slide onto the dirty, blue carpet next to him.

Ian drags his arm over my shoulder, and I curl into his side.

"Don't cry," he says as I soak his shirt. How can I still love him when I hate him so much? How can I still feel this way after everything I've been through with Salvador? I'd gotten to know what it would be like without him; how good that could be. So, what was I still doing here? Why won't this damn curse just let me go?

Ian nuzzles my cheek with his nose, and though I used to yearn for any affection from him, internally, I cringe. Perhaps the cringe wasn't as internal as I thought because Ian pulls away his face tightening. But while he's irritated, I'm stunned by my body's response to his affection. My heart might still be trapped, but my body recoils at his contact as if rejecting him for me. It's the first sign of hope that I might have learned something from the death wish.

Even if I could never see Salvador again, he was also there in my heart, reminding me that it had all been real and good. I would just need to give myself time to detach. But that time was like a ticking bomb inside, warning me to get out before there were any more beatings.

When Gabby texts me that she's outside, I exhale. *Finally.* She's late. I look at the clock, but it turns out she's not late. "I, uh, gotta go."

"Now?" Ian's eyes become slits as he watches me pull on my shoes.

"Yeah ... I'm still grounded for skipping, so this visit was conditional."

"I still don't understand how you could skip school and not come here to see me." There's an edge to his voice, like he wants to say more, but he doesn't.

I wave a hand toward the window, saying, "I just wanted to hang out with Gabby."

Cocking his head, his jaw shifts to the side. It reminds me of the way a snake can unhinge its jaw. "You could have done that with me. I've never had a problem with your family."

I stiffen because his words cause a flashing warning in my gut to tread lightly. "Yeah, sorry."

He gets up and kisses me. It feels weird, like kissing Grant.

"What the hell was that?" He grabs my wrist and squeezes it tightly. He's so much quicker to anger this time, his grip threateningly tight in a way that reminds me of the bruises I still have from his last beating, which was technically only days ago.

"What was what?" I ask, raising my voice as I yank my hand away. His eyes widen like he doesn't recognize me at all.

"Why do you keep acting like you don't want me to touch you?"

I didn't think he was capable of seeing anything beyond himself.

"Maybe because you hit me? People tend to not want to be touched by those who hit them."

Like a robot, his eyes dart back and forth between mine. I imagine him thinking through all the techniques he could use to control me—charm, guilt, redirection—before finally landing on his newest method. He jerks at me like he's going to hit me, and I flinch.

He laughs.

I have got to take anti-flinching lessons or something. I'm

two inches tall because Ian's aware he has the power to scare me.

"I have to go." My voice is embarrassingly small. I wait for some sign that he'll allow me to leave because this feels dangerously similar to the last time he hit me. The time that had led up to my death wish. If I'd learned anything from that experience, it was to trust my gut. It could happen all over again if I turn before he's ready. All his apology texts didn't mean he would never do it again.

"Well, go then." He dismisses me, pressing the door open.

I turn, walking as casually as I can down the perpetually dark hallway alone. I'd somehow lost and won at the same time. I wish I could talk this through with the other Gabrielle, if only because she already knows everything.

Once in the front yard, I race to the Mustang the way I ran from the monsters.

"Are you okay?" Gabby asks, still watching my every move like something big is about to happen.

"Yeah." I can't keep the shakiness out of my voice or hands as I pull my seatbelt on. "Do you think you could just drive around for a while? Maybe play some music?"

"For real?"

"Yeah ... I don't think Mom would mind." I spent much less time there than she probably would have expected since the thirty-minute time limit was actually my invention.

Gabby is more than happy to get in the driving practice, though I occasionally press the imaginary brake on my side of the car. I'd gotten so used to other Gabrielle and her months of training.

After Gabby circles the Bluff once, I direct her to the highway.

"Are you sure?" She glances nervously at my braking foot.

"I'm positive."

I didn't know where we were going. Or perhaps I always

knew but didn't want to think about it directly until I had her turn into the university.

"I didn't know you wanted to go here," Gabby says. "I thought you wanted to leave town for college."

"I do." I direct her to Salvador's dorm, my heart racing as the light stone comes into view.

Once she parks, I get out, asking her to wait in the car.

I walk toward Salvador's dorm, unsure if he even goes here in this life. I pause halfway up the sidewalk. Then start walking again.

At the end of the sidewalk, there's a familiar laugh.

Two guys come down the stairs of Salvador's dorm. Instantly, I recognize the back of one of their heads.

Salvador.

I freeze my heart racing and aching. It's not him, not really, but my body doesn't know that the way my brain does.

He's getting into his truck ... the same black Ford I know, when he seems to feel my gaze on him.

He turns and finds me. A slow, half-smile grows on his face, and my stomach flutters.

But his eyes ... they don't recognize me.

"Hey." He raises a hand to wave.

"Hey," I mumble before turning to go. Tears stream down my face back to the Mustang, and I don't even bother trying to hide them from Gabby.

Why did I think I could come here? What did I think would happen? I'm with Ian in this life. I'd invested all my time in him, hoping he'd change. My Salvador didn't even exist in this world, and he never would.

I'd run from two guys today, and neither one made me feel the way I knew I could.

chapter forty-one

A couple of days later, I returned from GameStop with Dad and Eric. I'd been obsessed with playing The Sims, trying to recreate a second life I'd never truly have back, and I wanted the supernatural expansion pack. Dad does not love video games, but when he'd said he needed to pick up the lotto, I'd invited Eric and myself along for the ride.

Both of them shrugged but didn't question it as I hopped in the truck.

I'm sitting on Eric's bed with my laptop in my lap when Mom walks by the room and does a double take.

"What are you doing in here?"

"Just playing Sims," I say without looking up. I'm trying, yet again, to recreate Salvador's face from memory, but this program can't get it right. Or maybe it's my mind that can't get it right. I slam my hand on the keyboard, causing Mom and Eric to jump.

Mom signals Eric to leave with a jerk of her head, and he sighs before saving his game.

Mom sits on the edge of the bed, and before she can say anything, I ask, "You ever think about Tita Mari?"

Mom's back straightens. "What makes you think about her?"

"I just wonder if you think about how different things

could have been between you two if she hadn't told Grandpa about the motorcycle incident."

"I don't see how that matters—"

"But it does matter!" I slam my laptop shut, shoving it aside. "Every little decision we make matters. Maybe you two would be close now, friends even ..."

"Yes, but I probably wouldn't have you or the rest of this family. She was the reason my parents sent me away to America. Well, her and the curse. They didn't want me to marry that boy."

I want to argue this point because my other mom still made it to America, still met my other dad, but I can't tell her those things without sounding ridiculous, so instead, I slump back against the headboard.

"What is all this about?"

I bury my face in my hands, sobbing. Mom grabs one of Eric's clean shirts out of a drawer and hands it to me to wipe my face.

When I'm calm enough to breathe, to speak, I say, "I just think about how different my life could have been if I hadn't met Ian." Mom sucks in a breath, but her face is still and unreadable. I can tell she's trying not to say anything that will anger me by not saying anything at all. "I'm thinking about breaking up with him. I'm just ... not strong enough yet. I wish I were in college already because maybe the distance would be enough ..."

Mom rubs my knee, silent for almost too long.

"He's been a part of your life for a long time," she says delicately. For once, there isn't anger toward me. She isn't recounting all the things that have gone wrong, all the changes in me since he and I had gotten together, and I'm relieved. It almost feels like a safe space, though I don't want to push my luck.

"Yeah, that's part of the problem." The time I'd invested in

Ian deflates my insides as if my worth is simply air escaping a balloon.

Mom's cheeks puff out as she exhales. Then she says, "Sometimes, I think about calling your Tita Mari up." I'm surprised at her direction, having assumed she'd want to trash Ian the first chance she got. "A few years ago, your grandma told me why Mari didn't live with us. Her mom took Mari from her because she thought your grandma was too young to raise a baby. Your tita must have seen me with our mom and dad, and thought they loved me more. I know I did. I was too young and naïve to even ask why, and people just didn't talk about things like that in the family."

"Maybe you should call her. Talk it through." I wipe my nose, feeling a calmness spread throughout me.

"Maybe it's too late," she says, raising a defeated palm up.

"You never know. You see things differently now that you know the truth. Maybe she does too. At least, you'll have tried."

Mom squeezes my hand before getting up.

At the door, she turns back to me.

"It's never too late for you as well, whatever you decide." Then she leaves, resembling my other mom for the first time since I'd returned to this life.

chapter forty-two

A week later, I get sick. I'm convinced my spirit is so low my immune system can't support me physically. I ask Ian to come to my house because I can barely move.

But he's got plans.

He won't even take fifteen minutes out of his day to see me. He would never meet me halfway again because he probably felt he'd done his part long before. I recall losing the embrace of his other arm many eons ago in my bed and try to remember if he'd ever held me like that again. What comes to mind are his two hands wrapped around my neck until blackness crept into my vision.

What was my life worth? What was my virginity worth?

Not this.

If I'd learned anything from Mom, it was my virginity was a commodity that couldn't be given without getting something eternally valuable in return. I was getting nothing.

"I'm worth more than this," I croak into the phone with raspy determination.

"If you think someone else out there is better than me, then go find him." He dares me.

"I will." I hang up, knowing we're done. The phone slips from my fingers like a dead weight falling from me. I did it.

We're really done. Then I turn my back on the device and fall asleep.

Mom comes in to check on me hours later. She's made my sick soup, *tinola*. She helps me sit up and asks me how I'm doing.

"I'm okay," I say, and I mean it for the first time in a long time.

Mom strokes my hair and hums.

"What's that?" I ask.

"You don't recognize it? I used to hum it when you were little. And my dad sang it to me."

"You made that song up, didn't you?" It's a line that would have set her off before, thoughtless on my part because I didn't want to fight. But instead of screaming, she thumps my forehead.

"*Gaga*," Mom says. *Dummy.*

I laugh and then cough.

It doesn't sound like a real song, but that's okay. Mom lies, and this one isn't hurting anybody.

When an *Aswang* finally kills its victim, it replaces her with a doppelgänger made of trees and moss. This imposter returns home, falls violently ill, and dies.

"Mom, do you know how to kill an *Aswang*?" Light, cut from the blades of my ceiling fan, dances across her bewildered face.

"You make a whip using a stingray's tail," she says matter-of-factly.

Rolling onto my sour stomach, I murmur into my pillow, "We might need one of those."

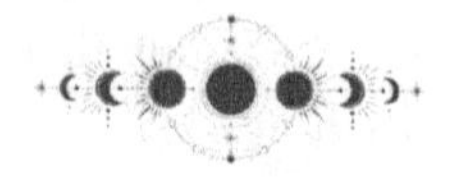

Of course, I didn't die.

What followed was a year of being so high on life that I am now a different person. I was free from my prison the way I had been when I'd first made my death wish. For the second time, I hadn't realized how genuinely miserable I was, until that misery vanished and what it left was spectacular—a life in full color. Only this time, it was a life that was entirely mine.

Still, I can never be the person I was before Ian or even the person I was with the other Gabrielle and Salvador. That's the thing about an *Aswang*, literal or metaphorical, once it attacks, one is never the same.

I am genuinely positive about others ... but not of myself. I tend to believe people dislike me and stay up nights replaying conversations while reminding myself it would be best if I talked less. When I'm upset, I don't dance around the reasons; I get straight to the point because I want to talk about it. Some people find that kind of directness abrasive, but I just don't want any more miscommunication. Because of the power they wield, I don't handle authority well without heavy internal reminders of my place. I am infected and battle the repercussions of that dark time every day to prevent infecting others. Mom was right about the curse; I was never the same even after it was over.

There have been more roads to walk, but I am never alone again. I cling to my mom and sister with everything I have and rely on Eric and Dad in ways I never thought I could. I know what life is like without them and the monsters that await me.

It took months, but Mom and I are finally starting to heal. I hate the time we wasted trying to figure out how to talk to each other. I'd like to tell you that being raised in different cultures created an emotional barrier between us, but that can't be it. After all, my sister never had these problems with Mom. No, there was something profoundly different in how we used language to convey intent that broke us. Had that barrier not existed, I might have made better choices like Mal.

But I also probably wouldn't understand the nuances of language as I do now, and I use my voice every chance I get to create the life I want.

These days when I tell Mom funny stories, she rushes to the bathroom so she doesn't pee herself. Such is the case when I recount how Gabby and I became known as 'The Trash Twins.'

Mom emerges from her room, her face red and her smiling lips pressed together, threatening to boil over with laughter. But before we all hit that breaking point, something catches our attention on the Filipino satellite. Within one of the telenovelas is the song Mom hummed to me the day Ian and I broke up. The same song she hums to my sister and brother when they're sick or sad. Gabby and I slow-turn to Mom, jaws open, the running joke that she has invented this song and imbued it with family history completely demolished.

Her chin raises triumphantly.

"Nobody wants to believe me!" Though we all believe her now.

Mom is not a liar.

Gripping the column textured with the notches that mark our heights, I recall all the ridiculous things she's said in the past, realizing one by one, through the news, through articles shared with the click of a button, through gossip, that Mom's warnings are her truth. People *can* die from pimple infections. People *do* get arrested for acting strange in stores. Road rage *can* get you shot. While she may have never said she was trying to keep me away from Ian because she viscerally felt he was evil, it was there in her intentions—I just wasn't listening.

epilogue

I've never been able to let my other life go entirely, but it constantly tries to let go of me. Every day my memories fade more, and that life, and those beautiful people, become just an ache in my heart. Anita was one of the things from my other life that I intended to have in this one, even if she wasn't the same person.

The week I broke up with Ian and felt good enough to return to school, I marched into English class and said, "What do you know about Filipino mythological creatures?"

Her eyes were amused as she said, "Not much. Why?"

"I just feel like it could be an interest of yours."

"What a WEIRD thing to say!" she exclaimed loudly. She absolutely loved it. And she should because that kind of bold weirdness is something I learned from her.

Now Anita, Gabby, Bentley, and I are together, enjoying *halo-halo* cups at the Selena statue downtown. Auntie Perlah opened a Filipino food truck just a few months ago, and we like to follow it around sometimes.

Every once in a while, I see the other Salvador—like I do tonight. My heart throbs at the sight of him in a way it hasn't since I'd last seen my Salvador through the portal. I always get near enough to gaze at this other Salvador, but I never talk to him. I'm just a stranger in the crowd, so my face blends into the background. But to me, his face is a singular star in the night—a sun a universe away.

I'm convinced that seeing his face in this life is the only reason I know it wasn't all a dream.

I lean against the metal bars surrounding the statue of the beloved, dead singer, looking down at the bouquets people have dropped at her feet when a hand grazes my arm.

I turn and drop my *halo-halo* cup—particles of green, purple, and yellow splatter against the cement.

Salvador.

My Salvador. My soul recognizes his soul instantly.

"How?" The intensity of his eyes pulls me in. They're the eyes of someone who's missed me as much as I've missed him.

"That's the first time I've ever heard your voice." Salvador's gaze flicks from my eyes to my lips.

I pull his head down to mine, pressing my lips against his, and kiss him like it's our last day.

REFERENCE GUIDE

Agimats- An amulet or charm, also known as an Anting. In Filipino occult, each agimat may serve a different purpose such as for protecting, warding off evil, attracting love, healing, or even to heighten or grant supernatural abilities.

Albularyo- A type of folk healer or witch doctor who heals people with homeopathic remedies like using herbs or hilot. Albularyos are thought to have supernatural healing powers and are extremely connected to nature.

Anak- child, a genderless term for one's offspring.

And true love mo is coming- Your true love is coming.

Ano- What

And ba- What the heck?

Aswang- An umbrella term for shapeshifter. Various types of Aswangs include witches, vampires, demonic spirits and werebeasts such as dogs, bats, birds, etc. Malaya uses this term very broadly when her story first begins because she still hasn't quite embraced her culture. As she becomes more knowledgeable, she uses more specific terms to describe specific Aswangs like the Tiktik (see Tiktik).

Ate- Big Sister; also used for older female relatives and respected friends.

Bagakay- A ten inch dart made of bamboo thrown in close quarters.

Bakunawa- A serpent-like dragon said to cause eclipses, earthquakes, rain and wind. Legend says there used to be seven moons, but Bakunawa ate all but one. This creature is associated with eclipses because in mythology, it always attempts to eat the last moon but must spit it out when defeated and be cast back into the dark ocean until the next time.

Balarao- A Filipino dagger with a leaf-like blade that was used throughout the pre-colonial Philippines.

Balikbayan box- Meaning 'returning to the nation,' this is a box containing an assortment of items generally from overseas Filipinos to their relatives and loved ones in the Philippine Islands. However, Balikbayan boxes may also be sent from the Philippines to loved ones outside of the country as well.

Balut- A fertilized, developing egg embryo which is boiled or steamed and eaten from its shell.

Bampira- Vampire

Berberoka- A swamp from *Apayao, Abra* and *Ilcos Norte* mythology. This creature will suck up all the water in a pond or damn a river with its ability to morph in size. When people are fooled into collecting fish flopping on the ground, the Berberoka will release the water to knock people off their feet. As the people struggle to get upright, the Berberoka picks them up to eat them. They don't like crabs.

Bobo- Stupid or fool

Buntot pagi- A whip-like weapon made from a stingray tail.

Dalaketnon- Beautiful, yet evil elf-like engkanto. They are said to be tall and have telekinesis. They are so evil they can control Aswangs, Tiyanaks, and even Manananggal.

Duwende- A humanoid trickster akin to a dwarf or gnome. They make homes in mounds of earth in the woods and when you pass their houses you must excuse yourself by saying tabi tabi po or face bad luck. Duwendes often move into homes and are responsible for residents losing items. To get them back, offer food on the floor and say tabi tabi po.

Filipino Broom- A walis-tambo is a soft indoor broom made of long, dried grass.

Gago or Gaga- Silly/Dummy

Halo-hal0- A popular cold dessert made of shaved ice, coconut milk or evaporated milk, ube, coconut strips, fruit, tapioca pearls, leche flan, sugar or syrup, sweet beans, sweet banana, jelly and more.

Hay naku- Oh my gosh

Hayop ka- A profanity meaning 'you animal.'

Hoy- Hey

Ilocano- A language and people belonging to the third largest ethnolinguistic group in the Philippines. They are generally found in the northwestern part of Luzon known as the Ilocos region.

Kadu Kadu- A small creature with pointed ears and a larger upper body than lower body.

Kali- The national martial arts of the Philippines known as the art of stick fighting.

Kaluluwa- One's soul

Kapre- A tree giant who likes to chill in tree branches and smoke. They are not necessarily evil, but they do like to play pranks on people.

Kapran- God and the Sky, husband to Maguyaen (Auntie Maggie) and brother to Maguayan (Yanny).

Karambit- A Filipino knife with a curved blade like a tiger's claw.

Kris sword- A wavy sword

Lampong- A two feet tall dwarf-like forest spirit with the ability to transform into a white, one-eyed deer in order to lure hunters away from the creatures they are hunting.

Lola- Grandma

Lumpia- Like spring rolls, Lumpia is meat and mixed vegetables rolled in a paper-thin wrapper.

Maguayan- (Yanny) God of the sea and Kaptan's brother

Maguyaen- Goddess of the winds of the sea, a Visayan Diety

Mamay- Mama; Another word for mom like Nanay

Manananggal- A demonic-like creature capable of separating its lower body from its torso, and sprouting huge, bat-like wings to attack its victims from the sky with its vicious fangs.

Mangkukulam- A sorcerer. This term generally has a negative connotation as it's someone who practices black magic and will help others seek revenge. However, there is a lighter side to Mangkukulams as they also practice natural magic like Albulrayos and can help heal people.

Minokawa- A giant dragon-like bird the size of an island which is capable of living in outer space.

Nanay- Mom; an affectionate term for mother like Mamay

Nilaga- A Filipino stew eaten with rice.

Nuno- Also known as nuno sa punso, is a dwarf-like nature spirit who lives in dirt mounds or anthills. If you cut down a tree or trespass without asking a nuno's permission, misfortune, illness or even death will befall you.

Opo- A way to say "yes" but with respect to elders.

Palitaw- A sweet, flat rice cake covered in coconut.

Pancit- A stir-fry rice noodle dish; a party favorite

Pandesal- A soft and airy bread roll eaten for breakfast

Patis- Fish sauce

Pero- But

Po- An honorific particle added to words or sentences to show respect to someone older than them.

Pugot- meaning decapitated one, derived from the Ilocos region. It can assume various shapes such as hog, dog or human but it prefers being a gigantic, headless being.

Quince- In Hispanic cultures this is a shortened term for quincenera/o which is a 15-year old's coming-of-age debut.

Sayaw sa Bangko- A dance from the Pangasinan province in which performers dance atop a narrow bench that is typically only six inches wide.

Sigbin- Also known as Sigben, is a nocturnal, blood-sucking creature said to look like a cross between a kangaroo and a headless goat. It walks backward with its head lower than its hind legs. It is capable of attacking someone by attacking their shadow. It will turn into clay when stored in a jar.

Sigbinan- A person of this lineage is said to have the power to command and possess sigbin. They can store a sigbin in a jar and it will change sizes to fit the jar.

Sinigan- A sour soup made of proteins, seafood, and vegetables.

Sirenas- Sirens, often portrayed as vicious mermaids, have an alluring and hypnotizing singing voice. They use their voice to lure humans into the water where they drown them.

Sulingkat- Baskets made of woven coconut leaves, derived from Tawi Tawi in the southern Philippines.

Tabi tabi po- Meaning excuse me or may I pass?

Tagalog- 1. The national language of the Philippines is Filipino, which is derived from Tagalog. 2. Tagalog people are largely from the Luzon region with their own culture which includes Tagalog mythology. This novel pulls mythology from many kinds of Filipino cultures.

Taglish- A mix of Tagalog and English, often used when code-switching.

Tanga- Stupid

Tikbalang- Werehorse; a tall, humanoid creature with disproportionately long limbs and the head and hooves of a horse. They are said to live in the mountainous and rainforest regions of the Philippines. They like to get people lost, so one must turn their shirt inside-out to avoid this.

Tiktik- A type of Aswang known for the tik tik noise it makes. When the noise is loudest, it is farther away. When the noise is quieter, it is close, and you are in danger. This shapeshifter will shift from its human form to something more grotesque with features that include wings, a proboscis like a mosquito used to suck out organs, and backward limbs.

Tinatawag ko ang mga halımaw mula sa kaharian sa ilalim ng tubig- I summon monsters from the underwater realm.

Tinikling- A traditional Filipino dance in which two people tap and slide long bamboo poles against the ground while the dancers avoid their ankles being snapped as they dance between the clapping poles.

Tinola- Chicken or fish soup with ginger broth served with rice.

Tiyanak- A vampiric shapeshifter that takes the form of a defenseless baby in order to lure its victims in before attacking.

Umupo ka- Sit down

Wakwak- A vampiric, bird-like creature which snatches humans at night as prey. Its leathery wings are as sharp as knives.

author's note

This story is written from the perspective of a mixed-race Filipino American. Malaya and I are not the same person. However, some of Malaya's experiences are drawn from my own lens as a biracial Filipina American. My characters may explore what it means to be mixed-race or BIPOC, but they do not represent the entirety of what it means to be multiracial or BIPOC. They cannot even represent Filipinos as a whole because the country is made up of more than 182 ethnolinguistic groups, and to encapsulate so many cultures in such few characters would be inaccurate and impossible. It would also be a disservice to anyone who is seeking Filipino representation to identify with or learn from. My hope is that you connect with this Filipino story which includes some, but not all Filipino mythology, and that it makes you want to seek out other Filipino stories.

acknowledgments

The theme of the importance of family would not be honored if I didn't first start with my everlasting thanks to my own.

To my husband, Victor: My writing career was over a decade in the making, and you supported me at every beat, twist, and turn. You were there for every rejection until the numbness set in and listened to every half-explained plot as I reasoned out seemingly insane ideas. Talking about being an author (to me) was akin to aspiring to be a rockstar—so far-fetched and fantastical. I am continually amazed at your faith in me.

To my sister, Danielle: I cannot believe you read seven versions of act one of *When Oceans Rise.* Do you know how to say no? LOL! I'm grateful you don't because this book wouldn't be what it is without you. More than that, a bit of you is in every story I write. You are in the most loveable characters because I can't imagine not sharing parts of you with the world. Thank you for continuing to read my work even though you hate reading. You must really love me.

To my sweet, sweet babies: You are wild and weird, and I'm here for all of it. I swear you were born to teach me more about love than I ever imagined. I love you in a way that is difficult to explain in words but inspires me to want to. I know you're probably going to draw in this book because you're six and three, and I will cherish it as a timestamp of this moment.

Thanks to my parents for allowing me to be so weird growing up and always taking the pictures to prove it. Thanks for pushing me to be a reader with the constant library visits and buying me books when we didn't always have the money. Also, a big thanks goes to Mom for answering my phone calls whenever I needed to ask about our culture! This book wouldn't have worked without you, and Dad couldn't have answered those questions.

Additionally, thank you to Auntie Lou and Grandma Salango for the calls from the U.S. to Morocco, to the Philippines to also fact-check my questions about Filipino culture. You both were wonderful for indulging me at all hours of the night because I had no clue what time it was in your countries!

Thanks to my brothers Deric, Matt, and Julio for showing me the many ways that men are not evil. But don't test me.

Thanks to my in-laws, Vera and Toti (Jose): Your support, and time with the kids, and beyond made this book possible. I love that I can lean on both of you.

To Mercedes Hobson: I'm devastated that we can't fulfill our plans for when I finally got published. We always talked about "when it happens" like it was just a matter of time because of your endless faith in me. But time wasn't on your side. I wish I could timeshift for you.

Thanks to Kandle and Kiahna for being there for the first-ever drafts of *When Oceans Rise* when it was just a baby short story. Your advice and encouragement kept me going. I'm also fortunate to have Kristin, Alexis, Leah and Diane, who believed in me at all stages of my writing career, even though I wouldn't share my crap writing with them!

I'd also like to thank editors Brianna, Ann, and Angela for their incredible insights. They helped shape and reshape *When Oceans Rise* into what it is today and did it all with honest yet kind criticism.

To the team at Creative James Media: I cannot thank you enough for taking a chance on me and *When Oceans Rise.*

Everyone at this company works so hard to put out the best books they can, and my book is no exception.

To my publisher, Jean Lowd: Thank you for loving this book from its premise to print! Your belief in this book helped lift me up when I was drowning in doubt.

To Staci, my editor: Thank you for the video chat of encouragement and for your insight.

I'd like to thank Dr. Laura Payne, my creative writing mentor. Without your amazing writing classes and incredible ability to prompt students to produce the story that already exists within them, *When Oceans Rise* might never have existed.

To Dr. Sarah Roche: You have this incredible knack for driving students to be the best versions of themselves. I couldn't have asked for a better advisor. Thank you for supporting my path in my writing career.

Thank you to everyone who follows my writing journey and general weirdness on TikTok. I'm not sure what I'll do if that ship ever goes down! Thank you to my street team for all you did to help get this book into the hands of readers. I couldn't have asked for a better group of people!

Finally, thanks to you, my dear reader. Thank you for taking a chance on this book and, by extension, me. I let my emotions, my humor, my fears, and my tears explode on the pages. I hope you didn't mind if I got a little bit on you.

about the author

Robin Alvarez is a beach bum living in the desert with her husband and two kids. Something of a career taste-tester, she has worked in news stations, made TV commercials, edited high-end wedding videos, crafted industrial animations, been a photographer, a painter, and an English teacher. After having kids, she switched to working from home by teaching Chinese students online and returned to school to get her masters in creative writing. Robin was co-editor of the literary magazine The Sage, in which her short stories have been published. She has written for a business magazine and currently works at Sul Ross State University.

In her free time, Robin enjoys watching K-dramas while doing face masks, singing karaoke, making her kids costumes, and swimming with her family. She will be best friends for coffee. You can connect with her on TikTok: @robiiehood or reach her at P.O. Box 421994 Del Rio, TX 78842-1994

CPSIA information can be obtained
at www.ICGtesting.com
Printed in the USA
LVHW030413100623
749337LV00002B/552